Trained as an actress, Barbara Nadel used to work in mental health services. Born in the East End of London, she now writes full time and has been a regular visitor to Turkey for over twenty years. She received the Crime Writers' Association Silver Dagger for her novel Deadly Web in 2005. She is also the author of the highly acclaimed Francis Hancock series set during World War Two.

Praise for Barbara Nadel:

'The delight of Nadel's books is the sense of being taken beneath the surface of an ancient city which most visitors see for a few days at most. We look into the alleyways and curious dark quarters of Istanbul, full of complex characters and louche atmosphere'
Independent

'Nadel's novels take in all of Istanbul – the mysterious, the beautiful, the hidden and the banal. Her characters are vivid. A fascinating view of contemporary Turkey'   *Scotland on Sunday*

'Inspector Çetin İkmen is a detective up there with Morse, Rebus and Wexford. Gripping and highly recommended'   *Time Out*

'A colourful and persuasive portrait of contemporary Istanbul'
Literary Review

'Nadel's evocation of the shady underbelly of modern Turkey is one of the perennial joys of crime fiction. İkmen is a magnificent character and I can't think of a better summertime read'
Mail on Sunday

'Nadel makes full use of the rich variety of possibilities offered by modern Istanbul and its inhabitants. Crime fiction can do many things, and here it offers both a well crafted mystery and a form of armchair tourism, with Nadel as an expert guide'
Spectator

'The strands of Barbara Nadel's novel are woven as deftly as the carpet at the centre of the tale... a wonderful setting... a dizzying ride'   *Guardian*

P9-DEV-255

Also by Barbara Nadel and published by Headline

The Inspector İkmen Series:
Belshazzar's Daughter
A Chemical Prison
Arabesk
Deep Waters
Harem
Petrified
Deadly Web
Dance with Death
A Passion for Killing

The Hancock Series:
Last Rights
After the Mourning
Ashes to Ashes

PRETTY DEAD THINGS

BARBARA NADEL

headline

First published in 2007 by
HEADLINE PUBLISHING GROUP

First published in paperback in 2008 by
HEADLINE PUBLISHING GROUP

1

Cataloguing in Publication Data is available from the British Library

ISBN 978 0 7553 3563 3 (B Format)
ISBN 978 0 7553 4515 1 (A Format)

Typeset in Times New Roman by Palimpsest Book Production Limited,
Grangemouh, Stirlingshire

Printed and bound in Great Britain by
Clays Ltd, St Ives plc

Headline's policy is to use papers that are natural, renewable and recyclable
products and made from wood grown in sustainable forests. The logging and
manufacturing processes are expected to conform to the environmental
regulations of the country of origin.

HEADLINE PUBLISHING GROUP
An Hachette Livre UK Company
338 Euston Road
London NW1 3BH

www.headline.co.uk
www.hachettelivre.co.uk

To my husband, my son, my mother and all my fantastic friends both in the UK and in Turkey.

Cast of Characters

Çetin İkmen – middle-aged İstanbul police inspector
Mehmet Süleyman – İstanbul police inspector, İkmen's protégé
Commissioner Ardiç – İkmen and Süleyman's boss
Sergeant Ayse Farsakoğlu – İkmen's deputy
Sergeant İzzet Melik – Süleyman's deputy
Metin İskender – young İstanbul police inspector
Hikmet Yıldız – young police constable
Dr Arto Sarkissian – İstanbul police pathologist
Fatma İkmen – Çetin İkmen's wife
Zelfa Süleyman – Mehmet Süleyman's wife, a psychiatrist, known professionally as Dr Halman
Dr Krikor Sarkissian – Arto's brother
Natasha Sarkissian – Arto and Krikor's cousin
Balthazar Cohen – ex-İstanbul police officer
Estelle Cohen – Balthazar's wife
Berekiah Cohen – Balthazar and Estelle's son
Hulya İkmen Cohen – Berekiah's wife, Çetin İkmen's daughter
Ahmet Aksu – successful style magazine owner
Emine Aksu – Ahmet's wife
Edmondo Loya – eccentric Balat resident and academic
Maurice Loya – Edmondo's identical twin brother, an architect

Ali Paksoy – Balat shoe shop owner
Handan Sarıgul – Ali Paksoy's sister
Rafik Sarıgul – Handan Sarigul's son
Esther Sinop – elderly Balat resident
Gazi Sinop – Esther's grandson
Juanita Kordovi – romantic novelist
Garbis Aznavourian – Armenian church custodian
Ali Tevfik – prominent İstanbul businessman
Kadir Özal – old hippy

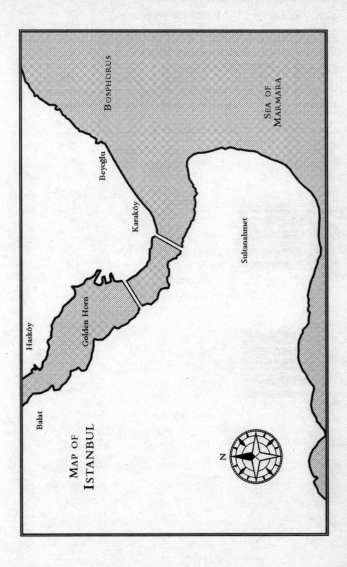

Prelude

'My wife, Inspector, is a tart,' the man said with what could only be described as amusement in his deep black eyes.

'As in . . .' the policeman began tentatively.

'As in she sleeps with other men as and whenever the mood takes her,' came the reply. 'Both Emine and myself are free spirits, Inspector.' He smiled. 'We are of the generation that first discovered the crazy world outside this country.' Then, holding up a large decanter filled with a light caramel-coloured liquid, he said, 'Whisky?'

The policeman, Inspector Çetin İkmen, placed one hand over his heart and said, 'No, thank you, sir. I am on duty.'

The man, who was a tall, rangy individual called Ahmet Aksu, shrugged his shoulders. 'As you wish,' he said as he topped up his own already rather full glass. He then paused in front of the large picture window that let so very much light into his vast sitting room and looked at the amazing view beyond.

Hasköy was not yet one of the more fashionable suburbs of the city of İstanbul. Situated on the northern shore of the Golden Horn it was a place of steep hills, narrow roads, and houses that ranged from tin-roofed shacks to elegant mini-mansions made of wood in the style of the nineteenth-century Ottoman Empire. In the past it was a district heavily populated by Jews

1

and gypsies. In the latter half of the twentieth century, however, many of the 'ethnics' moved away and Hasköy became the preserve of poor migrant workers from eastern Anatolia, who came to the city to find employment and to make their fortunes. Now, the fifty-seven-year-old İkmen reflected, Hasköy was experiencing a different kind of incomer. Ahmet Aksu, İkmen decided, was about his own age, though better preserved. He was the owner of a glossy lifestyle magazine. Elegant and media savvy, Mr Aksu and his wife had purchased one of the Ottoman mini-mansions and had turned it into what İkmen imagined the inside of a Zen Buddhist temple might look like. Not that a mere Turkish policeman like İkmen had ever had the opportunity of seeing a real Zen Buddhist temple – he had rarely left his country and when he had, it was only on business. He did know, however, that Zen minimalism was 'in' because Mr Aksu had told him that it was. Mr Aksu had also told him that his home was a perfect example of this style and philosophy, but Çetin İkmen found that sitting so close to the floor, even on large pad-like cushions, was not comfortable. It made his knees feel very sore and meant that in order to smoke effectively he had to crouch inelegantly over the ashtray Mr Aksu had given him. He must look, he felt, like some sort of dark, scruffy hobgoblin – especially when compared to the pristine Mr Aksu.

'Mr Aksu,' İkmen said as soon as he saw the other man move away from his view of the Golden Horn and the teeming suburb of Ayvansaray on the opposite shore, 'you mentioned that you were of the generation who discovered some crazy world beyond this country . . .'

Ahmet Aksu laughed. 'Ah, yes,' he said, 'in the 1960s.' With a youthful effortlessness, Aksu lowered himself on to the cushion across from the long, low table in front of İkmen. 'You were there too, I imagine, Inspector,' he said, 'when

2

the hippies, flower children and drop-outs arrived from Western Europe.'

'Yes . . .' İkmen wanted to smile too, but he didn't. Long, long ago he'd loved a 'flower child', a British girl called Alison. Even now, in 2005, the memory of her, long since dead, still gave him pause.

'At first I would go down to the Pudding Shop in Sultanahmet where they all used to gather, and just watch them,' Aksu said as his eyes shone with the memory of it. 'Later, groups formed. We all talked incessantly. They taught me a lot. Conversations with them about everything from drugs to psychoanalysis to music improved my English. I learned that growing one's hair was not a sin – even though my father begged to differ – that men could wear flowers and still be heterosexual, and, of course, I met a kindred spirit in Emine. We both committed to explore free love in 1969.'

'I see.' İkmen was a little shocked by this admission and turned his head to one side. He remembered the old hippy café and hangout in Sultanahmet called the Pudding Shop. As a young constable he'd raided it for drugs on more than one occasion and had himself seen quite a few curious young Turks within its walls. He knew that some local people took to the hippy lifestyle like ducks to water, but he'd never had a great deal to do with such people himself. Not until now.

'We married eventually, in 1974,' Aksu continued. 'But that didn't change anything with regard to how we lived our lives. Emine and I take lovers, Inspector. I call her a "tart" as a term of endearment. In reality I am as hungry for sexual adventure, if not more so, as my wife. You may disapprove but—'

'Sir, my only concern is for the safety of Mrs Aksu,'

3

İkmen replied. 'If, as you say, she has been missing for two weeks—'

'Two weeks and a day,' Aksu corrected. 'And Emine has gone off before, Inspector. In fact, last year she spent three weeks on the south coast – at Bodrum, as it turned out. First in the company of a young conscript, then an Israeli kayaking instructor, and then an artist from İzmir. I didn't hear from her until the eighteenth day of her absence. But I was never worried.' His slim face suddenly clouded. 'Not like this.'

Frowning, İkmen said, 'Like what?'

Aksu shrugged. 'I can't really articulate it,' he said. 'It's only a feeling. But this time, I am uneasy. There's something . . . wrong. I . . .'

'Tell me about it,' İkmen said as he rocked painfully back on to his thighs and then lit a cigarette.

A moment of silence ensued, after which the elegant media man said, 'Emine left home two weeks and one day ago to go, I know, to meet someone. After all these years, I know the signs and I could see that she was excited.'

'You didn't ask whom she might be going to see or where she might be going?'

'That was never part of the deal, if you like, Inspector,' Aksu said. 'My wife and I come and go as we please, as the spirit takes us. We always have. But this . . .' he leaned forward his face now set and serious, 'this was different.'

'In what way?'

'I don't know!' Aksu said. 'Call it a feeling, an intuition, some sort of emanation from the unconscious, or second sight, but something was . . . wrong.'

İkmen knew all about 'second sight'. 'Did you tell your wife that you were concerned about her? Did you express your fears to anyone, Mr Aksu?'

'No!' He shook his head, his eyes beginning to fill with tears. 'She would have thought that I was stupid.' He took a long slug from his whisky glass and said, 'I thought I was being stupid.'

Çetin İkmen sighed. How many times had he seen intuition ignored in this way? How many times had he known, to the bottom of his soul, that it shouldn't be so easily discounted? He put out his cigarette and consulted the notes he had taken from Mr Aksu earlier. Emine Aksu was fifty-five years old, slim, blonde, and apparently without noticeable inhibitions. 'Mr Aksu,' İkmen said as he looked at the finer details of his notes, 'your wife's mobile phone would seem to be out of action.'

'Yes.'

'So it's not likely that we can trace her via that method.' Not that technology was anything that İkmen generally placed great professional faith in. In his experience, the more complicated a system was, the more delicate and temperamental it also could become. 'Mr Aksu, do you know in what direction your wife went when she left you two weeks and one day ago?'

Aksu looked towards the window at the grey, now slightly autumnal-looking waterway beyond. 'Across the Golden Horn,' he said, 'towards the old southern neighbourhoods. I can't be any more precise than that, Inspector. I'm sorry.' And then with a certainty that İkmen found chilling, Ahmet Aksu said, 'Emine is dead, isn't she, Inspector?'

İkmen didn't answer.

As if suddenly struck by a thought even more disturbing than his wife's death, Aksu looked at İkmen and said, 'It was as if she was a girl again. When she left here that afternoon it was as if she was her old self, years ago, going off to meet me in Sultanahmet with her most beautiful clothes on and her brain full of strange ideas. Actually, Inspector, there is just one thing. I don't know if it is significant . . .'

Chapter 1

Çetin İkmen was sitting in the Pudding Shop with his friend and colleague, Mehmet Süleyman. After they had bought their coffees, he turned to the other inspector. 'Young people can do a lot of things these days which were just not possible thirty years ago. They can talk to each other endlessly on their mobile phones, wander around wearing iPods that allow them to listen to the music tracks of their choice – they can even afford Prada and Versace clothes and accessories. One of the things they can't do, however, is go on the hippy trail from İstanbul to Kathmandu. The conflict in Afghanistan and the instability in Pakistan, not to mention the practical difficulties for independent travellers in post-revolutionary Iran, have rendered travelling the trail an act of madness. In the sixties and seventies it was a very "hip" thing to do. Getting to Kathmandu, finding enlightenment in a Hindu ashram, having a lot of sex whilst stoned and doused in Patchouli oil, were definitely where it was "at" back then. Much of the initial "tuning in" and "dropping out" began at the beginning of the trail in İstanbul. In fact, it began right here, in this small, seemingly insignificant eatery.'

The Pudding Shop had been started in the 1950s by two brothers from the Black Sea coast. It had specialised in cheap milk and rice puddings, ideal for those afflicted by the ravages of cannabis-induced hunger. Cheap and friendly, it also provided

7

an information sharing system, in the form of a notice board as well as by word of mouth, for all of the freaks, heads and seekers headed East. It was, for a time, where the Flower Children first learned what it meant to be on the trail, where the excitement, as well as the drugs, first really and truly kicked in.

'It was a lovely dream while it lasted,' Çetin İkmen continued as he stirred four sachets of sugar into his frothy cappuccino. The Pudding Shop did still sell bog-standard old Turkish black tea, but many of its youthful customers now openly preferred designer coffee, which was not exactly 'roughing it'. 'I mean I know I took part in searching this place for drugs on several occasions, but that didn't mean I didn't sympathise with the hippies' goals. Finding oneself or rather some sort of satisfaction in life, by whatever means, is an admirable aim. And some of the young people were absolutely gorgeous . . .'

'Then,' his younger, taller and far handsomer companion raised a warning finger before tipping his head back towards the left-hand side of the restaurant. 'Now, however . . .'

İkmen looked up to see what or who Süleyman was indicating with his head. It was a man, probably, of indeterminate age. Crusted with filth, his features were nevertheless fine and narrow like those of an English or Frenchman. His bare arms were, significantly, threaded with livid and, in some cases, bloodied track marks.

'I think that he probably found something of a rather more malignant nature than a lot of them,' İkmen said.

'An eternal appointment with Dr Heroin,' his companion replied. 'Çetin, a great many of them ended up that way.'

'Yes, well . . .'

'I know that the girl you liked, Alison, didn't do drugs until they were forced upon her by those dealers but . . .'

İkmen lowered his head once again. Inspector Mehmet Süleyman was one of the few people in his life who knew about his brief and innocent dalliance with a young English hippy girl back in the 1970s. Married with children, İkmen had been a constable and was basically happy, as he was now, with his lot in life. The attentions of a pretty and funny foreigner had, however, been flattering. He had never slept with Alison, or had anything more than rather superficial conversations with her, and he had only ever kissed her once. But somehow a connection had been made and when he learned many years later that she had died at the hands of drug dealers when her personal trail eventually finished in Pakistan, it had affected him profoundly. In spite of 'busting' more than a few hippies for drugs in the seventies, İkmen still possessed an irrepressible admiration for those early heads, freaks and seekers of Nirvana. The drugs aside, there was a lot about their rejection of materialism in favour of the world of the contemplative and unseen that chimed positively with Çetin İkmen. As the son of a woman many had consulted as a seer and a witch during the course of his childhood, İkmen knew all about looking 'inside'.

'Drug casualties are littered along the old hippy road to Kathmandu,' İkmen said. 'We naturally have our share of these ghosts of the sixties and seventies.'

Mehmet Süleyman offered his friend a cigarette before lighting one up for himself. 'I can remember being warned about this place when I was a teenager,' he said. 'My mother believed that if you so much as set foot in here you became a drug addict.'

İkmen laughed. 'By the time you were a teenager the

glory days of the Pudding Shop were very nearly over,' he said. 'In the late sixties when you were still at primary school, I was pulling lumps of hashish the size of bookshelves out of backpacks. By the late seventies raiding this place for a few grams of Lebanese Gold wasn't worth the effort, not when compared to what you could pick up from all the wandering dealers in the streets behind here and up towards the Grand Bazaar. Pudding Shop drugs were largely recreational. What came after that time – well, that was different.'

'Now the trade is controlled by Mafias,' Süleyman said with a sigh. 'Russians, Chechens, our own . . .'

'And is, as a consequence, a business,' İkmen continued. 'Nothing to do with enlightenment or even just plain honest fun.'

They both sat in silence for a short while. At the pristine self-service counter, a very smartly dressed young assistant sold cappuccino and cake to a respectable middle-aged couple from Berlin as well as a cup of tea to a very scrubbed-looking backpacker from Israel. Times had changed since the days of the hash-smoked walls of the Pudding Shop of yesteryear.

Süleyman cleared his throat. 'So why did you ask to meet me here specifically, Çetin?' he asked as he pulled one hand through his thick, slightly greying black hair.

İkmen dug one thin, yellowed hand into the pocket of his jacket and took out a photograph of a woman. He put it on the table in front of Süleyman and said, 'This is Emine Aksu, wife of the magazine owner Ahmet Aksu.'

The other man looked down at the picture and raised his eyebrows. 'Attractive.'

'She's fifty-five years old, childless, and she's a missing person,' İkmen said. 'Been gone from their home in Hasköy for – according to her husband, whom I saw this morning – two weeks and one day.'

Süleyman frowned. 'He's only just now reported it?'

İkmen, in a rather more lowered tone than was usual for him, told Süleyman about the Aksu's 'open' relationship and then said, 'Ahmet Aksu met Emine here in the Pudding Shop back in the sixties. Given their espousal of free love plus the faint whiff of cannabis smoke I picked up in their house in Hasköy, I don't think that either of them has ever really left since. Take away Mr Aksu's suit and his wife's designer clothes and I think that you'll find pure hippy underneath. I know it's supposed to be fashionable now, but even their home is decorated in the Buddhist style – or so he told me. I mean Buddhism was almost the state religion of the hippies . . .'

'I thought that a lot of them became Hindus . . .'

'Well, in addition to Hinduism,' İkmen said. 'But that is by the by. Look, Mehmet, I don't have to tell you that I am my mother's son, do I?'

Süleyman smiled. Everybody knew that Çetin İkmen was the son of Ayşe İkmen, the famous witch of Üsküdar. Originally from Albania, Ayşe had been an odd choice of wife for Çetin's academic father Timür, and indeed for some years she had been very out of place in the Asian suburb of Üsküdar. But as her experiences of second sight as well as her other demonstrations of occult knowledge grew, so did her fame and standing in the local community. Not that any of this lasted for any great length of time. Çetin was only ten when his mother died, but she left him with her considerable gift of insight. He used it more often than even he would sometimes admit to himself in his work.

'I have a distinct feeling of foreboding where Mrs Emine

11

Aksu is concerned,' İkmen continued. 'It is a feeling that Mr Aksu shares.'

'Well, as you said yourself, Çetin, he is a hippy at heart and such people do tend to believe in such things.'

İkmen knew that Süleyman was not implying that he didn't himself believe in 'such things', but was just simply making an observation on Ahmet Aksu. What Mehmet Süleyman believed or did not believe about the world unseen was still very open to question.

'Yes,' İkmen said. 'What Mr Aksu also believes, or rather what he observed in his wife the last time he saw her, could be, he thinks, something to do with her old hippy past. He said that when she left their home just over two weeks ago, there was a girlish quality about her. After I quizzed him further, he told me that his wife had intimated that she might be going to meet someone from her distant past. The Aksus apparently knew – amongst others – a lot of drug dealers and other assorted criminal types back in their old hippy days. Now, this makes Ahmet Aksu distinctly nervous. He claims to remember very few names and when he did dredge one up it was with great reluctance. I suspect the Aksus have moved on socially even more than their polished outward appearances would suggest.' He pulled a slightly sour face. 'What rich kids do or did for fun, eh?'

Süleyman put his cigarette out and then almost immediately lit another. 'Are Mr and Mrs Aksu both from wealthy families?' he asked.

'Nouveaux riches,' İkmen said with a smile. 'Compared to yourself, I mean, my dear Mehmet.'

'I see.' The handsome, arrogant face hardly moved. But then İkmen knew it was just a game his friend played with him at times like this. To look blank and unmoved was an

Ottoman prerogative and Mehmet Süleyman was most decidedly an Ottoman. Although the Sultanate of Turkey had been abolished by Atatürk back in 1924, prior to that what was then the Ottoman Empire had been ruled by the monarch, supported by an assortment of relatives, ministers and significant families. One of those connected to the royal house by marriage was the family that became known by the surname Süleyman. Mehmet, the son of a man older people in their home neighbourhood still called 'Prince' Muhammed Süleyman, was one of a very noble, if now impoverished, breed. Those with money, at least in the eyes of some of the old families, could only be nouveaux riches with all the connections to lack of taste and coarseness that such a term included.

'In the late sixties many of our own youngsters, particularly those with money and education, discovered the hippies,' İkmen said. 'I remember it distinctly. Looking in here and seeing a few pale Turkish faces amongst a sea of red and brown Europeans. They were nervous at first – it was all so alien – but once they got going on the hash, read a few pages of *On the Road* and discovered sex, inhibitions soon came crashing down.'

'I'm sure they did,' Süleyman replied. 'And so you think that this Mrs Emine Aksu may really have met someone from that time, do you, Çetin?'

'I think that it is one possibility,' İkmen said. 'Looking at her past acquaintances from that period is certainly a place to make a start in the search for Mrs Aksu.' Then he leaned across the table and smiled at his friend. 'How do you fancy a trip back to the 1960s, Mehmet?'

A quiet life wasn't something that Mr Ali Tevfik had thought anything much about until he reached the age of thirty. Up until that time he had spent most of his waking hours hanging out in the cafés and bars of Sultanahmet in the winter and then doing much the same thing at the seaside resorts on the southern Mediterranean coast in the summer time. Ali, to the eternal shame of his diplomat father, devoted his time entirely to parties, women, drink and drugs. In the forefront of the nightclub scene in places like Antalya, it was only when one of his young female conquests commented upon his 'advanced' age that Ali began to question what he was doing. Up until that moment being thirty had meant very little to him. Suddenly being told that he was 'old', however, set him thinking and within a year he had enrolled on a business studies course in London and made his father very happy. Now he nominally ran one of the most successful car hire firms in the country, had been married for twenty-five years and had two daughters both of whom were at university in the US. Mr Ali Tevfik enjoyed reading, pottering in his lovely garden which led down to the Bosphorus, and, occasionally, a little relaxed game of golf with other semi-retired friends. In short, he enjoyed a life of very deliberate quietness. It was not a style of being that prepared him in any way for the appearance of a rather scruffy policeman with news from his distant, disreputable past.

'I understand', Çetin İkmen said as he sat down in the garden chair his host had gestured him towards, 'that you know Mr Ahmet Aksu and his wife, Emine.'

'I know of them,' Ali Tevfik replied as he sat down opposite the policeman. The Bosphorus was very blue and calm on what was a very fine evening and the view of it which his seat afforded him made him smile. 'Ahmet Aksu owns *Fabulous Homes*, that lifestyle magazine.'

14

'He does indeed.' İkmen smiled. 'However, Mr Tevfik, when I said that you know the Aksus, what I should have said is that you knew the couple, years ago.'

Ali Tevfik frowned.

'Back in the late sixties and early seventies, according to Mr Aksu, you and he were part of a group that met in the Pudding Shop in Sultanahmet,' İkmen said.

'Ah.'

'Like a lot of young Turks at the time you were fascinated by all of the European hippies who descended on the city during that period.' He moved his hands through the air as if casting a spell. 'Mysterious travellers on their way to seek enlightenment.'

'Well, er . . .' Mr Tevfik looked down at the floor in a way that made İkmen feel that he was embarrassed by this conversation.

'But then that wasn't always the case, was it?' İkmen said. 'Many of them just wanted to get high, didn't they? I arrested a few of those back then, in the Pudding Shop. Maybe Mr Aksu, his wife Emine Öz, as she was then, and you were even present when that happened. I mean, you must have seen a few – what did the hippies call drug raids?'

'Busts,' Ali Tevfik said as he looked up with a sigh. 'We called them busts. What on earth is all this about, Inspector? I haven't done anything wrong. Why are you asking Ahmet Aksu about my past?'

İkmen told him about Emine Aksu and the fact that she was now officially a missing person.

'Back then, in the sixties, Emine was wild,' Ali Tevfik said. 'Before she even met Ahmet there was this Dutch boy, and, well . . .'

'And there were a lot of drugs,' İkmen said. 'According

15

to Mr Aksu your particular preference, for both taking and dealing, was LSD. Having an "acid trip"—'

'He had no right to bring that up! That was a very long time ago!' Ali Tevfik's eyes blazed. 'We all did it back then! Everyone took, even the whiter than white dealt on occasion! You can't arrest me for something I did when I was twenty!'

'Nor would I want to, sir,' İkmen said. 'You are now a very respectable man whose company contributes considerably to the economy of this country.' He looked up at the large nineteenth-century Ottoman villa behind them and then continued, 'And to your own wealth, of course, too.'

'Then . . .'

'Mr Tevfik, I know from Mr Aksu that it wasn't just a Dutch boy upon whom Emine Öz bestowed her favours back in the sixties. You were also, shall we say, intimate with the lady. Is that not so?'

Ali Tevfik lowered his very dark brown eyes. 'Yes. Although not for very long. Ahmet came along and . . . well, back in those days most of us preferred the Western girls anyway. Emine was a lot of fun, but she was too Turkish . . .'

'Too Turkish? What do you mean?' İkmen said.

'Well, materialistic, I suppose you would say,' Ali Tevfik replied. 'Inspector, back then the Westerners – and some of us, too – were all against materialism; it was the fashion. The fact that you had to have wealthy parents to do what we did, didn't occur to us. So going to India to "find yourself" or getting high in order to look inside your own head were the things that obsessed our minds. Oh, and getting laid was important too, but . . . our "ordinary" countrymen were fixated only on making money.'

'Yes, sir,' İkmen said a trifle testily. 'Because they were, if you recall, poor. Most of us were.'

Turkey in the late sixties and seventies had, as Mr Ali Tevfik knew only too well, been another country. There had been no tourist industry to speak of back in those days and most people, though not deprived of the necessities of life, had enjoyed few luxuries. Western Europe, and particularly the US, had been viewed as places of almost impossible comfort and were either envied or emulated accordingly. People like Çetin İkmen had scraped a living – just.

Mr Ali Tevfik waved a hand in front of his face as if pushing thoughts of the 'poor' away from him. 'Yes but Emine came from a wealthy family and so she didn't really *need* anything. Unlike the Western girls, she was always on about the latest new dress, about her hair, her handbags, make-up, the shoes that seemed to change every day. She did drugs because it was fashionable to do drugs, not because she thought she might learn something from the experience. She was a spoilt little rich kid.' And then he smiled. 'But then you probably think we were all spoilt little rich kids, don't you, Inspector?'

İkmen did but he didn't pass any comment on it. 'Mr Tevfik,' he said, 'my only concern is for Mrs Aksu who has been missing from her home now for fifteen days.'

'Missing? You mean she's gone off or something?'

'We don't know,' İkmen said. 'Mrs Aksu is, as she was when she was young, a free spirit. Her husband is accustomed to her frequent absences from their home. However, this absence has persisted and he is worried, which is why he contacted the police.'

'So why are you asking me about it?' Ali Tevfik said. 'Emine and Ahmet are not people that I know now.'

İkmen looked out at the perfect lawn which stretched down

17

to the great broadness of the Bosphorus at the end of the garden and said, 'Mr Tevfik, Mrs Aksu is still, according to her husband, a very sexually adventurous woman. Mr and Mrs Aksu possess an understanding about such things and, in general, experience no problems in this regard. However, apparently when Mrs Aksu left home this last time to go about her "adventures", her husband felt uneasy. In addition, Mrs Aksu gave her husband the impression she was not going off to meet a new lover but someone she had been with before, someone from her past.'

'And you think that I—'

'Your name was just one of several that Mr Aksu gave us,' İkmen said. 'As you will appreciate, sir, we have to follow all and any leads we are given.'

'Inspector, I have been very happily married for twenty-five years now,' Ali Tevfik said gravely. 'I am of course aware of Ahmet and his magazine and, in fact, my company has in the past advertised our chauffeur service in it. I've seen both Ahmet and Emine at a couple of business functions over the years and I have spoken to both of them. But I haven't had an affair with Emine, if that is what you think.'

'No spark left over from the old days . . .'

'Not a bit of it!' he looked around first to make sure that no one else was in the garden before he leaned forward towards İkmen and said, 'I last saw Ahmet and Emine two years ago. There was a dinner organised by the Touring and Automobile Association at the Pera Palas Hotel. I was there with my wife. I had a few very pleasant words with Ahmet and, after the dinner, a lot of the guests went into the bar for drinks. It was there that I spoke to Emine. Ahmet had gone off to speak to some other media types and my wife was talking to a friend so we were alone. Emine, after what can only have been at most five minutes, propositioned me. She always was a mischief maker. *She* came on to *me.*'

'Did she.'

'Yes!' he whispered. 'She said that if I wanted to come up to the room she and Ahmet had taken for the night she'd – well, she'd have sex with me. For the sake, she said, of old times . . .'

'And did you?' İkmen asked.

'Well, of course I didn't!' Ali Tevfik replied. 'I love my wife.'

'And yet Emine Aksu is a very attractive woman,' İkmen said. 'And you have, by your own admission, slept with her before.'

'Back in the sixties, yes,' he said as he again looked around to ensure that no one else was about to join them in the garden. 'But I left all of that behind years ago. Emine Aksu is still, I will freely admit, a very attractive woman, but she isn't any more for me now than she was back in 1968.'

'Why is that, sir?'

'Well, because of her abiding materialism,' Ali Tevfik said. 'I mean, I know I like money and I love to have nice things, but . . .' he lowered his voice again. 'Between you and me, at one point she did suggest that we go outside, round the back of the hotel and "do it" out there. In the old days we both rather liked that sort of thing. And, well, I admit I was tempted, I—'

'You went outside with her.'

'Yes! Please, please don't let this go any further . . .'

But İkmen neither confirmed nor denied whether he would comply or not.

19

'I kissed her, I admit,' Ali Tevfik said. 'But then when it came to, well, sex and . . . there was a bit of a performance about how we might be able to protect her Versace skirt during the course of the proceedings and then when she took her shoes off so that she wouldn't accidentally scuff them against the wall behind her . . .'

'Your ardour cooled.'

'Yes.' He put his head down again, seemingly in shame. 'I told her what I thought, she swore at me, and I went back to the bar. I haven't seen Emine Aksu since.'

'Are you sure?' İkmen asked.

'Positive. But I have heard a few rumours,' Ali Tevfik said.

'Oh?' İkmen replied. 'And what might they be, sir?'

According to her husband the only clue that Mrs Emine Aksu had given him about her destination on the day that she apparently disappeared, was that she was headed towards those old neighbourhoods on the southern side of the Golden Horn. Balat, Fener and Ayvansaray – Mehmet Süleyman knew them all for various reasons. Fener was where one of the many daughters of his colleague Çetin İkmen lived. In a big old house up by the Greek boys school, Hulya İkmen lived with her small son Timür as well as her mother and father-in-law and her husband, Berekiah. Not that Hulya, who was only just nineteen, was in her house very often. Eighteen months previously Berekiah had been badly injured in the terrorist attack on the Neve Şalom Synagogue in Beyoğlu which had resulted in the partial paralysis of both of his arms. Until that time Hulya and her in-laws, the Cohens, had lived opposite the synagogue. After the bomb, however, the Muslim daughter-in-law and her Muslim son had moved with her Jewish husband and his family to Fener. There they all lived while Hulya worked punishing hours in a variety of jobs in order to keep everyone. Prior to the violent events of November 2003, Berekiah Cohen had worked as a jeweller in the Grand Bazaar. Understanding as his old employer had been, no one could really use a jeweller with no strength or movement in his hands.

Ayvansaray was not a place that Süleyman visited frequently. One of the first cases he had worked on with İkmen, back in the days when he had been the older man's sergeant, had taken place on the edge of this district. But it wasn't somewhere that he knew well. Balat, on the other hand, was somewhere he was familiar with. It was also a place that, in spite of its connection to several murder cases he had worked upon over the years, was a district of which he was very fond. Until comparatively recently, it had been a predominantly Jewish quarter and it still, if one looked hard, possessed a considerable number of synagogues both large and small. Now, however, Balat was a district in transition. There were and had been for some time a large number of migrants from central Anatolia in the area. They were now being joined by certain rather bold members of the artistic middle classes. By dint of a large grant from UNESCO, Balat had been designated a world heritage site and was, so some believed, on the up.

However, Mehmet Süleyman in his smart dark suit still looked out of place. Children of dubious cleanliness eyed him suspiciously. He imagined quite a few of them were gypsies. In fact, several of the children were familiar to him for just that reason. One of the more recent incomers was a gypsy artist called Gonca. Tall, big-boned and beautiful, Gonca was also the mother of twelve children, most of

21

whom looked vaguely hostile much of the time. But that was understandable. Mehmet Süleyman had had a brief but intense affair with their mother some years before. However, as he looked around at the listing buildings hung with great swathes of dark green creeper, he put Gonca and her delights firmly from his mind. The task at hand was to look around and talk to people about Mrs Aksu who must have looked, Süleyman felt, just as out of place in this environment as he did.

He went into a small grocer's shop, passing as he did so an old flat-capped man snoring in the evening sunshine on a low stool outside. Just like village shops all over Anatolia, which always had at least one elderly man lurking around outside, this establishment sold everything from vine leaves to plastic toys and smelt strongly of bread and spices. As he entered, another flat-cap-wearing man behind the counter ushered his heavily veiled wife into a dark room at the back of the premises. Probably her husband, he was obviously protecting her from the gaze of the strange suited outsider who had just come into the shop.

The man, who was old, looked at Süleyman with an expression of open suspicion on his face.

The policeman in his turn, smiled. 'Good evening, uncle*,' he said as he picked a packet of Winston cigarettes up from the counter in front of its elderly owner. 'I'd like to buy these cigarettes please.'

The old man shrugged and named his price and, as Süleyman passed the bank notes over to him, he showed him his police identification. The grocer swallowed hard. Traffic

*'Uncle' is used by Turkish people as a term of respect for their male elders.

22

cops and the occasional passing uniformed officer were rare, but a smart man in plain clothes with a very posh accent was distinctly worrying. Such officers were, or could be, so he had heard, concerned with very frightening things like terrorism or the pursuit of traitors.

'Sir, I don't know what you want—' the old man began.

'We're looking for this woman,' Süleyman said as he placed a copy of the picture Ahmet Aksu had given to the police of his wife on the counter in front of the shopkeeper.

'Mmm.' Elderly eyes coped better when assisted by spectacles which the shopkeeper put on now. 'An attractive lady,' he said. 'Very wealthy, by the look of her. Not like the ladies who live around here.' He handed the picture back to Süleyman.

'This lady, Emine Aksu, doesn't live here,' Süleyman said. 'But this area is where she was apparently due to meet someone when she was last seen.'

'When was that?'

'Two Mondays ago, 9 May. In the afternoon or early evening, we think'

The old man, still looking at the photograph in front of him, shook his head. 'No,' he said. 'We don't get ladies like her around here.'

'Not even amongst the artists who've come to live in the area?' Süleyman asked.

'They don't come into shops like this,' the shopkeeper responded darkly. 'They get what they need in the smart shops on İstiklal Street or in one or other of those mall places they have these days.'

'Maybe, but you'd see such people on the street nevertheless.'

'Possibly. But', the old man said with what sounded like

23

considerable certainty in this voice, 'not this woman in the photograph.'

Süleyman tried another tack, something İkmen had told him the woman's husband had spoken to him about. 'This lady was wearing very distinctive shoes . . .'

'Shoes or no shoes, I've not seen her.'

'You're sure?'

The shopkeeper said that he was, and, in fact, he wasn't the only Balat resident to deny having ever seen Emine Aksu. Süleyman found that those who deigned to speak to him appeared to be almost disgusted by the photograph in his hands. Traditional country values and moralities were obviously very powerful forces in modern Balat. But then in all probability wherever Emine Aksu had gone on that fateful afternoon in May it had to have been to someone or some people like herself. Recent Anatolian migrants to the old Golden Horn districts were unlikely to have attracted a woman like her.

Süleyman left the shop, opened his new packet of cigarettes, lit up with a sigh, and then began the long climb to the top of the hill and the more 'artistic' inhabitants of the area.

There was and had only ever been room for one. Now that there were two, everything was impossible. There wasn't room – at least, not enough to be able to move around easily. And one had to be practical. He'd been a fool and he said so in no uncertain terms.

The reply when it came nevertheless was not unexpected in any way. 'I had to.'

It was true.

'BUT NOW THERE'S A PROBLEM. YOU MUST SEE THAT SURELY.'

'Of course I do!'

'WELL THEN YOU'LL HAVE TO DO SOMETHING ABOUT IT, WON'T YOU?'

'We *will*. We *will have to do something about it.*'

That, too, was true.

Chapter 2

Hulya İkmen Cohen was so tired by the time she got home that even the sight of her little boy Timür, his arms spread wide to cuddle his mummy, couldn't cheer her.

'I'm so sorry, my soul,' she said as she bent down to kiss the child lightly on his forehead, 'I'm too tired to pick you up. Mummy's exhausted.'

Standing up, she took the glass of tea her mother-in-law was offering to her with gratitude. 'Thank you.'

Just the look of Hulya these days made her mother-in-law, Estelle, want to weep. Prior to the synagogue bombings of 2003, Hulya had been a beautiful and blooming young wife and mother. Her husband, Estelle's son Berekiah, had a good job as a jeweller in the Grand Bazaar and life was very pleasant. But now that Berekiah was effectively crippled, everything had changed. Ever since the great earthquake of 1999, Estelle's own husband, ex-Constable Cohen, had been unable to work due to the injuries he had sustained during the course of that natural disaster. He had lost both his legs. Estelle had adjusted to it, and had taken work as and when she could. But now that Berekiah was unfit for work the pressure had increased. Now Hulya was the main breadwinner for the family and she did this by holding down a variety of jobs. First thing in the mornings she served breakfast to tourists at a small pansiyon in Sultanahmet; this was then followed by clerical work for the rest of the day at a travel agency in Beyoğlu. Then, twice a week, as on this particular occasion, she did a short stint waitressing at one of the bars on Nevizade Alley, behind the old fish market up in Beyoğlu. She was still very young and there could be quite an exciting buzz to working in the Kedi Bar even on the early evening shift. But it could also be rough and sometimes she got groped – usually by severely intoxicated customers from former Eastern bloc countries. Not that she told her husband, who would have been both furious and humiliated in equal measure. And besides, she was a policeman's daughter and so, for all her tiredness and fragility, Hulya could handle herself. She sat down just as her husband, Berekiah, walked into the room. Instinctively, she made to rise and go to him.

'Oh, don't get up, my love,' Berekiah said as he watched his mother go into the kitchen to begin preparing Hulya's evening meal. 'You're tired.'

He lowered his head briefly in order to kiss her lightly on the cheek and then sat down in a chair on the other side of the room. Hulya and Berekiah rarely sat close to one another these days. She watched him as, smiling at the child playing in the middle of the room, her husband leaned back and let his all but useless arms flop heavily to his sides. The fanatics who had blown up the Neve Şalom Synagogue as well as all the homes and businesses that had surrounded it had also, Hulya bitterly observed, taken the physical side of her marriage away with all that death and destruction. If things didn't improve, Timür would be the one and only child they would ever have.

But as usual, none of this was talked about and the couple just spoke of this and that, the minutiae of their respective days, until, at just past ten o'clock, Berekiah's father Balthazar called out from his accustomed position in the little room with the television, nearest the front door.

'Someone's in the garden!' he called out huskily through a deluge of cigarette smoke. 'Estelle! Estelle!'

Even since the bomb attack Balthazar, who now lived for little beyond idle gossip and the television, had become obsessed with security. 'Quick!' he shouted, panicking. 'I think whoever it is, is at the door!'

With a sigh of impatience – such incidents happened all the time these days – Berekiah rose painfully to his feet and said, 'It's all right, Dad. I'm coming.'

'If it's one of those bloody terrorists, I want to see his face before he tries to kill me this time!' Balthazar shouted.

But, just as Berekiah knew it wouldn't be, the person outside the front door was not a terrorist. It was Mehmet Süleyman.

'I was in the area and so I thought I'd come and see how everyone is,' the policeman said as he first embraced Berekiah and then kissed him on both cheeks.

'Oh, it's so good to see you!' the younger man said. 'It must be—'

'Who is it?' Balthazar Cohen called from his TV room by the door. 'What does he want?'

'It's Mehmet, Dad,' Berekiah replied.

'Mehmet? My Mehmet? Mehmet Süleyman?'

'Yes.'

'Oh, Mehmet!' A woman's voice, elderly but full of life, now joined in what was becoming an entire chorus based around just one name.

'Estelle!'

She rushed forward, took the tall, handsome policeman in her arms, and kissed him hard on both cheeks. 'Oh, Mehmet, you've come at just the right moment,' Estelle said. 'I'm preparing food for Hulya, who has been working all day and half the night, poor girl. You must join us!'

'Er . . .'

Many years before, when the Cohens were still living back in Karaköy, Mehmet Süleyman had lived with them in their small and often riotous apartment. When his first marriage to his cousin Zuleika came to an end, he was both in disgrace with his own family and broke. Estelle had taken him in and cared for him as one of her own for several years while he got back on his feet again. Then, later, it was Mehmet who had been instrumental in helping to rescue Balthazar, Estelle and Berekiah from their shattered apartment opposite the bombed Neve Şalom Synagogue. Such vast and deep history meant that all and any contact between them was significant. Also Mehmet knew of old that getting away from the Cohen household without sharing a meal with them was impossible.

'Let me just go and see Balthazar and then I promise I'll be in to eat your food immediately,' Mehmet said as he kissed Estelle on her cheeks and then pinched her chin lovingly between his fingers.

'It's only bulgur and a little chicken,' Estelle said as she made her way back towards her kitchen. 'If only I'd known that you were coming, Mehmet!'

'It's not a problem, Estelle, it—'

'Mehmet! Mehmet!' Balthazar called. 'Stop talking to women and get in here with me!'

It wasn't always easy for Mehmet Süleyman having what amounted to a second family. His own blood relations and his wife could be quite difficult enough to deal with on their own without the problematic and demanding Cohens in his life too. But he loved them and so, after taking his leave of

Estelle and Berekiah, he went into the smoke-filled television room that was home to his old friend Balthazar.

Roughly the same age as Çetin İkmen, Balthazar Cohen nevertheless looked a good ten years older. Even allowing for the fact that both his legs had been amputated due to the injures he had sustained in the earthquake, ex-Constable Cohen was a small, thin man. His skin was heavily lined and coarsened by constant smoking, and he now bore little relation to the rather piratical and very funny man Mehmet Süleyman had patrolled the streets with at the beginning of his career. Back then he'd had a cheeky swagger and intense, sparkling black eyes which his many, many mistresses had found irresistible. Now his injuries and the bitterness that had resulted from them had reduced him to an angry and frustrated creature still hankering after his long lost sexual glory days.

'Mehmet! Mehmet!' he said as his friend bent down to kiss him on both cheeks. 'We haven't seen you for a long time! To what do we owe the pleasure now?'

'I was just passing.' Süleyman sat down in the chair opposite his friend and lit up a cigarette. Balthazar, as usual, already had a smoke in one of his yellow, clawed hands.

'Passing? You? Up here?' Balthazar narrowed his eyes. Süleyman lived out in the smart Bosphorus village of Ortaköy. He was hardly likely to be 'just passing' any of the old neighbourhoods along the Golden Horn at this time of night.

Seeing the look of suspicion on his friend's face made Süleyman smile. 'All right,' he said, 'I'm working.'

'Oh.' It was said in such a way as to indicate interest of a mild nature. But Süleyman knew that Balthazar's curiosity about his old profession was very far from being unenthusiastic. Balthazar loved hearing about his old work and the lives and loves of his old colleagues. And so, because Emine Aksu's disappearance was now a recorded fact, he told Balthazar about it and even showed him a photograph of the woman. After all, being housebound, Balthazar sometimes spent long periods of time staring out of the window watching the world go by. He could possibly have seen Emine Aksu. Not that Süleyman had come to the Cohen house to question its occupants. He had just literally dropped in on his way back to his car after what had been a very fruitless afternoon and evening. Emine Aksu, it seemed, may well have disappeared into thin air somewhere along the Golden Horn Bridge.

'Nobody's seen or heard anything about this woman, I suppose,' Balthazar said, more as a statement than a question.

'No.'

'This area doesn't change,' the older man said darkly. 'When my brothers and I used to scream in terror because our drunk of a father beat us senseless, no one ever heard or saw a thing. These neighbourhoods have always been close and that is irrespective of the type of people who might live here. When I was a kid all of our neighbours were also Jews, but these Muslims from Anatolia are no different. Hear, see and say nothing. If it was a definite murder, now that may be different, but . . .'

Mehmet Süleyman knew that his friend had been born in Balat but that he had then moved with his father and brothers to Karaköy when he was a youngster. Now that he was almost back to where he had started, it was obvious that Balthazar still retained many negative feelings about the place.

'Are many of your friends from your childhood still in the area?' the policeman asked once Estelle had been in to remind him that his food was nearly ready.

'No.' Balthazar shook his head. 'There're a few. Old Esther Sinop still lives down by the Ahrida Synagogue. Then there's Moşe Levi, whom I went to school with. He's still around. The Loya brothers . . . there were still a few shops in Jewish hands until recently – maybe there still are – clothing and shoes, mainly. But I don't see anyone and no one bothers to come and see me.'

Ignoring this brief foray into self-pity, Mehmet asked Balthazar what the district had been like in the 1960s. They were, after all, talking about Emine Aksu whose glory days the sixties had been. Not for the first time it occurred to Süleyman that perhaps the reason why Emine had gone to meet her paramour in this area was because it was in Fener/Balat that she had originally met him back in her hippy days. Her husband had, after all, been given the impression that his wife was going to meet someone from her past.

'Ah, the 1960s!' Balthazar smiled. 'Now that was my era, Mehmet. Sultanahmet alive with girls with long blond hair, vans full of hippies singing Rolling Stones songs driving by, and me – young, fit and very interested in that "free love" thing they all spoke about!' He laughed.

'Yes, but Balthazar here in Fener—'

'What, hippies here in these neighbourhoods? No. They might have passed through here, but . . . even now people don't stay in Balat, do they? We've one hotel here in Fener down by the Golden Horn, but this generally isn't a tourist destination, is it?'

'No.'

'Although I suppose it's possible that your missing woman, because she is Turkish, may have met her lover back here in the 1960s. You don't know if he was a Jew or . . . ?'

'We have no idea who he is or even if this idea of Mrs

33

Aksu meeting an old lover from the past is accurate,' Süleyman said. 'Çetin İkmen is working his way through her known contacts, although as yet he's not come up with very much.'

'Ah, but he will,' Balthazar said with a confident nod. 'My daughter-in-law's father is the best police officer in the world.'

Süleyman smiled. Çetin İkmen was indeed a legend amongst Turkish police officers, although whether his fame had yet spread across the world was less certain. But then Balthazar Cohen, as well as being related by marriage to the inspector, had always been one of his greatest fans. İkmen had, after all, covered for Balthazar – whose sexual adventures back then often took some time – on more than one occasion when they were both young officers together.

'Well, Balthazar, that is true,' Süleyman said as he rose to go and make his way out to the living room. From the polite coughing that was coming from the hall, he deduced that Estelle had finished preparing the food. 'But your wife has cooked and I must go to eat . . .'

'Mmm.'

He bent down in order to kiss his friend on the cheeks once again. As he pulled away, however, Balthazar said, 'The idea of hippies, even Turkish hippies, around here is intriguing. Let me see if I can speak to a few people. Get me away from these four walls.'

Süleyman gave Balthazar a doubtful look. To his knowledge his friend never went out anywhere these days, however local.

'I have a wheelchair and Estelle to push me if I want. She won't mind,' Balthazar said in answer to his friend's unspoken question.

'Yes, but you never—'

'Then perhaps it is time that I did get out,' Balthazar said firmly. 'I could go and see Moşe Levi and the Loya brothers. I could go and see if those clothing businesses are still going. There was Mr Madrid the haberdasher he . . .'

Süleyman left him to his reverie and went to get some food. Later, rather apologetically, he spoke to Estelle about Balthazar and his newfound desire to go out. He thought she might be angry that now, suddenly, he wanted her to get that great big wheelchair they had brought out from under the stairs and to push him around like a nurse. But Estelle said she didn't mind. 'Maybe going out will help to alleviate his misery,' she said as she kissed Mehmet goodbye at the door. 'Maybe it will also bring some reality back into his life. Mr Madrid the haberdasher died way back in the fifties. I think his shop was taken over by a couple from Bursa. The man, I think, made and mended shoes.'

Sleep did not come easily to Çetin İkmen that night. Putting aside the fact that his wife Fatma kept on throwing the sheets off their bed because she was so hot, İkmen was disturbed. Maybe it was remembering the sixties and early seventies that was unsettling him. But, despite his brief and very innocent dalliance with the English flower child, Alison, during that period, it had been a good time. And even that hadn't been bad, in retrospect. At the time it had been exhilarating. No, the sixties and early seventies had been good for İkmen. He'd been young and fit, as had Fatma, and they had been new parents. Passion had been frequent and energetic. Now he placed one hand on his gently snoring wife's back and remembered. Before the real hard-core political violence took hold in the mid to late seventies, his life, though lacking materially, had been really very good. It was the remembrance of

35

the sixties and seventies that was indeed unsettling him, but not for any personal reasons. What he was feeling was to do with Emine Aksu, or rather the impression that he was getting of her from her friends and relatives.

Although he'd never tried it himself, İkmen didn't have anything against the concept of free love. He was not a religious man, and so he could not object to free love on the grounds of faith. And if all concerned were happy with the situation, where was the harm? There was none – at least that was the case provided human emotions were not involved. The previous afternoon, İkmen had spoken to two men who had loved Emine Aksu in the past; Ali Tevfik, the car hire boss – who had heard rumours that his old love had maybe found someone 'special' – and a man called Nesim Arseven, who had turned out to be old and drunk and very graphic in his speech. Apparently, during the height of her involvement with hippy culture, Emine Aksu had been passed from man to man just as the Western girls had been at that time. It seemed odd to İkmen that at a time when women were supposed to be gaining more freedom from men, they were still allowing themselves to be used by them simply for sex. The men were still in control even if they were stoned out of their minds.

İkmen sat up in bed and lit a cigarette. Now that Fatma was finally asleep, he knew that it was unlikely to wake her. She was – and had been for a number of years – going through her change and was frequently dogged by night sweats. For hours she would shuffle uncomfortably about in their bed, unable to get cool and therefore rest. Then eventually, usually in the early hours of the morning, she would finally drop off, snoring and utterly exhausted. Having seen her go through pregnancy and childbirth nine times during the course of their married life, İkmen felt that the lot of women was not something that was easy. Their lives were, as far as he could tell, dominated by their biology. But then with regard to the girls who gave themselves to the hippy men, maybe that was the point. Maybe their promiscuity was connected to their biological imperative to reproduce – at any cost and with just about anyone. But then again, perhaps it all happened simply because they were all stoned off the planet. İkmen puffed heavily on his cigarette and, vaguely wondering what cannabis might be like and whether it really was as relaxing as people said it was, he let his mind drift on.

Emine Aksu and her husband were an attractive and well-off couple. As far as İkmen could see, they had everything they could possibly want – with the exception of children. But perhaps that was by choice rather than biological misfortune. After all, if one spent much of one's life in pursuit of pleasure – and in the case of Emine, at least, some mischief too – there was going to be little room for any children on the scene. Youngsters, as he knew only too well, were not good for either the looks or the energy levels. Not that he regretted having any of his children, however difficult they might be or have been. He loved them all, which was why his mind now turned away from Emine Aksu and on to the subject of his daughter Hulya. He knew how hard she was working and it worried him. Her mother-in-law Estelle did her bit, going out cleaning and occasionally helping at her brother's shop in the Egyptian Bazaar. But Estelle was getting on in years and couldn't work like a youngster any more. That was down to Hulya who was, to her father's way of thinking, looking decidedly drawn these days. How he hated those people who had rendered his son-in-law unemployable! And yet he was also acutely aware of how useless and without point his hate actually was. Nothing was going to change what had happened to Berekiah. There was no time machine that one could get into, go back in to put things right. No such thing existed in reality. But then it occurred to İkmen that this was an incorrect assumption on his part. People like the Aksus revisited their misspent youths all the time. They did as they pleased, played around and exhibited, to İkmen, much that was in common with spoilt children. Even their clothes, Emine Aksu's at least, were frivolous. In many ways they had never grown up. Whether they realised it or not they were stuck, probably for ever now, in the sixties and seventies. At least Ahmet Aksu was. Emine, as İkmen had felt almost from the start, was way beyond such idle musings now.

Moving her was so easy. There was so little left that in a way what had happened, albeit by reflex more than anything else, had been for the best. Not that her condition, or the condition of any actual body living or dead, made any real difference. She was just awkward; angular and difficult. She had been so very sexy for so very, very long.

'*What a wonderful model of car this was! So stylish. What innovation!*'

A 1972 Fiat 124 BC coupe.

'*I'M WONDERING WHERE TO PUT HER.*'

'*I think that the car should take her wherever is appropriate. Let it decide.*'

'*THAT'S VERY BUDDHIST.*'

'*What?*'

'*GOING ALONG WITH EVENTS, ALLOWING FATE TO MANIPULATE WITHOUT RESISTANCE.*'

'*Kismet.*'

'*PLEASE DON'T BRING ISLAM INTO THIS. IT IS BOTH SACRILE-GIOUS AND INAPPROPRIATE.*'

'*As you wish.*' A pause. '*Then there's that very naughty idea that was put forward. Very wicked. Very appropriate, though.*'

'*EVIL.*'

'*At night the place should be deserted. Such an appropriate place, I think. Cool, like here?*'

'*VERY COOL.*'

But loading her into the back of the car was not as easy as it might seem. When her head hit the handle of the outside of the back left-hand door it came off and hit the ground with a dull thud. Luckily it was quickly and easily replaced at the top of her spine with a spot of glue.

Chapter 3

In most people's lives there are three, maybe four, events which stand out as truly remarkable. For people in some professions, however, events of this type are likely to occur with more regularity just because of the nature of the job concerned. Police officers fall often into this category and Çetin İkmen more than most.

After getting in close to what was really only a skeleton, İkmen stood back in order to look at what had to be one of the oddest crime scenes the İstanbul police force had ever attended. On Voyvoda Street, which was in the old banking quarter of Galata, there was a very attractive but strange legacy from the district's financial past. Donated to the city by the Jewish banking family Kamondo, the staircase known as the Kamondo Steps represented a strange fusion between utility and art. Unashamedly art deco in design, the short stairway ran up from Voyvoda Street to Kart Cinar Street in two symmetrical curving ares. In the middle of what some would call an 'exhibit' rather than a staircase, was a large, vaguely tulip-bulb-shaped flower bed. Under normal circumstances the residents of Galata were accustomed to seeing a small and, frankly, sickly looking bush inside this feature. But not now. Not at five o'clock in the morning with İkmen and other police officers rubbing their tired eyes in disbelief at the sight of the thing.

41

'Well, as a method of corpse disposal it is most original,' İkmen said as he lit up a cigarette and then inhaled deeply.

Süleyman, who, together with his sergeant İzzet Melik, was also in attendance, said, 'This is less corpse disposal and more display, if you ask my opinion.'

It was bizarre. A skeleton, covered in places by what looked like a selection of rags, was sitting up in the flower bed, its legs splayed out to either side of its torso, grinning. From the rather large amount of dry brown hair that still clung to its scalp it would seem that the skeleton was that of a woman.

'Not Mrs Emine Aksu though,' İzzet Melik said through a lot of cigarette smoke and even more luxuriant moustache.

'No.' İkmen leaned in towards the skeleton and said, 'No, this is old. Or rather, I assume that it is. Dr Sarkissian will be able to tell us more about it when he gets here.'

Arto Sarkissian, the police pathologist, had been called by İkmen as soon as he had arrived at the site. An ethnic Armenian, Dr Sarkissian was İkmen's oldest and closest friend. He was also an expert in his field as well as being a very diligent and caring professional. Not everyone, as İkmen knew from the reactions he'd got from the two young constables who had found the skeleton, could easily cope with such epic levels of oddness as this. Since police had arrived in some numbers just over half an hour before, he had seen a few people cringe in terror while others burst out laughing – but not in a happy way. Shock, as İkmen knew only too well, could be a very strange creature indeed.

'Of course,' Süleyman said as he put his head on one side so that he could better see the grinning skeletal face, 'this "person" has not, necessarily, been killed unlawfully.'

'True.' İkmen nodded. 'Although I think that the chances of this person having met a natural end are slim. This body has been placed in a very public and attention-grabbing way. Why do such a thing if the body concerned is not either one's handiwork or a statement of some sort?'

'Maybe whoever put it here dug it up from one of the cemeteries,' Süleyman said. 'Perhaps an act of spite against a deceased rival or, as we think in this case, her family.'

'Whether he killed her or not, whoever put her here needs to be caught,' İzzet Melik said. 'Digging up the dead and messing around with them is a seriously disturbed thing to do.'

'We'll need to check out all the cemeteries in the greater İstanbul area,' İkmen put in wearily. 'Laborious work, but there's no way round it.'

'I can make a start on that,' İzzet Melik said with just a brief glance over at his boss.

'If Inspector Süleyman feels that is appropriate . . .'

'Yes, of course,' Süleyman said. 'Get back to the station and start listing cemeteries and ringing around, İzzet.'

'When Sergeant Farsakoğlu gets in at seven I will instruct her to assist you,' İkmen said.

'Sir.'

İzzet Melik left with a smile on his face, buoyed up, Süleyman thought, by the prospect of working with İkmen's very attractive female sergeant, Ayşe Farsakoğlu. Many years previously Süleyman had had a brief affair with Ayşe, but that was now in the past and he was now happily married. Not so Ayşe Farsakoğlu, however, who, Süleyman knew, would not relish the thought of time spent in company with a middle-aged macho man like İzzet. Not that Sergeant Melik's heart wasn't in the right place; he was just rather old fashioned in his attitudes towards women – not something of which a woman like Ayşe could approve. If she knew how crazy he was about her, would it change her attitude towards him? Süleyman felt that, sadly, it probably wouldn't.

'So,' İkmen said to Süleyman once İzzet Melik had gone, 'we've one missing ex-hippy woman, a barely clothed and seemingly ancient skeleton, and the English and Italian football lunatics haven't even started to arrive in the city yet!'

Süleyman smiled. Liverpool football club were playing AC Milan in the final of the UEFA Champions League at the Atatürk Olimpiyat Stadium, which was just outside İstanbul, on the following Wednesday, 25 May. It was now Friday 20 May and the first 'football lunatics', as İkmen termed them, were not due to arrive in İstanbul until Saturday at the earliest.

'I don't see why the arrival of a horde of football fans should disrupt what we are doing,' Süleyman replied.

İkmen gave his friend a deeply cynical look.

'I've heard that the department has the policing for the event under control,' the younger man continued. 'I've no reason to doubt—'

'Several thousand young English and Italian fans roaming the streets, fuelled by oceans of beer, do not easily follow instructions or entreaties to get out of the way when one is in a hurry,' İkmen said. 'Mark my words, Mehmet, before this thing is over and done with you and I will have altercations with football lunatics.'

Still smiling to himself, Süleyman said, 'Yes, Çetin. If you say so.'

'I do.' He then folded his arms angrily across his narrow chest.

İkmen was that rarity amongst Turkish men; a man who hated football. In spite of having had a father and, currently, a son who were both fanatical Galatasaray Football Club supporters, not to mention friends who supported a variety of clubs, İkmen was unmoved. Not a sportsman himself, unless heavy smoking could be regarded as a sport of some sort, İkmen couldn't see the point of such activity and hated the passion and violence that supporting football teams so often brought. Even one as urbane as Mehmet Süleyman had his club, which was also Galatasaray. In fact, most people that İkmen knew supported what was arguably the city's most famous team. The exception to this rule was the breathless and very overweight man hurrying towards them now.

'Good God,' Dr Arto Sarkissian said as he hastened up the steps towards the grinning skeleton, 'who on earth put you in there?'

Arto, who predictably received no reply from the dead body in front of him, supported Beşiktaş Football Club. But then, as İkmen's football-mad son Bülent was heard to say to his 'uncle' Arto some weeks before, somebody had to.

There had been a time when none of the Cohen brothers, Balthazar, Jak or Leon, had been able to walk through the streets of Balat without talking to at least three different groups of friends. As youngsters the boys had been pitied by many of their neighbours because of their poverty. Their mother died young giving birth to a fourth brother who did not survive. This left the three boys in the care of their brutal alcoholic father whose habit kept his sons hungry, ragged and frequently dirty. But two of them had come out comparatively unscathed. Balthazar went into the police force while Jak headed for England and a very successful career in the London nightclub scene. Only Leon, who now lived out in one of the shabbier tower blocks just to the east of Atatürk

Airport, had followed their father's example and become hopelessly addicted to drink.

'There! You see there?' Balthazar said as he waved a long, thin hand towards a group of men outside a grocer's shop on a street corner. 'Those men there! Listen to their speech. Just listen to it!'

Estelle who was trying to be patient as she pushed her complaining husband around in his wheelchair, sighed. Balthazar was light, but the chair was heavy and Balat was, like most of the city, characterised by many hills, slopes and broken pavements. But in spite of this she did as her husband asked and listened, or tried to listen, to what the group of men were saying. Not that she had much success in this venture.

'Kurdish!' her husband said by way of explanation. 'They are speaking Kurdish. Outside Eskenazi the grocer's, these men are speaking Kurdish!'

Now their rather guttural tones made sense. 'Ah, well,' Estelle said, 'that explains it.'

Her husband turned stiffly around in his chair to face her. 'And that doesn't bother you?'

'That they're speaking Kurdish? No. They are Kurds. Why shouldn't they? We speak Ladino.'

'Not on the street,' Balthazar retorted. 'Amongst ourselves. There is a time and a place. We know where those are.'

'And these men don't?'

'No.'

But Estelle knew that it wasn't the fact that the men were speaking Kurdish that was bothering her husband so much as the idea that they were from somewhere he neither knew nor understood. Eastern Turkey, where so many of the more recent migrants to the city came from, was a total mystery to someone like Balthazar. Turks, Armenians, Greeks, he understood their languages – he spoke Turkish most of the time after all – only going into Ladino, the language of the Sephardic Jews, on very rare occasions. These people, to him, were of 'his' city; they were İstanbullus irrespective of their ethnic origins. The Anatolian country people, whether Kurdish or not, were 'other', folk from 'out there' in a place Balthazar neither knew nor wanted to know.

'But outside Eskenazi's place . . .'

Not that the little grocer's shop on the corner of Vodina Street still belonged to the Avram Eskenazi whom Balthazar remembered from his childhood. The old man had sold up years ago, back in the fifties. Since then it had been taken over firstly by a local Turkish family and then by the current owners, Kurds from Diyarbakır. Estelle knew that deep down inside Balthazar had to know all of this – he had, after all, worked all over the city until 1999. But his choosing to ignore reality was nothing new and so Estelle just carried on pushing in silence until finally and thankfully they came across one of her husband's old friends.

Edmondo Loya was, as he was always quick to point out, the older of the identical Loya twins. His brother, Maurice, was a full minute and a half younger. It was something Edmondo never let him or anyone else forget. Balthazar was well aware of this and so when he saw him coming out of the shoe shop that was next door to the Kurdish grocer's he said, 'Ah, the elder Loya! Edmondo! How are you? Are you well?'

Estelle pushed the wheelchair over towards the thin, elderly-looking man who was holding a bag containing what looked like a new pair of shoes.

47

'God still sees fit to keep me on earth,' Edmondo said in the lugubrious fashion which those who knew him recognised as his style. 'My arthritis is a trouble, but what can one do? My young brother suffers also. It must be in the blood.'

'Your father suffered too, if I remember rightly,' Balthazar said as he lit up a cigarette and then coughed very heavily on to the back of his hand.

'You should give that up or it'll kill you,' Edmondo observed gloomily. And then looking up at Estelle he said, 'Hello, Mrs Cohen. Are you well?'

While Balthazar smarted under his friend's exhortation to stop smoking, Estelle passed the time of day with Edmondo pleasantly enough. They carried on with the subject of health for a while and then passed on to the weather at which point a still-needled Balthazar said, 'Yes, but I didn't come out today to talk about the blasted rainfall!'

'Ah . . .'

'No.' He shifted awkwardly and painfully in his chair. 'Edmondo,' he said, 'do you remember whether there were any hippies here in Balat or in Fener back in the sixties and seventies?'

'Hippies?'

'Those European kids who came here on their way to India,' Balthazar said. 'Took a lot of drugs and' – he looked around briefly but warily at his wife – 'had sex a lot and—'

'Oh, all the crazy kids who came to Sultanahmet,' Edmondo said. 'Yes, I remember them. I spent quite a bit of time over there in those days. Some of the hippies were very well read. I remember a marvellous conversation I had outside the Aya Sofya with a German girl about Kierkegaard. It was wonderful . . .'

'Yes, but do you remember whether any of those kids came here? Whether they hung around?'

'No!' Edmondo shook his shaggy grey head emphatically. 'Not here. No one came here then.' And then, turning around to face a short, stocky Turk coming out of the shoe shop behind him, he said, 'Ali, you remember the hippies; I know you do. They didn't come up to this part of town back in the sixties, did they?'

'Hippies?' Ali Paksoy's face, which, like the rest of him, was in its mid-fifties, briefly wrinkled at the word. 'No. Why?'

'My friend Balthazar is asking,' Edmondo said. And then, turning back to the Cohens he asked, 'Why do you want to know about hippies here, Balthazar?'

Balthazar thought about telling them about Mehmet Süleyman and his investigation and then thought better of it. After all, he didn't know precisely what Mehmet had said about it to those locals he had interviewed and Balthazar was still too much the police officer to want to ruin any line of inquiry for a colleague.

'Oh, I'm just busying myself after all these years looking at a little history of my neighbourhood.'

'Nothing to do with the disappearance of a Turkish lady who, it is said, used to be a drug taker, then?' Edmondo asked. 'I've not been told a name or—'

'Er . . .' Balthazar had forgotten how news had always travelled fast in a place like Balat.

'A very handsome policeman was asking around last night,' Edmondo said. 'You know Juanita Kordovi? Married a rabbi, then had an affair with a pharmacist, writes bad romantic novels?'

Balthazar knew the name and the dubious reputation even if he didn't know the woman.

'She saw this policeman. She said he was asking about a missing woman who had been a hippy. You were once in the police force, Balthazar . . .'

'Yes, but, well . . .'

'A Turkish woman who was a hippy?' Ali, who had been listening with a deeply furrowed brow, said. 'That's rare. Are you sure?'

'So it is said,' Balthazar replied.

'But not unknown,' Edmondo Loya said. 'Not unknown.'

'Well, no,' Ali said. 'No, I . . .' But he didn't say anything more; he simply cleared his throat.

A tall, very slim young man wearing a Liverpool Football Club T-shirt came and stood next to Ali and said, 'What are you talking about?'

'Nothing of any interest to you,' Ali replied with rather more heat in his voice than Balthazar felt was appropriate.

'Oh,' the young man said, and then, obviously cowed, he moved back in the direction of the shoe shop.

'My nephew,' Ali said once the boy was out of earshot. 'He helps me in the shop but his only real interest is football.'

'Rafik, Ali's nephew, supports the English club Liverpool,' Edmondo added. 'Quite why—'

Ali put a finger to his head and then shook it violently. 'Crazy boy,' he said. 'A little bit simple, as some would say. But he can fetch and carry boxes of shoes, and he's neat and practical, so he's a good enough help to me in my work.'

'He must be excited that Liverpool are playing over in the Atatürk Stadium next week,' Balthazar said.

'Oh, yes, he's very excited about that,' the Turk replied. 'He hasn't got a ticket, of course, who can afford such things?

50

But he'll watch it on the television with all of his football-mad friends. He's not a bad boy.'

It wasn't an assertion Balthazar felt was in accord with the way in which Ali had spoken to Rafik earlier. But then maybe the shoe seller was just a gruffly spoken man. Balthazar himself was frequently guilty of such harsh behaviour with his own son. Not that any of this was relevant to what he was supposed to be doing, which was finding out, if he could, some local information for Mehmet Süleyman. Edmondo and this Ali claimed to have no memory of any hippies in the district and so maybe it would be best if Balthazar moved on to possibly more fruitful encounters. However, there was something that he had to ask his friend and the shoe seller first.

'Your shop,' he said as he tipped his head towards the Turk, 'it is Madrid's haberdashery, isn't it?'

Behind him Estelle sighed with what sounded like impatience.

'My father bought the shop from Mr Madrid's widow back in the fifties,' Ali responded with what looked very much like a somewhat patronising smile.

'Your family came from Bursa,' Estelle said.

'Yes, Mrs Cohen, they did.'

She smiled. 'Balthazar and I lived away from Balat for many years. In Karaköy. We . . . er . . . we lost touch with the quarter.'

She was trying hard to cover up her husband's obvious inadequacies with regard to local information. His status as a disabled person coupled with his recent reluctance to face current reality was something she felt she had to explain. She meant it kindly lest people think that he was stupid. But Balthazar felt bitter towards her anyway. She got out and about on legs, as he had once done, and just the thought of it made him jealous. And besides, life had been better when Mr Madrid had run the old haberdasher's shop. Then almost every face on the street had been familiar to him and the shop window he was looking at now had been draped with rich velvets and shimmering silks. It was more than a bit of a change from the cheap rubber boots and the odd pair of spangly flip-flops that were currently displayed in the shoe shop window.

As if by way of an apology for his cheap and rather sparse wares, Ali said, 'We used to hand-make our shoes in the old days. But now there's no call for it any more. People just want cheap things now. Rubbish. It's sadly the modern way. My father had such ambitions for this shop, but they all came to nothing.'

Balthazar grunted his agreement. The world, and especially his city, was indeed regressing.

Ayşe Farsakoğlu replaced the handset of her telephone down on to the receiver and sighed. None of the workers out at the city's biggest cemetery, the Karaca Ahmet in Üsküdar, had seen or heard anything odd over there during the night. As far as they could tell, all of the graves were intact. But in order to be absolutely certain they would have to do a detailed search of the whole site which was, Ayşe knew, a massive job. She looked across at İzzet Melik who was just finishing a similar conversation with the custodian of the great Eyüp Cemetery at the northern end of the Golden Horn. A favoured place of burial for pious Muslims, Eyüp was another vast space that would take probably days to investigate in anything approaching any detail.

'Nothing?' she asked as Melik, too, replaced his handset.

'No.'

'Unless we get very lucky, this is going to take a long time,' Ayşe said as she held up a packet of cigarettes and then asked her colleague if he would like one.

İzzet Melik first smiled and then leaned forward to take one from her packet. He wanted to smoke, like his boss Mehmet Süleyman, there were few things that he preferred over a cigarette. A smile from Ayşe as she shared a smoke with him, however, was one of them. He didn't often get the opportunity to work with İkmen's deputy but whenever he did he was inevitably consumed with lust. Not that he could show that in any way. Ayşe Farsakoğlu was a very 'modern' woman, concerned with female rights and privileges and other things İzzet only had the vaguest notion of.

'Dr Sarkissian couldn't find much earth on the body,' he said as he lit his cigarette and then inhaled deeply. 'He said that given the fact that he felt the skeleton was old, it should have been caked in soil. But it wasn't.'

'Maybe it came from a mausoleum above ground.'

'If she were a wealthy non Muslim*, maybe.'

'Maybe she was.' Ayşe frowned. 'Not that her status is relevant to this. The poor woman, whoever she was, has been dug up, maybe violated . . .'

'Dr Sarkissian has only just started his examination,' İzzet cut in. 'We don't really know anything about her yet.'

'No, but . . .'

'Ayşe, she may or may not have been violated. We can't jump to conclusions before we have the facts.'

Ayşe looked down at the floor and said, 'No.'

---

*Muslims believe that corpses must be buried directly in contact with the soil.

Two seemingly contradictory things had been happening in the police force across Turkey. On the one hand more women were joining up and were consequently gaining positions of increasing influence. On the other hand, or so it was rumoured, more male officers of a religiously conservative nature were joining too. Ayşe, it was well known, shared her boss Çetin İkmen's strong views about the necessity for a secular state and was, as a result of this, very touchy around men she felt did not share her views. Although traditional in that he did have an essentially patriarchal take on life, İzzet Melik was not a man who needed or even wanted the women in his life to be covered. Quite the reverse was in fact true and now, possibly, was the time when he should make Ayşe aware of this.

'Sergeant Farsakoğlu,' he said addressing her by her formal, professional title, 'I think that I should tell you that I may not be precisely what I seem.'

She looked up fearfully at him.

'In spite of outward appearances,' he pointed to his large and very black moustache, 'I am a reasonably modern guy. I know that women, a lot of women, sometimes get a rough deal from some men—'

'An understatement,' Ayşe said.

'Yes, but—'

'Yes, but I can see what you're trying to say, Sergeant, and I do appreciate your saying it.'

He smiled.

But of course Ayşe was no fool and knew only too well that İzzet, though indeed not a religious person, was a fairly unreconstructed macho man. He liked a drink with his male friends, enjoyed sexist jokes, and he could very often be found goggling at pictures of semi-naked models in the cheaper type of newspapers down in the squad room. Not that any of this made him a bad person; it didn't. It just made him a person she could never in a million years find attractive. That he in his turn found her so alluring was just sad for him and really rather embarrassing for Ayşe.

'We'll see what Dr Sarkissian comes up with after the autopsy,' Ayşe said by way of mollification.

'Yes . . .'

At that point the door to what was actually Süleyman's office flew open and, preceded by a large body of smoke, İkmen entered. Without preamble he said, 'Well, Dr Sarkissian has confirmed that our body is indeed female. Just one look at the pelvis convinced him. Amazing to be so knowledgeable about anatomy . . .' He smiled. 'But anyway, I have left him to his grim task and we will no doubt find out more later. Any ladies not in their graves that should be?'

'No, sir, not yet,' Ayşe replied. 'Sergeant Melik has been concentrating mainly on the cemeteries on this side of the Bosphorus, while I've been working on those over on the Asian side, including the Karaca Ahmet.'

İkmen threw himself down into Süleyman's very clean and comfortable leather chair. 'My parents are buried over there,' he said. 'I was born in Üsküdar.'

'Well, sir, so far, the Karaca Ahmet would seem to be OK.'

'Mmm. But it's a big site.'

'It will take the custodian and his workers some time to investigate the whole area . . .'

'Well, let them know that they can have officers to help them if necessary,' İkmen said as he stubbed his cigarette out and then instantly lit another. 'I don't like people who desecrate and disturb the dead. Whoever, to quote Inspector Süleyman, "displayed" this lady's corpse for us this morning is quite obviously not the sort of person who should be wandering our streets at liberty. God, if you're not even safe when you're dead . . .'

Station legend had it that İkmen's first case after he had been promoted to inspector had been the investigation of a suspected necrophiliac. It had apparently left him with a particular antipathy towards such people and their activities.

'In the meantime, however,' İkmen continued, 'I must also carry on with my investigations into the disappearance of Mrs Emine Aksu. The living, as our esteemed commissioner has been very quick to point out to me, taking quite rightful precedence over the dead.'

Not that İkmen felt that Emine Aksu was probably still alive – he didn't. But his boss, Commissioner Ardiç, had been adamant that what he called the 'oddness' on the Kamondo Steps should not distract from what could be a very high-profile missing-person case. In addition, and something that wasn't actually said by either İkmen or his boss, there was also the question of solvability. Grave desecration always had been, and remained, a serious crime, but offenders were notoriously difficult to apprehend and not all of those working on such cases felt that a long-dead victim warranted time and money that could be spent upon the living. Added to this was the fact that İkmen and his colleagues now worked much more in line with their counterparts in the European Union – which meant case clear-up targets with the emphasis firmly upon dealing with those who may be a danger to life. Those attacking the dead, therefore, though not regarded as exactly benign, were not seen as a present danger to the living.

'Sergeant Melik and myself will continue making contact with the cemeteries,' Ayşe said.

'Yes.' İkmen stood up. 'If I can leave this in your very capable hands . . .'

'Sir.'

'Having had little success with Mrs Aksu's old hippy friends, I now find that I am obliged to swim in somewhat deeper water,' İkmen said.

Ayşe Farsakoğlu frowned.

'Those of our countrymen who have remained hippies,' İkmen said. 'Men in some cases even older than myself.' And then, noting the look of deep distaste on her face, he added, 'Yes, it is tragic. I think of myself with long hair and maybe even a kaftan and I don't know whether to laugh or cry.'

And then, with a slight bow towards İzzet Melik, İkmen left. Tragic had been an apt word for the type of person he was going to meet now. However, it was also a term that could have been equally well applied to the look on İzzet's face as he surveyed the lovely Ayşe. The poor man didn't stand a chance with her and yet he longed for her in a way all the world could see only too clearly.

Chapter 4

It had been at about eleven-thirty in the morning when Ahmet Aksu had telephoned the police station to talk to İkmen. But the inspector had already gone to his rather ill-defined appointment with some of Turkey's remaining hippies. It was therefore Mehmet Süleyman who spoke to Aksu and he, too, who went out to Hasköy to see him in person. Mr Aksu, now standing in front of his huge front window over-looking the Golden Horn, had remembered something.

'The man I think my wife may have been seeing was, I believe, as I've said before, someone from our past,' Ahmet Aksu said as he watched Süleyman sit down and then light a cigarette. 'I don't know who, although I understand that Inspector İkmen has been looking into my wife's old contacts.'

'Indeed.'

'Not easy for me. A past I . . . well . . .' Ahmet Aksu sighed. 'But there's something else. Something that may or may not be of any significance.'

Süleyman nodded. 'Anything you can tell us, Mr Aksu, is most welcome. Sometimes things that one may perceive to be entirely unconnected may indeed have an important, if not a vital, part to play in the solution to a crime or a disappearance like this.'

Although slightly pale, most probably due to lack of sleep and possibly too many cigarettes, Ahmet Aksu was an attractive and very well-groomed man. As stylish as his state-of-the-art home, he also moved with a fluid grace that impressed the much younger and considerably less graceful Süleyman. Ahmet Aksu moved towards the set of thick floor cushions opposite Süleyman and sat down.

'In the weeks leading up to her disappearance, Emine laughed a lot more than usual,' he said as he, too, lit up a cigarette.

'She laughed.' If, Süleyman thought, he'd come all the way over to Hasköy just to talk about a middle-aged women being a bit happier than usual, he wasn't going to be too pleased.

'As if she were responding to some sort of private joke.'

'And was she? Did you ask her?'

'No. I found it a little odd and disconcerting, maybe, too, but it didn't bother me. No, of her own volition, Emine supplied a partial explanation for her mood.'

'Which was?'

'She said she'd been "hanging around", to use her own words, with someone she knew and I would never guess whom.'

Süleyman frowned.

'She didn't say whether it was a man or a woman or whether or not she was sleeping with this person. So I don't know if the person I am talking about now is relevant to her disappearance. What I can say with some certainty, however, is that the person who made her laugh was someone we had known and laughed at before.'

'When you were young hippies?' Süleyman asked.

Ahmet Aksu shrugged. 'Maybe. We knew lots of odd and sometimes really quite pitiful people back in those days, Inspector. So many kids – not just rich ones like Emine and me – wanted to get in on the hippy scene; children of reli-gious people, mummy's boys, the mentally ill, the sexually desperate maybe even deranged . . . Emine promised to tell me whom she'd come across soon. She said I'd laugh my head off when I found out who it was.'

'But you didn't take too much notice?'

'No. I will always freely and openly admit to being a hippy when I was younger. But it's over. I am a businessman now. That's all.' Ahmet Aksu lifted his arms up helplessly and then let them drop to his sides. 'I knew that she was seeing someone romantically and this just seemed like a rather irrelevant little sideline. But now that I think about it, now that I think about every word we spoke to each other over those last few weeks, I have to consider that the person at whom she was laughing may also have been the man that she was bedding, too.'

'Yes, but sir, if your wife had contempt for this person, would she have found such a thing exciting with someone who was so risible? You said yourself that this last affair was one that she was finding very exciting.'

'I wouldn't have said so, no,' Ahmet Aksu replied. 'But who knows? Maybe this old acquaintance had changed. People do. Maybe that was the surprise, that someone like Murad the Mummy's Boy or that terrible little dope-head, Erdoğan something or other, had transformed into a rich, attractive, desirable citizen.'

'Like you?'

Ahmet Aksu smiled. 'You mean, Inspector, that my wife was looking for adventure and all she found at the end of it was her husband or a facsimile thereof?'

'Maybe.' Süleyman also smiled. 'Mr Aksu, as you know, Inspector İkmen, has interviewed several of your male friends who shared your unconventional past. None of them have seen Mrs Aksu for quite some time – or rather, that is what they would have us believe, and in truth we have no reason so far to doubt their stories. Inspector İkmen is at this moment with some of your more distant acquaintances, a man called Kadir—'

'That junkie!' Ahmet Aksu shook his head in disbelief. 'Now there is a breathing joke if ever there was one!'

'So maybe—'

'Emine and Kadir? Impossible! Inspector, Kadir shoots up heroin, has done for years. And if there is one thing that Emine and myself agree upon it is that we never, ever sleep with junkies. The risk of disease is just too high!'

'Yes.' AIDS being the most awful possible result of such a mating as Süleyman knew only too well. Although entirely clear of the disease himself he had, some years before, had sex with a prostitute who had been an HIV positive heroin user. He had done what he did in a moment of great weakness for which he had nearly paid with his life. Never again. He could fully understand how Aksu and his wife felt on this issue.

'So if not this Kadir, is there anyone else in your old circle of friends whom you can name that was odd or awkward in some way?'

Ahmet Aksu thought for a few moments before replying. 'I can't remember them all. I know there was an Armenian boy – he had a horse – but I can't recall his name to save my life. However, what I can recall . . . mmm . . .' He sighed. 'I'm not saying that any of these really quite pathetic specimens as I knew them, have harmed Emine in any way . . .'

'But they might know whom she is with or whom she was seeing when she left?'

'Exactly.' He first put his fingers up to his lips and then

said, 'Well, there was a boy called Bekir who had terrible acne. We used to call him "Mountain Face" on account of his appalling spots. I think he came from Bebek. His father was a doctor, which just added to his problems because the rest of us found the idea that he could have a face like that with a doctor for a father very funny. Talk about a bad advertisement. Mountain Face fancied Emine, badly, but then who did not? There was a boy from Aksaray, I can't remember what he was called, but he walked with a limp and took far too much acid. I think he ended up in an institution . . .' He paused. 'Inspector, there were so many creatures like this. Tea boys who wanted to get high, randy taxi drivers . . .'

'The son of the doctor should be easy enough to find,' Süleyman said. 'I know there are quite a few medics in Bebek, but they all know each other . . .'

'An older man whose name was something like Abdullah . . .'

'But not Abdullah?'

'Abdulrahman. That was it! Abdulrahman! He must have been about thirty in the late sixties. But he could speak English and he hung around the Pudding Shop just like everyone else. He must be getting on now. He liked Emine. They used to talk philosophy together. I assume he wanted her body as well as her mind and maybe he even got it. But we used to laugh at him, too. He seemed old to us.' He paused for a second before continuing, his face marred just slightly by a frown. 'There was also a Jew,' he said. 'Clever.'

'Was he, this Jewish man, old?' Süleyman asked.

Still frowning, Ahmet Aksu said, 'No. Although he seemed it. He was actually young like the rest of us. But his conversation was so learned and his clothes so very conventional that he gave the impression of being older than he was. Now what was his name?'

'Do you know where this Jewish man came from?'

He answered immediately. 'Balat,' he said. 'There were still a lot of Jews there in those days. Now what was his name . . . Spanish . . .'

'You and your friends laughed at this Abdulrahman and the Jewish boy?'

'For different reasons, yes. Abdulrahman was a little too desperate to hang on to what remained of his youth and the Jewish boy was – well, he was quaint. I liked him. He was clever, serious and, well, quaint.' And then suddenly Ahmet Aksu's eyes shone with recognition. 'I have it!' he said. 'The Jew's name. It was Edmondo! Edmondo Loya.'

'There were so many takers. Even in the old days,' the middle-aged man with the half-closed eyes said to İkmen. 'People who didn't know Ginsberg from a hole in the road.'

'And do you, Mr Özal?' İkmen asked. 'Do you know your Ginsberg from a hole in the road?'

Kadir Özal turned a lizard-like eye upon his interrogator and answered with a very slow and bad tempered, 'Yes.'

Roughly İkmen's own age, Kadir Özal saw himself as the apogee of hippy life in İstanbul. Clearly stoned on something (hashish, from the smell of his place, but heroin from the look of him, İkmen felt), he was listening to Jefferson Airplane's 'White Rabbit' on the antiquated stereo that fitted very well into his Afghan rug-covered flat in Sultanahmet. In fact, Kadir only lived around the corner from İkmen's own apartment on Ticarethane Alley. That 'hippy central' had been not only down the stairs from his own apartment but also just across the road from police headquarters had always been something that had amused the inspector greatly.

'So, Emine Aksu,' İkmen said as he continued the conversation they had been having earlier, 'what was your relationship with her?'

Kadir shrugged. 'She was cool, back in the day. Very flirty, liked to stir things up, make a bit of trouble from time to time. We had a thing together for a while.'

'You had a relationship with Mrs Aksu – or Miss Öz, as she was then?'

Kadir Özal smirked, rather unpleasantly, İkmen felt. 'We had sex,' he said.

'I see.'

'Then she went off with Ahmet Aksu and they got married.' It was said with ill-disguised disgust. 'Not cool. I know that Emine and Ahmet still sleep around, but even so . . . hardly the action of people "mad to live" as Kerouac put it.'

'Maybe they just grew up,' İkmen couldn't resist saying.

Kadir Özal viewed him acidly over the top of his round, pale blue spectacles and said, 'That was a cheap shot, Inspector.'

'Yes, I know I—'

'Listen, man, I choose to live like this,' Kadir said in the heavily American-accented English he liked to use. 'When the hippies came here to Turkey it was, for me, like someone turned the light on. Know what I mean?'

In a way İkmen did. Although not nearly as outré as Kadir he was fully aware of the contribution those early Western visitors had made to his city.

'Emine Aksu is missing,' İkmen said. 'We have reason to believe that she may have gone off with someone from her past.'

'Not me,' Kadir replied with a very final tilt of his head.
'No?'

'No.' He smiled. 'Without wanting to cause offence, Emine and women of her age, they don't do it for me. I mean, why have a hen when you can have a chick?'

Like a lot of the old hippy men whom İkmen had met over the years, Kadir preferred young girls. It was understandable, from the hippy's point of view. What İkmen could never, however, really appreciate was what the girls saw in such men. Old and drug-raddled, they were not often wealthy (although Kadir Özal was, or so it was said) and they were probably more patronising to the girls than even the oily carpet dealers in the Grand Bazaar. Maybe it was the romance of the 'old days' that attracted them? All this vinyl instead of CDs, talk of Ginsberg and Kerouac, not to mention the perception-altering properties of the drugs on offer was very much at odds with a world that İkmen recognised and acknowledged as superficial. For the more spiritual young person the modern world was extremely daunting and some wanted to hark back to what had been a much simpler time. Some of them, of course, just wanted to get high, but then that wasn't a topic that İkmen wanted to explore even in his own head just at that moment. He had his own issues with youngsters, young men, getting high.

'Have you seen Mrs Aksu around and about in Sultanahmet of late?' İkmen asked.

'I saw her walk past the Pudding Shop with a boy about six months ago.'

'Did you speak to her at all?'

'Yeah.' He smiled. 'I asked her who her "friend" was and she said he was a twenty-four-year-old Italian.'

'She was sleeping with this boy?'

'What else would she be doing with him?' Kadir said. 'Just because she's a woman doesn't mean that Emine cannot like young flesh just like me.'

'Her husband thinks that the man she was going to meet when she disappeared was an older man, someone from their past.'

'Who she was sleeping with?'

'Yes.'

He shrugged. 'It is possible, I guess, but I don't know of such a person.'

'Do you see that many people from the "old days"?' İkmen asked.

Kadir Özal looked down at the floor with a grave expression on his face. 'No. There are not that many of us left, to be honest. Life in Sultanahmet, even sanitised as it is now, can be . . . tough . . .'

'A lot of drug casualties,' İkmen said as a statement of fact.

The hippy looked up at him with undisguised fury in his eyes. 'People have to die from something,' he said. 'Why not the trip of a lifetime? I can think of worse ways to die!'

'Can you?'

'Yeah!' He pushed a great hank of grey-black hair over his shoulder and then said, 'Don't judge what goes on here, Inspector. Don't lay any of your moral and religious—'

'I am not and never have been religious, Mr Özal,' İkmen replied. 'In fact, with the exception of your reliance upon body- and mind-destroying drugs, I am very much impressed by many of the things that hippies regard as important. I love the idea of physical travel as well as the exploration of the mind . . .'

'But not through drugs?'

'No.'

'Why not?'

'Well, Mr Özal,' İkmen said, 'as you yourself intimated, many of those on drugs are now dead. And –' Luckily he stopped himself from saying what was far too personal to be professional, just in time. '– it is illegal.' He cleared his throat. 'But anyway, Mr Özal, there are few older people, like yourself, in or around the hippy scene in Sultanahmet these days?'

Kadir Özal slipped into what turned out to be very cultured Turkish and said with some bitterness, 'As you have observed, Inspector, most of us are dead now. Emine Aksu, to my knowledge, amused herself with boys. That's all.'

And in part it was true. Emine Aksu did like young men. But given even the slightest opportunity with an older man, she was accustomed to taking that too. Ali Tevfik and his encounter with Emine at the Pera Palas Hotel was a case in point. Basically, the woman went with almost anyone and had to be as a result, or so İkmen felt, really quite jaded sexually. That said, Ahmet Aksu had been very adamant on the fact that his wife was excited by this latest lover; someone from her past . . .

At the beginning of their interview, İkmen had asked Kadir Özal where he had been on the day that Emine had disappeared. He'd said he'd been with a 'friend', some child half his age, in the lovely Bosphorus village of Yeniköy. So İkmen now asked for her name and address and also requested that Kadir tell him what they had been doing in such a pretty and select place.

The hippy lowered his head for a second time as he said, 'I took her to visit my mother. She's got, er, we have a . . . it's a kind of a palace and . . .'

So it was true what was said about Kadir Özal and his wealthy background.

When he finally left the small dope-and-joss-stick-scented flat in Sultanahmet, İkmen couldn't resist observing that perhaps not all of Kadir's life could be described as 'rock and roll'. The hippy viewed him with some malice as the policeman disappeared out into the hall in front of his apartment. He then took his mobile phone out of the pocket of his kaftan and made a call.

The body that Arto Sarkissian had dubbed the 'Kamondo Stairs Lady' lay curled up on the pathologist's dissection table like one of those ancient 'bog' people from Scandinavia. Brown with age and stripped of whatever bits of clothing it had once possessed by the forensic scientists, the Lady was now the preserve of the Armenian, his assistant and a rather reluctant-looking Sergeant İzzet Melik.

'The forensic institute found a little soil on the corpse,' Arto said as he made a preliminary sweep of the body with his eyes. 'It would seem that it came from the flower container she was found in on the Stairs.'

'Not from a grave?' İzzet asked.

'No.' The Armenian sighed. 'And there is also the issue of her head to contend with, too.'

'Her head?'

'At some point it has either been removed or, more likely, knocked from its bed at the top of her spine.'

'But . . .'

'It is where it is now, Sergeant, due to the application of superglue,' Arto said. 'Applied quite deliberately and, I must say, liberally to the base of the skull. Possibly the person who knocked her head off did not want that to happen again.'

He smiled. He often smiled at what seemed to the rest of the world inappropriate moments, like now. 'Maybe it would have disordered his "display", as Inspector Süleyman put it, of her.'

'You think that this person, whoever put her there, is very disturbed?'

'How should I know?' the Armenian responded lightly. 'I deal with physical reality not psychological mumbo jumbo, Sergeant. Solving crimes is your job, not mine, thank God.' He sighed. 'I just cut up what other people have killed and tell you about the beastliness I have observed.'

For a moment he looked quite sad. Completely unlike his usual light and often irreverent self. But then, as Süleyman had once told him, İzzet Melik knew that Dr Sarkissian had been a police pathologist for a very long time. Like İkmen, in his late fifties, the Armenian had to have seen more than his fair share of 'beastliness' over the years. Maybe it was finally beginning to get to him. But then again maybe he had other problems the policeman knew nothing about. Also it was almost five o'clock now and the doctor as well as Melik and everyone else associated with this desiccated body had been awake and busy for a very long time.

'Are you going to watch this football match between the Italians and the English next week?' the doctor said as he gently lifted pieces of bone and other, less identifiable tissue, with his scalpel.

'On the television, yes,' Melik replied. 'Can't afford a ticket.'

The doctor looked up from the corpse and smiled. 'Like to go, would you?'

'It's AC Milan and Liverpool, what red-blooded football fan would not?'

'You know my brother has several tickets for the match. He's a great friend and supporter of Beşiktas,' the doctor said.

İzzet Melik, who was a staunch supporter of the third great İstanbul football team, Fenerbahçe, remained silent. Beşiktaş might be all right for the Sarkissian brothers to support, but it was quite, quite wrong for him.

'My brother', the doctor continued as he leaned down to look closely at the ragged ribcage of the corpse, 'offered one of his tickets to me. But sadly I am on call next Wednesday evening. However, if you wanted to go in my stead, Sergeant, I am sure that could be arranged.'

İzzet Melik felt his face suddenly flush with blood. Dr Krikor Sarkissian, the pathologist's brother, was one of the foremost addiction specialists in the country. Rich, clever and very well connected, Dr Krikor would not be going to the match with a bunch of loud 'pals' who would spend their time shouting and swearing at the referee. Nice, reserved men and women of the medical profession who barely uttered a word during the proceedings would more than likely be his companions.

'Oh, well, Doctor, well that's very kind and . . .' Melik muttered. He couldn't go to a football match with people like that! He'd make an idiot of himself! They would look down upon him and probably with good cause!

'Then that's settled,' the Armenian said. Then, looking up from the body in front of him, he added, 'Oh, and by the way, this woman was stabbed.' He pointed with his scalpel at what looked like a notch on the corpse's breast-bone.

'In the chest?' İzzet Melik asked.

'The weapon nicked the side of her sternum,' the doctor said. 'Left-hand side. Possibly he stabbed her through the heart. How dramatic, eh?'

71

'Yes . . .'

'Of course when I say "he" I am making an assumption,' the doctor continued. 'To stab a person through the chest does take considerable power and force and a woman would have to be strong in order to do it. But a female killer is not impossible.'

'No . . .' But Melik's mind was still largely on that very wanted but also very not wanted ticket to the Liverpool/AC Milan match. How on earth could he go with Dr Sarkissian's brother? 'Doctor . . .'

'And she's been dead a long time,' Dr Sarkissian said. 'I won't know exactly how long until the forensic tests are complete, but it is years – unburied.'

'So the murderer, maybe, had her body lying around?'

'Possibly. There are very few Christian mausoleums in the city and so it's doubtful she came from one of those, I think.' The doctor shrugged. 'As Inspector İkmen is wont to say, there is no limit upon the strangeness of humans. Quite honestly, the thought of having a dead body around me and mine is not one that appeals.'

'And the glued head?'

'Who knows, Sergeant? Why, how and for what purpose are not questions I can answer. One can speculate, but' – he frowned – 'that could lead to levels of strangeness I, personally, am not willing to plumb.'

'No.'

They both stood in silence, one to each side of the body, for a few moments. İzzet Melik was just about to try and find a way of tactfully refusing Dr Sarkissian's offer of a ticket to the UEFA Champions League final, when the medic spoke again.

'I envy you seeing Liverpool and AC Milan in the flesh,

as it were,' he said. 'It's going to be very exciting.' And then he smiled broadly. 'But you'll enjoy it, Sergeant, I can tell.'

He then turned away towards his instrument bench while İzzet Melik smiled sheepishly.

Visiting the graves of the mother and the father, which were in Eyüp, had turned out to be both frightening and instructive. Men in woollen caps, ancient custodians of the cemetery, were poking about amongst the graves.

'THEY'RE LOOKING TO SEE WHETHER OR NOT SHE CAME FROM HERE.'

'No they're not! They can't be! That would take for ever!'

'YES. GOOD, ISN'T IT? BECAUSE WHILE THEY'RE LOOKING HERE . . .'

'They're not looking anywhere else.'

'EXACTLY.'

It had to be a puzzle. Nothing had appeared in the newspapers or on the television as yet, but the police had to be involved by now. She was no longer where she had been left, so she had been found. What can they have made or be making of her?

It had not been ideal, what had been done. It was, in fact, quite alien really, but it had been necessary. There was no way she could have gone on any longer. Not just because of the space issue, but also because she really wasn't needed any more. Like this cemetery, she was old and dry and what she had once been or even later represented had begun to slip from memory. She had just simply worn out. And so the weird and, some felt, faintly creepy custodians of the cemetery, carried on looking for disturbed earth, some indication of the existence of a perverse crime almost beyond imagining. They would not and could not find a thing. What had been done, with a lot of pleasure, it had to be said, had been done elsewhere.

Chapter 5

'Tell me about the Loya brothers,' İkmen said as he offered his old friend yet another cigarette.

Balthazar Cohen looked briefly across at Mehmet Süleyman before taking what İkmen offered. 'Why?'

'You know we can't tell you that, Balthazar,' İkmen said. 'If it's to do with this missing woman . . .'

'Balthazar,' Mehmet Süleyman said, 'we shouldn't even be here, as well you know. The name Loya has come to our attention for reasons we cannot discuss. We're only here because we know that you are friends with the Loya brothers.'

Balthazar Cohen lit up the cigarette İkmen had given him and then said, 'You want me to snitch on old friends.'

'No!' İkmen, who also now lit up a cigarette, sighed. 'Not unless you know something, well, distasteful about them. No, Balthazar, we just want to know what they're like, what you know about them.'

'Snitch.'

'Yes, if you like, "snitch",' Mehmet Süleyman said. And then quite independently of his host, he turned the sound down on Balthazar's ever-on television. As usual, it was showing some football match somewhere in the world.

Balthazar cast his friend a brief, venomous look before, as usual, he acquiesced to the demands of his old colleagues. Looking beyond the television and into the darkening garden beyond he said, 'The Loya family have been here in Balat since the beginning.'

'Since 1492?' İkmen asked, citing the year when tens of thousands of Jews were expelled from Spain and Portugal by their respective monarchs and the Holy Inquisition. They, or as many as could get there, were given unconditional asylum within the Ottoman Empire.

'Yes. They came from Toledo,' Balthazar said. 'One of those posh families who can still tell you what church was on the corner of their street back in the "old country". The Loyas have always been Balat "royalty", you know? The boys' father, Nat Loya, was a dentist, very well respected.'

'And the "boys"?' İkmen asked.

Balthazar once again threw him an acid glance. 'I'm coming to them!' he said bitterly. 'Give a man a chance!' He sighed. In spite of the fact that he had known Mehmet for many years and was related by marriage to Çetin, he was not comfortable talking about his 'own' to gentiles. 'Edmondo and Maurice Loya are twins,' he said. 'Edmondo is the older by about a minute and has always looked far more "intellectual" than his brother.'

'Is he? Intellectual?' Mehmet Süleyman asked. The rather geeky Jewish man whom Ahmet Aksu remembered had been a clever, if risible, figure.

'Edmondo has a degree in philosophy from this university here,' Balthazar said, meaning İstanbul University – the institution in which İkmen's father had taught modern languages. 'His brain is enormous. Always talking, talking. About ideas, about theories, about shit no one else can understand . . .'

'Including his brother?'

Balthazar shrugged. 'Maurice is quite different. Maurice

is more like me!' he laughed. 'Wine, women and song is Maurice! But for all that he looks about a hundred years younger than Edmondo. When we were all boys together, Edmondo looked like a man of forty. He was born middle-aged!'

Which fitted, Mehmet Süleyman felt, with the picture of the young-old man that Ahmet Aksu had painted of Edmondo Loya. In the normal course of events he would have gone straight away to interview the Jew and not bother with this business with Balthazar. But when he'd told İkmen what Aksu had told him and how he had recognised the Loya name, İkmen had felt that to do what they were doing now might be prudent. In a sense, Balthazar and his family were İkmen's family too, and the Jews of Balat were a small and quite closed community now. If they did indeed have a murderer in their midst, the police would have to act with an air of caution. Ever since the bombings of the synagogues, the community had, quite naturally, been sensitive to all and any changes in their lives.

'What do the Loyas do for a living?' İkmen asked.

'Maurice is an architect,' Balthazar replied. 'He's done some lovely houses for the rich and famous out of town.'

'And Edmondo?'

Once again, Balthazar shrugged. 'What can I say? Nothing! Contemplates the infinite as he once told me himself, does Edmondo. The dentist Loya left his sons fairly well provided for, it is said, and so there's no great issue of money, I think.'

Edmondo, therefore, could well have spent his otherwise empty days hanging around with the hippies of Sultanahmet in the sixties. Just at that moment a young, very pretty face peered around the door into the TV room at İkmen.

'Hi, Dad,' Hulya said. 'Mehmet.'

Mehmet Süleyman smiled.

'Hello, sweetheart,' İkmen said as he rose briefly in order to kiss his daughter on the cheek. And then as he smoothed her hair away from her eyes, he said, 'Do you have to go out to work tonight?'

'I've been given an extra shift,' she replied with a small, if strained smile. 'I can't say no. I might never get overtime again.'

'I know.' Her father kissed her again and then she left.

Once she had gone, Balthazar said, 'She's a good girl, your daughter.'

'I know,' İkmen repeated.

And then, his face flushed a little with the acute embarrassment his lack of ability to finance his family produced, Balthazar said, 'We – I – don't deserve such a girl, she—'

'So when did you last see Edmondo Loya, Balthazar?' İkmen cut in partly in order to save his friend's obvious and painful embarrassment.

'Yesterday,' Balthazar replied. He then looked across at Süleyman. 'He told me he'd heard you'd been going around asking questions about a missing woman.'

'Did he?' İkmen frowned. 'And how was he when he was talking to you? Was he OK?'

'He mentioned it in passing,' Balthazar said. 'Casually. He told me he used to hang around with the hippies in Sultanahmet for a while. I would never have guessed.'

'Where does Edmondo Loya live? Do you know?' İkmen asked.

Balthazar said, 'Down by the Balat ferry stage. Mürsel Paşa Street.'

'On the main road?'

'Yes.' Mürsel Paşa Street was the main road along the

Golden Horn at Balat. It was noisy, dirty and its few resi-
dential dwellings had always looked, to İkmen, very down
at heel. 'The house looks nothing, like an old wreck,' Balthazar
confirmed. 'But that's just the outside. Inside is like a palace,
full of antiques. They live very well on Mürsel Paşa Street.'

'They?' Mehmet Süleyman asked. 'Edmondo lives with
someone?'

'Yes, with Maurice,' Balthazar responded simply. 'They
have always been inseparable. More so after their parents
died. Maurice, of course, works and does a certain amount
of his drinking and probably whoring too, away from the
house. But in general the brothers are always together.'

İkmen knew that a lot of people felt slightly ill at ease
around identical twins. He himself was one and, as he looked
across at Mehmet Süleyman's rather doubtful face, he knew
that he was another. Two middle-aged brothers living together
was odd, but identical twins, too . . . Maurice, according to
Balthazar, would seem to sort himself out with regard to sex,
but what about Edmondo? According to Ahmet Aksu he had
been the butt of many jokes amongst the rich locals and the
hippies back in the sixties. Edmondo, Aksu had recalled, had
publicly declared his love for Emine in the middle of the
Pudding Shop. Ahmet had thought absolutely nothing of it.
Everyone, including Emine, had laughed.

İzzet Melik wasn't a native of İstanbul, so walking past the
great Karaca Ahmet Cemetery in Üsküdar had no great
emotional resonance for him. That he was in its vicinity,
many kilometres away from his small apartment on the Golden
Horn, and after hours, too, was a measure of his professional
involvement in the Kamondo Stairs Lady case. He'd spent
much of the day around other cemeteries and bodies and,

oddly, he was loath to go home. Though was it odd, exactly, to not want to go back to a bleak rented apartment shared with a younger, recently divorced and extremely grumpy brother?

A native of the southern city of İzmir, İzzet had come to İstanbul to work with the city's police department shortly after his own divorce two years before. At forty-seven he was older than his superior, Süleyman, and saw little opportunity for promotion in the future. Not that it was the job that really bothered him. He had always wanted to be a police officer and he had achieved that ambition with some distinction. The job, for all of its shortcomings, was just fine. It was his personal life that was a mess. His divorce had been acrimonious, had cost him a considerable amount of money, and it meant that he only very infrequently saw his children. Also he was lonely. Lack of sex and the more basic aspects of relationships aside, İzzet was lonely. It wasn't the big things that he missed, that created this desolate feeling he was experiencing now. It was the tiny comforts, like the way his wife Suzan had always brought him a bottle of Efes from the fridge when he was watching football on the television. Things like the big AC Milan/Liverpool game next Wednesday brought such 'lost' beers to mind. Because when Suzan went so did the comforting sight of her carrying his beer into the living room for him. Maybe, in spite of the misgivings he had about the company he might have to keep, being with Dr Krikor Sarkissian and his posh friends at the match was not such a bad idea? But then he looked down at the cheap shirt he had bought, like all the rest of his shirts, at the cheap market behind the Yeni Valide Mosque and wondered yet again how on earth he was going to cope. Although he knew that such a detail wouldn't bother a person like Dr Krikor, just the thought of who the addiction specialist might bring with him made İzzet shudder. Other medical consultants? Lawyers? Media people? What would they think about a humble policeman in their midst and, more to the point, what would they think of Dr Krikor for bringing one along? Dr Arto Sarkissian had always been good to İzzet and the last thing he wanted to do was shame his family in any way. Now if he could have somehow arranged to take Ayşe Farsakoğlu with him . . .

İzzet paused in front of one of the large gated entrances to the cemetery and lit a cigarette. He'd come all the way out here ostensibly to think. But he wasn't doing that clearly. A beautiful woman like Ayşe wasn't going to look at him. She didn't. In fact, quite often, he could feel her disdain for him permeating the air. Not that he could blame her for that. İzzet, good at his job as he was, nevertheless remained virtually penniless. By his own admission he possessed few social graces beyond his Italian language skills and as for fashion, well . . . In addition to being clueless about clothes, he was also far too hard up to look like anything more sophisticated than a standard middle-aged macho man. Moustache, standard haircut, grey suit, cheap shirt, old tie. Not the sort of man a woman who bought her clothes in designer shops with foreign names was going to consider.

It was just starting to get dark now and İzzet noticed that parts of the great cemetery were beginning to look hazy and indistinct. In this particular portion of the huge graveyard the stones were of the antique tall column variety. Unintelligible to most modern Turks the inscriptions were written in the old Ottoman script which had used the Arabic alphabet. Together with the veil for women and the fez for men, the Arabic script had been abolished with the coming of the

Republic in the 1920s. The first and most famous president of the Republic, Mustafa Kemal Atatürk, had devised and then taught an entirely new Roman-style alphabet to his people which they had been using ever since. People like İzzet knew nothing different and would look at inscriptions in the old Ottoman script with pained lack of comprehension. In effect, these 'antique' dead were now entirely inaccessible to all but Ottoman scholars. The look of these stones with their unknown, nameless owners made İzzet feel a little sad. Not that namelessness was anything unusual amongst the dead. One of the custodians of the Karaca Ahmet had earlier in the day told him about several quite large areas of the cemetery given over to the unknown and unknowable. Graves for the disappeared where, unless some evidence were found to identify her, the Kamondo Stairs Lady's body would be eventually laid to rest. It was not a nice thought. Unmarked graves were both sad and infuriating because whoever they covered they were just never good enough. Everyone needed and deserved a name. The Kamondo Lady needed that. She needed justice, too, not just for her death but for the strange journey her oddly superglued body seemed to have been making for such a long, long time.

In an act that for him was almost without precedent, İzzet Melik began to weep. Appalled and yet at the same time so glad that he was alone, İzzet wondered how and why this particular body was affecting him so badly. If indeed his tears were about the body. Maybe he was crying also for himself and his loneliness in this place of death and mist and namelessness?

What struck İkmen first about the Loya house, apart from its dilapidated exterior, were the swords. Behind the rotting front door was a large, square hall with an elegant staircase rising from its rear. On the walls of the hall hung swords; many, many curved, straight, long and short swords.

Watery eyes, the skin around which had crinkled with intense concentration, regarded İkmen particularly with interest. 'Our ancestors came from Toledo,' Edmondo Loya said. 'Hence, what you see here.'

'Toledo swords? These are all Toledo swords?' İkmen asked.

Swords made in the Spanish city of Toledo have always had a reputation as weapons of quality and provenance. It is a manufacture that has been taking place in Toledo for many hundreds of years. It is also one that possesses its own secrets, legends and skills. Toledo swords, it is said, were forged under the influence of spells and incantations. They were also said to be so sharp that just laying a silk scarf along the blade of such a weapon would rend it in two.

'Yes.' Edmondo Loya seemed surprised and almost offended that İkmen would ask.

'Mr Loya, did your ancestors bring . . .'

'What, in 1492?' Edmondo Loya huffed impatiently. 'They were lucky to bring themselves out of Spain, let alone any artefacts! Like most Jews my ancestors came here with the clothes they stood up in and nothing more. These swords' – he raised a short, thin arm upwards to the wall – 'are what my father collected.' And then, turning back sharply towards İkmen and Süleyman, who had accompanied him, he said, 'What do you want with me?'

'Emine Aksu, or Emine Öz, as I think you knew her, is missing,' İkmen said as he watched Edmondo Loya's face colour.

83

'We are, as a matter of course, interviewing anyone who may have had a connection with Mrs Aksu – either now or in the past,' Süleyman added. 'We believe, Mr Loya, that you were one of a group of local people who liked to meet with the Western hippies in Sultanahmet back in the late sixties. Mrs Aksu and her husband were also part of that scene.'

Edmondo Loya looked down at the small, scruffy carpet at his feet and then said, 'You'd better come and sit down.'

He led them through to a room that would not have looked out of place in one of the city's nineteenth-century palaces. On the highly polished hardwood floor lay an enormous Ottoman court carpet. All deep pile and gorgeous flower motifs, its age seemed to enhance its already considerable beauty. Cabinets and shelves, loaded with what looked like antique books, lined the walls. Carved in wood inlaid with metal and shell these items of furniture were also used to display artefacts which ranged in style and period. An ornate seven-branched candlestick or menorah sat alone and magnificent on one shelf while others held rustic pottery from Cappadocia, large crystal brandy glasses from Moravia and even an ikon of the Virgin and Child from the Greek island of Chios. The entire room, rather dangerously in a partly wooden house, was lit by huge, church-like candles. As the two policemen were ushered into large leather-covered chairs, İkmen pondered on the fact that ex-Constable Cohen had not been wrong about the Loyas' place. It was indeed a treasure house.

As if reading what was on İkmen's mind, Edmondo Loya said, 'I suppose Balthazar Cohen told you about me? He's been asking around about the 1960s. We have spoken, he and I.'

'Your name was given to us by Mrs Aksu's husband,' Süleyman said, both answering and not answering Edmondo Loya's question. 'But he had difficulty remembering your name, sir. Your activities in the sixties, it would seem—'

'I knew a lady was missing, but I didn't know it was Emine Öz,' Edmondo Loya interrupted. And then, changing the subject rapidly, he said, 'I used to go to Sultanahmet in the sixties, for intellectual discourse. I went with a friend, an older man called Abdulrahman. He's dead now, I think. Some of the young Europeans were very well read.'

'And Mrs Aksu, or rather Miss Öz, was very beautiful, wasn't she?' İkmen said.

The Jew regarded him blankly.

'Mr Aksu', İkmen continued, 'distinctly remembers you declaring your love for Emine Öz in the Pudding Shop many years ago.'

Edmondo Loya's face, which had been red, was now very white.

'When did you last see Emine Aksu, Mr Loya?' İkmen asked.

A clock, which Süleyman recognised as an English grand-father clock, chimed the hour: ten.

'I haven't seen Emine since I left the Pudding Shop for the last time on 4 September, 1969.'

It was a very precise memory that this man had. But then, if Ahmet Aksu were to be believed, it must have been quite a significant event in the life of quiet Edmondo Loya. He had proclaimed his love for Emine Öz, which must have taken some courage, and he had been humiliated. It was the sort of event that did tend to stay with a person, particularly a rather cloistered and intellectual individual like Edmondo Loya.

85

'I imagine that because you have spoken to Ahmet, you know what happened, or rather didn't happen, between Emine and myself on that date,' Edmondo Loya said.

'Your—'

'She laughed at me,' he cut in bitterly. 'I declared my affection for her and she laughed at me. I was a figure of fun, you see,' he said as his eyes visibly filled up with tears. 'People like me . . . I think there is an American word for it now. Geek. I was a geek, and therefore a person of no sexual or emotional activity.'

İkmen looked at Süleyman who was no doubt thinking the very same thing. Edmondo Loya, geek, had never got over it. Probably he never would. But whether this meant anything with regard to their current investigation or not . . .

'I didn't kill Emine,' the Jew said as if almost on some sort of clichéd cue.

İkmen, also wrapped up in the same almost stagey set-up, said, 'I didn't say that Mrs Aksu was dead, Mr Loya. I didn't even hint that anyone had murdered her, much less yourself. She is missing. She has been missing for over two weeks. My colleague and I are merely following up on her contacts, both past and present.'

Edmondo Loya simply continued to look at İkmen with blank but startled eyes.

The policeman continued. 'When one is investigating a disappearance it is quite routine to interview those who may have had issues with the person who is missing.'

'Issues?' Edmondo Loya's face scrunched up into a small and mean arrangement of features. 'I don't and have never had issues with Emine. I was in love with her until I discovered, on the very day I declared my love for her, what she was really like. Hard and cold and a maker of trouble just

86

for the sake of her own amusement. Then I had nothing but contempt for her and have continued to do so.'

'Do you hate her?'

'No!' His face was half shrouded in the shadow thrown by the heavy candle-lit furniture. Suddenly Edmondo Loya, after looking quickly at his grandfather clock, stood up. 'And if that is all, I'd rather you went,' he said. 'My brother will be home soon and I don't want him to find you here. It might worry him.'

'Well, Mr Loya,' İkmen said, 'far be it from me to cause you any distress.' Both he and Süleyman rose from their seats. 'I don't suppose that your brother knew—'

'My brother never knew anyone in Sultanahmet, ever!' Edmondo Loya snapped. 'Please leave!'

İkmen shrugged. 'Of course,' he said. 'But Mr Loya, if we have to ask you any more questions—'

'Then you may do so,' Loya said. 'Now will you please leave? Maurice is due and he's been working. He gets very tired these days.'

'I have a lot of responsibility,' an almost identical voice said from the door into the ornate room. 'You, for one thing, brother.'

İkmen and Süleyman turned to see a smiling, fresher-faced version of Edmondo Loya standing in the doorway.

'Maurice,' Edmondo said, his face whitening yet again as he spoke, 'you're back early.'

'We must be careful not to succumb to the many clichés that seem to exist within what we've just seen,' İkmen said as he placed his glass of beer down on the table in front of him. 'Identical twins to us non-twins can seem rather peculiar at times.'

'I think it's just a physical thing, though, don't you?' Süleyman replied as he lit up a cigarette. 'Two people looking exactly, or almost exactly, the same is quite unnerving. One wonders what tricks they may choose to play upon the rest of us. I don't know whether I hold with the notion that they possess telepathic powers, however.'

'I, too, am unsure about that,' İkmen said. 'I know very little about it, to be honest. To my knowledge, we have never had any twins in the family.'

They were sitting in the conservatory of the only hotel in the Fener-Balat area, the Daphnis. Although on the very busy road that is a continuation of Mürsel Paşa Street, where the Loya brothers lived, the Daphnis, and particularly its conservatory, had fabulous views over the Golden Horn. And even though it was dark, the two men could still see the lights from small boats passing along the great waterway as well as those from the districts of Kasımpaşa and Hasköy across the Horn. İkmen wondered what that very elegant Hasköy resident, Mr Ahmet Aksu, was doing at that moment. Not for the first time he wondered whether Ahmet had perhaps had a hand in the disappearance of his 'tart' of a wife. After all, hippy or no hippy, Ahmet Aksu was still a Turkish man with all the pride and machismo that went along with that state.

'Nevertheless,' İkmen said as he took another gulp from his glass and then lit a cigarette of his own, 'Edmondo Loya knew Emine Aksu, was at one time in love with her, and has never married since.'

'Neither has Maurice,' Süleyman put in.

'True. But Maurice works and is altogether far more in the world than his brother,' İkmen replied. 'I expect that, as Cohen told us, he has women. But as for Edmondo . . . I know it's a fiction-detective cliché, but Edmondo did seem either to know or assume that Emine Aksu was dead. Murdered. Even *we* don't know that.'

'Although you suspect it, Çetin.' It was said as a statement of fact.

İkmen looked down at the surface of the table and then said, 'The witches' blood that runs in my veins tells me that Mrs Aksu is probably beneath the ground, yes.' He looked up and smiled. 'Although, as ever, I would tell no one but you, my dear Mehmet.'

Their superior, Commissioner of Police Ardiç as well as many of their colleagues, did not hold with such 'superstitious nonsense'. Those of an entirely atheistic nature, as well as the devoutly Muslim, were inclined to find such phenomena either unintelligible or threatening. And although Süleyman didn't always understand or even quite believe in what İkmen was experiencing, he respected what the older man went through. He also knew that İkmen and his 'hunches' were usually frighteningly accurate. Emine Aksu's 'death' was probably no exception.

'What about the husband?' Süleyman asked, bringing İkmen back to his previous line of thinking.

'Ahmet Aksu?' İkmen sighed. 'I don't know. His wife, seemingly with his approval, has been passed from man to man for years. I've interviewed old hippies who've had her, businessmen who were old hippies . . . but now, at least according to the old hippy Kadir Özal, she amuses herself with younger men as opposed to elderly rockers.'

'And yet her husband seemed to think that she was seeing someone from her past.'

'If Ahmet Aksu is telling the truth, yes,' İkmen said. 'We have no proof either way, however. Apparently, Emine was seeing some young Italian boy about six months ago, but that is on the say so of a junkie. That's the trouble with all this, really.'

'Drugs?'

'Kadir Özal is a junkie. Mr Aksu himself obviously enjoys his cannabis. Emine herself, we've heard from several sources, liked to make mischief, and possibly this included telling lies about her movements, et cetera. Old reformed flames don't want anything to do with the woman or her disappearance and Edmondo Loya and his brother are distinctly odd.'

'You thought that Maurice Loya was strange, too?' Süleyman asked.

'Didn't you?'

He shrugged. Alongside the twitching, geeky Edmondo, Maurice Loya had appeared to Süleyman to be a perfectly normal person. That Edmondo had been nervous as if tiptoeing around Maurice was probably understandable, given the circumstances; Maurice effectively kept his brother who was, it seemed, though physically like him, quite different psychologically. Edmondo was in effect, if not in actuality, autistic in comparison to the easygoing Maurice.

'Initially, I found it odd that it was Edmondo and not Maurice who got involved with the hippies,' İkmen said. 'But then I suppose Maurice is rather a different type of good-time boy. I see him in bars and around women, but not whilst discussing freedom or with a sheaf of articles by Hunter S. Thompson in his hands. No, it was Edmondo's fear of him that got me thinking.'

Süleyman took a swig from his glass of beer and then said, 'You think that Edmondo is afraid of Maurice?'

'On some level, yes.'

'I didn't get fear, rather deference. As if Maurice were the father figure, Edmondo the somewhat stupid child.'

'I don't know,' İkmen said. He looked at the gently drifting lights of the boats on the Golden Horn and briefly recalled in his mind how this area had been back in the sixties. The Horn had certainly had a very different aroma in those days. If chemicals plus dead rat had a smell all of its own, that was what it had been.

'So do you think that Edmondo has killed Emine in an act of extremely delayed revenge?' Süleyman asked.

İkmen, roused from his brief reverie, said, 'With her body lying rotting somewhere in the Loya brothers' palace? It's possible, I suppose, but why now? Why kill Emine after all this time?'

'Who knows? Edmondo is not as other men,' Süleyman said with a smile. 'What has significance for him may not be obvious to others. Maybe Emine did meet up with him again – and spurned him again, too.'

'Maybe. But with no sightings of Emine since her disappearance, plus only the word of her husband upon which to rely, you know what we have to do next, don't you, Mehmet? You know what Ardıç will absolutely insist that we do?'

Mehmet Süleyman sighed. Yes, he knew. It wasn't something that he or anyone else liked to do very much. 'Lift Mr Aksu's floorboards,' he said wearily.

'Lift, as you say, Mr Aksu's floorboards,' İkmen agreed with a slight, equally tired nod.

Chapter 6

The two sets of opposing football fans were being separated at the airport. If you were in İstanbul for AC Milan you went one way; for Liverpool, you went another. A third, less organised route through the terminus was for those oddities who had come to the city for reasons other than football. It was a system which should work provided the aircraft from the UK and Italy were not overflowing with drunks. Drunks were, as everyone knew, unpredictable.

'Foreigners out of their heads all over the city,' Commissioner Ardiç mumbled impatiently as he shuffled through a sheaf of papers on the desk in front of him. 'It could so easily end in misery.'

His large face, which was set in an expression of permanent pessimism, drooped even further than usual. He liked football as much as the next red-blooded Turk but when it came to foreign football in his city he became very nervous. Not that the local fans who, in the past, had greeted some foreign teams with banners reading 'Welcome to Hell' were a whole lot better than those from abroad. Not lately. The days, unfortunately, of the Galatasaray and Beşiktaş fans singing playfully innocent supporters' songs while peaceably playing small drums were long gone. But this time the locals were not involved. This time Ardiç and his colleagues had only to deal with Italians and Englishmen. Only.

Ardiç looked up at the officers in front of him, Inspector Süleyman and Sergeant Melik, and said, 'So the last thing that we need right now is another obscenely displayed skeleton in a public street. What's happening?'

Süleyman hadn't slept for very long the night before, due, in part, to his late visit to Edmondo Loya's house. And although he hadn't forgotten about the Kamondo Stairs Lady, she had not been at the forefront of his mind until he had arrived at the station that morning; İzzet, who looked as if he hadn't changed his clothes since the previous day, had filled him in on some details.

'It is the opinion of the pathologist that the woman was stabbed through the chest,' Süleyman said.

'Murdered.'

'Yes, sir. But then her body was kept somewhere for some time. Dr Sarkissian still isn't sure for how long, but he reckons it's years as opposed to months.'

Commissioner Ardiç's many chins wobbled with disgust. 'Does Dr Sarkissian venture an opinion as to why this woman's body has lain unburied for so long?'

'No, sir.'

'Oh, and there is the glue too,' İzzet Melik put in.

'Glue? What glue?'

'The head of the skeleton became detached at some point, sir,' Süleyman said. 'Whoever was in possession of the body glued it back on at some time for some reason.'

'God!' Ardiç shook his head before he placed the small stub of cigar that had been on his desk back in his mouth and said, 'What is this? Some sort of necrophiliac at work?'

'We don't know, sir,' Süleyman replied. 'We may know more once the forensic institute have completed their tests on the corpse itself and fragments of its clothing.'

'We've no reports of any desecration activity in any of the city graveyards,' İzzet Melik said.

'Well, if the body wasn't buried, we wouldn't, would we?' Ardiç snapped back angrily.

'Sir—'

'Yes, yes, I know you had to check anyway, but . . .' He lit his cigar stub and leaned back heavily in his large leather chair. 'Any ideas about why this body was placed where it was on the Kamondo Stairs?'

'Not as yet, sir,' Süleyman replied. 'The Kamondo family who built the Stairs were, as you know, sir, a wealthy Jewish banking family who left the country many years ago.'

'Mmm.' Ardiç hadn't known, and Süleyman knew it, but no matter. 'So Jews . . .'

'Unless the corpse's DNA connects her to anyone known to us, we don't know who she is apart from the fact that she is female. Once we have some clear idea about when she died we can begin looking at missing-person records.'

'Dr Sarkissian thinks we are probably looking at at least twenty-five years ago, probably more,' İzzet Melik said. 'So I've made a start on some old records.'

'It would help if we could find anyone who saw anything the night the body was placed,' Ardiç said and then added gloomily, 'But I suppose that's too much to ask.'

Although Voyvoda Street had once been at the centre of the Ottoman banking trade and was still lined with very impressive financial buildings, that was all firmly in its past. Now, although only on the edge of what had become the Karaköy red-light district, it was still rather in its orbit in spite of the strenuous efforts of the city authorities to clean the district up. No one hanging around that area at night would really want to own up to it. Although there were always exceptions.

'A Mr Emin telephoned this morning to say that he'd read about the body in the papers and although he didn't see anything suspicious, he was in the vicinity of the Stairs in the early hours of the morning,' İzzet Melik said. 'I'm going out to see him this afternoon; he lives in Tahtakale.'

'Doesn't sound hopeful . . .'

'Yes, but we must try to remain positive, mustn't we, sir?' Süleyman said through clenched teeth. Ardiç had always had a tendency towards gloominess but this was excessive even by his standards. Perhaps his fears about imminent football-related violence were colouring his perception of everything?

Without so much as a glance his in direction, Ardiç said, 'Well, Melik, get about your work, then. Stop idling around here.'

Süleyman briefly raised his eyes at his colleague as he left. But once Melik had gone, Ardiç asked Süleyman to sit down. It wasn't often that people did that in his presence and so the inspector took immediate advantage of it.

'Süleyman,' he said, 'let me ask you something.'

'Sir?'

'How do you feel about this country's application to join the European Union?'

It wasn't the usual sort of question that Ardiç asked. In general his queries revolved around the job of policing and why his officers were not doing it better. Süleyman wondered why he was asking such a seemingly unrelated thing when they were so busy. 'I'm generally in favour of it,' he replied. 'Although whether it will ever actually happen is another matter.'

'You mean because we have to continually "prove" ourselves worthy and up to the task?'

'Compliance with some European legal procedures and a lot of the legislation on working hours, et cetera, are things that I think will benefit Turkey,' Süleyman said. 'But yes, sir, it is annoying, and also at times humiliating, that we are required to jump through so many hoops with no guaranteed result at the end. And some of the legislation on food seems crazy. I mean, the prospect of living without kokoreç*, well . . .'

'Life without kokoreç would not be something I would want to consider,' Ardiç responded gloomily.

'Sir, why are you—'

'One of the unofficial ways in which the Europeans are assessing our performance with regard to EU entry is the treatment of their citizens in this country,' Ardiç said. 'Specifically at this time, these English and Italian football fans. Our prime minister is very close to both Mr Blair and Mr Berlusconi, both of whom support Turkish entry into the EU. Nothing has been said directly, but I know, as I have already told İkmen, that every officer in this city is now under intense scrutiny. Whether you are involved in the policing of the football match or not, I am watching you.' He fixed Süleyman with a very hard gaze. 'All of you.'

'Sir.'

'So, if you see English or Italian fans getting drunk in the streets of this city, you do not intervene,' Ardiç said. 'Provided they are not causing trouble, we leave them alone.' He smiled, but not pleasantly. 'We want them to have a good time. A good experience.'

'Yes.'

'We don't want them coming across unburied corpses in the street,' Ardiç reiterated his earlier entreaty. 'I know I've said this to you before but' – he suddenly moved his large

---

*Kokoreç is a popular Turkish snack of cooked strips of spiced lamb intestines.

head further across the desk towards Süleyman and lowered his voice – 'I've had a call from the forensic institute,' he said. 'They have found traces of semen on that skeleton.'

'Oh.' Quite why he hadn't mentioned this in front of İzzet Melik, Süleyman didn't know. But then Ardiç although no prude, was rather more comfortable when speaking of sexual or other 'delicate' matters to officers he had known for many years. Melik was comparatively new to İstanbul and his current job. 'So then it would seem that we could indeed be dealing with a necrophiliac,' Süleyman said.

'Yes.' Ardiç cleared his throat. 'I've told Dr Sarkissian, although I didn't get to talk to him much. Something about his teeth . . . We didn't get around to the glued-on head.' He pulled a disgusted face. 'Sick bastard!' Then he leaned back in his chair and pointed his cigar at Süleyman. 'Find him,' he said. 'Find him before he finds some unfortunate drunken Italian to kill and then have his way with.'

'But sir, I—'

'Yes, I know this woman has been dead for years, but that semen wasn't old. And anyway, I now have this nightmare to contend with which involves one of these foreigners falling victim to this lunatic. Pictures of the unfortunate victim, once found, are beamed all over the world and we, or rather I, personally, am held responsible for the outrage. Once again, Turks are labelled barbarians and we will never gain entry to the EU.'

Süleyman smiled inwardly to himself. Ardiç had always created worst-case scenarios in his head way before they were even a possibility. It was in his nature. It was why he took, or so it was rumoured, tranquillisers on an almost permanent basis.

'I don't like mad, sick people making trouble in this city,' Ardiç said.

Süleyman, in as soothing a voice as he could muster, said, 'Don't worry, sir, we will catch him. And I will, I promise, try to make sure that no Englishmen or Italians are caught up in either my investigation or that of any of my colleagues.'

'Mmm.' Ardiç regarded the younger man with an intense and somewhat disbelieving eye. Poor Ardiç – if one could feel sorry for such an explosive creature – no wonder he was both feared and pitied in almost equal measure by his officers.

Over in Hasköy there were not, as yet, any young men or women wandering around in either AC Milan or Liverpool football strips. It didn't mean, however, that things in that district were not threatening. For Mr Ahmet Aksu things had taken a sudden and decisive turn for the worse.

'So you suspect me of killing my wife,' he said to İkmen as he stood in the middle of his super-cool living room, his back to the sun-touched Golden Horn. 'What about the person I told you she was going to meet that day? What about Emine's old flames?'

'Mr Aksu, this investigation is, I have to assure you, quite routine,' İkmen replied. He stood, together with Ayşe Farsakoğlu, at the head of a small squad of uniformed officers. 'If a missing person does not appear after weeks as opposed to just days, we search the premises where they used to reside. It is almost immaterial who now lives in those premises. This is unfortunately something that we have to do.'

'And my objecting to this will do me no good?'

'Not at all,' İkmen said. 'Basically, sir, we can conduct the search whether you like it or not. But your co-operation will make it easier and also less distressing. I have instructed my officers to tread carefully and be respectful of your property.'

Ahmet Aksu, in response to a very pretty smile from İkmen's deputy, shrugged his shoulders and then said, 'Well, if you must. Would you like to start in Emine's bedroom?'

That the Aksus had separate bedrooms was not something that İkmen had anticipated. He had imagined that their extra-marital adventures added excitement to their own marriage – it was what he thought Ahmet Aksu had said when they had first met. But, now that İkmen really thought about it, he hadn't said anything of the kind. The Aksus' marriage, it would appear, was not something that involved the two of them having a lot of sex with each other.

'Yes, sir, that would be good,' İkmen said. 'Sergeant Farsakoğlu, could you please go with Mr Aksu to do that? I think that a woman searching a woman's room is rather more appropriate, don't you, sir?'

'Er, yes, er . . .'

Ayşe Farsakoğlu put on a pair of plastic gloves and said, 'Mr Aksu, if you'd like to lead the way . . .'

'Oh.' He smiled at her, obviously, in spite of everything that was going on, smitten by the sight of a pretty face. But then he looked at İkmen and the uniformed officers and said, 'And you? What will you be doing, Inspector?'

'I would like to send some of my officers out to the garage you have at the back of this property, Mr Aksu,' İkmen said. 'Constable Yıldız and myself will start in the kitchen.'

It was always a good idea to start in a kitchen, İkmen felt. Mainly because the guilty always felt so secure about such an innocuous area. The guilty always imagined that they had cleared every scrap of their victim's blood from a kitchen. In all his years of experience with murderers, İkmen knew that this was almost never the case. He'd been in kitchens where whole areas of floor were covered in gore. The stupidity of people neither shocked nor surprised him any longer.

'If you wish,' Ahmet Aksu responded coldly. Then, turning back to Ayşe Farsakoğlu with a smile, he said, 'Would you like to follow me, Sergeant?'

In the presence of Ayşe Farsakoğlu, Ahmet Aksu hardly looked like a man frantic with worry over his missing wife. What he did look like was a much older man lusting after a young woman. İkmen wondered how often Mr Aksu had indulged in 'free love' since his wife had disappeared. Once Mr Aksu had gone he sent all of his officers, apart from young Hikmet Yıldız, out to the garage behind the house. Then, with a sigh, he put on a pair of plastic gloves, beckoned Yıldız to follow him into the kitchen, and opened the top drawer of one of the units. Inside was an array of large carving knives.

'Çetin İkmen's first case after being made up to inspector involved a necrophiliac,' the doctor said. It was an utterance that was very quickly followed by a low moan. 'Oh why does dental anaesthesia always wear off so quickly?'

Süleyman nodded sympathetically. 'I don't know,' he said to the short, plump man holding a large handkerchief up to his swollen face. 'What did you have done?'

The doctor moved the handkerchief away from his mouth and said, 'A filling. I wish I hadn't bothered. It didn't hurt until I went to the dentist.'

They were sitting in his office, a room permeated by the smell of blood, sweat and surgical spirit. The doctor's laboratory, not to mention several cadavers, were less than two meters from where the two men were drinking coffee – in Arto Sarkissian's case, this was with the aid of a straw.

'Doctor, to get back to the subject of necrophilia . . .'

'I can't remember the details of Çetin's case now; you'd have to ask him,' the Armenian said through his handkerchief.

'Yes, doctor, I appreciate that,' Süleyman replied. 'But what about your own experience? I mean, working in this environment . . .'

'Oh, one comes across them!' the doctor said knowingly. 'Not generally amongst members of my own profession, you understand, but I've had a few odd assistants in the past. Young men very eager to learn. Quiet youngsters who profess to follow a religion of some sort with considerable passion always arouse my suspicions.'

'For example?'

'Ow!' he took the handkerchief away from his face again and then very gently rubbed his jaw. 'A Greek lad I had a few years ago. In church every day, quite attractive, but covered in spots. Dr Mardin caught him kissing the corpse of a female heroin overdose.' He shook his head. 'Poor inept creature. He was young, with sexual needs, spurned by women and girls alike. He turned to the dead. Not that I am excusing his actions, you understand. Plenty of teenage boys are awkward and needy around girls, but few of them turn to corpses for their pleasure.'

'So was there something different about this particular boy?' Süleyman asked. 'Did something mark him out from other inept teenagers? I ask simply because if we are looking at a necrophiliac offender here, I need to know something about how he might think.'

'Then you could do a lot worse than talk to your wife,' the doctor said.

Zelfa Süleyman, Mehmet's Turko-Irish wife, was a practising psychiatrist.

'My understanding is that necrophilia is a fetish,' Arto Sarkissian said. 'Just like those people who can only achieve sexual satisfaction if they are wearing opposite gender clothes or looking at women's shoes, the necrophiliac is a fetishist. He or she doesn't have control over his or her sexual compulsion.'

'Do you know how fetishes come about? I mean there are a lot of young men out there who are difficult around women. Few of them resolve that problem by kissing corpses.'

'Again, Zelfa is the best person to ask,' the doctor replied. 'But from my own experience and from the little that I've read on the subject I can tell you this. There is usually either a moment of shock or revelation in the backgrounds of these people. My little Greek boy was nephew to this city's only Greek undertaker. Dr Mardin told me that apparently the boy told her his moment came when he saw a very pretty girl on his uncle's embalming table. At fourteen he was adolescent, impressionable and instantly aroused by the sight of her. The boy, so he says, fell in love. He kissed her passionately and she did not either laugh at him or push him away, which was how his experiences had been with girls up to that point. Shortly afterwards the girl was buried and there were no more pretty girls because, as you know, the Greek community in this city is very small. He came to work here, unbeknown to us, in order to have access to more lovely dead girls.'

'So did you tell his family?'

The doctor rubbed his jaw yet again and said, 'Of course, I had to. I know his uncle and his father. They were appalled.'

'And now?'

'And now, apparently, he works in an office in Nişantaşi.

103

As soon as I told them his father and his uncle took him to one of the old brothels in Karaköy and, it is said, his dalliance with corpses is at an end.'

Süleyman looked into the doctor's eyes and said, 'But you're not sure, are you?'

Arto Sarkissian sighed. 'I don't know, I really do not,' he said. 'It's probably all the fault of psychiatrists – some will tell you that fetishes can be corrected while others will tell you they cannot. As is usual with psychiatrists they give lay people like us far more choices and options than we can handle.'

Mehmet Süleyman smiled. His wife was forever saying things about 'absolutes' being 'illusory', about the concept of a 'cure' for anything being a nonsense.

'But all of that aside, if you're looking for someone who might be a necrophiliac, then you should know that they are not usually killers,' the doctor said. 'In fact, those like the boy I told you about, and another one I came across a couple of years after that, are generally timid. They have been shocked, humiliated or driven in some other unnatural way to this kind of behaviour and their main aim in life is to keep it as secret as they can.'

'So you wouldn't expect this type of fetishist to display a corpse he has defiled . . .'

'No, no. No, your offender in the case of the Kamondo Stairs woman is, though undoubtedly aroused by her, something else too, I feel.'

'Like what?'

The doctor shrugged. 'That I can't tell you. But if he killed her, I suspect it was not just to have sex with her. As Çetin will tell you, necrophilia may be part of a murderer's repertoire, but it is rarely the point of a killing. A killer like this, if indeed we are dealing with the actual killer here at all, is driven by multiple needs, drives and inadequacies. There won't just be one revelatory moment, there will be a build up of drives and tensions leading up to the moment of destruction. Contrary to popular belief, it takes a lot to kill another human being.' He smiled. 'It takes quite a bit just to cut them up when they're already dead.'

Süleyman smiled again. It was well known that fascinated by his work as he was, Dr Sarkissian was also frequently disturbed by what his job revealed about the murkier side of the human soul. It was said that these days he suffered with several stress-based ailments directly attributable to his profession. Some, although significantly not the doctor himself, were speaking of retirement.

The younger, fitter man rose to his feet. 'Doctor, I will leave you to your work now,' Süleyman said. 'Oh, DNA, on the semen . . .'

'No matches,' the Armenian said. 'Whoever it belongs to isn't known to us, sadly.'

Süleyman sighed. 'Oh, well, thank you for your assistance, Doctor. No doubt we will be talking about the Kamondo lady again soon.'

'Yes.' Arto Sarkissian stood up and just briefly embraced the policeman who, over the many years they had worked alongside one another, had become, albeit a rather formal one, a friend. 'Give my regards to Zelfa,' he said. 'And do talk to her about fetishes. Psychiatrists are so much better at explaining such phenomena.'

'I will.'

He left the laboratory quickly. Although crimes of death were his speciality, Mehmet Süleyman did not like being in close proximity to either the dead or the dying. He disliked laboratories and, probably even more so, hospitals. They made him feel afraid, vulnerable and sometimes vaguely sick. That his wife worked in such an environment was not something that the couple routinely discussed. Now, however, he would have to talk to Zelfa about her work. If not for the benefit of the case itself, he needed to know for his own sanity why a person would want to violate the dead in the way that Dr Sarkissian had described. As he walked out onto the street he saw two Western men stroll past wearing red Liverpool T-shirts. It was a very pleasant, warm day; still and fairly quiet for İstanbul, but these men were already drunk. As Süleyman crossed the road to get into his car one of them shouted at him 'Woah ho, Abdul!'

He was just about to go over and remonstrate with the man when he remembered Commissioner Ardiç's words about only intervening with the foreigners if they caused trouble. The man who had shouted at him was, he now saw, smiling.

'Hello,' he called back in English. 'Enjoy your time in İstanbul.'

'Thanks, pal,' the man replied. 'I think this is a right nice town, this.'

'Oh aye,' his wobbling and rather red-faced friend agreed, 'top place, this.'

And then they both weaved unsteadily, if with very good humour, down the road. People, Süleyman thought, for the umpteenth time in his life, were so very rarely what they seemed.

For a moment, İkmen watched as the old man, the district's linen seller, placed a pile of tea towels in a basket which the headscarved woman living opposite had lowered down to him from her third-floor apartment. If the transaction ran true

106

to form the woman would now inspect the goods, take what she wanted, and then send the rest, plus the required money, back down to the seller in the basket. Not so many years ago, such transactions had been common in İkmen's own neighbourhood of Sultanahmet. In fact, together with the cries of the old yoghurt and water vendors, it was one of the aspects of the district that the European hippies had found so charming. But ever since the area had been extensively 'improved' in the 1990s, such old-world features had been few and far between. Back to himself again now, İkmen gently dipped a finger into the small pot of white powder Ayşe Farsakoğlu had placed in his hand and then put the finger into his mouth.

'Cocaine,' he said to a drawn-looking Ahmet Aksu.

Ayşe, whose find the narcotic had been, nodded in satisfied agreement with her boss.

'I don't know anything about it,' Ahmet Aksu said. 'Your inferior,' he looked across arrogantly at Ayşe, 'found it amongst Emine's belongings.'

'He says his wife, and she alone, is the user, sir,' Ayşe Farsakoğlu put in.

'That may well be the case,' İkmen said. 'Were you aware of your wife's habit, Mr Aksu?'

Ahmet Aksu lowered his head. 'Inspector İkmen,' he said, 'may I talk to you alone, please?'

İkmen turned to Ayşe Farsakoğlu and said, 'Sergeant, would you please go outside and take Constable Yıldız with you? See what the other men are doing.'

'Yes, sir.' It wasn't the first time a suspect had asked to speak to İkmen alone. It also wasn't the first time that İkmen had acceded to such a request.

Ahmet Aksu motioned İkmen over on to one of the great

low cushions in his living room and the two of them sat down.

İkmen lit a cigarette and said, 'Well?'

The lifestyle magazine publisher also lit a cigarette and, as he exhaled, said, 'Inspector, you must, I am sure, know that when a person reaches a certain age, energy levels can drop quite dramatically.'

'I know that only too well, Mr Aksu,' İkmen said. 'You, your wife and myself are of an age. I do not, however, take cocaine in order to artiticially enhance my energy.'

'No, well . . . er . . . Look, as I said before, Inspector, I don't take it.' He leaned forward across his super-cool Buddhist-influenced coffee table and said, 'It is Emine, she—'

'You knew that your wife was taking cocaine.' It was said as a statement of fact because both of the men in the room, their profiles outlined against the waters of the distant Golden Horn, knew the answer to that question.

'Yes. I did. But she did it', Aksu said, 'in order to continue to have the sexual pleasure she had always had in the past.' He leaned in even closer across the table. 'Women of her age, with the menopause, well, they don't get as much out of sex as they did.'

İkmen began to think about his own wife, a contemporary of Emine Aksu, but then he turned his mind away from her and back to business. 'So your wife took cocaine in order to have a better sex life with you?'

'Well, not just with me . . .'

'With you at all?' İkmen asked. 'You sleep in separate rooms, Mr Aksu.'

'Some of the time, yes.'

İkmen regarded the man in front of him with a critical eye. 'Some of the time?'

'Well . . .'

'Your wife took cocaine for her lovers, didn't she, Mr Aksu?' İkmen said. 'Not for you. She rarely bothered with you.'

He turned his face slightly away to one side. 'I have other women, pretty girls . . .'

'Yes. And so why carry on with a middle-aged woman who no doubt costs you money for clothes and certainly costs in terms of her cocaine habit? I know that you were both hippies when you were young, but this is still Turkey, Mr Aksu; your wife cuckolds you, she is a drug addict—'

'I love her.' It wasn't said emotionally but it was said with a warmth that was unmistakably genuine. 'You can't be expected to understand our lives now, or our past,' Aksu said. 'But Emine and myself, although, OK, we don't sleep together and, in fact, rarely even touch, still care about each other, and my life without her is, believe me, nothing. It is she who has given me the courage and the dedication to do what I do. Without Emine I am nothing.'

'And yet you didn't try to get your wife to stop taking cocaine? That stuff can kill you! You didn't try to save her life?'

'Oh, I tried all right!' He flicked his handsome head impatiently to one side. 'But when Emine wanted something she always got it. It was always that way. She was, she *is*, very strong willed.'

For a moment İkmen just sat and listened to the sound of what remained of old Hasköy around him. The simit* seller, shouting out the name of his seeded bread rings to

*Simit is a bread ring covered in sesame seeds. It is a popular snack in Turkey.

the residents of the district, the seller of cherries with his handcart piled high with a pyramid of deep black fruit from the orchards around İzmir, the excited babbling sound of a passing group of colourful gypsy dancers. These people, the Aksus, and those like them, wanted to change for ever the nature of old neighbourhoods like Hasköy. They wanted to gentrify them, render them 'cool' and clean and neutral. But then maybe that was and always had been the end point of the hippy, multicultural, free-love ethos? Maybe in a sense it wasn't quite such a bad thing. At least, maybe it wasn't provided you were not poor . . .

İkmen hit his host with what only he and the young man who had been working with him knew. 'Mr Aksu,' he said, 'I have to tell you that Constable Yıldız found traces of dried blood at the back of one of your kitchen work surfaces and under a tile on your en-suite bathroom floor. We will be comparing the DNA found in the blood against your wife's DNA which we have already sampled from her clothes. Lying to me about this would therefore not be very intelligent. Now—'

As he looked into what was now the open-mouthed face of Ahmet Aksu, İkmen's mobile phone began to ring. 'Excuse me,' he said as he took the telephone out of his pocket and answered the call.

'Ah . . .'

'İkmen,' the policeman said. He was then silent, listening for a least five minutes. Ahmet Aksu saw the man who had been his increasingly aggressive interrogator turn a rather alarming shade of grey. And even when he had finished the call, İkmen, or so it seemed, needed several moments to gather his thoughts before he spoke again.

'Inspector?' Ahmet Aksu said. 'What—'

110

'Mr Aksu,' İkmen said as he rose swiftly to his feet, 'there is no easy way to tell you this. Someone has confessed to the murder of your wife, Emine.'

Ahmet Aksu's eyes widened as he clapped a hand over his mouth in order to stifle his scream.

Chapter 7

Edmondo Loya did not, he said, either want or need a
lawyer.

'I did it, and so there's nothing to discuss,' he told İkmen
as the latter sat down in front of him in interview room
number 2. Across the coffee- and cigarette-ash-stained table,
underneath the naked 40-watt light bulb, the man whom
İkmen knew as a friend of Balthazar Cohen looked pale and
exhausted. Dressed in a frayed brown raincoat, with an equally
dishevelled beret on his head, Edmondo Loya was the very
picture of a man at the end of his tether.

'You should still seek professional representation,' İkmen
said as he motioned to Ayşe Farsakoğlu to sit down in the
chair beside him.

'Professional representation!' Edmondo Loya snorted. 'By
this I take it you mean some over-paid, sharp-suited creature
who will charge me a fortune to tell me that "everything will
be all right" provided I say nothing.' He shrugged his arms
in the air and said, 'I've come to confess. There's nothing
more to be said.'

'Confession or not, you still have rights of which your
lawyer, should you appoint one, will make you aware,' İkmen
said. 'Now—'

'Emine Aksu decided, out of the blue, that it would be a
tremendous laugh to humiliate me all over again; I couldn't

113

take it and killed her. I threw her body into the Golden Horn. End of story,' Edmondo Loya said without, İkmen noted, even the slightest shred of emotion.

'In addition, from our side of things, we have to be certain that you really have committed this offence, that it was not committed under duress—'

'I killed her,' Edmondo Loya cut in simply. 'Me. Edmondo Loya. I killed Emine Öz and threw her body into the Golden Horn.'

He didn't look as if he could easily carry an ordinary-sized briefcase much less a really rather meaty middle-aged woman. But then, as İkmen knew only too well, people in the grip of strong emotions could often do very surprising and out-of-character things.

'Why?'

The middle-aged Jew squinted over the table at İkmen. 'Why what?'

'Why did you kill her, Mr Loya?'

'Well, because she humiliated me, I—'

'No. No,' İkmen said. 'That she humiliated you, I think Sergeant Farsakoğlu and myself understand. What I'm asking, Mr Loya, is what exactly triggered off the attack or action that caused Mrs Aksu to die. You do not strike me as a violent man. Something must have caused you to lose your temper, to snap . . .'

'I am a man and I will not be trifled with,' Edmondo Loya said as he sat up straight in his chair. 'Emine tempted me, as she had done in the past, and then she failed to deliver.'

'She offered sex and then changed her mind?' Ayşe Farsakoğlu asked.

'Yes.' He looked at her and then looked away very quickly

114

as if embarrassed. 'She had no right to do that! Men have needs, animal needs!'

'Yes, and women have the right to say "no" if they feel threatened or exploited,' Ayşe responded hotly. She wasn't the only feminist in the station but she was probably the most vocal. İkmen actively encouraged her to be vocal, although not on this occasion. On this occasion he wanted to work his way towards the truth. He was finding it difficult to believe that mild-mannered Edmondo Loya could so much as kill a rat, much less a human being.

'Edmondo,' he said as he placed a restraining hand briefly over Ayşe's wrist, 'tell me how you killed Emine. Tell me the sequence of events.'

'I stabbed her . . .'

'No, no, not how you did it, how it happened,' İkmen said. 'Emine did what? She took her clothes off, you got on top of her, she changed her mind and tried to get up, you hit her . . . ?'

'I, well I, I started, you know, to . . .' He looked first at İkmen, then at Ayşe Farsakoğlu, then back at İkmen again. 'Couldn't we have a male officer?'

'No.' If Edmondo was lying, İkmen was disinclined to do anything to help him and if he really was a murderer he deserved precious little in the way of concessions. Let him feel uncomfortable around a woman! It was after all nothing compared to the discomfort he was going to feel in prison. 'Please continue, Mr Loya, if you will.'

Edmondo Loya, momentarily taken aback by İkmen's aggression, cleared his throat. His old friend Balthazar had worked with this man for many years and only had praise for him. Why, he couldn't understand. İkmen seemed now to be nothing other than an insensitive bully.

'I, well, yes, as you say, I tried to er, get on top of – I tried to enter Emine, as it were . . .'

'You attempted intercourse,' İkmen said. 'Were you aroused?'

'Well, yes, of course I was!' his face was suddenly puce to the ears.

'Just checking.'

'Sometimes men kill because of their own impotence,' Ayşe Farsakoğlu said. 'Their own inability to maintain an erection causes them to become angry and to lose control.'

'Yes, well, I don't have any trouble keeping an – what you said, an . . . Emine suddenly refused to go on with it,' he said. 'She said she'd only been teasing and that she wanted to go home to her husband. She laughed. She got up and she actually laughed!'

İkmen opened up the file on the desk in front of him and said, 'What was she wearing, Edmondo, on the day that you killed her?'

'What?' He looked both strained and puzzled which is exactly what İkmen wanted him to be. The inclusion of sudden, factual, if seemingly trivial, questions in an interrogation was a recognised way of checking the veracity of a suspect's story.

'Emine,' İkmen said as he looked down at the file that was now in his lap. 'What was she wearing on the day that you killed her?'

'Oh, er . . .'

'Was it a dress? Or trousers? Blue? White? Black? Did she wear shoes or—'

'Oh, she wore shoes all right,' Edmondo said. 'Little black peephole toe things with high, transparent heels. Her dress was pink, showed her curves, and she wore a shawl just as

116

she always had done when she was young. Black again, but sparkly with sequins or something.'

İkmen, still looking down at the file in his lap, said, 'Going back to the shoes, Edmondo, was there anything else, anything unusual . . .'

'You mean what was in the transparent heels? Floating in some sort of liquid, I think?'

'Yes?' İkmen looking up now viewed Edmondo Loya closely. 'In the heels, in liquid . . .'

'Little models of the Eiffel Tower!' Edmondo Loya said. 'Yes! They went up and down as the shoes moved! A gimmick, a . . .'

İkmen passed the file over to Ayşe and pointed silently to something on the page he had selected.

'. . . a designer gimmick. Silly.'

She looked up at İkmen and then at Edmondo Loya with an expression of shock on her face.

Mr Bülent Emin was no longer a young man.

'I gave up going to prostitutes before you were born,' he said in answer to İzzet Melik's slightly veiled question regarding what the old man had been doing in Karaköy on Thursday night and Friday morning. 'Last time I went to a whore I think I was probably still in the army. I wasn't even married then, I don't think.'

The policeman was with Mr Emin in a small office at the back of his shop on Hasircilar Street which ran at a ninety-degree angle away from the Spice Bazaar and parallel with the shore of the Golden Horn. The shop was like many of the smaller premises in the teeming ancient streets around the Spice Bazaar in that it specialised in only one product. In the same street there were shops selling ladies' corsets, cigarette lighters and their various fuels, and foreign perfume that was almost certainly fake. Bülent Emin's shop specialised in buttons. Every shape, colour and size imaginable was contained in his seemingly endless array of cardboard display boxes. Buttons could be made, İzzet Melik had discovered since his arrival, not only from materials one would expect to see, such as bone or plastic or metal, but also from materials that one would not immediately think about, such as stone or human hair.

'In countries like England and France in the nineteenth century, people made a big thing of funerals,' the old man had said when he showed İzzet an example of a button made from human hair. 'Mourners would put on black sometimes for years and have special jewellery made for the funeral, often containing clippings of the dead person's hair. They also made buttons, like these, with hair embedded in a glass capsule on top of the piece. To good Muslims this is very strange, but to Christians who sometimes do not bury their dead for weeks, it is quite normal.'

İzzet had been appalled, especially when Mr Emin had told him that demand for such grisly oddities was high. 'Collectors of buttons, like collectors of anything, can be odd,' he said as he led the policeman out through the back of his shop and into his office. Now, a glass of tea, several cigarettes and a lot of buttons later, İzzet was asking Mr Emin to remember everything that he could about the night in question. Mr Emin had not been over in Karaköy for what many would regard as 'normal' business at a 'normal' time of day.

'I was with one of the button lunatics I told you about,' Emin said with a wave of a nicotine-stained hand. 'He has buttons from everywhere. One of Sultan Reşad's buttons from one of his shirts, a button from a dress that belonged to Marilyn Monroe, a row of tiny pieces from a glove worn by Queen Victoria of England . . . He is obsessed.' He shrugged. 'But old. Even older than me, may God protect him. From time to time I take him pieces I come across that he may be interested in and we talk. I generally go over to see him about once every three months and I always go in the evening when the shop has closed. Sometimes we go on a bit; he sees very few people now and is quite disabled. I must have finally got away at about 2 a.m.'

'Your friend, Mr—'

'Mr Adnan Osman.' And then, having given his friend's name away, he said, rather guiltily, 'You won't need to speak to him . . .'

'Mr Osman lives at the house on Midilli Lane . . .'

'Just above Voyvoda Street, yes,' Mr Emin said. 'Where that body was put. Not that I saw it with my own eyes, thanks be to God.'

He wore the knitted woollen cap, so often sported by those of a religious turn of mind. He also invoked or thanked God at every available opportunity as he spoke.

'So what did you see or hear, Mr Emin, on Thursday night that made you telephone the police station now?'

Bülent Emin sighed. 'Not a lot, I'm afraid, officer,' he said. 'I was in a hurry, to be honest. Rushing to get home to the comfort of the bed God sees fit to allow my poor old body to rest upon. Leaving Adnan's house I go down on to Voyvoda Street on my way back to the Galata Bridge and home.'

'So what happened?'

'That was suspicious? Nothing,' Mr Emin said with a smile. 'As I told you, officer, I saw nothing bad going on. What

119

was a surprise, however, was the vehicle that I saw on Voyvoda Street that night.'

'Vehicle?'

'A 1972 Fiat 124 BC. Beautiful car. I used to have one myself! In my younger days I was very enthusiastic about cars,' he said, his smile broadening as he obviously warmed to his subject. 'And this Fiat was in wonderful condition for its age. In fact, I would have, in spite of the lateness of the hour, gone up and had a closer look had it not been for the arguing.'

'Inside the vehicle?'

'Yes. Men's voices,' Mr Emin said with a frown. 'That time of night, who knows what might happen if one talks to strangers? These days you hear such stories! I just walked on. But it was very unusual, the Fiat 124, very unusual.'

'And there were definitely two men in the car, arguing?' İzzet Melik asked.

'Oh, yes,' Bülent Emin replied. 'I didn't see them, you understand; I didn't get that close. My eyes are not so good . . .'

'What were they arguing about? Do you know?'

Bülent Emin smiled again. 'My ears are not so good either,' he said. 'I'm seventy-five years old!'

'And yet you knew the car. You appreciated the car.'

'Oh, I would know a 1972 Fiat 124 in the dark, officer,' the old man said. And then, looking from side to side to make sure that no one else had come into the room without his knowledge, he added, 'You never forget the car that you really, truly loved, do you? I laugh behind my hands at people like Adnan, who loves his buttons with a passion. Sometimes I admonish him that he is practising a form of idolatry. The Koran is very clear upon the fact that good Muslims should

120

not be in thrall to material things. And we all try to be good Muslims but . . . that car was my god. I once took a lady, a Spanish tourist, for a ride in it many years ago. She took a shine to me and although nothing improper happened – well, it is a memory that I treasure.' He then looked up with a very serious expression on his face and said, 'Officer, I would know a 1972 Fiat 124 if I was dead. And there was one on Voyvoda Street at just past two o'clock last Friday morning.'

As far as Ahmet Aksu could remember the last man his wife Emine had undoubtedly been with was the young Italian whom the hippy Kadir Özal had told İkmen about.

'His name is Francesco Vitali,' Ahmet Aksu said. 'He came to live with us for a time, when Emine's passion for him was at its height.'

'One of the sources you yourself named, a Kadir Özal, said that your wife was stepping out with an Italian boy about six months ago,' İkmen said. 'Same or different boy, Mr Aksu?'

He sighed. 'Oh, same one. Francesco was very attractive and athletic, according to Emine.'

'Kadir Özal said he actually saw the Italian with your wife about six months ago.'

'Francesco went back to Venice three months ago,' Ahmet Aksu said.

'So your wife, by your own admission a sexually predatory woman, didn't see anyone after—'

'Oh, she wasn't on her own for very long!' Aksu said with some bitterness in his voice. 'This "thing" with this unknown man has, I reckon, been going on for two months.'

'So your wife took cocaine for, or with, this new man?'

'My wife took cocaine with anyone and everyone who had

121

her!' He crossed his arms angrily over his chest. This marriage of the Aksus was not as 'open' as, İkmen felt, they might like people to think. He suspected Mr Aksu was unfashionably jealous.

'And you yourself do not take, and never have taken, cocaine?'

'I've told you, no!' he snapped. 'Emine took it, she needed to. I neither want nor need the filthy stuff!'

'We can run blood tests . . .'

'Well, run your fucking blood tests and have done with it!' Aksu said. And then as he slumped back into the hard, straight-backed station chair he murmured, 'Just tell me about this person who has confessed to her murder and let me get out of here. That is all I ask.'

Unbeknown to Ahmet Aksu, the slumped little Jewish man in interview room 2, the room right next door to where he and İkmen were now sitting, was the person who had confessed to the murder of Emine Aksu, his once darling wife. Although by no means an open and shut confession, Edmondo Loya had given İkmen such an accurate description of the clothes that Emine had been wearing when she disappeared that he had to take what he had said seriously. The clothes concerned had been so particular, so very individual, especially the shoes. There was, as yet, no body, but then if Edmondo had indeed consigned Emine to the waters of the Golden Horn she could be almost anywhere. Bodies not quickly picked up in the Horn could be swept out into the Bosphorus or even the Sea of Marmara. From then on they were usually lost. Soon İkmen would have to tell Ahmet Aksu who had confessed and why. They knew or had known each other. It was not going to be easy. And even though it was Ahmet Aksu himself who had given the name of Edmondo

122

Loya to Mehmet Süleyman, İkmen doubted whether he had seriously considered the Jew to be her killer, İkmen himself was struggling with the idea.

'Speaking of tests, Mr Aksu,' İkmen said, 'we are still going to run them on the blood traces found in your kitchen and bathroom.'

'Just because you have a confession doesn't mean that you rule out – what is it you call it, "other lines of inquiry"?' Ahmet Aksu leaned across the table wearily. 'I can understand that. Inspector, have you found Emine's body?'

İkmen shook his head. 'No.'

'So it will be difficult to decide whether this person who has confessed to her murder is telling the truth or not?'

'We have been given, by this person, a certain scenario and a possible site for the disposal of the body . . .'

'Which is?'

'Mr Aksu,' İkmen said, 'all I can tell you at this point is that the person who has confessed to your wife's murder says that the body was dumped in water.'

'In the bloody Bosphorus!' Ahmet Aksu flung his long, slim arms in the air in exasperation. 'So it's lost? How will you find it with the current and tides . . .'

'Sir . . .'

'God!' He stood up and, weeping now, put his head in his hands.

İkmen let him cry. If his tears were genuine, then he had a lot to shed them over. His wife was in all probability dead, and recovering her body from any of İstanbul's great waterways was indeed very unlikely. However, he did now know where Edmondo Loya claimed to have dumped the body, to the side of the Fener ferry stage, and so he would be sending divers down into the immediate vicinity. But if that proved fruitless he would just have to wait and see what the Golden Horn, the Bosphorus and the Sea of Marmara produced. He would, however, in nearly three weeks since her disappearance, have expected something of Mrs Aksu to appear somewhere by now. One of her Eiffel Tower shoes caught up in a fishing net, perhaps? But then İkmen was not wholly convinced by Edmondo's story. In its favour was the ancient grudge he so obviously still held against her combined with the intimate knowledge he had of her clothing on the day that she disappeared. But, on the other hand, there was Edmondo's physical frailty plus his inability to adequately describe the act of murder itself. The precise details remained fudged.

'I am going to send divers down,' İkmen said as he offered Ahmet Aksu a cigarette from his almost empty packet of Maltepe. 'But sir, about the blood in your house, I must ask you if you know—'

'No,' he wiped the tears away from his eyes with the cuff of his crisp, white shirt and then took a cigarette from İkmen. 'No I don't know how it got there,' he said. 'Maybe Emine cut herself.'

'In the kitchen, yes,' İkmen said as he lit both his own and Ahmet Aksu's cigarettes. 'But in the bathroom? Underneath a floor tile?' It smacked of concealment.

'Well, maybe it's my blood,' Aksu said as he sat down, a little calmer now. 'I cut myself shaving occasionally. At my age I know how inept that sounds but . . . or maybe the blood is Emine's. Or even Francesco's.'

'The Italian cut himself shaving?'

'Or maybe his sexual atheleticism caused him to fall,' Ahmet Aksu momentarily closed his eyes against the vision this idea was producing. 'Sometimes Emine and Francesco would . . . I would hear them in the bathroom . . .'

124

'You know, Mr Aksu,' İkmen said, 'we are going to have to contact this Francesco Vitali.' He took his notebook out of his pocket. 'Venice, did you say?'

He sighed. 'Yes. I don't know his address, but I'm sure I can find it amongst my wife's things.'

They looked at each other, the policeman and the arbiter of modern taste. Both of them were connected by the fact that they had individually sorted through the effects of the same woman, now thought to be dead. Nothing else tied them to each other; in every other way they were worlds apart. And indeed this sudden, unlooked-for closeness would have been even more intense had the one not suspected the other. Edmondo Loya's confession could be one hundred per cent genuine, for all İkmen knew, but while he didn't actually *know* it to be so, anyone and everyone was fair game. And that included Ahmet Aksu, the missing woman's husband, the rich man, the cuckold.

'Thank you,' İkmen said as he steadily observed the shifting eyes of the man in front of him. 'That will be most appreciated.'

Chapter 8

Zelfa Süleyman was only half Turkish. Her mother, Bernadette, had been Irish and Zelfa had herself been brought up in Dublin. Back there she was still known as Brigit and, in spite of the fact that her father was Turkish, she had been raised a Catholic. Not that she went to Mass these days. The son she had with Mehmet Süleyman was, like his father, being raised a Muslim. She was also, by her own admission and like many psychiatrists, an agnostic. And so it was with some surprise that Mehmet saw his wife coming out of the Catholic Church of St Anthony of Padua on İstiklal Street.

'What are you doing here?' he asked as he watched her take a scarf off her head in the lee of the red-brick gothic building. Set back from the road behind a gateway, as nine-teenth-century Ottoman law demanded churches to be, St Anthony is nevertheless one of the largest and most visible Christian centres in the city.

'I went in with them,' she said as she tilted her head towards a small group of red-shirted skin-heads who had also just come out of the church. Then, switching into English, she held one thumb up to the men and said, 'Well, now we've the Blessed Virgin on our side, we can't help but win, can we?'

'I'm made up, darling!' One of them answered back a little drunkenly. 'Proper made up, me!'

'Ah, God love you and bless the dear boys!' Zelfa said.

Mehmet Süleyman frowned. 'You don't support Liverpool Football Club,' he said. 'They're an English team.'

'Yes, they're English, but . . .'

'But what?'

Under the now very watchful gaze of her husband, Zelfa's erstwhile football friends were walking back on to the main street once again.

Zelfa stopped in her tracks, put her hands on her hips and sighed. These foreigners, her father included, just didn't understand. And when they were young like Mehmet, too, well . . . 'Look, if you live in Liverpool you either support Liverpool or Everton,' she said. 'It's very old and very complicated but basically if you support Everton you're a Protestant and if you support Liverpool you're a Catholic of Irish origin.'

'But you are not from Liverpool.'

'No, but I am Irish and so I have a duty to support other Irish Catholic teams.'

'But you are not religious.' He took her arm, steering her away from a group of rather loud Italians who had also just left the church. 'And these Italians, they are Catholics too . . .'

'Yes, but—'

'Zelfa you don't even like football!' Mehmet said. 'You laugh when your father watches it on the television.'

'That's Turkish football,' she said as, once out of the church precinct, she took a cigarette out of her handbag and lit up. 'This is Liverpool and AC Milan. Liverpool Irish against the world. This is serious.'

Mehmet didn't know a lot about football, especially not about foreign teams. But what he did know was that not many Liverpool players were actually from Liverpool. Most of them, like so many players in a lot of the big English teams, came from places like Brazil, Russia and even, sometimes, Turkey. But then, like so many aspects of life in Western Europe, it was something he found hard to understand. Zelfa's past life in Dublin was, when she occasionally spoke about it, a bit like a somewhat labyrinthine and dark fairy tale to Mehmet. Peopled by black-clad priests, enormous families of poor folk and decorated with numerous statues of the Madonna and the saints, Dublin in the fifties and sixties was a place that, in spite of his wife's descriptions, Mehmet found hard to even imagine.

'Ah, well, all the lads and lasses are arriving for the match in force now,' Zelfa said as she looked at the growing number of people in football shirts on İstiklal Street. 'By Wednesday we'll be full to bursting.' She looked quite pleased about something her husband so obviously viewed with horror. 'What are you doing up here, Mehmet?'

Her practice office was up near Taksim Square in the centre of the relatively new and largely nineteenth-century part of the city. Her husband, based over in old Sultanahmet, was often across the Golden Horn in Beyoğlu or Karaköy, but it wasn't every day that he managed to see Zelfa. In fact, working on a Saturday as he was now, seeing her was even less likely. But she did on occasion, as today, have the odd patient or two booked in at the weekend.

'Officially I'm at lunch,' he said. 'I came over to pick up a book in English about Ottoman armour for my father. They're holding it for me at Robinson Crusoe bookshop.' Mehmet's father, the old prince, was retreating ever further into the once-glorious world of his ancestors. 'Actually, Zelfa, if you have time, would you like to have a coffee with me?'

She knew he had an ulterior motive, she'd always been able to read him, and he knew that she knew it. He bent

129

down to kiss her and said, 'I won't waste either your time or mine taking you to a cheap place.'

'You'd better not,' Zelfa replied. 'If this doesn't mean Patisserie Markiz, then I'll be charging you the same hourly rate as my patients.'

'Fetishism is not what you think it is,' Zelfa said as she spooned the froth from the top of her cappuccino into her mouth.

Mehmet stirred his plain black coffee and said, 'You don't know what I think fetishism is. I haven't said.'

'No. That was unfair of me,' Zelfa replied. 'You're not thinking about voluptuous women dressed in leather, are you?'

'I may be thinking about you like that,' he said with an entirely straight face. 'It's an idea.'

She laughed. 'I'm glad we're holding this conversation in English,' she said.

'I am glad that you mentioned voluptuous women in leather.'

Still laughing, she shook her head. Probably over half of the smart, well-heeled people in Patisserie Markiz could understand every word of their conversation. But it didn't matter. Markiz people were generally not shocked by much. Those devoted to delicious cakes and dark, sinful coffee rarely are. Patisserie Markiz was original Art Nouveau; the age of Toulouse Lautrec, of absinthe and of young Ottoman princes dying of their self-imposed vices. A little sexual deviance was not going to bother these descendants of the İstanbul demimonde.

'The oldest and, for want of a better expression, traditional meaning of "fetish" is that it is an inanimate object its owner

130

believes procures the services of some god or spirit within it. The owner or keeper of this thing treats it with almost irrational reverence, to the point and sometimes beyond of worship.'

'So, if a fetish is a religious object, why does everyone always talk about sex?'

Zelfa sighed. 'There has probably always been a sexual element to reverence for inanimate objects. For instance, some of the dances that people like the Dogon of Mali perform in the presence of their elaborate carvings look, to us, very sexual. Having said that, most things do look sexual to tight-arsed monotheists.'

It wasn't often that Mehmet's comprehension of English failed him, but this was one of them.

'Monotheism,' Zelfa explained. 'Worshipping one God as Christians, Muslims and Jews all do. We're all a bit puritanical, especially when it comes to sex. The Hindus are a lot more relaxed about such things as are many of the animistic faiths. But that aside, sexual fetishism in the modern psychiatric sense of the term is all about a pathological sexual attachment to an inanimate object.'

'The object has to be inanimate?'

'Yes. Clothes are very popular, particularly shoes, for some reason. Childhood toys, jewellery, grooming equipment like a hairbrush or nail extensions. Generally fetishism is a solitary and harmless pursuit.'

Mehmet Süleyman looked down at the highly polished wooden table and, for once, felt glad that he hadn't bought one of the patisserie's wonderful cakes on this occasion. 'What about fetishism of the dead?' he asked.

There was a short pause before his wife answered him.

'Necrophilia?' She sighed again, but this time on a long,

slow stream of breath. 'Well, that is another matter alto-gether,' she said.

'Why?'

'Well, because strictly this, too, is just simply straight-forward fetishism. The object at issue is inanimate. No person is harmed. But it wasn't always that way. The dead were once the living and to defile them is both a criminal act and a sin in all major religions.' She leaned across the table and took one of his hands in hers. 'We're talking about the body found on the Kamondo Stairs here, aren't we?' The story had, of course, been all over the newspapers. 'You didn't tell me you were working on that!'

'No.' He didn't always tell her about his work. In fact, most of the time he was expressly forbidden to do so. But this time he was consulting her as a professional under the guidance of the police pathologist, no less. The fact that they were conducting their meeting in a smart café was just rather more pleasant than talking at her office or at home around her father and their young son. 'So can necrophiliacs be dangerous? To the living, I mean.'

Zelfa let go of his hand and leaned back against her chair once again. 'Not that I've heard,' she said. 'Most fetishists, if disturbed when about their "business", may become first agitated and then possibly violent. But most of the time when they're found out, fetishists are just ashamed. I had a patient once with a "thing" for his wife's jewellery. It was pitiful. Every time she found him at it, he just cried.'

'Mmm.' That did sound sad. Sad and pathetic. It did not, to Mehmet Süleyman, easily equate with that obscenely displayed corpse on the Kamondo Stairs.

Amazingly, to Mehmet, Zelfa ordered a large slice of tiramisu cake before she continued to tell him basically what

Arto Sarkissian had told him before about the genesis of sexual fetishes. What never ceased to amaze the policeman was how his wife, and almost every other medic he had ever met, could eat with such gusto around such grisly sights, sounds and topics. Policemen generally didn't, not even Çetin İkmen. Like most of them, he just smoked himself to a standstill. And so in an act of solidarity with his absent colleagues, as well as just because he wanted to, Mehmet lit up.

'Necrophiliacs rarely kill,' Zelfa said, underlining yet again the opinion of the pathologist. 'And if you say you think this offender may have had this one body for some time . . . whoever she was may have been meaningful to him – a wife or a sister or . . . this could well be someone who murdered, maybe spontaneously, a crime of anger or passion, and then became attached to the body, possibly by guilt. Then again, not all fetishists fetishise just one thing.'

'What do you mean?'

'Well, look, I know that I do have a tendency to extend connections sometimes beyond what is realistic but . . .' Zelfa pushed a large piece of tiramisu into her mouth. A paper-thin model-like woman at the table opposite looked on in disgust. 'Sometimes the fetishist may be aroused by a number of items. Jewellery and shoes is not an unheard of combination. Maybe your necrophiliac killed this woman because he wanted her clothes or her make-up.'

'And then, once he'd taken possession of those things, he killed her? That seems unlikely,' Mehmet said. 'Why would he then hold on to her body?'

'Because her association with the fetishised items was too strong for him to part with her!' Zelfa said, her eyes becoming big with excitement as she spoke. 'Maybe he only realised it once he'd killed her. But suddenly he couldn't part with her, because without her the fetish, the clothes, make-up or whatever, didn't work!'

'And you've come across cases like this? You know that this is a possibility?'

Zelfa, her eyes shining, looked down. 'Well . . .'

'It is a theory is it not?' her husband said as he tried, without success, to catch her eye.

'Yes, I . . .'

Zelfa Süleyman was a good psychiatrist in as much as she was always thinking about her subject, always looking at and mentally pushing the boundaries of what the minds of others might be doing. That a lot of her ideas were pure speculation wasn't a bad thing per se, but from a policeman's point of view her musings were not always exactly helpful.

'Zelfa, I need to know roughly what type of person we are looking at,' Mehmet said. 'What is your profile for the "average" lover of the dead?'

After forking what remained of her cake into her mouth and then lighting a cigarette, a weary-looking Zelfa said, 'Sad loner, physically unattractive, unsuccessful, may or may not be religious, and if so, in a weird and twisted way. There're nearly always parental issues, too. The parent either smothered the child with attention, affording zero independence, or bullied him, made him feel inadequate, unworthy – so he turns to the dead for validation, for want of a better word. Oh, there's also a very bad smell they have about them.'

At this last item of information, Mehmet looked up at his wife and gave her a small, grim smile. 'Irish humour, yes?'

'No, fact,' she replied. 'When I was a medical student back in Dublin we had one in our morgue, as it turned out, and he stank. But then you would, wouldn't you?'

So no real deviation from what Dr Sarkissian had told him. They were looking for a sad, lonely, inadequate man. Mehmet Süleyman silently wondered how many of them were currently in this city, or any city come to that. Although he didn't groan out loud, he felt himself do so inwardly.

Rumours spread quickly in what is left of the Jewish community of Balat. It was said that Maurice Loya himself started this one. Friends for many years with Moşe Levi the baker, he then told old Esther Sinop who then just happened to meet the novelist Juanita Kordovi in Ali Paksoy's shoe shop. Esther, though decidedly on the 'sensible' side of things when it came to shoes, was just as extreme in her use of language as the silver high-heeled pump-wearing diva, Juanita.

'From Maurice's own lips!' she said as Ali Paksoy's nephew brought her yet another box containing a pair of broad, brown shoes. 'Thank you, darling.' She smiled at the boy who put the box down on the floor and then went away. 'His brother Edmondo, a killer. Of a woman!'

Juanita Kordovi, authoress of fifteen romantic novels featuring the fictional Turkish chieftan, Osman Bey, cleared her throat. 'Well, anyone can kill, darling,' she said, 'read the papers!' She pointed at the huge sheaf of newspapers on her lap. She bought almost every paper published in Turkish every day. She'd lose most of them during the course of the day but she still went on buying them. 'And if it was a woman he murdered then it was almost certainly a crime of passion.'

'A crime of passion? Edmondo Loya? But he's a thing surely without passion, Juanita. Edmondo Loya, he's like a eunuch!'

'A eunuch? Who's like a eunuch?'

Both women looked up in response to the male voice that

had suddenly cut in to their conversation. Ali Paksoy stood above them, smiling, holding the pair of red stilettos Juanita had seen in his shop window earlier.

The novelist beckoned him down to come and sit next to herself and Esther. 'Mr Paksoy, maybe you haven't heard.'

'Heard what?' he sat down and then handed the heavily made-up romantic writer her chosen shoes.

Juanita Kordovi took her silver high-heeled pumps off and threw them carelessly on the floor. Her greedy eyes were now well and truly focussed on the new and exciting red shoes. 'Edmondo Loya', she said, 'is a murderer!'

'Well, we don't actually know whether he really did do it,' Esther Sinop put in at first, a little nervously. However, she very quickly warmed to her subject and said, 'But he, Edmondo, he confessed to the police, or so Maurice says. But then Maurice is his brother and he should know.'

'But what woman?' Juanita Kordovi said as she pushed and shoved one of her seriously swollen feet into a delicate red shoe. Normally Ali Paksoy would have come to her aid under such circumstances and at least offered her a shoe-horn. But on this occasion he did not.

'That woman who has been missing for a while. From over in Hasköy,' Esther replied.

'Aksu, the magazine owner's wife,' Ali Paksoy said quietly.

'Yes, that's it,' Juanita Kordovi said. And then losing patience with the shoe dangling uselessly from her toes she asked, 'Mr Paksoy, you don't have this style in a thirty-eight do you?'

'No . . .' He didn't even go to look and see whether this was really the case. But then Ali Paksoy had the reputation of knowing his stock inside out. He was, however, very, very white.

'You've been good friends with Edmondo for many years, haven't you, Mr Paksoy?' Esther said.

There was a pause. 'Eh . . .'

'You and Edmondo Loya, you've been friends for a long time,' Esther reiterated.

Ali Paksoy looked up into Esther Sinop's worn, pleasant old face and said, 'Yes. Yes, Edmondo and myself have been close, Mrs Sinop. He is a – a good man . . .'

'Mr Paksoy *do* you have anything else in red?' Juanita Kordovi asked. 'I'm going to a luncheon with some very eminent romantic novelists from abroad; from England and America, and I must have the right shoes to go with my new ruby-coloured dress.'

'I'll, er, I'll have a . . .'

'I can still remember you and Edmondo and that boy whose father owned all those horses – Armenian, I think he was . . .'

'Garbis . . .'

'Garbis, yes! When you were teenagers you'd all go off wearing those wide-bottomed trousers the youngsters liked to wear then. I know your poor late father disapproved . . .'

'Mr Paksoy, red shoes?' Juanita Kordovi was not accustomed to being put last or even second to anyone. But then suddenly she saw something outside the window of the shoe shop that made her drop the small red stiletto on the ground and run barefoot towards the front door. The newspapers that had been on her lap flew to the ground. Just before she let herself out into the street she pointed in the direction she was headed and said, 'It's Mrs Cohen, the policeman's wife! She'll be able to tell us some more about Edmondo Loya!'

And then she was gone, her voluminous yellow-flowered skirt flapping in the breeze behind her.

'I liked it here back in the sixties,' Esther said as both

137

she and Ali Paksoy watched Juanita Kordovi nag, badger and eventually pull Estelle Cohen towards the shoe shop. 'It was,' Esther continued, 'less complicated back then. Of course, I was younger myself, too . . . what a world it is now! Computers and those mobile phones everyone has! Miserable with them, miserable without them! And the terrorism and the murders! And now Edmondo Loya!' She shook her head sadly. 'Clever Edmondo Loya. Who would have thought it, Mr Paksoy? Who would have thought it of Edmondo Loya.'

But Ali Paksoy didn't answer her. He just watched as the crazy old novelist pulled the policeman's wife almost kicking and screaming into the shop. He would, he thought, have to try and speak to Estelle Cohen once all the old women had gone.

There were two divers, both ex-marines, and both called İsmet. It was one of those coincidences that other people, as opposed to those actually involved, found odd and maybe even slightly spooky. İkmen, nominally in charge of the operation, actually found it quite useful. He only ever needed to speak to them both together and so shouting out 'İsmet!' and immediately getting the attention of both of them was quite useful. That Ardiç had organised divers at such short notice was good, although it was now mid-afternoon and, although spring was well and truly established in the city, the light was dimming somewhat. But then, as Ardiç had said, this was only a first attempt. The divers had been available and were available for the following day, too. Just now the mission was to get into the Golden Horn via the jetty at the Fener ferry stage and see what might remain of Emine Aksu at the place where Edmondo Loya said he had deposited her body. He did not have great hopes of anything being there, but he'd had the stage closed down for a couple of hours anyway which had not made him the most popular person with the small group of locals who liked to use the ferry. But that wasn't a homicide detective's problem. He left all that to the rather angry man in the ferry ticket office who was now glaring at İkmen and his team with some venom.

'İsmet!'

The two black-clad divers flopped their way in flippers over to where İkmen was standing.

'There is a chance that even if the body isn't present, you may find the murder weapon,' İkmen said.

İsmet 1, as İkmen had dubbed him, who was the taller of the two men, said, 'What's it like, this weapon?'

'A straight dagger, approximately twenty centimetres blade length. It has quite an ornate handle, I understand, and it's made of Toledo steel. The man who has confessed to the murder claims to have thrown the weapon into the Horn with the body. Oh, and look for women's shoes, too,' İkmen said. 'High-heeled, unusual, transparent heels . . .'

'Down there, Inspector, with respect,' İsmet 2 said, 'a shoe is a shoe is a shoe. You know? Just lumps . . .'

'We'll bring up whatever we find down there,' İsmet 1 said in a rather more gentle tone of voice than that of his colleague.

İkmen sighed. 'Do what you can,' he said as he first offered a cigarette to Ayşe Farsakoğlu and then took one for himself.

İsmets 1 and 2 made their way over to where the support team were waiting for them at the edge of the jetty. Some talk between the İsmets and the others then ensued, after which the two men disappeared backwards over the side of the jetty. A man, a headscarfed woman and a large goat in a small motor launch passing by the end of the jetty looked on with puzzled expressions on their faces.

'Do you really think that the divers will find anything down there, sir?' Ayşe said as she inhaled deeply on her cigarette.

'You mean do I think that Mr Loya really killed Emine Aksu?' İkmen replied. 'My gut feeling, Ayşe, is that he could not and did not. He couldn't have got her body down here without help. Mrs Aksu is not, or was not, a small woman. However, the knife Mr Loya claims to have killed Mrs Aksu with, or some knife at least, is missing from the display on the wall of his house. He did have "issues" as people say these days with Mrs Aksu, and he does not have an alibi for the afternoon and evening of her disappearance. I don't know what İsmets 1 and 2 will find. I really don't.'

There was nothing save a few bubbles to show where the divers had submerged. It was a typical spring afternoon in İstanbul, neither very cold nor very hot, and yet the water of the Golden Horn, close to the shore, looked oily and dingy. Unlike the fast-moving water of the Bosphorus, this generally looked a little tired. Until comparatively recently the Golden Horn had been filthy. But now that the industry and businesses lining its shores had cleaned up their acts it was a lot more savoury than it had once been. This did not mean, however, that it was entirely empty of rubbish. Substances as well as 'things' still ended up in the Golden Horn and so looking for certain, specified things, including dead bodies, was not going to be an easy task.

'If they don't find anything this afternoon, will the divers go down tomorrow, sir?' Ayşe asked.

'I don't know,' İkmen said. 'It will depend upon Commissioner Ardiç and, of course, Mr Edmondo Loya.'

'Loya?'

'Were he to recant his confession we could all go home. Or, of course, if Mrs Aksu were to turn up, which I don't think is possible . . .'

'Sir!' Ayşe flung out a hand and gripped İkmen's arm hard. 'Isn't that Edmondo Loya?'

'What?' İkmen looked about him with narrowed, confused eyes. 'What?'

'Look over there!' Ayşe said as she pointed inland towards a group of people standing silently to one side of the ferry stage. 'Next to that short woman with the blue headscarf.'

For a moment İkmen squinted into the distance. He really was beginning to need spectacles now. But the figure that he saw next to the small woman was familiar. It was also, incongruously, smartly dressed.

'That isn't Edmondo Loya; it's his brother, Maurice,' İkmen said. 'They're identical twins, remember?'

'Oh, yes of course.' Ayşe put a calming hand to her own chest. 'Just for a moment there . . .'

'Twins can be disconcerting to those of us who are not twins,' İkmen said. 'To have a copy of oneself, as it were, seems wrong somehow. Why don't you go over, Ayşe, and ask Mr Loya to join us.'

Ayşe frowned. 'Do you think that's a good idea? This is a police operation, sir. What if a body—'

'İsmet and İsmet will give us due warning about any bodies,' İkmen said. 'Go and get him, will you, Ayşe.'

She did as she was asked while İkmen stared back out over the water once again. What Maurice Loya was doing gawping at a police operation, headed by the man who had

141

taken his brother into custody, he couldn't imagine. If İkmen had been Maurice Loya, he would have kept a low profile, knowing what Edmondo had done, in giving himself up to the police. But here was the architect, in what looked to be a very good suit, as large as life, walking towards him with Ayşe Farsakoğlu.

'Mr Loya.' İkmen extended his hand to Maurice. They had of course met briefly before when İkmen had been to see Edmondo with Mehmet Süleyman.

Maurice Loya took İkmen's hand for a tiny fraction of a second and then said, 'You are, I take it, looking for what my brother may have thrown into the Golden Horn.'

'You think that your brother Edmondo threw something into the Golden Horn?'

'You have him in custody,' Maurice Loya said. 'You tell me?'

His manner was punitive, but then, given his current situation, it was probably bound to be. Not that Maurice Loya needed to be where he was at this moment. He didn't. His aggressive persona therefore was not entirely welcome.

'I can't tell you anything about why we are here or what we are doing,' İkmen said. 'This is a police matter and we alone have an interest in it. But, Mr Loya, the fact that you are here I find interesting. And also the fact that you claim your brother has thrown something into this waterway . . .'

'A woman's body,' Maurice Loya said, making no effort as he did so to soften either the tone or volume of his voice. A couple of people in the crowd on the shore beyond the fence turned and looked at him. 'Emine . . .'

'Sir, let us not yell out names in a public place, shall we?' İkmen said as he pulled the sleeve of Maurice Loya's coat towards him. He lowered his voice. 'Your brother, as I know

142

you know, has confessed to the murder of a woman.'

'Yes, he . . .'

'I will need to speak to you about the night your brother claims he killed this person,' İkmen said. 'But now is neither the place nor the time. What are you doing here, Mr Loya?'

'I was going to catch a ferry . . .'

It was perfectly possible, although İkmen doubted whether it was true. There was a faint mocking expression behind the smooth and confident face of this man. İkmen was getting the feeling that Mr Loya had the idea he was having something over on the policeman. Quite why he should want to do such a thing, İkmen couldn't imagine. But that he did appear to be doing it was obvious to him.

'Mr Loya—'

'Sir! Sir!'

İkmen looked around at Ayşe Farsakoğlu. Pointing excitedly at the water below the jetty, she said, 'It's İsmet, sir! He's got something!'

Quite which İsmet she meant, İkmen didn't know. But, after excusing himself to Maurice Loya, he went over to his sergeant and was just about to ask her what she meant when he saw one of the İsmets holding something over his head in the water. To İkmen it looked very much like a knife.

'Things are better now. Settled. I feel settled.'

There was nothing except the sound of the engine revving as the accelerator was pressed down gently. This was as it should be. This felt good. It had also provided relexation after considerable anxiety.

'Normality has been resumed. Nothing is wrong. I have done nothing wrong. Life is as it should be.'

143

Later on, much later on, the back of the old garage, the bit that hung like a house at the end of the world over the edge of one of İstanbul's seven hills, shut its doors and the sound of the engine's revving ceased. Shortly after that the front of the garage opened and then shut very quickly for what it was hoped was going to be some time. People were about, it was dangerous. Someone could possibly have seen the car drive in, or, after that, this visit to the garage now. A quick getaway was essential.

Sometimes, if one looked very quickly across one of these back-street scenes, one could almost imagine that it was 1970 again. 1970, before death came to stay. That was an altogether happy and attractive notion.

Chapter 9

'R ossoneri means red-black,' İzzet Melik said. 'It is one of the names the AC Milan fans give to themselves. They also call themselves The Devils, too.'

It was Sunday morning and Melik and his boss Mehmet Süleyman were driving along İstiklal Street watching as even more people than usual went in to and came out of the two Catholic churches on that thoroughfare. Red- and black-shirted Italians, plain red-shirted Englishmen.

'Both sides praying for victory,' Süleyman said with a shake of his head. 'You know, İzzet, my wife told me that Liverpool is a very religious city.'

'Is that so? Well, it's not like Milan, then. In Milan I think they worship only at the altars of Versace and Ferrari.'

İzzet, who originally came from the southern city of İzmir, had been taught Italian by one of the Italian-speaking Jews who still inhabited that city. The man in question, a Mr Levi, had also taught İzzet a considerable amount about Italian life and culture. Football, prayer, fashion and cars.

'What about Fiat?' Süleyman asked as they drew level with and then parked in front of the Church of St Mary Draperis.

'As a company? Fiat is for poor people,' İzzet said.

'And yet this Mr Emin you spoke to yesterday . . .'

'Mr Emin had a thing about the 1972 Fiat 124. Some

145

people become fixated on ordinary cars. He had a Fiat 124 when he was young and so is nostalgic about them. Not that the 124 is exactly ordinary. It was very advanced for its day, but . . . whether the Fiat had anything to do with the dumping of the Kamondo Lady, we don't know. But I've issued a statement to the press as you instructed, Inspector.'

'Good.' Süleyman got out of the car just as a large wave of red and black shirts disappeared into the church. 'We have very little besides that at the moment; just some unknown DNA. Both that of the woman and her – well, let us call him her assailant, is unknown to us. So the car, well . . .'

'I'm not sure what we're doing going back down to Voyvoda Street now, Inspector,' İzzet said as he closed and then locked up his car door.

'Because it never hurts to revisit a crime scene,' Süleyman said as he lit up a cigarette. 'I know the men were all over the Karaköy area and up here in Beyoğlu just after the woman was discovered, but that first sweep very rarely catches everyone. Some people are out when we first come along, some people take a few days to think about and perhaps interpret what they have seen at the scene of a crime. Sometimes things only make sense when one thinks about them calmly after an event.'

'Mmm.' After enabling the car alarm, İzzet joined his superior as they began to walk down İstiklal towards the Tünel funicular railway which takes people up and down the steep Karaköy Hill. Built in the nineteenth century to transport the wealthy European merchants who traded in the area past the less savoury parts of the city, Tünel is the oldest underground railway in the world. Not that İzzet Melik and Mehmet Süleyman were headed for the railway today. They wanted to speak to people, which meant that they had to hit the streets.

146

'You don't think that we're going to just get swamped by these football fans, do you?' İzzet said as he watched a pair of Italian men throw a bottle of grappa between them like a basketball.

'I hope not,' Süleyman said.

Suddenly, and with monstrous loudness, two waves of men, one group wearing red and the other wearing red and black shirts, streamed out of the Tünel terminus at the bottom of İstiklal Street, singing. And although neither side was overtly threatening, most of these Liverpool and AC Milan fans were drunk.

'I think that maybe you spoke too soon, Inspector,' İzzet Melik said.

The knife the divers had found in the Golden Horn the previous afternoon was now at the forensic institute. Both Edmondo and Maurice Loya had identified it as one of the weapons from their home, a Toledo steel dagger, and Edmondo had confirmed it was the weapon with which he claimed he had killed Emine Aksu. His brother Maurice had not been in the house on the night Edmondo said that he had killed the woman. He had been out to dinner with a client in Nişantaşi. In fact, no one at all had seen anything odd happening in or around the Loya house that night. No one had seen anyone push a body in a handcart, admittedly wrapped in a large tarpaulin, towards the Golden Horn and then drop it in. For a small man like Edmondo the effort involved in such an enterprise would seem to be considerable. Such an operation alone would surely have caused him some distress and some amount of physical pain.

'I've yet to hear of anyone who really thinks that Edmondo Loya killed that woman,' Balthazar Cohen said as he looked

147

beyond his garden and down the hill leading to the shores of the Golden Horn. His son Berekiah was at the bottom of the garden bending down to smell some blooming spring flowers. 'What about people out in boats that night?'

İkmen shifted himself awkwardly in the uncomfortable cane chair Estelle Cohen had given him and said, 'No one saw or heard anything untoward. And with no body, there is no way in which I can either confirm or deny Edmondo's story. When the dagger comes back from forensic, we will know more.'

'If the woman's blood is on it.'

'Yes.'

Balthazar Cohen, still nodding his head gently as he watched his crippled son move slowly and carefully amongst the flower beds, said, 'And if there are no traces of her blood or DNA on the knife . . . ?'

'Then I only have Edmondo's confession,' İkmen said. 'And thankfully, the days when just a confession was good enough are long past.'

'Because you believe that Edmondo Loya is innocent.'

'Not exactly,' İkmen said. 'What puzzles me is how he can be, as he was, initially so convinced of his own innocence and then, just one day later, turn himself in as a murderer. The conversation he had with you for, instance. He only just admitted to going to Sultanahmet in the sixties. I mean, has someone got to him or . . . ?'

'You mean Maurice?' Balthazar smiled grimly. 'That is possible. Maurice was always the more forceful of the two. But I think that Maurice would only lean on his brother to give himself up if Edmondo were actually guilty. I mean they carp and rage at each other all the time, but they are genuinely devoted to each other, too. After all, just from a selfish point of view, why would Maurice pressure Edmondo to do something that will bring him grief also? People in general do not like murderers, or their families, and Balat folk are probably less forgiving than most. If he isn't already, Maurice may well be shunned, at least for a time. This rumour that it was Maurice who told the world about his brother's so-called crime is nonsense!'

'So if Edmondo is lying . . .'

'I can't think why he would,' Balthazar said. 'He's a quiet and, yes, admittedly, socially awkward man who has probably never had sex in his life. But—'

'But maybe this is his moment,' İkmen said. 'What age is he now?'

Balthazar shrugged. 'Fifty-eight, nine . . .'

'So maybe he looks at his life—'

'Edmondo has done a lot of academic stuff,' Balthazar said as he shuffled a little painfully in his wheelchair. 'He's researched, written things. That is what he always wanted to do.' But then he caught what was to him a significant look in İkmen's eyes and said, 'But maybe he hasn't lived very much, is that what you think, Inspector?'

'You said yourself he's probably never had sex,' İkmen said. 'I know it's strange and ultimately destructive, but maybe Edmondo wants the world to believe he is a sexual being of some, any sort, before it's too late.'

'Yes, but murder? To involve murder in such a story?'

İkmen spread his arms wide and said, 'A woman he knew was missing, the opportunity presented itself.'

'Yes, but this Emine Aksu could just turn up . . .'

'True. But maybe that is a gamble Edmondo is willing to take. You were on the force for years, Balthazar, you know that some people just confess.'

149

He shrugged. 'Yes.'

'Admittedly, most of those who do so, do so habitually,' İkmen said. 'But maybe, as I said before, Edmondo feels the weight of years piling up on him. Maybe he wants to be viewed as a "man" before he dies.'

'He's not old . . .'

'No, but he isn't young, either,' İkmen said, 'and at the moment I can't think of any other reason why he might confess to something he hasn't done.'

'Unless he did do it,' Balthazar looked long and hard into İkmen's eyes. 'I never knew this Emine Aksu. I'd left Edmondo and Maurice and all the rest of them back in Balat years before he met her. It's only recently I've been in touch with him and his brother again. I spoke to him the other day, as I told you, and he was fine; seemingly without a care. But I don't know accurately what he's like these days, not really.'

'Friends?'

'Acquaintances,' Balthazar corrected. 'Edmondo knows a few people a bit. Although I do remember that years and years ago he did spend some time with that old friend of Dr Sarkissian, the one who is the custodian of that church . . .'

'The church in the Fish Market. Garbis. I know him,' İkmen said. 'You don't recall anyone called Abdulrahman, I suppose? An older man? Edmondo reckons he's now dead.'

'No . . . No, that name isn't familiar at all.'

İkmen dug a hand into his jacket pocket, took out his cigarettes and, after offering one to Balthazar, he lit up both their smokes. As he did so, Balthazar's son Berekiah limped painfully up the garden and back into the house. Hulya, Berekiah's wife, was working, as usual. As he usually did at times like this, İkmen felt very sorry for his perpetually tired daughter.

'To go back to Balat and what people may or may not feel about Edmondo,' Balthazar said, 'Estelle was pulled aside and pumped for information yesterday.'

'By whom?'

'Some women. Esther Sinop and that mad old writer woman, Juanita Kordovi. They, or rather the writer, pulled Estelle into that shoe shop that used to be Madrid's Haberdashery. Ali something, now he's a friend or acquaintance on some level of Edmondo's, owns the place, runs it with his young nephew. The two old bitches were asking my Estelle question after question while that Ali looked on. They think that because she's a policeman's wife she'll know something.'

'What did Estelle do?'

'Well, she told them nothing,' Balthazar said. 'She knows nothing! Everyone knows that Edmondo gave himself up to you; she knows that, but she knows nothing more about it. She just pushed her way out of there.'

'Mmm.'

'Bloody Balat! I'd forgotten what it was like when we came back to live here,' Balthazar said gloomily. 'When I was a kid, everyone wanted to know your business. My father didn't move our family over to Karaköy just to be nearer to the bars when my mother died – although of course his drinking was a big part of that. He moved us to get away from the gossip over here. Balat people are always trying to find out what's going on in your life!'

'With some success?' İkmen asked.

'Oh, they can tell you who is sleeping with whom and if and when the Levi family ate a leg of pork!' Balthazar said. 'So your suspicion about Edmondo could be true from that point of view. If he left his house with a handcart in the

151

evening, someone would have seen him. But on the other hand, big things get missed here in the neighbourhood of the trivial.'

İkmen frowned.

'Of course I'm only talking about old Jewish Balat, which is a very small place now,' Balthazar said. 'But the new incomers from the East seem very similar to my old people. Some ten-year-old was apparently married off to some old man on Vodina Street last year. Nobody knew, you lot the least of all, for months! The child, it's said, was locked away for the pleasure of this dirty old bastard . . .'

'I heard about it,' İkmen said sadly. 'I know one of the officers involved in that operation. The child was kept in some sub-basement wasn't she? It was terrible.'

'Yes, and nobody knew,' Balthazar said. 'Either that or they turned a blind eye. A lot of people had those sorts of cellars years ago. I still do not to this day know whether that was the case with the rabbi's daughter back in the early fifties. Someone apart from him must have known.'

'The rabbi's daughter?'

'Rabbi Behr. He locked his daughter up in his emergency cellar.'

'Emergency cellar?'

'Yes. I don't know what you'd really call such a place. That's my name for it. But anyway, during the Second World War there were a lot of shortages. Although we were not ourselves at war, there was rationing.'

'Yes, my father told me about it,' İkmen said.

'OK. Well, what he may not have told you is that it was at that time that the minorities in this country were squeezed by the Government for tax. Ourselves and the Christians, had it tough.'

İkmen lowered his head. Although neutral during the Second World War of 1939–45, Turkey did suffer shortages and those members of minorities perceived to have considerable funds were taxed heavily by the then cash-strapped administration. It was not a time of which the majority of Turks, including İkmen, were proud.

'Some people built cellars under their cellars in which to hide precious stuff like sugar and tea,' Balthazar said. 'People still find old rancid sugar bags in these secret places to this day around here. Some people even hid themselves in there just in case the Turks suddenly decided to side with the Nazis. After all, a lot of people knew what was going on with the Jews in Germany, didn't they? Turkish diplomats were rescuing as many Jewish children as they could get out of Europe and bringing them back here. But who knew what would happen? Not Rabbi Behr, for sure. When the war started he had a sixteen-year-old daughter. He had a cellar dug inside his cellar, a secret place just for her.' He looked up, frowning. 'The rabbi's relatives only found her when the old man died in the early fifties. Screaming and hammering on the roof of her prison. Hungry and thirsty.'

'She'd been there all that time?' İkmen asked.

'Since 1942,' Balthazar replied. 'She was a pretty young girl and he feared that if we were invaded by the Nazis they would rape her, then kill her. When the war ended the world was in such turmoil, even here, that he was too nervous to let her out. When the girl did finally come out, she fell totally silent. She stayed that way until she killed herself. That was sometime back in the sixties.'

'That's extraordinary,' İkmen said. 'I—'

'The point I'm making, Inspector, is that this neighbourhood is old and nosy, but it's also a place riddled with a thousand nooks, crannies, cisterns, cellars and bolt holes,' Balthazar said. 'God Almighty, Inspector, this is one of those districts where people still actively search for Byzantine remains! We Jews are newcomers compared to the Greeks! Who knows? Maybe Edmondo had some secret way of reaching the Golden Horn you don't know about.'

'Well, so far the room he said he killed the woman in would appear to be entirely clean,' İkmen said. 'Forensic can find no blood traces of any kind. Edmondo says he killed Emine on a rug which he burnt after he disposed of the body. But there's no trace of that either. The only blood belonging to Mrs Aksu we have found is in her own home, the kitchen and the bathroom.'

'Then maybe her husband killed her and not Edmondo.'

'I have considered and continue to consider that possibility,' İkmen replied. 'Sergeant Farsakoğlu is making further inquiries to that end.'

'But then again maybe if Edmondo killed her, he did it in his secret passageway to the Golden Horn,' Balthazar said with a mischievous smile on his face. 'You know, Inspector, the one he doesn't want you to know about, the one his neighbours – long-time residents themselves, too, I believe – will never ever reveal to you. You are an outsider, aren't you? Just like the woman who is missing.'

Frowning, İkmen said, 'These emergency places, they didn't really reach down to the Golden Horn, did they?'

Balthazar laughed. 'No,' he said. 'Not that I know of. You'd need an engineer, I think, to do something like that. But hidey holes did and probably still do exist in Balat from the war years. And who knows, maybe people as wealthy as the Loyas did have an escape route out to the waterway. We

Jews, if nothing else, know all about the value of a good escape route.'

'Liverpool, Liverpool, Liverpool! Liverpool, Liverpool, Liverpoo-ool! Liver . . .'

The owner of the radio, television and general electrical goods store slammed the front door of his shop shut with a bang.

'So now we have this great Olympic-sized stadium out in İkitelli and who uses it? Foreigners.' He shrugged. 'Foreign football hooligans clogging up the streets.'

Güren's electrical shop on Banker Alley was about as near as any shop could be to the Kamondo Stairs. And although Mr Güren, who lived on the premises with his wife and grandson, had initially said he knew nothing about the appearance of the gruesome body on the Stairs, now he wasn't so sure. As soon as he had shut the door on the great crowd of red-shirted men and boys outside, he turned back to Süleyman and Melik and said, 'I did hear voices that night. Late.'

'How late?'

Mr Güren shrugged. Policemen, quite rightly, always wanted to know exactly when this, that or the other thing had happened. The taller and younger of this pair was also very superior and posh about everything. It was irritating.

'I don't know exactly,' Mr Güren said tightly. 'It was the middle of the night and I was half asleep at the time. Two, maybe. Two. I don't know!'

'And the voices?' İzzet Melik asked. 'What were they like?'

The shop owner shrugged. 'Men.'

'What did they say?'

'I don't know. I wasn't listening! Men talking in the street

155

at night. It happens, it's not unusual. Just like a noise, you know.'

'And did you look out of the window to see who was talking?' Süleyman said.

'Not on purpose, no,' Mr Güren replied. 'But on the way back from the bathroom, I glanced outside and I saw a man.'

'Alone?'

'Yes. Running, he was. I can see the Kamondo Stairs from my bathroom window. He was running down them and when he got to the bottom he went and got into a car.'

'What kind of car?'

'How should I know! It was the middle of the night!'

'But the body was not on the Stairs . . .'

'Not that I could see.' He shuddered just a little at this point. 'Do you think I wouldn't have called you people if it had been?'

'It was definitely one man that you saw and not two?'

'It was definitely one. I didn't think anything of it at the time. Still don't, really. The man I saw wasn't doing anything wrong.'

After visiting the electrical shop, Süleyman and Melik spent just over another hour talking to people on and around Voyvoda Street. Although it was now no longer cordoned off, the two policemen nevertheless noticed that people were actively avoiding using the Kamondo Stairs.

At just before eleven, Süleyman decided that he needed a glass of tea. It was a pleasantly warm morning and so the two men decided to get their drink at the small tea garden which was in the lee of the nearby Galata Tower. Although Karaköy and its environs were heavy with interesting buildings and monuments of all sorts, the Galata Tower was probably the most famous and certainly the most prominent. Built originally in the thirteenth century by the Genoese, the present tall, cylindrical structure was largely of nineteenth-century construction. Over the centuries the Galata Tower had been used as a look-out post, a fire-watching station, and as the launching pad for the first Turkish aviator, Ahmet Çelebi. In fact, Çelebi, who launched himself from the tower and then landed safely across the Bosphorus in Üsküdar, was not only Turkey's first aviator. His flight, using artificial wings, had taken place in 1638, making Çelebi the first recorded flying man in the history of the world.

Süleyman and Melik had been sitting for some minutes beneath one of the large trees in the Galata tea garden before they noticed Ayşe Farsakoğlu at the next table. When they first arrived all they saw was a couple, to whom they paid no heed. But when the young man left, they saw that the woman was Ayşe. In view of what he had just seen, coupled with his romantic feelings for her, İzzet was a little over-formal when she acceded to Süleyman's invitation to join them.

'And who was your friend, Sergeant Farsakoğlu?' İzzet asked in the high-handed tone of one who feels himself very superior to the person he is addressing.

Süleyman shot him a brief, disapproving look. It was all right for İzzet to have feelings for Ayşe, but she had her rights too, including that of being able to have tea with whomsoever she pleased.

'That, Sergeant Melik,' Ayşe responded with equal arrogance, 'was business. The young man you saw agreed to talk to me about the disappearance of Mrs Aksu.'

'Oh.' Süleyman smiled and then asked her how that investigation was proceeding.

'The man I've just been speaking to, Mr Vitali, is Italian,'

Ayşe said. 'He's here, coincidentally, for the football match on Wednesday. He'd had a relationship with Mrs Aksu—'

'I can speak Italian,' İzzet cut in, now more than a little embarrassed as was evident by his red face. 'You should have asked me to translate.'

'Mr Vitali speaks English, thank you,' Ayşe said tightly before turning back to Süleyman once again. 'Apparently young Mr Vitali was with Mrs Aksu for some months. He even went to live with her and her husband for some of that time. Part of their so-called "open" relationship.'

İzzet Melik shook his head at the weirdness of such an arrangement.

'According to Mr Vitali, however, the Aksus' relationship was not as open as Mr Aksu would want us to think,' Ayşe said.

'Meaning?'

'Meaning, sir, that Mr Aksu was jealous. I know Inspector İkmen has suspected it for some time. And although he never did anything untoward to Mr Vitali, Aksu and his wife did fight often and, apparently, blood was sometimes spilled.'

The men's drinks arrived, placed rapidly down in front of them by a very over-worked tea-boy. The garden was suddenly teeming with what looked like an army of young, trendy Italian men.

'As Inspector İkmen may or may have not told you, sir,' Ayşe continued, 'we found some of Mrs Aksu's blood in their kitchen and on the bathroom floor. In the bathroom, we think there may have been some attempt to cover it up . . .'

Süleyman's mobile telephone rang and so, in order to be away from as much loud Italian talk as he could, he took himself away from the garden and walked out on to the street.

Ayşe, now alone with a man she knew to be in love with her, pointedly turned to look up at the Galata Tower. İzzet, though not exactly 'rough', was hardly her type and she didn't want to get into any sort of awkward conversation with him. Besides, every time she saw him when another man or men were present, especially her ex-lover Süleyman, he looked so miserable and hurt it was almost beyond her tolerance. She did feel sorry for him and would have been quite happy to be chatty and kind to him, but she knew that any tiny act of compassion on her part would be misinterpreted. And so the two of them sat in silence until a frowning Süleyman fought his way through the hordes of AC Milan fans outside the Tower and sat down once again.

'That was Dr Sarkissian,' he said as he took a sip from his tea glass before lighting a cigarette.

İzzet tore his eyes away from Ayşe's lovely profile and said, 'Oh?'

'Yes,' Süleyman continued. 'Our Kamondo Lady. He has more forensics. She was in her mid-twenties when she died. She was also' – he cupped his chin in his hands and sighed – 'very sick.'

'But she was stabbed . . .'

'Oh, yes, it was a blade that killed her,' Süleyman said. 'But, according to the doctor, she was not long for this world anyway. She had cancer.'

'So . . .'

'So maybe whoever killed her actually did her a favour,' Süleyman said. 'And putting aside what we know has happened to that body subsequently, maybe the initial act was one of mercy.'

'Yes, but with a blade!' İzzet shook his head in disbelief.

'A blade wielded with such force it pierces the sternum? Inspector, she may have had cancer but—'

'But, yes, I accept what you say, İzzet,' Süleyman said. 'But our victim did have cancer, it was advanced, and it's an interesting slant to this case we hadn't considered.'

'Mmm.'

They all sat in silence for a few moments then. It was Ayşe who eventually broke it. As she stood up to leave she said, 'But, whatever the motive, someone still exhibited that body in an obscene fashion. Someone had sex with it, too. Good luck with catching this sicko, gentlemen.'

Süleyman sighed and as he watched her go he said, 'She's right, of course, İzzet. Why and how doesn't really matter. Stopping it is what counts and as soon as possible.'

Chapter 10

Fatma İkmen knew exactly what her husband was up to.
'Keeping an eye on your daughter is nothing to be
ashamed of,' she said as she watched him check his jacket
pockets for money and cigarettes in the hall of their apartment. 'I don't like Hulya working in that bar. Alcohol
and . . . just don't use her as an excuse to disappear into a
bottle of rakı yourself.'

'I won't.'

Not so many years ago he had drunk habitually, although
he'd never been that keen on rakı, the local aniseed-flavoured
spirit Turks drink with jugs of iced water. Çetin İkmen had
always been a neat brandy man himself.

'Because I know what it's like around Nevizade Alley and
all those other streets in that part of Beyoğlu,' Fatma
continued. 'Why Berekiah allows his wife to work in such
a place . . .'

'They need the money,' İkmen said as he bent down quickly
to kiss her on the cheek. Fatma didn't like any overt displays
of affection when her younger children were looking on. 'And
besides, do you honestly think that Berekiah or anyone else
could tell a child of ours what to do?'

Kemal, Çetin and Fatma's youngest son, standing in the
living-room doorway, smirked.

'That is with the exception of your mother and myself,'

İkmen told the boy as he rudely pointed into his face. 'If we say jump, then you jump. And if you give your mother the slightest bit of worry while I'm out this evening, I will be down upon you like the anger of God.'

Kemal was not a bad boy. But both Çetin and Fatma had detected worrying trends in his behaviour that reminded them of one of Kemal's older brothers who had been very difficult. And so it was with an admonishment on his lips that İkmen left his apartment and made his way across the Galata Bridge to Beyoğlu. But it was not to either Nevizade Alley or the Kedi Bar that he went when he arrived. İkmen went to the Fish Market – or, rather, to the Armenian Church of the Three Altars which was approached via a small door in one of the side walls of the ancient fish bazaar. Before he saw his daughter, İkmen wanted to speak to a man called Garbis Aznavourian, the custodian of the Three Altars church.

After he had left Balthazar Cohen's very pleasant garden earlier in the day, he had gone back to the station and spoken yet again to Edmondo Loya. In light of what Ayşe Farsakoğlu had told him about the opinions of Emine Aksu's Italian boyfriend, he wanted to be absolutely certain that Edmondo was the genuine article. After all, by evidence alone at the present time, Ahmet Aksu looked like a far more plausible murderer than Edmondo Loya. So, once again, İkmen and Edmondo had conversed about the killing of Emine Aksu and, once again, Edmondo had managed to explain away all and any anomalies in his story. He had burned the rug upon which he killed Emine; the tarpaulin he had wrapped her body in to carry it to the Golden Horn had been thrown into the water, too, and the handcart he had used to transport her had been burned along with the rug. Such excessive caution seemed to suggest that Edmondo had not initially been keen to get caught. So why, after taking such elaborate precautions against detection, should he confess to the crime now? His brother Maurice had, he said, no understanding of it. But then he was just simply focussing on his own disgust for what his brother had done. What was needed was a friend to maybe enlighten İkmen about Edmondo's character and possible motives for either murder or lying or both. Garbis Aznavourian, whom İkmen knew slightly through Arto Sarkissian, had been a friend, according to Balthazar Cohen, when both he and Edmondo were young.

They must have been an odd pair when they were youths, İkmen thought as he walked past great round trays of sardines and squid tentacles. If Edmondo had looked middle aged forever, then Garbis had been the old man of the pair. Of course, having arthritis very early on in his life had not helped. In reality, Garbis was only one or two years older than İkmen, but ever since Arto had introduced the policeman to him, probably forty years before, everyone it seemed had treated the Armenian as if he was an old man. İkmen told Garbis what he wanted to know as soon as he arrived and the Armenian began his story.

'My father had horses,' Garbis said as he offered İkmen a seat beside him in the small wooden office outside the church. 'You remember, Inspector, when many, many business people had horses.'

'Yes, indeed.' İkmen sipped his tea from the tiny tulip glass Garbis had given him. The smell of wax from the vast array of candles in a box beside the crippled Armenian wafted gently and softly up at him. He liked candles, they reminded him of his youth at home with his parents and brother in their own candle-lit house in Üsküdar.

'It was through horses that Arto Sarkissian and myself

met,' Garbis continued. 'Otherwise what would we have had in common?'

'You are both Armenians?'

Garbis shrugged. 'What is that when one is rich and one is poor? Arto's father, old Dr Sarkissian, liked to ride. My father as well as supplying horses to business people also kept them for wealthy folk. He had fields out by Yedikule, when the old city walls were still surrounded by country.'

İkmen smiled. He remembered Arto's father, Uncle Vahan, and his horse out by the city walls – all apartments and shopping centres these days. And yes, there was always another Armenian man with him, an old one, Garbis Aznavourian's father. 'I remember your father, Garbis,' İkmen said.

'But as I grew older I tired of my father and much of his world, as young people do,' Garbis said. 'To be honest, I took to "borrowing" horses from my father from time to time, which was when I met Edmondo Loya. It was when all of that hippy business started back in the sixties. I began riding around the streets of Sultanahmet, searching for adventure, I suppose. I used to spend most of my time in and around the Pudding Shop with the foreigners and their friends. I was young and I amused some people. I got in with a group which included Edmondo Loya. Sometimes I used to ride over to Balat to meet Edmondo and his friends and then we'd all travel over with whatever horse I had that day to the Pudding Shop and the rest of our friends.'

'Who else was in this group?' İkmen asked.

'Apart from Edmondo? Well, not his brother Maurice, I can tell you! Maurice Loya was very, very anti-hippy back in those days! He thought that all the philosophising was pretentious and he was very anti-drugs.'

'Did Edmondo Loya take drugs?' İkmen asked.

Garbis shrugged. 'We all smoked a little cannabis back in those days, Inspector, Edmondo included. Some took harder things – that woman you say Edmondo has admitted to killing was one. But Edmondo, and the older man – someone from the university I think he was – they didn't, and neither did Ali the shoe maker's son. We all smoked a bit, made asses of ourselves. The woman Edmondo says he killed, this Emine Aksu, you know I was there in the Pudding Shop when she rebuffed his affections.'

'Really?'

'Yes.' Garbis offered İkmen a cigarette and then took a smoke for himself. 'It was sad. Edmondo was so awkward. I said to him afterwards that it was better to go with European girls than some rich, spoiled local. I myself had several European girlfriends, as did Kadir Özal and Ali Paksoy the shoe maker's son.'

Kadir Özal, the man whose mother embarrassingly for him owned a palace, was the hippy friend of Emine Aksu whom İkmen had consulted very early on in the investigation. He hadn't met Ali Paksoy. But connections were being made in what was turning out to be the small world of the local aged ex-hippy community.

'But Edmondo was so serious about everything!' Garbis continued. 'He wanted something formal and "of value", as he used to put it. European girls came and went and he didn't want to get hurt in that way.'

'Hurt?' İkmen said. 'I thought the local men just used the foreigners and then left them?'

'People like Kadir, yes,' Garbis said. 'And that man who's now very rich, in cars, provides chauffeurs . . .'

'Ali Tevfik?'

'Yes. He was part of our group for a while. He used to

165

love and leave European girls. But some of the boys got hurt. Ali Paksoy was devastated when the little girl, I think she was from Wales, left him. Quietly desperate he was, after she left. And he has never married. Some of the things that went on at that time went deep, Inspector. Edmondo was very, very hurt by Emine Aksu.'

'Yes.'

'You say that, but you have to understand how she was,' Garbis said. 'Emine went with all the boys. She finally married Ahmet Aksu, probably because he was the only one apart from Kadir Özal who had a lot of money at that time and she was always materially greedy. But Emine slept with everyone who wanted her. She went with Ahmet, of course, Kadir, Ali Tevfik, and even that older man whom Edmondo used to go around with.'

'But not Edmondo?'

'No,' Garbis finished his cigarette and put the stub out on the floor of his office. 'Of the Turkish contingent she slept with everyone but Edmondo and Ali Paksoy. Ali didn't want her and used to get very roundly teased because of it, and she rejected Edmondo, as you know.'

'Why?' İkmen, too, stubbed out his cigarette and then lit another. 'Why reject Edmondo in particular?'

Garbis Aznavourian sighed. 'She thought him ugly,' he said sadly. 'An ugly hook-nosed Jew is how she used to describe him. She said that if she slept with him she feared she might be sick.' He shook his head slowly. 'Sorry as I was to hear about Emine, I can't be too upset, Inspector. She was not a nice person. She called herself a hippy, subscribed to all the free-love business, but she did not have peace and love values. She looked down on people for all sorts of reasons and she was very brutal about it.'

166

'You speak as if Emine were already dead, Garbis. She's missing.'

Garbis Aznavourian smiled. 'Well spotted, Inspector,' he said. 'Maybe I just wish that Emine Aksu were no more. Maybe I'm not a nice man.'

'Emine Aksu was not a nice woman.'

'No. She hurt Edmondo and after that, after he had declared his love for her and she had rejected him, things were never the same.'

'In what way?' İkmen asked.

'Well, the group split up shortly after that,' Garbis said. 'Kadir and some other men, whose names I can't remember, went off to India. Ali Paksoy drifted back to Balat and memories of his Welsh girl, Edmondo disappeared into his own head, and Emine and Ahmet got married. I got married too but—'

'You haven't mentioned whether you slept with Emine or not, Garbis,' İkmen said.

There was a pause during which Garbis smiled. 'Oh, yes,' he said, 'I slept with Emine.' And then, leaning in towards İkmen, he whispered, 'She was an awful person but very good at sex. Very good.'

With the exception of her sexual prowess, İkmen was building up a very negative picture of Emine Aksu in his mind. Spoiled and selfish, shallow and yet possessed of pretensions. İkmen was sure he would have hated her, too.

'Garbis,' he said after a pause, 'do you think that one very old slight could make a person take revenge after so many years?'

'Not usually, no,' the Armenian said. 'Things like what happened between Emine and Edmondo happen every day. Life moves on.'

167

'But in this case?' He had picked up a troubled expression now settling on Garbis's face.

'My friend Edmondo Loya is a very intelligent, kind and concerned individual,' Garbis said. 'I love him dearly. I did not love Emine Öz as she was in those days and, to be honest, I cannot summon up much sympathy for her now. But I realise this is a very important question you are asking me, Inspector.' He moved what were now permanently sore knuckles around in their sockets. 'The truth is I don't know if Edmondo has or could kill Emine. What I will say is this, however, and may God forgive me for doing it. Edmondo was damaged by Emine Öz. To my knowledge he has not touched a woman since. Edmondo is as sensual as the next man and so that is sad. His studies sustain him, to some degree. But his brother is cruel. Maurice Loya taunts Edmondo, Inspector. Calls him a eunuch – all sorts of abuse.' He sighed. 'Maybe Edmondo met Emine again for some reason or by accident and being with her was just too much for him. Maybe she rejected him yet again or maybe the bitterness of that past event and how it has subsequently damaged his life finally made him snap. Sadly, yes, I do think that Edmondo Loya could have killed Emine Öz.'

Mehmet Süleyman didn't suggest that he and İzzet Melik go to the Kedi Bar just because İkmen's daughter Hulya worked there. Though admittedly it was nice to see the girl and a good thing to keep a watchful eye upon her as she was mobbed by up to a dozen thirsty Italians at a time. It was especially fortuitous that İzzet spoke Italian, too, but for the main purpose of their visit to Nevizade Alley, namely to drink away a little of the day's horrors, it was as good as any of the other bars on the street.

Both men agreed that it would be pleasanter to drink outside and so when they arrived they both sat down on rickety wooden chairs set out on the narrow, uneven pavement. As they sat, Süleyman waved to Hulya, who indicated that she'd be with them as soon as she could. Although music, which Süleyman recognised as Robbie Williams, was pounding out of a bar three establishments away, the sounds played in the Kedi Bar were cool, unobtrusive and unrecognisable. After dismissing, with a flick of a hand, the young and rather sleepy-looking almond vendor who almost immediately came to their table, Süleyman said, 'So, if Dr Sarkissian's dating of the death of our victim is correct, we're looking at 1980 or thereabouts.'

İzzet Melik, after first sighing, took his notebook out of his pocket. 'So, missing women, 1980 . . .'

'Nineteen seventy-nine and 1981, too,' Süleyman added. 'And İzzet,' he offered his colleague a cigarette and then took one for himself, 'foreigners as well as Turks.'

İzzet gave his boss a look that spoke volumes about his feelings regarding this task. Looking back at missing-person records, especially records from that long ago, was laborious and, most of the time, boring.

'There is no way of telling whether the Kamondo Lady is local or not,' Süleyman said as he smiled at an approaching Hulya. 'She is above average height for a local girl at that time, but that doesn't necessarily mean she is a foreigner. Ah, Hulya!'

'Hello, Mehmet,' Hulya said as she placed a hand on the shoulder of this long-standing family friend. 'Sergeant Melik.'

İzzet Melik tipped his head in greeting. 'Mrs Cohen.'

'Our Italian friends—' Süleyman began.

'We're completely out of grappa, and if you want

Limoncello, you've come to the wrong place,' Hulya said as she took her order pad out of her pocket and moistened the tip of her pencil. 'Our Italian friends are in a deeply patriotic mood.'

'You have beer?'

'What the English didn't manage to drink at lunchtime, yes. Efes only, though.'

Efes Pilsen, the local Turkish lager, would do and so Süleyman ordered for himself and İzzet Melik. Once Hulya had gone, he spent a few moments looking up at the darkening sky before continuing his conversation with his inferior. Nevizade Alley, particularly the upper storeys of the buildings along its length, had a distinctly Gallic feel. Built in the nineteenth century largely for the expatriate European community, this part of Beyoğlu could, Süleyman felt, very easily be some rather down-at-heel but trendy quartier of Paris. The art nouveau street lamps, the broken and stained-glass canopies covering the lower storeys of the buildings, the odd wrought-iron balcony leading into rooms containing, sometimes, a man, a woman and an unmade bed . . .

Mehmet Süleyman shook himself back into the present with a shudder.

'To go back to our Kamondo Lady,' he said, 'when she died may not necessarily concord with when she went missing.'

İzzet Melik frowned.

'I mean', Süleyman said, 'that maybe to begin with she went willingly with the person who eventually killed her.'

'You mean, that perhaps she went to live with this man?'

'It's possible,' Süleyman replied as he dragged heavily on the last dense centimetre of his cigarette. 'Assuming, of course, that the person who kept her body and abused it was the same person as whoever killed her.'

'Yes, but if he wasn't the same person, then how did the second man get hold of her body?'

'He could have dug her up. Just because she is unsullied by earth now doesn't mean that she was always that way.'

İzzet made a deep and soulful sigh. 'So I—'

'You need to look at burials of young twenty-something women in the city from 1979 to 1981. I—'

'God.' İzzet first threw his cigarette end on to the ground, then put his head in his hands. At the next table four very intoxicated Italians looked on with sympathy. They knew mental pain when they saw it. One even had tears in his eyes.

'Beyond looking for men who fit the "typical" profile of a necrophiliac, we have no way in to the state of mind that might produce something like this,' Süleyman said. 'One of our witnesses heard two men apparently arguing in a 1972 Fiat 124, while our other witness, though he also saw the Fiat and heard two voices, saw only one man and an apparently empty car. What was man number two doing?'

'I ran a check on any 1972 Fiat 124 BCs registered in the city and there were none,' İzzet Melik said. 'All gone, pushed out by the Mercedes, Minis and other favourites you İstanbullus feel you deserve these days.'

'Old cars still predominate in İzmir?' Süleyman asked.

'If he says yes, he's lying,' another, older and very smoke-dried voice cut in.

'Çetin!' Süleyman stood up in order to embrace his colleague and friend, Çetin İkmen.

'I've just come from visiting Garbis Aznavourian over at the Three Altars,' İkmen said as he dragged an empty chair from the Italians' table over to Süleyman's. 'You İzmir boys

171

are just as keen on your fancy cars as we are,' he said to İzzet Melik at he sat down heavily. 'I am the only person I know who is stupid and just plain poor enough to own something like a 1972 Fiat. You might find one or two out east, in places like Kars or Van. Why do you want to know about them?'

After Hulya had brought their drinks and then gone to get another beer for her father, Süleyman told him.

'I know the Fiat may or may not have anything to do with the dumping of the body,' Süleyman said, 'but it's, well, it's I suppose almost kind of, well, I won't say ghostly, ephemeral . . .'

Çetin İkmen frowned.

'I think what the inspector means is that we can't trace this Fiat, sir,' İzzet Melik said. 'There isn't one, officially, in the city. But there was one on Voyvoda Street the night the body was dumped on the Kamondo Stairs. It's almost as if the car came from and then went back to oblivion.'

İkmen, now puffing heavily on a cigarette, said, 'Mmm, disappearing cars. Rather more my province than yours, my dear Mehmet. But then I, too, have my weird and possibly scary mystery.'

'Your missing Aksu woman,' Süleyman said. 'We saw Sergeant Farsakoğlu this morning. She said you were once again focussing on the husband.'

'Yes,' İkmen said, but he sounded doubtful.

'The confession by the Jewish man is confusing you?'

İkmen waited until his daughter had given him his beer and he had chased several Italian 'stallions' away from her before he answered. 'Most people in Balat think that Edmondo Loya is incapable of murder,' he said. 'Garbis Aznavourian, a man who really knows him, however, is of the opposite opinion.'

'He thinks that Edmondo Loya is telling the truth?'

'He thinks it's possible,' İkmen said. 'Mrs Aksu, apparently if inadvertently, damaged Loya's life very badly. To her the rebuttal of him was just a joke, but to him . . .' He sighed. 'Not that shy and retiring Edmondo Loya chimes with the image of the rather exciting man from her past whom Emine told her husband she had met.'

'I thought the man in question was supposed to be something of a joke?' Süleyman said.

'Yes, but not in Edmondo's league, I don't think,' İkmen replied. 'According to Garbis, Edmondo was mentally scarred for life when Emine flung his love for her in his face. As far as we can tell, Edmondo Loya had never been with a woman. A woman like Emine would not have found that exciting. And yet she was excited . . .'

'Sergeant Farsakoğlu said that the Aksus' relationship was not as "open" as they would have had the world believe,' Süleyman said. 'Mr Aksu was very jealous of his wife's Italian lover.'

İkmen looked around lugubriously at the massed ranks of manicured and well-dressed Italians on Nevizade Alley and said, 'Yes, but look at them. Who would not be?'

'Yes, but—'

'Edmondo's house has given me absolutely no forensic evidence at all,' İkmen said. 'Mr Aksu's house has. Edmondo had confessed, Aksu has not. In my opinion neither of them is telling the whole truth about this business, but why that is and whether it has anything to do with Mrs Aksu's disappearance, I don't know. But I am doing something about it.'

'What's that?'

'Tomorrow I'm going to tear Mr Aksu's lovely house in Hasköy to pieces.' He smiled grimly. 'I'm also going to take Edmondo's place apart, too, from below ground upwards.'

'Below ground?' Süleyman asked.

İkmen told a somewhat startled Mehmet Süleyman and İzzet Melik about Balthazar Cohen's 'emergency' cellars of Balat. When his colleague had finished, Süleyman said, 'I knew there were difficult times for the minorities during the Second World War, but I didn't realise they hoarded goods, that they were afraid.'

İkmen shrugged. 'This was a neutral country during the war, our government could, theoretically, have jumped either way. People were scared.'

'But surely these old sub-basements, or whatever you call them, were blocked up years ago,' İzzet Melik said.

'I expect a lot of them were,' İkmen replied. 'But if some of them are not then it is possible they may be being used for nefarious purposes.'

'So Edmondo Loya killed Mrs Aksu below ground and then lied to us about killing her in quite another place?' İzzet Melik snorted. 'That, with respect sir, doesn't make any sense.'

'No,' İkmen said. 'Very little about anything Mr Loya has told us so far, beyond his enmity towards Mrs Aksu, does make any sense.'

'So why search his place again?'

'Because I want to frighten him,' İkmen said. He frowned. 'I don't think that Edmondo Loya has actually killed Emine Aksu. But I know he's happy about the possibility of her death and I feel he knows something about her disappearance that he isn't telling us.'

'But why would someone like Edmondo, accustomed to considerable material comfort, want to go to prison?' Süleyman asked. 'I mean, we are talking life here, aren't we?'

'Yes.'

'Well, opposed as I was to the old death penalty,' Süleyman continued, 'personally, I think I'd rather die than spend thirty years in prison. Someone like me wouldn't survive! And Edmondo Loya is a lot less capable and considerably older than I am.'

İkmen sighed. 'I, too, cannot image what his motive might be.'

'Unless he did actually kill her,' İzzet Melik put in.

Both İkmen and Süleyman looked at him blankly until the former said, 'We're going round in circles.'

And then they all turned away in order to watch a large group of AC Milan fans dance what İzzet Melik at least recognised as a rather rudimentary tarantella in the narrow street outside the bar. After several minutes of this it was İzzet who finally broke the silence with, 'But then maybe that's what we're supposed to do.'

Both İkmen and Süleyman frowned.

'Go around in circles,' he expounded. 'Maybe that's all part of the plan.'

'A confession has been made. A confession to the police.'

'THAT'S GOOD, IT WILL END IT.'

'Yes, but there's still no body, is there?'

'DOESN'T MEAN THAT EDMONDO LOYA DIDN'T KILL EMINE AKSU DOES IT? IF HE IS CONFESSING THEN EVENTUALLY EVEN IN THE ABSENCE OF A BODY, THEY WILL HAVE TO ACCEPT HIS STORY. THE POLICE HERE ARE LAZY, THEY'LL ACCEPT.'

'So the pleasure continues?'

'OH, YES!'

Way, way down below street level, it was cool and merci-fully silent. The whole city, it seemed, had been taken over

175

by Italians and Englishmen. Had the visitors all been young and hip and into peace as opposed to tribal football violence, it would have been nice. Like the old days.

The face of Mary, the Madonna, the mother of Jesus, looked on. Both the Liverpool and the Milan supporters were Catholics. People said that the fans were going to churches all over the city to pray for success. This was one, under the street, bathed in blackness and reeking of unwilling sex, that they were going to miss.

Chapter 11

The fact that the rising of the sun over the Golden Horn had tinged the windows of his house a deep, shining copper did nothing at all to mollify Maurice Loya.

'It's Monday morning! It's my custom to be at my office in Taksim by nine,' he said as he looked impatiently at his watch. 'It's seven-thirty now and I still haven't had a shower!'

İkmen, Ayşe Farsakoğlu and three uniformed officers had knocked on the door of the Loya house at exactly seven o'clock. After a long pause a very sleep-sodden, pyjama-clad Maurice Loya had opened the door. It had taken a considerable amount of time to make him understand what they wanted.

'But you've seen the bloody basement!' he said as he shuffled across the hall towards a shelf above the place where visitors, in accordance with Turkish etiquette, left their shoes when they entered the house. On the shelf was an almost full packet of Marlboro cigarettes. 'You saw it last time you were here!'

'We need to look at it again, Mr Loya,' İkmen said as he watched Maurice Loya light up a cigarette with some envy. He'd only just put one out, but to have another one now would mean that he'd have to ask for Maurice Loya's permission to do so and he couldn't be bothered. Like taking his shoes off in the Loya house, asking politely was something he didn't feel Maurice entirely deserved.

'I need to see it again,' İkmen said calmly. Then with a flick of his head he indicated that Constables Yıldız, Hakan and Roditi should head down the staircase at the end of the Loyas' dark, heavily wallpapered hall.

'But I need to go to work!' Maurice reiterated, watching İkmen's men retreat into his basement. He lit up a cigarette. 'When—'

'Mr Loya, I don't know when we might be finished,' İkmen said. 'I have no idea.'

'Yes, but what are you looking for . . . ?'

'If I knew that,' İkmen said as he finally gave in to his cigarette urge and lit up without asking, 'my life would be a lot easier.'

'My brother has admitted to a crime and, presumably, given you some details about it,' Maurice said as he paced nervously across the hall. 'It must be enough for you to hold on to him! If he'd told you nothing you would have dismissed him as a crank and thrown him out on his ear!' When İkmen failed to respond he looked down the hall towards the staircase that led underneath the house. 'And why down there? What are they doing down there?'

He began to walk determinedly towards the basement staircase.

After first looking meaningfully at Ayşe, İkmen said, 'Mr Loya, I am fully aware of the fact that you have a considerable cellar area underneath this property.'

Maurice Loya had reached the top of the staircase. 'What of it?'

'Sir, are you sure that you know the exact extent of this area?'

178

Maurice Loya, rather than descend the staircase, stopped. From down below the sound of hard, stone wall being hit with something reached his ears.

'Are your men—'

'Mr Loya, the warrant I gave you to look at allows my men to test your walls for cavities,' İkmen said.

'You mean—'

'Mr Loya, do you know of, or have you ever heard rumours of, other, deeper chambers underneath this property?'

'Deeper, "other" chambers?' Maurice Loya cried. 'Are you mad? There's a cellar. What more do you want? Secret passageways? This is not, Inspector, some sort of haunted house in an American theme park!'

'So you are quite happy for our men to test the walls down there, then, Mr Loya?' Ayşe Farsakoğlu asked.

For a moment Maurice Loya looked at her blankly, not understanding. Then suddenly, with a burst of energy that looked as if it should have been beyond him, Maurice Loya bounded down the stairs and into the basement without another word.

Going through lists of missing persons was a very tiring business. Of course, now that such things were recorded on computer, it was far less onerous than it had been. İzzet Melik, however, was being treated to how things had been done in the 'old-fashioned way' with his brief to look at records of missing women between the years 1979 and 1981. Records of such cases still unsolved were housed in a very deep, dark and dusty room way, way down in the forgotten depths of police headquarters. İzzet had little doubt that he was the first person to enter this particular room in at least the last five years. Just the dust on its own was a clue to that apparent fact. Every time he picked up a new cardboard file, great cloaks of the stuff would rise up into the air and settle across his shoulders like a shroud.

Dead. He looked at a small, faded passport photograph of a Swedish girl – missing, last seen in Beyazit district in 1979 – and knew that she was so certainly dead he could almost see her corpse. Kids like that – from rich families, well fed, pretty – they didn't just disappear. OK, they might, whilst in thrall to some ideal like that of 'getting back to older cultures' or 'free love on the road', go missing for a bit, but when the dirt and the smell of patchouli oil and the sheer lack of under-standing that men exhibited to them on the road kicked in they would go home, bathe, get jobs in shops and offices, and marry. When they didn't go home it generally meant that someone else was preventing them from doing so. İzzet, like most western Turks of his generation, had grown up seeing the hippies cross and recross his country. He knew these girls and the boys they had either followed or pulled in their wake towards the mystic East. Some of them now of course, the ones who had stayed and somehow survived, were getting on. Middle-aged junkies who looked thirty years older. But not this Swedish girl. This one had gone and, so far, just for 1979, he had a stack of at least ten others who had also 'gone' too. Added to this there were also two Turkish girls, but both of them were probably too short to be real contenders for the Kamondo Lady. And besides, although sparse, the clothes had been, Dr Sarkissian at least had decided, hippy-ish. Back then, maybe with the exception of Inspector İkmen's missing woman, there had been very few local hippy women.

Entombed. When he looked around the room at the shelf-encrusted walls of this place, that was what he felt. Buried alive, screaming inside, well before his time. Even the theme

180

from *The Godfather* seemed innocuous by comparison. İzzet picked up his mobile phone and answered it.

'İzzet.' It was the smooth, cultured voice of Mehmet Süleyman. 'It would seem that our 1972 Fiat 124 has finally come to light.'

İzzet Melik lifted his eyebrows. 'Really?'

'Really,' Süleyman said. 'It's a very attractive car.'

'Are you there with it now, or . . . ?'

'Oh, yes, I am here with it now,' Süleyman said. In the background İzzet could hear what sounded like a lot of men's voices shouting, although he couldn't work out what. 'I suggest you come and join me, İzzet.'

'Join you? But Inspector, what about this missing-person job you gave me?' He was shuddering with the cold of that place now, the cold and the pictures of the dead underneath his hands. 'Where are you, Inspector?'

'In Fener,' Süleyman said. 'Just off Sancaktar Street by the Greek boys' school, there is a row of wooden garages. You won't be able to miss myself and my . . . companions.'

'Your companions?' İzzet frowned. It sounded as if Süleyman were in the midst of a crowd of possibly thousands.

'You'll see us,' Süleyman said and then he cut the connection and the line went dead.

İzzet Melik put his mobile into his pocket with a cold, blue hand. Then, just before he left, he turned to the next file on the heap of missing girls' details he was supposed to be working through. She, this pretty dark-looking girl, had been only eighteen and her name, he noted, had been Madeleine Driscoll. Dead. Shame. He left the tomb in the basement for the rare delights of a rediscovered 1972 Fiat 124 BC. İzzet, like most men, was even a little excited. Dead

181

people were one thing, but cars, however dead, could be resurrected. Maybe that was why some people got so close to their vehicles. Maybe that was why so many cars were allowed to secretly condemn nefarious one-time owners. Killing a person was one thing, but destroying a car . . .

Moving slowly high, low and across the centre of each portion of wall, the uniformed officers tapped first gently and then with rather more gusto. Watched all the time by Maurice Loya, a man clad only in pyjamas who, in spite of the dankness of the cellar, was sweating heavily, the men were also watched by a narrow-eyed Çetin İkmen.

'Mr Loya,' he said after about fifteen minutes had passed, 'if there is anything you want to tell me . . .'

'About what?' Maurice Loya threw an exasperated arm into the air. 'This is a cellar, Inspector İkmen. I believe that my brother said he killed this woman, or claims to have done so, upstairs. What you're doing down here is, well, I—'

'Sir!'

It was Constable Yıldız, a young and enthusiastic officer in whom İkmen at least had considerable confidence. Ayşe Farsakoğlu walked over to the youngster and said, 'Constable?'

He tapped the wall in front of him, an action which produced a distinctly hollow sound.

'Go below.' As İkmen, his team and Maurice Loya looked on, Yıldız tapped the wall below where he had tested before and elicited the same, empty noise. Knocking above the place had the same effect. Ayşe Farsakoğlu looked expectantly at İkmen. 'Sir?'

İkmen looked at a now extremely sweaty Maurice Loya. 'Sir?' he said.

The man, so alike and so unlike his brother, turned, smiling for some reason. 'Yes?'

'Sir, I am going to ask my men to make a hole in what I'm sure you agree is a hollow wall. I have to do this. Your brother has confessed to the crime of murder. But we have found no body as yet . . .'

'But you were diving,' Maurice said, 'in the Horn.'

Everyone else in the room stayed still and silent except for İkmen who now walked towards a visibly shaking Maurice.

'Mr Loya,' he said, 'we have some problems with your brother's account of his part in this "murder". I have to explore every possibility, which includes every centimetre of this house before I commit Edmondo for trial.' He put his hand on the other man's shoulder. 'Maurice, we are very, very far from the truth at the moment. I must get beyond that wall and—'

'But what is there has nothing to do with Edmondo!' Maurice cried, tears now springing from his eyes. 'It has nothing to do with me! It was our father!'

İkmen suddenly felt completely at a loss. 'Your father? Your father what?'

Maurice Loya bent double under the weight of something no one else in the room understood, and screamed in what appeared to be agony.

'Maurice?' İkmen put a hand out to comfort the man who pulled away sharply from it like a burnt finger. 'Mr Loya?'

Maurice Loya put his head in his hands. İkmen was just about to give the order for Yıldız and the others to knock the wall down anyway when he lifted his head and said, 'Don't judge me, or Edmondo, by what's in there. We were babies. We – I've never thought that you would – that any of us were ever in real danger but . . .'

İkmen understood – or thought that he did. 'Mr Loya, if your father built somewhere to hide goods or even your family during the Second World War, then I do understand. I know about this phenomenon. Turkey was neutral and—'

Maurice Loya was laughing. In the deep dankness of that cellar it echoed very strangely. 'A hidey hole?' he said. 'You think we have one of those hidey holes other Jews had around here?'

'Yes, well . . .'

'Oh, it's rather more than that, I can tell you!' Maurice Loya said. 'Oh yes, rather more than that, Inspector!'

For a few moments İkmen just watched Maurice Loya, giving him time if needed, to perhaps expound on his somewhat hysterical utterances. But when nothing but a sort of gentle undercurrent of laughter ensued from the man, İkmen just turned to his officers and said, 'Break the wall down. Now.'

Just before pickaxe hit wall, Maurice Loya screamed out, 'No!'

Signor Rossi and Signor Ferrari (no relation to the car, as he would keep saying in broken English) had failed to sober up from their drinking exploits of the night before. They had been staying in the Hotel Daphnis which was also in Fener, but on Sadrazam Ali Paşa Street rather than Sancaktar Street, and had got lost in the early hours of the morning. Amid much hilarity, which was unintelligible to the rest of Fener, the two Italians had stumbled about the quarter for quite a few noisy hours looking for their hotel. It was only when it became apparent to them that they were never going to find it during the hours of night time that snuggling down amid a load of old garages became a viable possibility. And it was only when a young man called Gazi Sinop – grandson of Esther – saw two drunken Italians in someone's open garage, sitting in a 1972 Fiat 124, that the police got involved with the two AC Milan supporters' lives. Gazi, who had several convictions for petty theft and was therefore no great lover of the police, went and got the nearest thing he could handle to an officer of the law: Berekiah, son of that old policeman Balthazar Cohen. It had been Berekiah, once he'd seen the car and got some sense out of the two Italians, who had called Mehmet Süleyman.

'You know, sir,' Mr Rossi said in English to Süleyman through a hail of grappa fumes, 'one of my first car, it is Fiat 124.'

'Is not like having Ferrari or Alfa Romeo,' Mr Ferrari added, also in broken English, swaying as he spoke. 'But Fiat 124, this is historical, like memory, er . . .'

'It is nostalgic for you,' Süleyman said in English with a smile and then, turning to Gazi Sinop who had, some moments before, returned to the scene, he reverted back to Turkish. 'The men didn't actually drive the car, did they?'

'No, Inspector,' Gazi said as he observed the outdated green car now out in front of its dilapidated garage. 'They were totally out of it, both of them. It's why I went to get Berekiah Cohen. I knew the Italians weren't actually doing any harm, but I didn't want someone else to call the police and get them arrested. I like AC Milan.'

Mr Rossi, on hearing the word 'Milan', raised his arms into the air and shouted '*Milano!*'

Süleyman, who had already had a deeply suspicious Ardiç on the phone, 'just checking' that he wasn't 'upsetting' the Italians in any way, was very grateful for Gazi Sinop's low-key actions.

One of the uniformed officers Süleyman had brought along with him encouraged both Italians to sit down on a nearby wall at this point.

'But then Berekiah told me about the Fiat you're looking for and I recognised it, so he called you,' Gazi continued. 'It's something to do with that body over on the Kamondo Steps . . .'

'Gazi, do you have any idea as to who might own these garages?' Süleyman interrupted. He didn't want to get involved in any sort of conversation about the Kamondo Lady, but he did want to find out what he could and then get Mr Rossi and Mr Ferrari back to their hotel. Still drunk, they were reasonably happy. Sober and hung-over, they might prove more difficult.

But Gazi, in answer to his question, just shrugged. 'No. They're old. I could ask my grandmother, if you like.'

'If you think your grandmother might know.'

'She may do.'

Balthazar Cohen who, during the last part of Süleyman's conversation with Gazi, had been wheeled towards the policemen by his son, cut in. 'This boy's grandmother', he said to Süleyman, 'is Esther Sinop. She knows everyone and everything and is on personal terms with both God and the Devil.'

'Balthazar.' Mehmet Süleyman bent down in order to kiss his friend on both cheeks.

'Well, go on, then! Go and get the lady Esther for us!' Balthazar said to the boy once Mehmet Süleyman had straightened himself up once again. Gazi Sinop headed off in the direction of the Ahrida Synagogue and his grandmother.

Once Gazi had gone, Süleyman greeted Berekiah and then

offered both men cigarettes. 'I know I've asked Berekiah this before,' he said to Balthazar, 'but do you have any idea about who might own these garages?'

'None,' Balthazar replied. 'But then we were away from Balat and Fener for decades, so what do I know? This part of the district was always the "posh" bit when I was a boy. Tradespeople, doctors and chemists had places up here by the school. Down there,' he tipped his head down towards the small, teeming streets of Balat, 'where we were, was where the scum lived, the nobodies, the unemployed, the drinkers . . .'

'Yes, but Dad,' Berekiah interrupted what was becoming yet another descent into his morbid past by his father, 'Mehmet isn't asking about you, he's asking—'

'I know what Mehmet is asking me about!' Balthazar roared. Several of the uniformed officers and both of the Italians looked over at the incensed man in the wheelchair with concern. 'I'm not a fool!' Balthazar continued. 'I know he doesn't want to hear about my disgusting childhood! Who does?'

Ever since he had lost his legs in the earthquake of 1999, Balthazar Cohen's bitterness about his lost childhood had been increasing. Addicted to the gossip of others as he had been all of his life, this did not, however, sustain him for weeks at a time. Too often there were great lakes and seas of time unaccounted for, time during which he could brood on his early life with his brutal, alcoholic father. This time however, his bitter anger blew itself out quickly and after a pause he said quietly, 'No, Mehmet I do not know who these garages belong to. Sorry.'

'OK.' Mehmet Süleyman smiled. Maybe the garages didn't belong to anyone any more. Maybe the person who owned the Fiat 124 and the person who owned the garages were not one and the same. After all, in a city of about ten million people, space was at a premium and people put their families, their possessions and their cars wherever they could. But if someone did know, it would give him somewhere to start. After all, no Fiat 124 BC was registered to anyone in İstanbul and so tracking the car's owner down from that direction was going to be difficult. Forensic were on their way to investigate the vehicle and dust for prints, but then most of those would belong to Mr Rossi and Mr Ferrari. The two Italians had, by their own admission, had a lot of fun playing with the controls, if not driving, a car they felt very nostalgic about. In spite of the fact that the garage had been unlocked, that the key had been in the ignition, and that they were drunk, Mr Rossi and Mr Ferrari had managed to resist the temptation to drive the car.

Shortly after Balthazar Cohen disconsolately settled down into his wheelchair once again, Süleyman saw İzzet Melik's Mazda coming up the hill towards the scene. The usual crowd that always gathered at possible crime scenes – old, covered women, dirty children and resentful-looking men – parted to let the car, and the small motorbike that put-putted in its wake through. In fact, it was the bike, driven by Gazi Sinop with his terrified wild-haired grandmother on the back, that got to Süleyman before his deputy who was busy parking his car.

'Esther!' Balthazar Cohen cried as he spread his arms wide to welcome the red-faced old woman.

Too arthritic to dismount the tiny bike of her own volition, Esther Sinop allowed her grandson to carry her off and then place her gently on to the dust-covered road. 'May God help me,' she said as she dusted down her cornflower-patterned dress. 'May God forgive you, Gazi, for nearly giving your old grandmother a heart attack!'

'Esther!'

'Mr Cohen,' she said as she looked across at Balthazar and then slowly smiled. 'And your lovely son!' Then, turning to Süleyman, she said, quite unbidden, 'Such a shame about the other Cohen boy.' She lowered her voice. 'In a mental hospital . . .'

'Yes.' Mehmet Süleyman said it tightly. Berekiah's elder brother Yusuf had indeed been in a psychiatric institution for some years. Süleyman knew that it wasn't something that either Balthazar or Berekiah had any desire to discuss. 'Mrs Sinop, these garages here . . .'

İzzet Melik had just drawn level with Süleyman and the old woman when Esther Sinop said, 'These?'

'Yes.'

She looked at the garages, and at the Italians lounging drunkenly outside them, with a critical eye. 'Oh, these belong to the haberdasher, Mr Madrid.'

Still smarting from what he had heard her say about his eldest son, Balthazar Cohen attempted to correct what he had only just recently learned to be true. 'But Esther,' he said, 'Mr Madrid is long gone; he went in the fifties.'

'Oh, well, his descendants, then.'

'Who are . . . ?'

'In Israel,' Esther said lightly.

'So this Mr Madrid', Süleyman said, 'clearly has nothing to do with these garages now.'

'No. Long dead, God protect him. But as for his family?' Esther Sinop shrugged. 'Madrid's is owned by one of your people now, young man.'

Süleyman frowned.

'A Muslim,' Esther Sinop said.

'Sells shoes,' Balthazar Cohen put in. And then he added rather sadly, 'Cheap ones.'

It was only once the dust had settled and İkmen was actually in the small chamber that led off from the Loyas' cellar that Maurice managed to finish his sentence.

'. . . there's a door into this room from the garden. We never use it, but there is a key. Somewhere.'

İkmen looked very small and lonely amid the many streaming dust particles that danced around both him and every other solid object in that dark, dank little chamber. Apart from the door to the garden, at which Constable Yildiz was now looking, there were a few shelves on the walls containing what looked like bottles, a blackened sink over by the door, and a table, large and dark and old in the middle of the room.

İkmen gave the shelves a cursory glance while Maurice Loya put his head in his hands. Ayşe Farsakoğlu, who had now joined her superior in the chamber, walked over to the table.

'You may confiscate it if you wish,' Maurice said through his fingers. 'I know it is illegal . . .'

There was a silence while İkmen moved in closer to the shelves. Ayşe bent down towards the table and flicked through some surprisingly undusty magazines that were on top of it.

'My father was a dentist,' Maurice continued through his fingers. 'He could easily get hold of it. It – it was an insurance, if you like, against – well, you know, what was happening in Europe at that time. We should have got rid of it years ago, but how does one do that?'

'Mr Loya, at the risk of speaking out of turn, I don't think

190

that your father was probably alive when this was put down here,' Ayşe said as she held a slightly faded if quite obviously lurid magazine aloft.

Maurice Loya took his hands away from his face and looked up. The magazine was called *Huge Breasts*. He gasped.

'Published in 2004,' Ayşe said. 'I imagine your father—'

'Mmm, I think, Sergeant, that you will find that magazine is as much a surprise to Mr Loya as it is to us,' İkmen said. And then, turning back to the shelves behind him, he went on, 'No, Mr Loya is, I think, referring to the large cache, though admittedly aged, of opium which he has here.'

Ayşe put *Huge Breasts* back down on the table. 'Opium?'

Maurice Loya, who had now moved forward in order to look at the magazine as well as other similar publications underneath it, said, 'I told you. Father got hold of it during the Second World War. It's not something I'm proud of. It reeks of lack of trust. It wasn't a patriotic thing to do.'

'Mr Loya, in light, as you said yourself, of what was happening in Europe, it is understandable,' İkmen said. 'I presume from the quantities here that your father intended to use it to commit suicide.'

'Yes. He needed a lot,' Maurice said. 'Back in those days there was my mother, my paternal grandparents, a couple of uncles and Edmondo and myself. We were just babies. When the war ended and the danger was past, Father still wouldn't let the stuff go. He never used it himself, you understand, but he wanted to have it – called it his insurance policy.' He flicked over the pages of *Huge Breasts* and pulled a disgusted face.

'And when your father died?'

'To be honest, I didn't know what to do with it,' Maurice said. 'I thought about taking it all to somewhere like the forensic institute and letting them dispose of it. But I didn't want to have to answer any questions about where it came from or anything. And as for just throwing it away, how can you do that? And where? If you bury it, will it infect the ground? You can't sell it, we've enough junkies in this city as it is! And anyway, according to my brother, Father wanted us to keep it, just in case.' He looked down at the magazine-covered table again and added, 'Seems my brother just wanted this place left alone for his own purposes.'

'These magazines belong to Edmondo?'

'Well, I can't think of anyone else they might belong to. We have no servants these days, can't afford them, and I prefer real, live women myself.' He looked up at İkmen. 'Inspector, even putting his "confession" aside, my brother is odd. I mean these magazines' – he shrugged – 'God, he has a bedroom! Why doesn't he keep them in there? I know he must have a sexual life of some sort, I'm not going to knock on his door and stop him!'

'You're sure these are Edmondo's?' Ayşe asked.

'No one else has access to here,' Maurice replied. 'Your own men missed the entrance from the garden when you came to search the first time. As I said before, I didn't want you to find this place. It's, well, it's awkward and it's shaming and—'

'We will have to remove the narcotics now.'

'Of course!'

'*Huge Breasts*, however . . .' Ayşe began.

'There is no law against that,' İkmen said. 'And at least we didn't find a dead body in here, did we?'

'You thought you might?'

İkmen shrugged. 'I didn't know, Mr Loya,' he said. 'Your brother says he has killed this woman and thrown her body into the Golden Horn. As you know, we found what he claims

192

to be the murder weapon in that waterway. But beyond that there is no sign of any body and it puzzles me, as, I imagine, it must puzzle you, as to how your brother got the body down to the Horn without being seen or collapsing under the weight. Edmondo is arthritic; he's not a strong man.'

'No.'

'So although I do not disbelieve your brother, I cannot entirely believe his story either,' İkmen said.

'Well, I don't know how I can help you,' Maurice said as he looked at the serried ranks of opium bottles on the shelves of his father's hidey hole. 'I have never, ever been close to my brother. He isn't easy to get close to. I mean, to come down here with these magazines! God, we don't come down here! Or at least I don't.'

One of the young constables, who was now tentatively fingering a magazine on the table, said, 'Your brother was having a—'

'Yes, I think that we all know what Mr Loya's brother was doing down here,' İkmen said as he ripped the magazine from the young man's fingers.

'Sir.' He stood back immediately and lowered his head.

İkmen looked down at his feet, idly shuffling them against the hard stone floor.

'Mr Loya,' he said, 'do you have any idea why your brother might want to admit to a crime he did not commit?'

'No.'

İkmen first fixed Maurice Loya with a hard gaze before he said, 'Do you know whether Edmondo might have been coerced into making a confession?'

'Coerced? By whom and for what reason?' Maurice raked his fingers through his greying hair and said, 'I don't know Edmondo's life, Inspector. I don't know who his friends are, if he has any. This woman he says he killed was someone from back in the days when he used to hang around Sultanahmet with all the hippies. I was never part of that. God almighty, if he used to come down here – with all these terrible jars around the walls, without my knowledge . . .'

'It can't be easy living with a person as closed off and distant as your brother,' İkmen said.

'No it isn't,' Maurice Loya crossed his arms over his chest and shook his head. 'He doesn't do anything! Drifts around, not talking . . . What goes on in his life is a mystery.'

'You pay for everything.'

'Who else is there?' Maurice said. 'Everyone else is dead! Our father left us money, but contrary to many people's belief, that is now all gone.'

Ayşe Farsakoğlu, who had been following what had been happening closely, turned away. She knew where İkmen was going with this even if, apparently, Maurice Loya did not.

'With some people you can have a conversation sometime, but with my brother . . .' He shrugged. 'It's impossible. Living like this, together and yet apart . . . God, but I'm so angry that he came down here! What did he think he was doing? It wasn't as if he used opium himself.'

İkmen picked up a powder-filled bottle from one of the shelves and looked at it. 'Didn't he?'

'No!'

'In his youth he was involved with hippies.'

'He smoked a bit of cannabis!' Maurice Loya said. 'He's too dull to have done anything more than that!'

'And you?' İkmen, still looking at the bottle, said.

'Take opium? Me?' He laughed. 'Are you insane? I have to work all the hours God gives in order to keep this place going and put food in our mouths! I can't be half asleep! I can't even be vaguely relaxed, most of the time. You try it when you get no help at all and are just expected to—'

'So if your brother were out of your life in some way, things would be a lot easier for you?' İkmen asked.

At last Maurice Loya fell in. With a heavy, weary sigh he pulled out one of the chairs underneath the table and sat down. Yet again he put his forehead in his hands. 'Oh, so now it's all my fault, is it?' he said. 'I made my brother confess to a murder he didn't commit in order to get him out of my life and have this house and everything in it to myself?'

'I—'

'Inspector İkmen, I will be honest with you,' Maurice Loya said, 'and tell you now that that idea, as a concept, has a lot going for it. If Edmondo goes to prison, I get everything, which will probably enable me to give up working completely. Fantastic! There are problems, however.' He recorded them one by one on his fingers. 'Firstly, as you have said yourself, my brother's story is clumsy and full of holes. I don't make mistakes like that – ask my clients! And secondly, much as he may drive me insane, I do care for my brother. I love him. I've looked after him for his entire adult life!'

'Which means that he, by his own admission, does what you want him to do most of the time,' İkmen said. 'He wants to please you.'

'Yes—'

'He is also, I think, rather afraid of you too, Mr Loya,' İkmen said. 'Intellectually clever and complex as I know he is, Edmondo is also emotionally fragile and—'

Maurice Loya stood up quickly. 'Inspector İkmen, if you want to make an accusation . . .'

İkmen casually waved his words away with one hand. 'No . . .'

195

'I was there, as you may recall, when the knife my brother claimed to have used on this woman was found in the Golden Horn,' Maurice Loya said. 'I felt at the time that you felt my presence there was suspicious in some way. It was not. Edmondo told me the ins, the outs and all the rest of it about his murder of this woman before he ever told you. It was me who agreed with him that he had to go to the police! The night you and that other plain-clothes male officer came here, Edmondo and I rowed. He told me what he'd done and I told him he needed to tell you. I don't know whether he killed this Emine woman or not! I wasn't here the night he claimed to have done so. If you can't find evidence of this woman in this house then . . .' He sighed. 'Yes, I can and do "bully" my brother, Inspector. If I didn't, Edmondo would do even less than he does do. But as for persuading him to confess to a crime he didn't commit –' he shook his head slowly. 'No. No.'

İkmen pulled another chair out from underneath the table and sat down opposite Maurice Loya. 'Sir,' he said, 'what would be helpful would be if you could go over, with me, as precisely as you can, the conversation you had with your brother about his supposed murder of Emine Aksu. Sometimes there are small things that people tell us which have a significance which at first we don't recognise.'

'Well, yes I—'

'Maybe something Edmondo has told you but hasn't told us,' İkmen said. 'Because if he is innocent and you have, as you say, no hand in his confession, then he must be doing it either to cover up for someone else or for some other reason we don't understand.'

'Sir,' Ayşe Farsakoğlu interjected. 'Mr Aksu's house?'

They were indeed due yet again to search Ahmet Aksu's

196

house as soon as they had finished in Fener. But then they were not on any sort of time limit and, besides, talking to Maurice Loya was something that was long overdue and potentially important.

'Mr Aksu can wait for a while longer,' İkmen said. 'Give the forensic institute a call while I have a chat to Mr Loya, please, Sergeant. Tell them we have some very old narcotics for them.' He then turned back to Maurice Loya and said, 'Now, sir, I want to help your brother and quickly, so let's talk, shall we?'

Chapter 12

Rafik Sarıgul had been deep in conversation with two of his friends about the up-coming football match when the police arrived. There were three in uniform and two other men, one very smart indeed, in suits. His friend Deniz, who far and away favoured AC Milan over Liverpool, had headed out of the back of the shop immediately, like a rocket. No one really liked the police very much, but Deniz had some particularly bad tales to tell about when he was younger, stupider and sniffed glue. The police had not been particularly 'sympathetic'.

'Do you want to buy some shoes?' Rafik had asked stupidly as his remaining friend, Adnan, had looked on aghast. 'This is a shoe shop.'

'Owned by a Mr Ali Paksoy, I understand,' the taller and smarter of the plain-clothes officers had said.

'My uncle, yes,' Rafik replied. He then looked up at the officers and, for some reason, he smiled.

'My name is Inspector Süleyman,' the officer said after a pause. 'I need to speak to your uncle. Can you tell me where he is?'

'Er . . .' Rafik knew exactly where his Uncle Ali was, which was down in the basement organising the stock. But faced with all of these policemen his throat was closing very quickly and he was having great difficulty getting anything very much out.

'Boy, are you hearing what the inspector is saying?' the rather rougher looking man in plain clothes said. He had a very large and intimidating moustache.

'Um . . .'

'Can I help you, gentlemen?'

It was a voice that brought considerable relief to Rafik. 'Uncle Ali,' he said as he pointed to the short, fleshy man now standing at the back of the shoe shop. 'Uncle Ali Paksoy.'

Inspector Süleyman smiled and said, 'Mr Paksoy, I understand you are the owner of three garages on Sancaktar Street in Fener.'

'That's right.' And then turning to Rafik and Adnan, he said, 'Why don't you boys go and get yourselves some lunch?' He put his hand in his pocket, took out a twenty-lire bank note, and gave it to Rafik.

For a moment the boy just stared down at the money in disbelief. Uncle Ali was, as a general rule, very mean. This was unprecedented.

'Go to Osman's kebab shop on the corner,' he said. 'You boys stay there a while.'

He wanted them out of the way. But then with twenty lire in his pocket, Rafik was happy to do just that. As well as having two enormous lunches at Osman's, twenty lire would also buy the boys cigarettes and possibly even some bottles of drink, too. They both left without another word.

'My garages on Sancaktar Street,' Ali Paksoy said, 'what about them?'

The shop, which seemed to sell little beyond cheap plastic shoes and boots, was small and oppressive. Süleyman told the uniformed officers to wait outside. This left only himself, İzzet Melik and Ali Paksoy.

'Mr Paksoy,' Süleyman said, 'do you read newspapers, watch the news on the television?'

Ali Paksoy's fleshy features frowned. 'Sometimes. Newspapers, that is. People leave them in the shop. Rafik likes to read the sports pages. I don't have a television. Why?'

'Sir, are you the owner of the 1972 Fiat model 124 BC we found in one of your garages this morning?' İzzet Melik asked.

'My father's car?' the shoe shop owner said. 'Green?'

'Green, yes,' Süleyman said. 'Just like the one we've been trying to track down since last week. The one we have been asking the public, via the media, to report if they see or hear of. A very rare car these days, sir, and one we think may have some sort of connection to an ongoing criminal investigation.'

Still frowning, Ali Paksoy said, 'Criminal?'

'A body was found, an apparently exhumed corpse in Karaköy,' Süleyman said. 'You may have read about it in the papers. The only lead that we have is the reported presence of a 1972 Fiat 124 at the scene of the offence. Now it may well be that the car has absolutely nothing to do with this outrage, but we have to eliminate it from our inquiries.'

'Absolutely.' Ali Paksoy rubbed his chin with his hand. 'Gentlemen, the car belonged to my father, now sadly deceased. I keep it, or rather my sister, the boy Rafik's mother, and myself keep it for sentimental reasons. It isn't registered.'

'And yet it is in perfect working order.'

'Gentlemen, why were you at my garages this morning, may I ask?'

Süleyman told him about Mr Rossi and Mr Ferrari and why, when he had seen their antics, Gazi Sinop had put things in motion to call the police.

When he had finished, Ali Paksoy sighed. 'But I always keep the garages locked.'

'The Italian gentlemen said that the doors into that particular garage were flapping open,' Süleyman said. 'It was why they went in in the first place. They're not criminals. They were just a little . . . slightly inebriated.'

'If the car isn't registered,' İzzet Melik said, 'presumably you don't drive it on the road, Mr Paksoy.'

'No.'

'And yet, although they, too, didn't drive the car, the Italians proved to themselves and to us that the vehicle is in working order. The engine fires, it has gasoline. The keys were in the ignition.'

Ali Paksoy first wiped some beads of sweat from his forehead and then shrugged. 'What can I say? It's not usual, I know, but to hang on to things isn't a crime. My sister and I keep the car because it reminds us of our father. Ask her! Handan Sarıgul – she lives above the baker's next door.'

'We will,' İzzet Melik said as he made a note of the woman's name on his pad.

'Neither of us drives that car,' Ali Paksoy continued. 'And I always lock it away in the garage if I go there to maintain it, or Handan and I just simply go to look at it. Only I have a key to any of those garages.' He sighed. 'You know, people collect old cars these days, it's probably worth money. If those doors were open, it can mean only one thing, that my garage was broken into.'

'When did you last go and look at the vehicle yourself, Mr Paksoy?' Süleyman asked.

Ali Paksoy thought for a few moments, lighting up a cigarette as he did so and then said, 'I think it must be about three weeks ago. Handan came with me, ask her; we cleaned the old thing, as we do from time to time. I turn the engine over for a few minutes.' He shook his head sadly. 'Her husband died when Rafik was only a baby and life ever since has been hard – for Handan and for me – I keep both her and Rafik. As well as being a possible investment, my sister and I are very nostalgic for that car. We had happy times in it long ago. It was cool, you know. I hate to think that someone may have used it for . . . for bad things.'

'Mr Paksoy, where were you on the night of the 19th May, last Thursday?'

'Here at the shop,' Ali Paksoy said. 'At night, in my bed.'

'Can anyone corroborate that?' İzzet Melik asked.

Ali Paksoy cleared his throat and then looked down at the floor. 'I live alone,' he said.

'I see.'

'Well, Mr Paksoy, you'll have to come and give us your fingerprints,' İzzet Melik said. And then, with a quick glance at his somewhat disapproving superior, he added, 'In order to eliminate your prints from any that may belong to whoever may have taken your Fiat.'

'Ah.' Ali Paksoy smiled, as did Mehmet Süleyman. The latter, although just as punitive and often crueller than İzzet Melik, was not in favour of intimidating as yet innocent members of the public. In his experience it made people nervous and not in a way that could be useful to an investigation. Many years before, his old mentor, Çetin İkmen, had expressed it as his opinion that intimidation was usually pointless. Those who were not guilty would own up to anything to make the intimidation stop and the guilty were usually too canny or too tough to be taken in or bothered by it. European Union standards aside, 'gentler' working was usually a much more productive approach.

'It may also be helpful to us if you could look at the gasoline used, Mr Paksoy,' Süleyman said. 'I mean, you keep the car in working order . . .'

'With only a tiny amount of gas,' Ali Paksoy said. 'Not enough to go anywhere. Is the tank full?'

'We don't know yet, we'll have to take the vehicle away for forensic testing,' Süleyman said. 'I do apologise, but—'

'You have to do your duty,' the shoe seller said. 'I understand. It's important to catch criminals. Do you know if my car stopped at a garage? For gas, I mean?'

'No. Although, as I am sure you must be aware, Mr Paksoy, one can put gas into a car without recourse to a garage,' Süleyman said.

'I do it myself, with a can,' Paksoy said.

'Absolutely.'

İzzet Melik first looked at Süleyman and then cleared his throat. 'Well, Mr Paksoy,' he said, 'the sooner we can take these prints of yours . . .'

'Ah, yes, you want me to come down to the police station. Now?'

'It would be better if you could come with us now,' Süleyman said.

Ali Paksoy smiled. 'I'd better get Rafik from the kebab shop at the end of the street. To mind the shop.'

İzzet Melik stood up and said, 'I'll go and get the boy if you like, sir.'

'Thank you.'

Melik left, leaving Süleyman and the shoe seller alone, and, for a moment, both sat in silence. Then slowly Ali Paksoy shook his head in what looked like disbelief. 'The things that go on these days!' he said. 'My poor father's car possibly used for something criminal! A local man, so I've heard, owned up to a murder! Threw some woman's body in the Golden Horn, they say.'

Süleyman, too, shook his head for a little while, but then suddenly he stopped and said, 'Who? Who says some man killed a woman and threw her body into the Horn?'

This very quick change into sharp businesslike questions seemed to catch Ali Paksoy unawares. Briefly he blinked in what looked like shock and then he said, 'Well, everyone round here, I imagine. Certainly all of the people who come into the shop. Police divers were in the Horn, looking for a body!' He moved in closer to Süleyman for a second and then whispered, 'I've heard tell it's Edmondo Loya, the Jew. I know him. I've known him for many, many years. Unbelievable.'

Ahmet Aksu lit yet another cigarette and then said, 'All right, so I was rather less keen on the "open marriage" concept than Emine was. I suppose that as some of us age, we want more stability in our lives.'

'Not your wife, though?' İkmen said.

Over Ahmet Aksu's shoulder, through the huge window behind his head, İkmen could see the slightly choppy waters of the Golden Horn. In the mild midday sun they were a pale, slightly brown-tinged blue.

'No,' Ahmet Aksu said. 'Emine is, was, whatever term will not land me in one of your prisons, Inspector, a woman with multiple sexual needs.'

'Her young Italian lover, Mr Vitali, says that you and your wife fought over just this matter while he was present,' İkmen said. 'He says you spilled your wife's blood, Mr Aksu.'

'It's not something of which I am proud!'

'I don't suppose it is,' İkmen said. 'But your wife is missing and—'

'And Edmondo Loya has admitted he has killed her!' Ahmet Aksu said. 'What my relationship was with my wife is irrelevant. Ask him! Ask Loya why he killed Emine! Little freak!'

'I have done that, sir,' İkmen said, 'many times. You know as well as I do what his supposed reasons are. But we still don't have a body or, in spite of his confession, any evidence to connect Mr Loya to a crime of murder.'

'Well, if you're looking to me as a possible suspect . . .'

'I can't overlook you, can I, sir?'

'Officially, my wife is missing.'

'Unofficially you have been convinced ever since you called us in that she isn't coming back!'

İkmen watched Ahmet Aksu slump back into his seat like a distressed and slightly sulky child.

İkmen lit a cigarette and said, 'Mr Aksu, I will be honest with you. I don't know where your wife is, what has happened to her, or who has had a hand in any of what may have occurred. Mr Loya's confession is, in my opinion, inaccurate on some level I do not yet understand. People are lying to me all the time and I include you in that group, Mr Aksu.' He held a hand up to stem the protest he could see forming in Aksu's head. 'Don't try to convince me you are not doing so because you are. You lied to me about your happiness with the "free love" concept your wife chooses to pursue. You failed to tell me that you and your wife had fought. I had to find her blood in your house, have it analysed and have my sergeant talk to a foreigner before you would talk about that. My people are delving into every dark part of this house as we speak because you lied to me.'

'But if I'd told you we had fought, you would have

suspected me!' Aksu said. 'A wife beater! How does that look!'

İkmen, finally infuriated by this conversation, stood up. 'At this moment, may I be forgiven for saying so, sir, that it looks a lot better than being a liar!' he said. Then rudely pointing into Aksu's face, he shouted, 'I will not and indeed cannot trust you again!'

'But—'

'The search will continue and when it is done we will speak some more,' İkmen said. 'Who knows, Mr Aksu, maybe you may even manage to stay out of prison.'

Then his mobile phone went off and so İkmen walked into Mr Aksu's not inconsiderable hall in order to answer it.

Rafik didn't like it when his Uncle Ali left him alone in the shop for long periods of time. On the plus side he could invite his friends in to chat about football and girls, but on the minus side there were the customers to consider and, sometimes, Rafik's own mother, too. When Ali was away Handan liked to keep an 'eye' on proceedings. This time, however, Handan Sarıgul hadn't come straight down from the apartment next door as soon as her brother left for the police station. She'd been obliged to talk to one of the officers herself for a bit. But now she was in the shop and she was gossiping.

Juanita Kordovi, who had come into the shop to exchange the red pumps she'd bought for a pair of rather more lurid, and cheaper, gold shoes, shook her head in disbelief.

'Well, Mrs Sarıgul,' she said as she tapped Handan roughly on the knee, 'I don't know what this district is coming to! People's garages broken into now! And your poor brother!'

'As I told the policeman, he dotes on that car,' Handan

Sarıgul said. Younger than her brother, she was aged about fifty. Handan was a slim woman who wore a full-length coat and tightly fitting headscarf, even indoors. She was not someone who liked to even think about change – it had, in her experience, always been painful in the past. So the police fetching up at her door was not something she had welcomed. 'It belonged to our father,' she said. 'Happier times.'

Juanita Kordovi waved both her wrinkled hands in the air. 'Tell me about it, darling!' she said. 'When your family came here after Mr Madrid died, God protect him, Balat was a different place. Your father was a fine man; honest, a craftsman.'

'Yes.' She looked down at the floor and frowned.

'And when he got that car, I remember it distinctly,' the old woman said, 'he let your brother drive it! It was a new car, and he let your brother drive it! What a trusting man, a gentleman! We used to have gentlemen in this quarter.'

'I know, Mrs Kordovi.'

'And you, Mrs Sarıgul,' Juanita continued, well and truly in her stride now, 'your father was so good to you! Not married off to the first boy that came along like so many of the – God forgive me for saying so – other little Muslim girls in this area. He waited, your father did, until God provided a good man for you, Mrs Sarıgul. Not like these greedy old men now pushing their little girls out there for big dowries!'

'No.' Still looking down at the floor, Handan Sarıgul was aware of the fact that her marriage hadn't been quite what Mrs Kordovi thought it had been. But she wasn't going to say anything. That was family business, which was private.

'And now the police come to persecute your brother whose only crime is to own a car some thief tried to steal!' She placed her heavy bundle of newspapers on to the seat beside her and then called Rafik over. 'I've put those red pumps back on the shelf, you can tell your uncle, Rafik,' she said. 'Just wrap up those gold ones on the counter and give me the three-lire difference, will you, darling?'

'Yes, Mrs Kordovi.' Rafik began wrapping the shoes up immediately. The old novelist was not a person one made wait even if she wasn't yet obviously on the move.

'You know what they say, the police' – Handan moved her head close in towards Juanita Kordovi's and whispered – 'our father's car may have been used to carry a dead body!'

'Oh!' Juanita placed a calming hand on top of her ample chest. 'Well, that is why, my dear, they have taken your brother away with them,' she said. 'For the fingerprints and—'

'Ah.'

'They call it "eliminating him from their inquiries",' she said. 'I have a friend in Şişli who writes contemporary crime novels, and who knows all about it. Nothing to worry about.' She lowered her voice now. 'Mind you, Mrs Sarıgul, I wouldn't be surprised if some of our newer migrants . . .' She gave Handan a meaningful look which the latter returned. 'You know, I heard the other day that down by the Greek Patriarchate there are a whole load of illegal people from all over.' She threw her hands in the air in a gesture of hopelessness. 'The police do nothing! As I said to that Mrs Cohen, Estelle, whose husband was a policeman and who knows them all, "They do nothing, you know!"'

'And did she . . . ?'

'Oh, well, what could she say?' Juanita said. '"They do their best". Well, I said, that isn't good enough, is it?'

'No.'

Rafik, who had now wrapped up the gold shoes to the best

209

of his ability, took the three lire his uncle owed Mrs Kordovi out of the till and walked over to give the old woman her money and her goods.

As he put the money into her hands, Juanita said, 'Oh, isn't he a good boy!' She then pinched one of his thin cheeks between her forefinger and thumb. Rafik, like most young men of his age, hated it when old women did things like this. Even his Uncle Ali's, albeit infrequent, towering tempers were better than this.

Juanita Kordovi stood up and clutched her large handbag as well as her brand new shoes to her chest. 'Oh, well, I can't sit about here gossiping all day,' she said. 'I have a book to write.' She leaned back down towards Handan and added conspiratorially, 'Osman Bey is currently in Kars. He's having a terrible time with the corrupt Russian governor.'

'Oh, well, I look forward to reading it,' Handan said, 'when you've finished.'

'If!' Juanita Kordovi said, laughing, as she made her way towards the shop door and the outside world. '*If*, darling! Writers never say when – it's tempting fate.' Then with a wave she called out, 'Thank you, Rafik!'

'You're welcome, Mrs Kordovi!'

And then she was gone. Rafik looked at this mother and then let out a long, tired sigh.

'Mrs Kordovi is a trying woman at the best of times,' Handan said as she lay a calming hand on her son's shoulder.

'Mad,' Rafik said. 'She only came in here to get the gossip about Uncle Ali.'

'Everybody knows that your Uncle Ali went with the police, Rafik,' Handan said. 'They also know, as Mrs Kordovi said, that it is only routine. Uncle Ali's fingerprints have to be on that car, the amount of time he spends cleaning it. They have to separate out Uncle Ali's prints from those of the men who found the garage open and look at what might be left after that. Maybe then they will find the prints of the person who stole the car.'

Rafik sat down next to his mother in the space Juanita Kordovi had recently vacated. 'Mum,' he said, 'you know the shop hasn't been doing so well lately . . .'

'Lots of new shoe shops in Beyoğlu and in the malls out at Ataköy and Etiler are squeezing shops like ours, yes.'

'Well, if Uncle Ali is so worried about money, why doesn't he sell the old Fiat?'

Handan sighed. It was a good question, given the fact that Ali never, ever drove the wretched thing. He cleaned it all the time but she, its supposed co-owner, only got to see the car very infrequently. She didn't want to. She never even touched the thing if she could help it. 'Rafik, the car has sentimental value. It belonged to your grandfather.'

'But Uncle Ali couldn't stand Granddad!'

'No, he—'

'Uncle Ali told me,' Rafik said. 'Last time he was having one of his tantrums. He told me, shouted at me, that I made him feel the same way Granddad had made him feel – like a useless piece of shit.'

Handan winced at the word. 'Rafik!'

The boy hung his head. 'Sorry, Mum,' he said. 'But I'm only repeating what Uncle Ali said to me. He said that—'

'Yes, I know what he said, you've told me,' Handan said. 'But why did he say it?' She lifted her hand and gently stroked away a stray strand of black hair from over her son's eyes. 'What had you done to upset your uncle so much, my soul?'

For a few moments Rafik had to think. His uncle didn't lose his temper very often, but whenever he did Rafik tended to try to put it from his mind. Uncle Ali was, for most of the time, a good, kind man, and Rafik didn't want to get into the habit of thinking badly of him.

'I think I sold a pair of shoes I shouldn't,' he said eventually. 'On order for someone, or something. I think Uncle Ali probably felt it would make him look stupid in front of the customer. I think Granddad made him feel stupid.'

'Rafik,' Handan cut in, 'that really is not your business.'

'No, but—'

She raised a hand in order to silence him. 'Now that is enough!' she said. 'You and I must look after the shop until your uncle gets back from the police station.' She stood up and as she encouraged her son to do likewise, she looked down at the seat next to him. 'Oh, goodness, Mrs Kordovi has left all those newspapers! Today's, too!'

'Oh, she's always doing that,' Rafik said with a casual wave of one hand as he stood. 'I'll look at the sports pages later. Only two more days to go now, Mum, to the big game!'

'Mmm.' Handan Sarıgul, less than enthusiastic about sport, rolled her eyes heavenwards.

It was the afternoon before İkmen managed to get back to the station and the prison cell currently occupied by Edmondo Loya. A lot had happened since he'd last seen him, including the fact that he now had the results on the Golden Horn knife back from the forensic institute.

'Mr Loya,' İkmen said as he positioned himself across the table from Edmondo Loya in interview room number 2. 'Now—'

'If you're going to harp on about getting a lawyer again, you're wasting your breath,' Edmondo said. In the few short days he'd been in police custody his face as well as his body had become noticeably thinner. But then the guards had reported that Loya wasn't eating anything and only drinking the very bare minimum to sustain life.

İkmen shrugged. 'Whether you decide to employ a lawyer or not is your own affair, Mr Loya,' he said. 'No, I've come to ask you some questions – again.'

Edmondo Loya's face assumed a disgruntled aspect and he looked up with a sigh at the nicotine-stained ceiling above.

'Mr Loya,' İkmen said as he lit up a cigarette, 'you argued with your brother Maurice after Inspector Süleyman and I left when we came to interview you at your home. Can you please tell me what that argument was about?'

For a moment, nothing happened. It was as if Edmondo Loya hadn't heard a word. In fact, İkmen was just about to ask him the question again when Edmondo said, 'What did my brother say the argument was about? You have spoken to Maurice.'

'I want you to tell me,' İkmen said.

'Yes, but', he looked directly into İkmen's eyes for the first time, 'what did Maurice say?'

This circular argument went on for some minutes before İkmen finally told Edmondo Loya that if he didn't tell him his own version of events he was going to have him moved from a single cell to one that he had to share with others. This produced first a visible shudder and then Edmondo's account of his argument with his brother.

'Well, Maurice first asked why you had come to see me and so I told him it was about Emine.' Edmondo cleared his throat. 'I didn't tell him immediately about what I had done. I'd only just seen you and so I was quite shaken. But then when Maurice began to ask why you had come to speak to me about Emine, well . . . I told him the truth. He is my

213

brother and he deserved to know, I thought. The argument of which you speak wasn't really an argument at all. It consisted of Maurice persuading me to give myself up. He's got nothing to do with this, my brother. He's a good—'

'Oh, I imagine he is a good man on a good day, just like the rest of us,' İkmen said. 'I bet the people he works for think he's a marvellous person.' He leaned across the table towards Edmondo. 'But he bullies you, doesn't he, Edmondo?'

'No.'

'He bullied you that night,' İkmen said. 'Going on about how ludicrous it was that a "eunuch" like you should be implicated in the disappearance of a woman. By his own admission he went on and on and—'

'Maurice wanted me to give myself up! That was what the argument was about! I was intransigent!'

'Oh, so you were the strong man, were you, Edmondo?' İkmen said as he stared hard into a pair of pale and frightened eyes. 'The murderer standing hard and firm against your brother's conviction that giving yourself up was the only way forward? Why didn't you kill him, eh? If he knew what you'd done, and only he, then you could have killed him and slipped out of the country the next day. You didn't have to come here and tell me your story!'

'Yes, but—'

'Edmondo, your brother laughed at you until you blurted out this ridiculous story about being a murderer,' İkmen said. 'Maurice laughs at you a lot and this time for some reason; you couldn't take it any more and so you made up this, this . . .'

'Ah, but then,' Edmondo Loya raised a finger in the air and wagged it tremulously at İkmen, 'then how did I know

214

what Emine had been wearing, eh? From your reaction to what I said I know that you were very shocked by that, Inspector.'

He wasn't wrong there. And in spite of the fact that Maurice Loya had told İkmen how he had effectively goaded his brother into his confession, the issue of how Edmondo Loya had known what Emine Aksu had been wearing on the afternoon of her disappearance remained. He had described her clothes right down to her strange little designer shoes.

İkmen threw his cigarette stub down on the floor and ground it out with the heel of his shoe. 'Mr Loya,' he said, 'I am not saying you didn't see Mrs Aksu on the day of her disappearance. Maybe you did, or maybe someone you know did and described her to you. After all, there are still people about with whom you used to hang around in your hippy days with Emine.'

'Abdulrahman is dead.'

'Oh, Abdulrahman is most probably dead now,' İkmen replied. 'He certainly doesn't work at the university any more. But what about your other old friends? What about Ali Tevfik, Kadir Özal . . . ?'

'Kadir uses heroin, I wouldn't speak to him, I have always disapproved of that,' Edmondo said. 'Ali Tevfik, well . . . Look, I didn't see them! I killed Emine! I told you that!'

'Then of course there was Garbis Aznavourian,' İkmen continued calmly. 'And in your very own district, of course, Ali Paksoy. Garbis only lives minutes from you and Ali Paksoy just up the hill.'

'I didn't speak, I –' His eyes were full of tears now, he was maybe close to breaking. Into what, İkmen didn't know; he still wasn't sure about Edmondo Loya, even now. 'Inspector, no, I didn't I—'

'My colleague Inspector Süleyman is taking fingerprint samples from Mr Ali Paksoy now,' İkmen said. 'Your friend, Mr Loya, could very well be implicated in the desecration of a corpse!'

Not strictly true. Ali Paksoy, as far as Süleyman had told him, had been brought in for purposes of elimination as a suspect in the Kamondo Lady case. But both İkmen and now Süleyman knew that Paksoy had known Edmondo Loya from way back in the sixties. Apparently he had been very shocked to learn that Edmondo had 'killed' Emine.

Looking up in order the gauge Loya's reaction, İkmen was faced with a visage that was alarmingly red.

'What?' Edmondo squeaked.

'A corpse,' İkmen reiterated. 'Dead body.'

'N – not, not Emine . . .'

'Emine, whom you threw into the Golden Horn?' İkmen crossed his arms over his chest and smiled. 'No. Someone else. But you were afraid it might have been her, Edmondo. You are afraid she'll turn up somewhere. You didn't kill Emine Aksu!'

'Mr Paksoy could have found her body! Taken it from the water . . .'

'Oh, pathetic!' İkmen lit up another cigarette and then leaned back heavily into his chair. 'God, you're an intelligent man, Edmondo! Can't you do better than this? Your own brother has admitted to me that he goaded you the night we came to see you. He also admits that he was, for a while, quite happy with the idea of you in prison and out of his hair. But he doesn't really, in the depths of his soul, believe that you did it. Edmondo, we found your father's old subbasement with all the bottles of opium.'

'Oh, God!' Edmondo began to cry.

'Ssh! Ssh!' İkmen looked him straight in the eyes and said, 'We also found your magazines, Edmondo.'

'Oh . . .'

'But what we didn't find *anywhere* in or around your home or in the Golden Horn' – he stood up quickly and with a dramatic scrape of his chair – 'was any sign of Mrs Emine Aksu. No clothing, no hair, no blood or DNA even on the so-called "murder weapon", no other bodily fluids.' He leaned down and whispered. 'She wasn't in your house, was she?'

'She—'

'There is no sign of Emine Aksu or any of her possessions in your home, Edmondo, because you didn't kill her.'

Edmondo looked up, his face shiny with tears. 'I did!'

'No you didn't,' İkmen said. 'You saw her, somehow, and I'd like you to tell me about that. But if you won't, there's no way I'm going to continue to hold you. You personally are innocent.'

Edmondo Loya first opened his mouth like a gasping fish and then said, 'You're releasing me?'

İkmen walked over to the door of the interview room and knocked on it to attract the guard's attention. 'Yes,' he said. 'We'll decide about punishment for wasting my time later on.' The door opened. 'I'm rather too busy for this at the moment. Get out, please, Mr Loya.'

And then, turning sharply on his heel, he walked through the open door and was gone. Edmondo Loya, alone now with his new-found freedom, continued to weep.

Chapter 13

Mehmet Süleyman replaced the handset of his telephone back on to its cradle and then rubbed his temples with his fingers. Eyes closed, he sat like this in silence for a while until he felt that İzzet Melik could probably take no more.

'Yes, that was Mr Paksoy again, desperate to have his beloved car back from the forensic institute,' he said. 'As you heard me say for, I think, probably the fourth time this morning, İzzet, I have absolutely no control over what the institute do, how long they take to do their work, or anything very much.' He sighed. 'God, but we need something to happen here, don't we?'

The distinct sense of gloom in Mehmet Süleyman's office wasn't just caused by its owner's obvious pessimism. His deputy, for reasons quite apart from the continuing confusion regarding the Kamondo Lady, was very far from cheerful, too.

The big match was only one night away now and Dr Sarkissian's brother had already called İzzet to check that he was still going to join their party.

'My cousin Natasha is coming from England, supporting Liverpool, of course,' Dr Arto Sarkissian's brother, Dr Krikor Sarkissian, had said. 'Natasha's a biochemist. Then there's the Arslans, lovely couple. Süleyman Arslan and his wife Hatice, both geneticists. My good friend Abdullah, he's a lawyer, Abdullah Ceylan. Deals mainly with domestic issues, but you may well have come across him professionally. Then there's you, İzzet.' There had been a momentary pause at this point where, İzzet imagined, Dr Krikor had wanted to say something patronising about how interesting policeman were. But instead he just said, 'We'll make a very jolly group, I'm sure! So, glad you can come.'

Of course İzzet was very happy to be attending the match. But with a group of scientists and a lawyer, he understandably felt quite out of place. After all, apart from his very good command of Italian, İzzet was in no way an intellectual man. In an ideal world he would have wanted to go to the match with the lovely Ayşe Farsakoğlu. But she didn't fancy him. That was ridiculous. She liked cultured men like his boss, probably like Dr Krikor and his friends. What would a woman like Ayşe want with someone who watched Italian porno films with his brother? God, it was all so depressing!

'If only Mr Paksoy could see it from our point of view,' Süleyman said as he cut into İzzet's gloomy thoughts. 'We need to know who has been in that car and what they may or may not have done in there as much as he wants the fucking thing back!'

Hearing Mehmet Süleyman swear wasn't something that one experienced every day, and for a moment it took İzzet somewhat aback.

'Inspector—'

'I know he's got his problems, looking after his widowed sister and his nephew, but . . .' Süleyman leaned back in his chair and sighed. 'You know that Mr Paksoy and the man who confessed to Inspector İkmen for the supposed killing of Emine Aksu were friends when they were young?'

'That's the man that Inspector İkmen released yesterday.'

'Yes.' Süleyman didn't bother to add that İkmen's deputy, Ayşe Farsakoğlu, was currently watching Edmondo Loya's house. He assumed, given İzzet's fixation on Ayşe and everything she did, that he would know this already. It wasn't as if, within the department, İkmen had made any secret of the fact that although he didn't believe Edmondo Loya had killed Emine Aksu, he was pretty certain that he knew something about her disappearance – hence Ayşe's undercover presence in his life.

'Mr Paksoy was another member of the group that contained the missing woman and her husband, Loya, and a few other hippy types. Inspector İkmen is interviewing him later on today, although I can't really see Mr Paksoy as a great lover of women, can you?'

'My understanding of the Aksu thing is that Mrs Aksu was having an affair with someone who used to be something of a joke but had grown up into a kind of a sexual athlete,' İzzet said. 'I can see Mr Paksoy as something of a figure of fun, but not as a person who could even loosely be described as sexy.'

Süleyman smiled and then almost immediately frowned. 'And yet for our purposes, putting Inspector İkmen's investigation aside, he could fit the profile for a defiler of the dead.'

'You think so?'

'He's single, careless about his appearance, is firmly attached to his past. I would say, while not even pretending to be a psychologist myself, that he does have an unnatural regard for that car. My wife and her colleagues describe such unusual attachments as "fetishes".'

'Doesn't that mean that the person has sex with the thing?'

'Not necessarily,' Süleyman said, and then he went on to

221

expound upon Zelfa's interpretation of fetishism and why necrophilia could be included within it.

İzzet grimaced. Psychiatrists like Süleyman's wife talked so normally about revolting things. He'd heard her speak on several occasions about states of mind that would make most people either want to flee in terror or be sick. Süleyman himself could sound fairly casual about such things now. It had to be down to living with Dr Halman.

'So do you think that Mr Paksoy is our man?' İzzet asked.

'I think he could be,' Süleyman replied. 'Mind you, almost any sad and lonely man with an over-riding passion for something could be, too. I suppose we'll have to wait and see what forensic material the Fiat presents to us. If there's evidence of that body present we'll have to DNA test our Mr Paksoy.'

'You know, Inspector,' İzzet said, 'Paksoy's sister was a little out of step with her brother about the car.'

'How so?'

'Well, all of this stuff about how he so loves the car because of its connection to their father . . .'

'Yes?'

'Mrs Sarıgul, Paksoy's sister, said that their father was a difficult man who liked to keep Ali down.'

'He let him drive the car, though.'

'Yes, he did,' İzzet said. 'Although apparently it was rather more to do with just simply wanting people to see that he had a car as opposed to letting Ali have it out of the goodness of his heart. Old man Paksoy was, apparently, one of those bitter self-made men who have things and even children just to make themselves bigger in the world. Sometimes those things don't measure up. I get the feeling that Ali and Handan fell into that category.'

'The migrants have been fixated on taking the gold-plated

streets of İstanbul and all her attendant wealth and power from us for decades,' Süleyman said. And then, remembering that İzzet himself was from out of town, he added, 'Well, the ignorant, unlettered type is what I mean, of course.'

İzzet, smiling behind his hand, said, 'Yes, Inspector.'

Famously, Mehmet Süleyman would rarely apologise for anything. Perhaps it was just something Ottomans, albeit Ottomans without power or influence, didn't do. But then İzzet understood what his superior had been saying rather clumsily. For decades people had been coming to İstanbul from the country to seek their fortunes. And although more often than was felt by some to be fair, they had met with disappointment, the people from the country always arrived with high expectations. Someone like Mr Paksoy senior had, when compared to most migrants, done very well. But as Handan Sarıgul had told İzzet, her father's dream had been to have a chain of shoe outlets employing a staff of skilled shoe makers. Then in the early seventies things began to change and people who liked good shoes began to buy them from smart foreign shops. Ali, to his credit, had apparently been all in favour of his father's plans, but both of them were swimming against the tide and so when Paksoy senior was diagnosed with cancer some time in 1973, the whole expansionist enterprise was mothballed. The old man died later that year, wracked with bitterness, only at almost his last breath allowing his daughter to marry the man with whom she'd been in love for over five years. Resentful of the old man even now, Handan Sarıgul did not visit her parents' graves. Her brother always performed that duty alone.

'Anyway,' Süleyman said as he rose from his seat and went over to his office window, 'I've told Mr Paksoy we will have to search his property in Balat.'

223

'All the garages?'

'His business and the apartment above it, too,' Süleyman said as he stared at what looked like a sea of red T-shirts in the street down below. The bloody football match again. 'After all, whatever that Fiat may or may not yield to us, it was almost certainly in Karaköy the night when the Kamondo Lady was dumped. We can't overlook either it or him.'

It was strange the way sometimes people with money just ignored certain things about their environment. Edmondo and Maurice Loya's property was, Ayşe knew, an absolute treasure house of fine fabrics and antiques inside. But from the outside it looked almost derelict. The front door, old and scarred and very much in need of a coat of varnish, looked as if it was hanging off and one of the windows upstairs was actually boarded up. But then maybe they left it as it was in order to deter burglars. Then again, İzzet Melik had told her that Inspector Süleyman had told him that a lot of the wealthy old families like the Loyas just didn't care. Home renovation was just simply beneath them. Both she and İzzet had laughed at this. One thing they did have in common was that both their families were no one and nothing. In fact, although she could in no way say that she found İzzet attractive, Ayşe had got to like him a little bit more in recent months. Maybe living in a sophisticated city like İstanbul was civilising him.

Ayşe looked across the road at the Loya house once again and then wound down her car window in order to get some air. Of course another explanation for the Loyas' lack of concern for the outward appearance of their house could be connected to their religion. Jews had always been safe and protected under the old Ottoman Empire and, under Atatürk, this happy relationship had persisted. But when the Second

World War came bringing with it a nervous neutrality, things must have seemed confusing for them. On the one hand Turkish diplomats in Europe were rescuing Jewish children and bringing them in to Turkey, while on the other hand the Government was still speaking on some level to the Nazis. Then when the taxes rose and rationing really began to bite . . . The forensic institute boys had taken a vast amount of old opium away from the Loyas' sub-basement. The old dentist had been totally serious about killing his whole family should the worst have happened. Pushing them gently out of that hideous world of the 1940s on as painless a wave as he knew how to create.

Edmondo Loya had been taken back to his home when İkmen had released him the previous evening. Still protesting his guilt, he'd been delivered into the care of his brother Maurice and hadn't shifted from the house, as far as Ayşe could tell, since. Having said that if, as İkmen had once hypothesised, some sort of passageway led from the Loya house down to the Golden Horn, Edmondo could have slipped out that way. But then that rather fanciful theory had been developed when İkmen was trying to work out how Loya might have killed Emine Aksu and carried her body down to the Golden Horn without assistance and without being seen. Now at least on the face of things, İkmen felt that Edmondo was entirely innocent of this as yet unsubstantiated crime. Ayşe wondered, as she lit a cigarette, what would happen to Edmondo if it were proved beyond doubt that he had been lying. Most false confessors were already known to the police and were generally being, at least minimally, treated for some psychiatric disorder. They were almost always debunked immediately. Edmondo Loya was not perhaps all that a grown man should be, but he wasn't a lunatic. In fact, Ayşe thought he was quite a nice man. His brother Maurice wasn't exactly the opposite of Edmondo – in that he wasn't an evil person – but he wasn't sweetness and light either. Just a busy man in reality, Ayşe thought. And yet there was something about the Loyas, something beyond the strange house, the Jewishness, the wildly divergent life histories of the two brothers. Ayşe didn't know why İkmen wanted her to keep a watch on Edmondo, but she could understand it and she knew that it was right even if she didn't know why. And then suddenly there was Edmondo, standing on his broken front doorstep. He wore a heavy winter coat, despite the now constant warmth of late spring, and a knitted woollen hat.

Ayşe Farsakoğlu picked up her handbag and prepared to leave the car in order to follow him.

'It's strange, you know, but I have little memory of this group of shops from years ago,' İkmen said as he looked around at the shelves of cheap men's and women's shoes in Ali Paksoy's shop.

'You used to live in Balat, Inspector?' The shopkeeper was approaching with a small glass of apple tea in his hands.

'No.' İkmen smiled. 'But we used to come over here, my mother, my brother and myself.'

'Oh? You had friends?'

'Yes.' Or rather his mother, Ayşe, the witch of Üsküdar, had. She had always brought her sons with her when she crossed the Bosphorus in order to see the gypsies of Balat and Ayvansaray. The boys, Çetin and his older brother Halil, generally amused themselves by playing with the poor little Jewish boys, the Cohens – Jak, Leon and Balthazar. Their mother and the gypsies read cards and coffee grounds, and talked of stars, fortunes and the vicissitudes of love. There had been no time for shops in Ayşe İkmen's short life.

İkmen took the tea from the shopkeeper's hand and then sat down. Ali Paksoy had temporarily closed the shop in order to talk to İkmen in peace and so the only other person present was his nephew Rafik who was packing up his rucksack in preparation for his own departure.

'Do you want me to take these newspapers out when I go, Uncle Ali?' he said as he pointed towards a big stack of the things over by the front door.

'Yes, you might as well,' Ali Paksoy said. 'I'll call you on your mobile when I'm ready to open again.'

Rafik picked up the papers and smiled. 'OK,' he said. 'Goodbye, Inspector, see you later, Uncle Ali.'

And then he left, putting a 'Closed' sign up at the door as he did so. İkmen lit a cigarette and then said, 'Mr Paksoy, I will come straight to the point. This being Balat, I am sure you know that I released Edmondo Loya from my custody yesterday.'

The shoe seller sat down, but without giving any indication as to whether he knew about this or not.

'I released Mr Loya,' İkmen continued, 'because in spite of his confession, I cannot find any actual proof that he killed anyone, much less Mrs Emine Aksu. Now, Mr Paksoy, I understand that you were part of the group, which included Mr Loya, who used to meet in Sultanahmet in the late sixties and early seventies.'

'Yes.'

'You are in fact the last living member of that group whom I have interviewed,' İkmen said. 'Apart from yourself, Mr Loya and the Aksus, there was also Garbis Aznavourian, Ali

227

Tevfik and Kadir Özal. Mr Loya's older academic friend has passed on . . .'

'There were a lot of foreigners about, too,' Ali Paksoy said. 'It was really to meet with them that we all used to go to the Pudding Shop back in those days. Anyway, what's that old history to do with anything now? Is this all because Edmondo confessed to killing Emine?'

'In part yes,' İkmen said. 'Mrs Aksu, prior to her disappearance, told her husband that she was seeing someone from their hippy past. She didn't say who it was. Just to clarify, Mr Paksoy, the Aksus have a so-called "open" marriage with—'

'I know what an open marriage is, Inspector,' Ali Paksoy said. 'We used to talk about things like that as part of the utopian world we wanted to create back in the sixties. You think that someone else in the old group may have done something to Emine?'

'It's a line of inquiry,' İkmen said. 'As I say, I've spoken to Messrs Aznavourian, Tevfik and Özal and so far their alibis for the day on which Mrs Aksu disappeared check out. What were you doing on the afternoon and evening of Monday the 9th May, Mr Paksoy?'

'I was here at the shop,' Ali Paksoy said. 'We may not have many customers, but just keeping the stock tidy is a full-time job. I'm always here.'

'Can anyone substantiate that?'

Ali Paksoy shrugged. 'I think so,' he said. 'I did have customers that day. I can look at my sales receipts.'

'And your nephew?'

'Rafik always has Mondays off. Although I imagine I must have seen him once or twice during the course of the day, I generally do. Inspector, are you saying that you no longer believe Edmondo's story, that you suspect other members of that ancient group of ours?'

'I don't know,' İkmen said. 'There are aspects of Mr Loya's confession that make me wonder whether it is true and aspects that seem to me to be utterly impossible. I don't even know whether this line of inquiry is even valid. Mrs Aksu could have been lying about who she was seeing. All we do know is that the last time she was definitely sighted she was moving towards this district on the afternoon of the 9th May, ostensibly to see an old flame from her past. After that she seems to have disappeared.'

'Well, I didn't see her,' Ali Paksoy said. 'And even if I had, I wouldn't have had anything to do with her.'

İkmen leaned back in the rather uncomfortable chair Mr Paksoy usually gave to his customers and said, 'You didn't like Mrs Aksu?'

He put his head down and said, 'Not really.'

'Why? Most of your friends—'

'They all – except Edmondo – slept with her, yes. But I didn't either. I didn't want to.'

Garbis Aznavourian had said Ali Paksoy hadn't wanted Emine.

'You had someone else?'

'Yes.' He said it without any further elaboration. 'And there was the shop, too. My father was alive then. We used to make the shoes. And although they were always very plain things, our shoes were well made, with good leather. My father and I would put in extra padding for comfort, soft leather tongues, things like that. It took up a lot of my time.'

'It must have done.' İkmen looked around again at the ranks of cheap, mainly plastic shoes on the shelves. He knew they were mass produced without being told.

229

'To be well shod is important,' Ali Paksoy said. 'And shoes that are beautiful as well as being expertly made are rare and fabulous things.'

'You know that Mrs Aksu was wearing a very unusual pair of shoes when she left her home last time?' İkmen said.

'Was she?'

'Yes. High-heeled pumps with, so her husband has told me, little replicas of the Eiffel Tower suspended in some sort of solution in the heels.'

Ali Paksoy shook his head in disbelief, but he was smiling, too. 'God, the things they think of these days!' he said. 'So cool! When I was young the most you could put on to a woman's shoe was a fancy buckle. But now . . . That's why the hippies were a revelation to me, you know.'

'Their shoes?'

'Marvellous!' the shoe seller said. 'All kinds of styles and colours and little cut-outs and leather trimmings! Innovation, that's what I admire! I would have loved to have been able to make such things!'

'Why didn't you?' İkmen asked as he stubbed his cigarette out into the ashtray Ali Paksoy had given him.

'Oh, it's not a big thing,' the shoe seller laughed. 'My father would only make very plain shoes, he was a very plain and traditional man. Then after he died, well, the industry changed and everyone began to want shoes from abroad, Eastern Europe mainly. Cheap shoes.' No longer cheerful, he shook his head sadly. 'Things that are both ugly and poorly made are truly worthless. Depressing.'

And in truth, even in the twenty-first century there wasn't much that was lovely in his shoe shop. Up in Beyoğlu and in the various malls that had sprung up over the years, the shops were crammed with gorgeous, expensive and lovingly made designer shoes. But Ali Paksoy and others like him couldn't possibly compete with them. The man and his shop had long since been left to tending only to the very poorest people in what was still, in places, a very poor district.

The mood in the shop had taken a distinct turn towards the miserable; it had also wandered way off the point of why İkmen was there. In order to regain Mr Paksoy's attention, İkmen cleared his throat. 'So, Mr Paksoy,' he said, 'you haven't seen Mrs Aksu for . . . ?'

'Years,' Ali Paksoy responded gloomily. 'Edmondo Loya comes into the shop from time to time because he lives locally. Garbis I still see sometimes, too. But the others? Kadir, Ahmet and Emine came from a different world to the rest of us. Rich people from smart parts of the city, they don't see us any more. Ali Tevfik, too. He was just messing around with the likes of us. He took a lot of drugs and got into a bit of a mess, but he's a big businessman now.'

'And the foreigners?' İkmen asked. 'You hung around in the Pudding Shop with foreigners. You had a girlfriend or . . . ?'

'Years and years and years ago!' Ali Paksoy shook his head while looking fixedly down at the floor.

'Who was the girl? I understand you were very taken with her,' İkmen said.

'Who told you that?' He frowned. 'Which girl?'

'Garbis Aznavourian told me you were very fond of a girl from Wales,' İkmen said.

'Wales?' The shoe seller looked genuinely nonplussed. 'Which girl?'

'I—'

'You know, Emine aside, most of us had a lot of girls, Inspector. Foreign girls, we preferred them. They would . . .'

231

Strangely he blushed, giggled just a little and blushed. 'They would do things . . . you know . . . but it was not serious, ever. Maybe there was a girl from Wales at some point whom I said I loved to Garbis.' He laughed. 'You know how young people are.'

İkmen did. He'd been there himself around about the same time. In love, if not in a physical way, with lovely blonde Alison from England. She, too, had worn extraordinary shoes – pink army boots – she had, she'd told him, coloured them herself. The hippies, yes the hippies had been inventive. If something didn't exist, they had made it. It was a pity that the poor frustrated shoe maker whom Ali Paksoy had once been hadn't rebelled against his father and made the shoes he had so obviously wanted to produce. It was then that İkmen glanced towards the shop window and saw a very white-faced Edmondo Loya looking in. Less than a second later his mobile phone began to ring. It was Ayşe Farsakoğlu. 'Edmondo Loya', she said as İkmen looked into that very man's haunted little eyes, 'is looking in the window of Paksoy's shoe shop.'

Chapter 14

They had remained friends – Ali Paksoy and Edmondo Loya, and, to a certain extent, Garbis Aznavourian, too. It was understandable, İkmen said, that Edmondo should visit Ali so soon after he was released from police custody. After all they had both known Emine, if not in a sexual sense.

'Unlike the rest of the city,' Mehmet Süleyman said as he fingered the thin piece of paper that İzzet Melik had taken off the fax machine and then given him just minutes earlier. 'Odd hippy people.'

'A long time ago,' İkmen said.

It was early in the morning, but the three men were already in the station for various reasons – İkmen because he couldn't sleep, Süleyman because he was due to search Ali Paksoy's premises in less than an hour, and İzzet because he was leaving early that day in order to see the Liverpool/AC Milan football match.

'This fax' – Süleyman held the paper aloft for İkmen to see and continued – 'is from the forensic institute. It tells me that the Kamondo Lady was definitely in Mr Paksoy's car.'

'Although whether he put her there—'

'Or whether the car was indeed stolen as he asserts,' Süleyman said, 'is a good point. There are some other prints on the car, apart from those of the two Italians.' He sighed and then leaned across the desk towards İkmen. Ever since the results had come through he had been dreading this moment. 'Çetin, they're Edmondo Loya's prints.'

'Edmondo's!' İkmen frowned and shook his head at the same time. 'Are you sure?'

'Certain.'

İzzet Melik, leaning against a filing cabinet across the other side of Süleyman's office, gave his superior a significant look. Their guest in the office this morning had only just let this Edmondo Loya go.

İkmen sighed and then leaned back in his chair and lit a cigarette. 'It still doesn't mean that Edmondo had anything more to do with the Kamondo Lady than Ali Paksoy.'

'No,' Süleyman replied. 'The car could indeed have been stolen as Ali says. But this morning, as planned, I am going to search Mr Paksoy's shop, his garages and his apartment.' He then looked across at İzzet and said, 'We'll have to ask Mr Paksoy for a DNA sample now, too.'

'Sir.'

'Yes.' İkmen shook his head, still not really quite believing what he had heard. 'My sergeant is assisting, isn't she?'

'Yes. It's a big job; it was very good of you to volunteer her, Çetin.'

'Well, I've little myself for her to do,' İkmen said. 'With the exception of Mr Aksu, I can't definitely place any known person in Emine Aksu's vicinity on the 9th.'

'Could Mr Aksu have murdered his wife?'

'In theory yes,' İkmen said. 'Her blood is, after all, present in their house. But then she did live there, didn't she! People do bleed. They fought by his own admission!' He put his head in his hands and groaned. 'Oh, I don't know! It's not enough to charge him. Like Edmondo, it is a partial case, a—'

'Odd the way Loya knew exactly what Mrs Aksu was wearing, sir,' İzzet Melik said.

'Yes.'

'He must have seen her on that day.'

'That or she was wearing those same clothes on another recent occasion that he saw her,' İkmen said. 'But while the stupid man protests his guilt, what can I do? I ask him when he saw Emine and he persists in this fiction that he saw her on the 9th, when he killed her.'

Süleyman leaned back in his chair and said, 'Why do you think that he is confessing to this, Çetin?'

İkmen shook his head. 'I don't really know. From what I have deduced from his brother, it seems as if Maurice might have goaded Edmondo into it. Not consciously, but I know that Edmondo has problems around his masculinity. I mean, those magazines we found in his basement, they were juvenile, the sort of thing a teenage boy would have under his bed. Emine Aksu undoubtedly hurt him and I would concur with Garbis Aznavourian in that I believe that Edmondo Loya is probably still a virgin. But a killer? I still don't really know. There's no evidence.' He sighed. 'In a way, he is rather like Ali Paksoy. I can see them in a car together. Although alongside a long dead body? I don't know. But they are both – well, not unfulfilled so much as unfinished . . .'

'Unfinished?'

'Partial,' İkmen said, 'like incomplete paintings. I suppose I mean that in both cases their development is incomplete. Somewhere in both their pasts, they stopped, but not in a comfortable place. For all that he irritates with his Californian English the old hippy Kadir Özal is very happy in his anachronism. He embraces it and it's really OK. Edmondo Loya and Ali Paksoy are both just stuck – in Ali's

235

case by the circumstance of having to care for his relatives – but it really isn't pleasant for either of them.'

'Maybe they both used the Kamondo Lady and then took her out for a spin,' Süleyman said unpleasantly. 'Men do that with girls.'

İzzet Melik pulled a disgusted face.

'Anything is possible,' İkmen observed. 'But with Edmondo I can't see it. He's an academic, that is his life; sex, I think, is confined to the pages of his magazines.'

'And Ali Paksoy?'

'The shoe seller. Mmm.' İkmen frowned. 'I don't know. He is far more relaxed on the face of it than Edmondo. But . . . there is a tension when he speaks about the past and the opportunities that he lost. He wanted to be much more than he was, he wanted to be a maker of shoes. But first his father and then economic change were against him. I had the feeling he was angry with time. What I mean by that is that I suspect he believes time has cheated him of what he should have done or should have been.'

The silence between them was only finally broken by the cry of the man selling simit bread rings from his cart down in the street. People were saying that soon street simit sellers were going to become a thing of the past. EU regulations apparently dictated that such practices were unhygienic and already a few dedicated simit shops had begun to appear across the city.

'Do you think that Ali Paksoy is desperate enough to desecrate a dead body?' Süleyman asked.

'I don't know,' İkmen said. 'But one question you should be asking yourself, Mehmet, is, whoever has done this, why have they given up this corpse now?'

'You mean because fetishists don't easily give up their fetishes?'

236

'Yes, if necrophilia is a fetish, although I'm sure you've already checked that out with your wife,' İkmen replied. 'I'm no expert, Mehmet, but one thing I do know is that these people don't give up their "things". Whether Paksoy is your man or not, whoever is has done what he has done for a reason.'

Having another day off was great if for no other reason than it allowed Rafik to stay in bed. Of course he did have a small twinge of anxiety about why he had been given yet another day off – Uncle Ali's place was being searched by the police – but only a very small twinge. After all, Uncle Ali himself had said that if letting the police search through all of his things meant that they left the whole family alone in the future, then it was worth it. It also gave Rafik plenty of time to prepare for the Big Match.

Everything had been planned some time before. His friend Adnan, who was also a Liverpool fan as was his dad, was having Rafik and another friend, Deniz, around to his place in Fener. Adnan's dad had one of those big flat-screen TVs and the boys were all going to watch the match with him and with his brothers, Adnan's uncles. They were all Liverpool fans, too, and so Deniz was going to be very much on his own, but then it was his choice. He didn't have to be an AC Milan fan. He didn't have to be anything if he didn't want to be – except, like everyone else, he *had* to be a Galatasaray fan. Big though the Big Match was it wasn't Turkish football and so it wasn't really that important. It wasn't life and death.

Rafik shuffled the newspapers that littered the surface of his bed. That silly old Mrs Kordovi had left a load of them in the shop but now he'd brought them home. There was a brilliant picture of Steven Gerrard on the back of *Hürriyet* and a whole squad shot on the back of *Zaman*. Not that he'd put any of these pictures up on his bedroom wall, that was reserved for only one team and that was Galatasaray. But he might take them over to Adnan's and hold them up, if Adnan's dad would let him, when the match was on. Deniz said he had an actual AC flag that an Italian supporter had given him in Sultanahmet Square. It was possible, there were loads of fans up there, although Deniz was known to lie quite a bit about lots of things. Adnan reckoned that Deniz had probably stolen the flag from an Italian.

'Ah, I think this is the police for your uncle now, Rafik,' he heard his mother say from in front of her stove in the kitchen. Cooking up some pilav rice to stuff vine leaves for her son to take to his friend's house later that night.

'He'll be all right, won't he, Mum?' Rafik called back, suddenly a little anxious. Uncle Ali was very kind, but he could have a terrible temper sometimes, and he hoped that he didn't lose it with the police. They'd put him in prison if he did and then where would they all be?

'Your uncle will be fine,' his mother said. When Rafik was little she'd reassured him in just the same way about his dying father. Rafik jumped across the newspapers and over to his bedroom window. Outside two police cars disgorged a lot of police officers, both uniformed and plain clothed. One of them was a very good-looking woman.

Officially Wednesday was İkmen's day off. That he had already been into the station first thing in the morning was just a measure of his agitation about the missing Emine Aksu. The bloody woman was nowhere to be found and he was beginning to wonder whether his early sense of foreboding about this case had in fact been misplaced. Maybe Emine wasn't dead at all? Maybe she was just off with some other nice young man? After all the city was full of them at the moment. As he turned off the street and into the Cohens' courtyard he was almost pushed over by a small crowd of barely clad Italian men waving an enormous red and black flag. Perhaps Emine was in the bed one or more of them had just left? İkmen smiled at this thought but then when he saw the state of the figure in front of him his face resolved into a thing of more sadness.

'Balthazar.'

'I was just looking at these plants,' the man in the wheel-chair said as he reached out to touch the petals of a very deli-cate blue flower.

He looked so hunched up and tiny, especially in compar-ison to the large expanse of garden he now had in front of his home. Estelle and Hulya had cleared and planted the garden almost single-handedly. Women with sick husbands, almost but not quite alone in the world. It wasn't what İkmen had wanted for his daughter, but then he'd wanted perfec-tion for all of his children, like most fathers.

'I'm not a plants man myself,' İkmen said as he walked over to his friend and then bent down to kiss him on the cheek, 'but I like the springtime. Nice time of year.'

'You let Edmondo Loya go,' the man in the wheelchair said.

'A garbled confession like his, unsupported by any actual evidence, becomes untenable,' İkmen said. He pulled a rather rusty garden chair over towards Balthazar and sat down. 'I still don't know whether I did the right thing.'

'Edmondo Loya is a poor creature,' Balthazar said as he offered İkmen a cigarette. 'Sometimes I think it's as if he and Maurice are not brothers at all. They look alike, but their brains are different. I mean, I know twins don't have to do everything together, think the same thoughts or whatever, but the Loyas are very, very different.'

Although he was a renowned gossip, İkmen knew that Balthazar always kept his counsel where the subject involved police business and so he told him about the sub-basement under the Loyas' house. 'There was enough opium in jars on shelves to kill that family several times over,' he said. And then as this statement obviously triggered off something else he pulled his phone out of his jacket pocket before saying to Balthazar as he dialled, 'Which reminds me, sorry, I must just call my sergeant.'

Balthazar shrugged.

Turning away a little from his friend, İkmen spoke as soon as Ayşe Farsakoğlu answered. 'Oh, Ayşe,' he said, 'look, I know you're probably in the middle of your search with Inspector Süleyman now, but . . . look, make sure you investigate underneath his property thoroughly . . . Yes, just like the Loya house . . . Maybe, maybe. Tell the inspector that the shop was once under Jewish ownership a –' he put his fingers up to his forehead and pinched the heavily lined skin, trying to remember something. He looked across at Balthazar and said, 'Who used to own Ali Paksoy's shoe shop?'

'Mr Madrid,' Balthazar said. 'A long time ago.'

'But would he have been in the property during the Second World War?'

'Certainly.'

'A Mr Madrid,' İkmen said into the telephone. 'OK?'

Obviously she was because he closed the phone up almost immediately afterwards. The two men sat in silence for a few moments then until İkmen lit up the cigarette Balthazar had given him.

'You suspect Ali Paksoy?' Balthazar said as he watched the smoke from İkmen's cigarette head in his direction. But İkmen didn't answer, mainly because he didn't know. Ali Paksoy only had a slim connection to the case upon which he was working.

'I hardly know him at all,' Balthazar continued. 'We left soon after that family came.' And then he leaned towards İkmen, across the arm of his wheelchair, and said, 'But I can tell you that the old dentist, the Loyas' father, was not alone in laying plans to kill his family during that time.'

İkmen frowned. 'Oh?'

'My grandfather, Moşe Cohen, he went out and bought a gun, it is said,' Balthazar whispered. 'If the Germans had got here,' he put two fingers up to his head and mimed a gunshot. 'Boom! The whole lot of us. You know, Inspector, some people say that some Jews responded like this because they were afraid our government might make an alliance with the Nazis. But that wasn't the real fear.' He shook his head slowly. 'No. The Nazis were in Greece, they were conquering everything and everyone. Neutrality can only hold if all parties respect neutrality. People wondered how long it would be before Hitler stomped into Aya Sofya. He was a megalomaniac. It was possible.' He moved away a little now, pulling himself up straight in his chair once again. 'It was always possible.' And then changing the subject suddenly as he often did, he said, 'So are you going to watch the football tonight, Inspector?'

İkmen gave him a very cynical look. Balthazar knew him well enough to know that football was most definitely not his thing.

241

'I bet your kids are going to watch,' Balthazar said, teasingly.

'Oh, of course,' İkmen said bitterly. 'My small apartment will be overtaken by long-limbed young men and women flopping about in front of my television set.'

Balthazar laughed. 'Why don't you come over here?' he said.

'Because I imagine you'll all be watching the wretched thing too!'

Balthazar shrugged. 'True. But Hulya isn't working this evening and she hates football. You can spend some time with your daughter out here in the garden or in the living room with Estelle. It's only me and my son who will watch. Come over!' He placed an affectionate hand on İkmen's back. 'Watch a while with Berekiah and me. Who knows, you might even like it?'

'I doubt it. Tens of thousands of lunatics looking at twenty-two over-paid men . . .'

'It's just a game!' Balthazar said. 'It's nothing, it's—'

'Balthazar, somewhere in this city, or beyond, there is a missing woman,' İkmen said. 'Alive or dead, I don't know. I thought I did . . .' He frowned. 'Emine Aksu knew a lot of people. I've spoken to all whom I have deduced could be of significance. But not one of them really fits. Even her jealous husband isn't right. I can't work out how Edmondo Loya might have done it . . .'

'So why don't you have an evening off?' Balthazar said. 'We have a lovely garden here. Share food with us. If I know your wife, she'll be running around with food and drink for all the youngsters all night long. She'll welcome the fact that you're out of her way.'

'Mmm.' İkmen knew that what he was saying was true.

242

Although devoted to him, Fatma also idolised all of her children and welcomed all and any of their vast hordes of friends. The baking, boiling and frying of tasty little morsels would be going on for hours. 'We'll see,' he said. 'We'll see.'

Ali Paksoy had been sitting in the front of his shop, trying to close his ears to the sounds coming from the basement for some hours. God alone knew what the police were doing back there! How many shoes was he going to have to re-box at the end of it all?

'Mr Paksoy?'

He looked up into the face of the attractive woman policeman at his elbow. 'Yes?'

'Sir, there is a door at the back of your basement store-room which we can't seem to find a key for.' Because he didn't respond in any way at all to this, Ayşe repeated, 'Mr Paksoy, a door, downstairs . . .'

He blinked. 'Ah, yes. I'll, er, I'll get it for you. It's Byzantine.' He stood up.

'Byzantine?'

'Underneath the shop.' He smiled. 'Probably goes further than that. Probably stretches underneath the baker's, too. I've never measured it myself.'

Süleyman, who had now also entered the shop and had heard the last bit of the conversation asked, 'What stretches underneath the baker's?'

'The Byzantine chapel underneath the shop,' Ali Paksoy said.

'Ah.'

'I'll get you the key.'

Almost anywhere outside the old districts of İstanbul the very idea of a Byzantine chapel underneath one's home or business would be cause for wonder. At the very least there would be a level of intrigue. But in the old districts of İstanbul the concept of living on top of the detritus of at least one other level of civilisation was common. The Byzantines had built all of their great structures – churches, palaces and shrines – in the Old City area. Why Mr Paksoy hadn't given the police the key to the 'chapel' in the first place was the only mystery inherent in this situation.

'There's no light down here,' Ali Paksoy said as he switched on a torch and ushered Ayşe and Süleyman into what turned out to be a very large space. Usually these 'chapels' were little more than tiny, rubble-filled hovels. Ayşe now switched on her own torch so that its beams joined with those of Süleyman and Paksoy. From floor to ceiling the space had to be at least four metres high. And although the little door that led into this place from the basement was still open, little could be heard of the officers who were now working way above their heads.

Entirely empty, its walls blackened by both time and what looked like a slightly oily, perhaps sooty, black substance on the stone, the chapel had a large arch at the end which was probably, Süleyman thought, underneath the baker's shop. The floor, which looked as if it was made from hard-packed earth, was clear of any ornamentation or artefact. The walls too, which Süleyman went around and methodically tapped, were plain with the exception of one thing.

'What's that over there?' Ayşe asked, pointing to a bulge of stone in one of the side walls.

'That?'

'Yes.' She began to walk towards it, shining her torch in its direction the whole time. As she drew closer, above the feature, something that looked a little like a disc came into view.

'I don't know,' Ali Paksoy said as he led the two officers towards the thing. 'It's like a trough of some sort. I don't know whether it used to contain something or not.' He pointed to the disc. 'But this is a fresco. Mary the Mother of Christ, my sister thinks.'

'Your sister knows about this place?' Süleyman asked as he leaned forward the better to see what was indeed a very faint and battered Byzantine fresco.

'Sometimes we played down here when we were children,' the shoe seller said. 'Not much though. My sister, being a girl, wasn't very adventurous and Dad wouldn't let other kids into our house. If I'd had a brother, I expect we would have had a lot of fun here. Children like places like this.'

Ayşe Farsakoğlu, shuddering at both the look and cold feel of the place said, 'I don't know about that.' She then leaned in to look at the fresco. It wasn't very good.

'Does the Ministry of Culture know about this?' Süleyman asked as he ran the beam of his torch from the fresco into the wide receptacle below. Where the stone of the unknown thing joined the wall there appeared to be some cracking.

'No.'

'Well, they should be told,' he said. And then, frowning, he put his hand into the space. 'This could be a Byzantine baptismal place. The Ministry would most certainly want to know, even if they don't want to develop the site.'

Sometimes archaeologists would be called into ancient ruins like this in order to catalogue and preserve structure and artefacts.

'I'd have to speak to the neighbours,' Paksoy said.

Süleyman leaned forward into the stone-sided receptacle

and scraped his hand along the bottom of the thing. Again the surface felt like packed earth but this was also covered with a few of what looked like small stone chippings.

'Mmm.' Süleyman looked at the fresco once again and then trained his torch up towards Ali Paksoy's face. Lit from below the shoe man looked snub-nosed and gnome-like. But then maybe that was just Süleyman's imagination getting to work in this place of ancient, underground darkness.

'Who else, apart from your sister, knows about this place?' Süleyman said as he straightened up again.

'My nephew. And I might have mentioned it to the odd friend here or there.'

'Edmondo Loya been down here?'

'Edmondo Loya?'

'We found his fingerprints on your car,' Süleyman said.

'Oh, my car, can I—'

'No, Mr Paksoy, you may not have your car back yet,' Süleyman said. 'Please answer my question. Edmondo Loya?'

Ayşe Farsakoğlu, still behind the two men, was continuing to peer at the fresco on the wall as well as the receptacle below it. Just very quickly Ali Paksoy let his gaze flicker over towards her and then he said, 'I don't know, Inspector. As far as I can recall, I've never taken Edmondo with me to the car. Maybe if the garage was unlocked he looked in there one day, decided to take the vehicle out . . . He's always wandering about, thinking. He does much absently . . .'

'In addition,' Süleyman said, 'we now have forensic evidence that clearly links your car with the Karaköy corpse. This means, Mr Paksoy, that you will now be required to provide us with a saliva sample.'

Ali Paksoy frowned. 'What for?' He clearly didn't have any understanding about DNA.

246

Süleyman explained in as simple a way as he could the principle behind this kind of testing. He did not, however, tell him to what his results were to be compared. When he had finished Ali Paksoy said, 'And if I don't want to give this sample?'

'The law will compel you.' He spoke strongly and with authority, the sound echoing powerfully, if slightly eerily around the darkened chamber. Ayşe Farsakoğlu looked up to the vaulted ceiling as if following the vibrations with her eyes. She'd been in the past to the odd Greek Orthodox ceremony; one of her best friends was an ethnic Greek. If Süleyman's voice was anything to go by, how wonderful the old priests' sonorous voices must have sounded in the past as they gravely intoned the words of their Liturgy.

In response, Ali Paksoy first looked down at the floor and then looked up and smiled once again. 'Well then, Inspector, I had better give you what you want, hadn't I?'

'Yes.' Süleyman made one last sweep around the chapel with his torch and then ushered Mr Paksoy back towards the stairs in front of him.

'This is all there is?' he asked. 'This chamber?'

'To my knowledge, yes.'

But Ayşe Farsakoğlu, who had lagged behind and was now standing in the centre of the space, said, 'Mr Paksoy, there was a Jewish family here before you, wasn't there?'

What she had seen in Edmondo Loya's basement had affected her. Never before had she come slap bang up against the raw reality of ethnic fear. If the Nazis had come, Nat Loya would have killed his entire family. İkmen had not needed to remind her of it earlier, and it was now, it seemed, almost always on her mind.

'Mr Madrid and his family, yes,' Ali Paksoy said.

247

'Did they know about this?'

'Oh, yes.' He smiled. 'They used to store things in here. My father once told me that Mr Madrid's widow said that it had felt funny to her living above a church. But Mr Madrid's family had always lived here. Apparently, his grandfather said that he could hear the ghosts of the old dead Byzantines moaning down here at night.'

'And can you ever hear them, Mr Paksoy?'

'Oh, no.' He mounted the stairs. 'That was just a story.'

'Or the wind?' Ayşe said as she moved to get closer to Süleyman and the stairs.

Ali Paksoy frowned. 'The wind? There's nowhere for it to get in.'

'Maybe there used to be,' Süleyman said as he followed him. 'Our sadly rather too frequent earthquakes can alter the lie of the land from time to time.'

'Yes. Yes that's very true.'

For just a moment Ayşe looked back into the great, dark space of the chapel as she swept her torch around its walls. Wholly self-contained with thick stone walls, the chapel was inaccessible except via the door at the top of the stairs. Mr Paksoy, although not volunteering the key to the door at the outset, had not attempted to then conceal the place from them. But Ayşe was nevertheless uneasy. She couldn't say why and maybe it was just as a result of having seen two rather mournful places under the ground in recent days. But then as Süleyman said just after the search was concluded and Mr Paksoy willingly gave them a saliva sample, the DNA comparison to the semen found on the corpse would convict or exonerate the shoe seller. Quite why Ayşe felt it was not going to be that simple, she didn't know. At Süleyman's request she went off to try and find Edmondo Loya.

Chapter 15

I n order to pick up his ticket and meet everyone else he was supposed to be seeing the match with, İzzet Melik had to go to Dr Krikor Sarkissian's apartment in Cihangir. Just to the east of İstiklal Street and the delights of Beyoğlu, Cihangir was a smart, convenient and very funky part of town. Popular with artists, writers and intellectuals, it was not the sort of place that a policeman, apart from Mehmet Süleyman, would feel at home in. But, by the time İzzet arrived, Cihangir, just like the rest of the city was heaving with football fans all either on their way to the match or filling up every bar, pub and tea garden in order to watch it.

'Ah, Sergeant Melik!' the doctor said as he opened the door to his guest. 'Come in.'

While İzzet took his shoes off at the door, he looked around at the hall of the doctor's apartment. He'd never been to a doctor's home before and if the hall was anything to go by – completely bare of any ornamentation apart from a carpet even İzzet recognised as worth a fortune – it was going to be quite an experience.

The living room, which was probably a little bit larger than the apartment İzzet shared with his brother was also minimalistic. Beautiful carpets, this time on the walls, were again the main features of the room. He'd once overheard Inspector İkmen telling Inspector Süleyman that Dr Krikor owned carpets that had once belonged to the Balian family. İzzet knew who they were. Armenian architects, the Balian family had been responsible for building almost every nineteenth-century palace in the city.

'Come and meet my cousin,' Krikor said as he took one of İzzet's arms gently in his hand. 'Natasha comes from England and is fascinated by police work.' He moved in closer to İzzet as if sharing a secret with him. 'She likes to read crime fiction; Miss Marple and all that.'

'Yes, but—'

'Oh, I know it's only fiction, but the English do love it and Natasha has lived all her life in that country.' He began to pull İzzet towards a small, rather attractive woman currently talking to Abdullah Ceylan the lawyer. But İzzet was resisting. 'İzzet? May I call you İzzet . . . what's the matter?'

'Dr . . .'

'Krikor. We're not at work here, it's Krikor.'

'Krikor,' İzzet gulped. 'No, I don't mind talking about my work, it's just that . . . I don't speak English very well. I . . . my parents, we lived in İzmir, they had me learn Italian.'

Krikor smiled. He had thought that this great lump of a policeman might be a bit awkward in this company, but he'd been willing to have a go nevertheless. Arto always maintained that İzzet Melik had a good heart and he did. It was also, Krikor felt, rather touching that this great ox of a man spoke such a delicate language as Italian.

Krikor patted İzzet affectionately on the back. 'Well, I think that your command of Italian is laudable,' he said. 'I wish I spoke it; such a beautiful language. But as for my cousin Natasha, you don't have to worry, she speaks Turkish.'

'Oh.' İzzet visibly relaxed.

They moved forward past a middle-aged couple, Süleyman

and Hatice Arslan – who were, Krikor said, geneticists – and a little black-clad maid who gave İzzet a large glass of champagne.

'Natasha!' Krikor said and he placed a hand on Abdullah Ceylan's shoulder. 'Can I introduce you to someone?'

The woman, who was probably in her mid-forties, extended her hand towards İzzet.

'Sergeant İzzet Melik,' Krikor said. 'He works for the police department. İzzet, this is my cousin Natasha.'

She was small and round and pretty. She had a nice smile which he liked very much.

'Sergeant . . .'

'İzzet.' He took her hand and shook it lightly. Krikor ushered the lawyer away to speak to the Arslans.

'I understand that you like crime fiction,' İzzet said, suddenly and painfully aware that he was the only man in the room wearing a suit. Over-dressed – the sure mark of a man with no money or taste.

Natasha laughed. Her eyes were, he noticed, a very strange shade of blue, almost purple.

'Yes,' she said, 'I do. But then growing up in England, how could I not? I was raised on Agatha Christie, Conan Doyle and, of course, all the modern stuff, too.'

'Right.' He didn't have a clue who Conan Doyle was. Though he knew that Agatha Christie had stayed at the Pera Palas Hotel in Beyoğlu, or so Inspector Süleyman had once told him.

'But I know it's not really like that, what you do,' she said. 'In fact, I've heard that in reality police work can sometimes be quite boring.'

'Yes.' He took a sip from his champagne glass. 'Yes, sometimes.'

251

'Ah.'

She was obviously expecting him to elaborate on this, but at that moment he couldn't. She was lovely, clearly bright, he was in a wonderful place with, now he looked across at the windows, fabulous views over the Bosphorus, and he had totally clammed up. What the hell was *he* doing there with his cheap suit from one of the stalls around the back of the Yeni Mosque? He should have followed his instincts and stayed at home with his brother and watched the match on TV. But it was just as his panic was threatening to over-whelm him that something wonderful happened.

Natasha took one of his arms in her hands and began to steer him towards the largest of the living rooms, which had three enormous windows. As they drew nearer, the intense blueness of the Bosphorus really became apparent, as did the various buildings, both famous and not famous, tumbling down the hill towards the great waterway below.

'I love the crazy higgledy-piggledy nature of this city,' Natasha said as she took a sip from her glass and then smiled up at him. 'Look at this! The Bosphorus with those marvel-lous old ferries still going strong, the great bridge, all those ancient houses and mosques and churches . . . so much of old İstanbul is intact, I love it.'

'Yes, it's, er . . .' Again the words just failed him.

'Where I come from, London,' Natasha said, 'vast areas of the city were bombed during the Second World War, so there's not nearly so much remaining from the past. Have you ever been to London, İzzet?'

'No. Venice.' It was the only foreign place he had ever been to.

'Oh, yes, Venice. It's lovely,' she said, 'but full of tourists these days. You can so rarely get to look at something alone in Venice. No, İstanbul fascinates because it has so many layers of history, so many nooks and crannies.'

And that was when he began to tell her about the chapel they had found earlier that day underneath Ali Paksoy's shop. He didn't give her any details, of course, just the fact that the thing existed and that its appearance was not that uncommon in the Old City across the Golden Horn.

'So people actually have chapels or Byzantine store houses or whatever underneath their homes?'

'Yes.'

Natasha's extraordinary eyes widened. 'God! That's amazing!' And then, tucking herself closely in to his side, she said, 'Hey, can any of these places be seen? You know, by someone like me, on—'

'I know a man in Zeyrek, where I live, who has a Byzantine cistern in his garden,' İzzet said. 'He is a taxi driver, a friend of my brother. I could tell you where it is if—'

'Oh, yes,' she said, 'that would be marvellous!'

'I could take you to see it myself,' İzzet said.

The maid came over then and recharged their glasses with champagne. From behind him İzzet could hear ripples of polite gossip and laughter from the other guests. But it didn't disturb him unduly. Slowly, he was beginning to feel just slightly more relaxed. She was helping, this large-eyed, enthusiastic little woman. She was not as young or beautiful as Ayşe Farsakoğlu, but there was definitely something . . .

'That would be nice,' Natasha said. 'If you don't mind.'

'Oh, it's no trouble at all,' İzzet said. 'It will be my pleasure, in fact.'

Natasha looked over her shoulder at the other guests and then, moving closer to İzzet once again, she said, 'I know they're all a bit academicy and boring, except for my cousin, of course, but you and I will manage, won't we?'

'Er . . .' He was smiling now, even though what she had just said did sound a bit odd to him.

'At the match!' Natasha said. 'I like a damn good shout, don't you?'

'Well . . .' İzzet took a sip from his champagne glass and then laughed. 'Yes, I do, actually.'

'Good!'

'And a cigarette,' İzzet said, and then feeling that he may well have just pushed it a little too far, he put his hand over his mouth. 'Sorry. Dr – Krikor doesn't—'

'No, but I do,' Natasha said. She then put her glass down on to a table nearby and added, 'There's a balcony off the dining room, I'll ask Krikor if we can have the key.'

'That's . . .'

'Oh and by the way I'm supporting Liverpool,' Natasha said, before tapping Krikor on the shoulder and then whispering into his ear.

The doctor first frowned and then took a small key out of his pocket and gave it to her. They shared a moment of humour which, İzzet imagined, was probably conducted in English.

When she returned she held up the key to İzzet and said, 'So, Liverpool?'

He sighed. It had been such a nice encounter until now, but he couldn't lie about this, this was football. 'Milano,' he said shaking his head as he did so. 'I'm sorry. I come from İzmir, my city has many connections to Italy. I speak Italian.'

Natasha sighed and shook her head in what he thankfully recognised as mock disapproval. 'Oh, well,' she said, 'if I must smoke with the enemy . . .'

*　　*　　*

Edmondo Loya was nowhere to be found. He wasn't at home and Ayşe couldn't see him anywhere on the street. She hammered on the door of his house, knowing how large it was, how long it might take him to answer. 'Mr Loya, it's the police!' she'd said. 'It's all right, but we do need to ask you a few more questions, about one of your friends.' Nothing.

Maurice Loya, so neighbours told her, had gone over to İkitelli to watch the football match with one of his rich clients. Before he left, however, according to the neighbours again, he had argued with his brother. So Edmondo must have been in the house until relatively recently. People were thin on the streets now, all getting off home to see the football. The only recognisable person she saw was Ali Paksoy's nephew, Rafik, going off to see the match at a friend's house. She asked him if he'd seen Edmondo Loya but he said that he hadn't. She gave him one of her cards and asked the boy to call immediately if he did see the Jew. Rafik, obviously deeply suspicious of a woman who had taken part in searching his uncle's house, mumbled that he would. Back at her car, Ayşe phoned through to Süleyman who told her to go off duty, he would take it from there.

She was tired. It had been a long day and she was still troubled by what she'd felt in that strange Byzantine space underneath Ali Paksoy's shop. There was nothing there! A void! And yet there was something about it . . . Maybe it was just because it was a church. Ayşe was hardly a *good* Muslim, but she did notionally adhere to the tenets of Islam and some-times, particularly when she was in trouble, she would recite appropriate Suras from the Koran. Feelings, like the one she'd had underneath the shoe shop, were not common for Ayşe. İkmen, she knew, had them often. It was therefore fortuitous for her that she noticed her superior's beaten-up old Mercedes parked outside the home of ex-Constable Balthazar Cohen.

Back when Cohen was still working, Ayşe and Balthazar had been colleagues. They had worked together on many occasions and he had always flirted with her. Now she imagined as she walked towards the door that led into the Cohens' courtyard he probably didn't do such things any more. She was wrong, but she did feel she needed to speak to İkmen.

'Sergeant Farsakoğlu now!' Balthazar opened his arms in greeting as he watched her walk towards him. 'Smart, too! Promotion suits you, Ayşe!'

She'd been a sergeant for a couple of years now, and he'd known it. Just any excuse to compliment and flannel a lady. Legs or no legs, Balthazar Cohen hadn't changed – at least not in his head. Physically he was, she could see, shrinking. When he'd first had that wheelchair he'd looked like a man, now he hardly fitted the thing at all, giving him the appearance of a small, wizened child. Beside him even skinny little İkmen looked huge.

'So are we three old officers of the law all going to watch football together?' Balthazar asked.

Ayşe, who knew that İkmen didn't like football, looked at him quizzically. 'Sir?'

İkmen sighed. 'Strange as it may seem, Sergeant,' he said, 'I have agreed to keep our old friend Balthazar company during the match this evening. The streets are choked with traffic. Getting home was going to be a nightmare.'

Ayşe looked nervously back towards the courtyard door. She, too, was supposed to go home. Over in her own district of Gümüşsüyü, her brother and his friends were waiting for her to return. Not that that was bothering her.

'What is it, Sergeant? You look worried.' İkmen said.

After he had found her a chair and Estelle Cohen had provided them all with more tea, Ayşe told İkmen and Balthazar all about the feelings she had experienced in Ali Paksoy's chapel.

'Ah, I see spooky witches' stuff rubbing off on you now, Ayşe,' Balthazar said with a wink after she had finished. 'You work with Inspector İkmen, well!'

Both İkmen and Ayşe ignored him. The former rubbed his now moderately stubbly chin and said, 'Well, not having been down into Mr Paksoy's chapel, Ayşe, I can't really comment. But as I have always told you, it is a poor policeman who does not listen to the feelings in his gut.'

'Exactly! But I didn't know what to say!' Ayşe said. 'Inspector Süleyman isn't easy to approach on that level. And I don't work for him.'

'Inspector Süleyman would have understood what you were getting at, although he wouldn't necessarily have allowed it to inform what he did,' İkmen said.

'Exactly!'

'In the event, I think that Inspector Süleyman has done the right thing for the time being,' İkmen said.

'Sir, I think if I'd come to you, you would have had arc lights in there, men hammering on the floor . . .'

'Ayşe, the way you describe it, the chapel is a large stone building with only one entrance. Did Inspector Süleyman tap the walls?'

'Yes.'

'Well, then, in the absence of any other evidence, he did what he could,' İkmen said. 'Ali Paksoy has, you say, been DNA-tested. When the results come through it will be clear as to whether his DNA matches that found in the semen on

257

the corpse. There's nothing else that can be done before that result is through. And if the match is positive . . .'

'Yes, I know!' Ayşe briefly put her head in her hands and then said, 'If only I didn't get the feeling there was something else!'

'Something else!'

Balthazar nudged İkmen in the ribs and said, 'Crazy. Just like you.'

Again they ignored him.

'There's something really wrong,' Ayşe said. 'Not just this corpse business. Whether it's to do with Mr Paksoy or not, I don't know, but I have this awful, awful feeling . . .'

'You have it now?'

'No. I had it in that place. The chapel.'

He offered her a cigarette which she took gratefully.

'I can't tell you what this feeling is or what it means,' Ayşe said. 'Just that something was very wrong . . .' She shook her head as her attempts to articulate what she meant came to nothing. 'Just wrong.'

'Do other people know about this chapel, apart from Mr Paksoy?'

'His nephew and sister. Plus a couple of Paksoy's friends, so he says. The sister is pretty innocuous, a widow with little money. The nephew? Well, he's a bit – well, not terribly bright,' Ayşe said. 'Sports mad. I saw him just before I came here, off to a friend's house to watch the football.'

'Do you get the impression this boy or his friends might have stolen the uncle's car?'

Ayşe sighed. 'I don't know. I don't know the boy or his friends well enough. But where would they have got the corpse from even if they had stolen the car? Kids do stupid, clumsy things in my experience and as we know, whoever stole this corpse covered his tracks very well. There are still no reports of any grave desecration and anyway, the body was totally without earth on it, wasn't it?'

'True.' İkmen smoked in a slow and concentrated fashion. 'Did Mr Paksoy give any opinion as to how Edmondo Loya's fingerprints came to be on his car?'

Ayşe knew that İkmen was still very unsure about having let Edmondo Loya go and so she told him the whole story about Ali Paksoy's seemingly genuine confusion over the matter. She also told him that she hadn't managed to find Edmondo.

'If he's had a row with his brother, he's probably sulking on his own in that house somewhere,' Balthazar said. 'He won't answer the door to you.'

'Do you think he might answer it to you?' İkmen asked him.

Balthazar shrugged. 'I don't know. Maybe.'

İkmen looked at his watch. It was still well over an hour until kickoff. There was certainly time, even if he and Ayşe did have to push Balthazar down the hill and, more importantly, back up again. Ali Paksoy's car had nothing to do with the case that he was working on and so Loya's prints on it were officially none of his concern. But they were another apparent mystery that surrounded the strange prematurely aged little Jew and his friend Ali Paksoy.

İkmen turned to Balthazar again and said, 'Fancy taking a trip down to Edmondo Loya's place?'

The two boys sat on the floor of Adnan's mum and dad's living room and Rafik spread his newspapers out before them.

'This squad picture in *Zaman* is good,' he said as he pointed the scissors Adnan had given him at the newspaper. 'We can hold it up when we score.'

'Yeah.'

'That'll piss Deniz off,' Rafik said as he began to roughly cut the picture out of the paper.

'Says he's got an AC flag,' Adnan said. 'If he has, he'll be wanting to wave that about. I'll have to ask my dad not to let him.' He reached across the floor towards a football magazine he'd thrown down earlier. 'Shall I cut out that picture of the Liverpool goalie?'

'If you like,' Rafik said. 'Although I've got a great shot of Steven Gerrard in *Hürriyet*.' He reached for it, throwing what was left of *Zaman* to one side. Who found the best or 'right' pictures was a very competitive thing between the two boys. Deniz aside, these two were also frequently at odds in a quiet, serious way. But then football was a serious business and it is in the nature of young men to compete.

'Well, I'll get the goalie anyway,' Adnan said. 'I've got Cissé, too.'

'OK.'

Adnan began cutting his magazine while Rafik tidied up before he snipped Steven Gerrard's picture out. After all, it wasn't his house and Adnan's mother was quite particular about mess. He was, he felt, really quite lucky with his mum when it came to untidiness. She didn't care very much, or didn't seem to, and so he and his friends could really make as much of it as they wanted. But in someone else's house it was only polite to do what they wanted and Rafik had always been a very polite boy. His uncle Ali had made sure of that. Moan and moan about *his* father, Granddad Faruk Paksoy as he did, Uncle Ali wasn't that much different from him. He didn't hit Rafik, but he did make him feel stupid and look down on him for much of the time. If his dad had lived, Rafik and his mother wouldn't have had to put up with any of that. Rafik gathered up bits of newspaper and began to put them into a pile. It wasn't that he was looking at any of the stories in the papers as he was stacking them; it was actually a picture that first caught his attention. It was of a woman, an old one, in Rafik's eyes, older than his mum. The police were looking for her, the story said.

Rafik Sarıgul had seen her.

'I wonder how Sergeant Melik is getting on with Dr Sarkissian and his friends?' İkmen said as he lit up yet another cigarette.

Taking Balthazar Cohen out for a push in his wheelchair was, İkmen and Ayşe Farsakoğlu were learning, no quick or easy option. Without actually saying the words, Estelle Cohen had let them know that her husband was now incontinent. Toileting prior to any journey, however short, was essential, as was the dressing up of her husband in various devices designed to save his dignity whilst out in public.

'I expect he's all right,' Ayşe replied. She was leaning against one of the heavy-stone walls that surrounded the Cohens' garden, also smoking. Like İkmen, she really just wanted to get down to the Loyas' house now and find out what was happening. But neither of them could go without Balthazar.

'I don't think you believe that any more than I do,' İkmen said. 'Krikor, even more so than our own Dr Arto, has got some very, very smart and intellectual friends. I can see poor İzzet just sitting about with his mouth open. And then, apparently, there's their cousin Natasha too, coming from England.'

'Why's that significant?'

'I don't know her well,' İkmen said, 'but I do remember Natasha when she was a little girl and she was a dreadful flirt even then! Clever woman, like all her family, but totally ruthless with men. Likes them a bit rough . . .'

'Like İzzet.'

'Oh, he'd be just her type!'

Ayşe shook her head. İzzet Melik wasn't a bad man. He was clumsy and very much unreconstructed, but she also knew that beneath the moustache and the bluster and the sometimes outright misogyny, he was very thin-skinned. 'I hope she doesn't hurt him,' she said softly.

İkmen raised an eyebrow. She seemed to mean it.

'I'm sorry! Holding everyone up!' Balthazar, now sporting a rug over what was left of his legs, was being pushed by Estelle from the house into the garden.

'It's OK,' İkmen said. 'Things have to . . . happen . . . for you . . .'

But before Estelle could get the chair over the doorstep there was a hammering on the great wooden door to the courtyard.

'Oh, someone at the door!' Estelle said impatiently. 'What . . . ?'

'Let me do it,' İkmen said as he gently took the handles at the back of the chair from her. 'You go and answer the door.'

She let him do it, shaking her head with impatience at the thousand and one things she always seemed to have to do as she went.

'Mrs Cohen! Mrs Cohen!' There was a great hammering on the door. She didn't recognise the voice. It was a woman, but . . . Estelle began to run as İkmen and Ayşe Farsakoğlu pushed and then finally lifted Balthazar's chair over the doorstep.

'There must be a knack to it,' İkmen muttered.

'No,' Balthazar said. 'Estelle is just strong. Always has been.'

'Are you saying that I'm weak, Balthazar?' İkmen teased.

'No. I'm saying my wife is like an ox when it comes to strength. Who is that at the door? What do they want?'

Looking up, İkmen saw a covered woman and a young man talking, in what looked like earnest tones, to Estelle in the courtyard.

'That,' Ayşe Farsakoğlu said after a moment, 'is Rafik Sarıgul with, if I'm not mistaken, his mother, Ali Paksoy's sister. I wonder what they want with Mrs Cohen?'

'"THE TIME HAS COME THE WALRUS SAID . . ." NO. NO, NOW IS NOT THE TIME TO SPEAK OF MANY THINGS. NOW IS THE TIME TO WRITE. WRITE.'

But no one answered and the pen didn't move. It had done a lot of moving about until now, but the conclusion that was essential just wouldn't come.

Looking around that small room now. 'I HAVE FALLEN DOWN THE RABBIT HOLE.' Echoing into nothing.

'BUT IN THE RABBIT HOLE IS WHERE I HAVE BEEN ALL THE TIME.'

'I HAVE NOT LIVED A LIFE IN ANYTHING ONE COULD CALL A "WONDER" LAND.'

'ALICE'S ADVENTURES WERE FAR FROM BENIGN.'

'"OFF WITH HIS HEAD! OFF WITH HIS HEAD!"'

And then the conclusion came – pen scratching furiously over paper – and with it, finally, a smile, even some laughter. 'NO MORE QUESTIONS. NOT ONE.'

Then stand up, climb on to the chair, hope to God that the explanation given was sufficient, and jump out into freedom. At last. That was the plan.

Chapter 16

Red on its own or red with black – of course – were the colours that met their weary eyes when they finally made it to their seats.

'I'm so glad I insisted we leave early,' Krikor Sarkissian said as he allowed his body to drop wearily into his seat. Then, turning to his cousin Natasha, he added, 'That journey, you know, should have taken no longer than an hour!'

'The police shut one of the access roads,' Hatice Arslan said. 'How senseless is that!'

'Do you know why one of the roads was shut?' her husband asked a very silent İzzet Melik.

'How would he know?' Hatice snapped at her husband. 'He doesn't work for the traffic division. Krikor told us. Don't you ever listen? God! Stuffed in that car for hours on end! My hair has gone flat, like old string!'

Krikor Sarkissian was embarrassed. It had taken him two and a half hours to get his party to the stadium and what should have been fun was turning into an orgy of frayed tempers. 'Sorry.'

They all, of course, muttered that it wasn't his fault; the roads were jam-packed with fans and the police, for reasons known only to them, had decided to close one of the access routes. If anything, the group ire was directed at İzzet Melik – all except that of Natasha Sarkissian. Hugging one of his

265

arms as she had started to do as soon as they entered the stadium, she whispered, 'Don't take any notice!'

'I . . .'

'Oh look!' Momentarily she let go of İzzet's arm and pointed across the vast green centre of the stadium towards the great ranks of seats opposite. 'Isn't that Diego Maradona? Over there in that box?'

Krikor, squinting over the top of his glasses, looked in the direction in which she was pointing and said, 'Oh, yes. Yes, it is! My goodness, but he's lost weight! Last time I saw him on television he looked like a football.'

'I think you'll find Maradona is commentating for the Spanish TV network,' Abdullah Ceylan said with the sort of sobriety of tone people expect from a lawyer.

'Oh.'

Natasha hugged herself still closer into İzzet's side and said, 'Isn't it exciting! I'm so excited now I'm here! Watching this match with you, a policeman!'

Aware of the fact that Hatice Arslan, at least, was looking at what Natasha was doing with some distaste, İzzet tried to put a little mental distance between himself and Natasha. 'I am still going to support Milano, you know,' he said.

It wasn't that he didn't fancy her. He did. But if he picked up on her very obvious signals and even began to reciprocate, that could spell trouble. Dr Arto Sarkissian was his superior and would not, İzzet felt, be very pleased at the idea of a nobody like him coming on to his cousin. What Mehmet Süleyman would think, and maybe even do about such a breach of etiquette, he didn't like to imagine.

'Well, I couldn't possibly respect a man who changed his footballing allegiances, even if it was for me,' Natasha said, pouting puckered, amused lips as she did so. 'Football is important.'

'Yes.'

Opposite, there was a great band of red, waving scarves, as the fans swayed and sang what Natasha, for one, recognised as 'You'll Never Walk Alone'. Liverpool supporters had been allocated approximately two thirds of the tickets to the Olimpiyat Stadium – the strength of their voices made their numbers sound far greater even than that. As soon as the elaborate opening ceremony was over and most of the players had crossed themselves, the two captains went to the centre of the pitch with the referee. It was time to see who was going to have the honour of kicking off.

'I didn't mean for you to get involved!' Handan Sarıgul said as she took a glass of tea from Estelle Cohen's hand. 'I – we – Rafık and me, we only came to see Mrs Cohen. For advice. Because Mr Cohen was a policeman, in the past.'

'But Sergeant Farsakoğlu and myself happened to be here,' İkmen said. 'And Mrs Sarıgul, whichever way you look at it, you would have been obliged to come to us at some point. What your son has told us could be very important.'

Ayşe Farsakoğlu handed Handan Sarıgul a tissue with which to dry her eyes. The last few minutes had been very emotional for the shoe seller's sister. Rafık, whilst cutting out football pictures from newspapers, had come upon the photograph of a face that he recognised. It was the woman he'd seen his Uncle Ali with down in the basement of the shop. He didn't know when he'd seen her exactly, just that it had been a Monday because that was his day off. He'd gone off to be with his friends as he usually did on a Monday, but then he'd gone back towards the end of the afternoon to pick up the new shoes he'd bought for himself from his uncle the previous Saturday.

'We were going to go out, Adnan and me,' the boy had told İkmen. 'So I went back to get my new trainers. The shop was shut, which was unusual, but I didn't think much of it. Sometimes, on a Monday, Uncle Ali does shut up because he is alone – to eat or count stock or whatever. I let myself in, heard some voices down in the cellar. Uncle Ali was with this woman, doing, having . . . well, you know . . . Her eyes were closed and . . . they didn't see me, either of them. I'd never seen Uncle Ali like that before! I . . . I left, without the shoes, quietly. I told no one until I told Mum just now. My uncle has a temper and I try not to upset him. Me seeing *that* would upset him, I think – not that I've ever seen him do *that* before. I wouldn't have told even my mum if this woman, this Emine, hadn't been in the paper.'

İkmen had been tempted to really crack into the boy about how important it was to read parts of the newspapers that were not just concerned with sport, but he restrained himself. In a country where entire newspapers were dedicated just to football he knew that he was swimming against the tide. With regard to his own viewing of the latest 'big match' he knew that that was probably now well and truly on the back burner. Mr Paksoy would have to be spoken to at the very least.

'Mrs Sarıgul,' he said, 'is your brother at home now, do you know?'

'In the flat above the shop? No,' she said, 'I don't think so.'

'Uncle Ali isn't watching the game,' Rafik said. 'He doesn't like football and he doesn't have a TV. When Mum and I came past, the shop was shut and everything was quiet. He could be out – or in the basement. He might be counting stock on . . .' He looked down at the floor, obviously disturbed by his recent memory. 'I don't know if it was the 9th when I saw that lady with him, Inspector,' he said. 'It could have been the week before.'

'It doesn't matter,' İkmen said. 'You saw your uncle with a woman who is missing and we need to talk to him about it.'

'Oh God! Oh God!' Handan Sarıgul said. 'What on earth is Ali going to say when he knows it was Rafik who told you? He pays our rent; my son and I will be out on the street!'

Estelle Cohen, who had been sitting next to Handan all the time, said, 'My dear, I'm sure that this is all perfectly innocent. Your brother is a good man. And if he can indeed account for his time with this lady, I'm sure that the inspector will explain to him why you did what you did. He will understand.'

Rafik, who wasn't so sure, but who also desperately wanted to get back to Adnan's house and the football, cleared his throat.

'The boy wants to get back to watching his football,' Balthazar Cohen said in a tone which suggested his own disappointment at not getting his own short trip out.

'If you, Mrs Sarıgul, will accompany us,' İkmen said, 'then Rafik, provided he gives us his shop keys, can go back to his friend.'

Ayşe Farsakoğlu looked at him doubtfully. This was very much against accepted procedure.

İkmen, well aware of what his deputy was thinking, turned to the boy and said, 'Rafik, I'll let you go provided you don't tell your friends anything about your uncle or what we've discussed here.'

'When I left I told Adnan that I'd forgotten something at

home,' Rafik said. 'I won't say a thing.' His face, alive with eagerness, almost shone in what was now the gathering dusk. 'I'll keep my mobile phone switched on so you can talk to me if you want to. I don't mind if you ring during the match.'

İkmen smiled. 'Well, that will be helpful, Rafik,' he said.

The boy stood up to go, but İkmen made him sit down for just a little bit longer. 'Just one more thing,' he said. 'You know that your uncle has a friend called Mr Loya, Edmondo Loya?'

'Yes.'

'Do you know if Mr Loya has ever been out to help your uncle clean his Fiat? Your grandfather's car?'

'Not that I know of,' Rafik said and then, jumping again to his feet, 'Can I go?'

'We all used to go out in that car years ago,' Handan Sarıgul said. 'Father let Ali drive and he would take a lot of us out from time to time. Myself, Garbis the Armenian, girlfriends the boys had, and Edmondo, too.'

'But you haven't seen Mr Loya at your brother's garage in recent years?'

'No. But then I'm not always with him when he goes to the car.'

'I . . . can I go now or . . . ?'

'Inspector, will you let the boy go back to his football!' Balthazar said. 'It's important!'

İkmen looked up into Rafik's pleading eyes and then said, 'Off you go.'

'Thank you!'

There had been a moment, when he'd first shown his mother Emine Aksu's picture in the paper when Rafik had thought he'd never get back to see the match. He thought at one point that he might have to confront Uncle Ali himself.

But happily that was now all in the past and he was going back to Adnan's. As he ran past the pretty young woman just walking in to the Cohens' garden from the street, he whooped with delight.

Hulya İkmen Cohen frowned when she saw the speeding Rafik and, looking across the garden at her father, she said, 'Dad? What is going on?'

'Your father, my friend, has just ruined my evening,' her father-in-law, Balthazar Cohen said, miserably.

Kick-off for the Liverpool versus AC Milan match was scheduled for 8.45 p.m. But ever since 8 p.m. the city had been visibly and audibly calming down. At 8.15, most of those due in to the stadium were inside and everyone else was either watching the action at home or in drinking establishments – both those that served alcohol and those that did not. By 8.30, only real oddities were still on the streets. That Çetin İkmen, Ayşe Farsakoğlu and Handan Sarıgul didn't consider themselves odd was neither here nor there, but as they walked through the streets of Balat towards the shoe shop, people in homes around and about looked upon them with incomprehension.

The same was true when Mehmet Süleyman arrived at the Loyas' house accompanied by a visibly reluctant Constable Yıldız. He had desperately wanted to watch the match. But he was also on duty and Süleyman had insisted.

'Come back when the match has finished,' one of the Loyas' neighbours said as he hung out of the window of his apartment. 'As I told that policewoman hours ago, Maurice is at the stadium.'

'And Edmondo?' Süleyman called up to the man.

'God knows!'

'You've not seen him come out?'

'That policewoman banged on the door fit to waken the dead!' the neighbour said. 'But there was no reply. I've not seen him go out, but that doesn't mean much. Weird man, creeping around, always has done. World of his own, that one!'

He then shut the window again and returned to the blaring television in his living room.

After what he considered to be a decent pause, Constable Yıldız said, 'Sir, it seems we're not going to have a lot of success looking for this man tonight.'

'On the contrary, Constable,' Süleyman replied. 'With the streets as empty as they are, this is the perfect time to move around easily.'

'Well . . .'

'And we will need to check and see whether in fact Mr Loya has returned to his home.' Süleyman pointed the young man towards the front door. 'You knock, I'll go around the back.'

The fact that he was smiling when he said it only made Hikmet Yıldız all the more irritated.

Up at Paksoy's shoe shop, Handan Sarıgul was opening the front door.

'Ali?' she called as she went inside. 'Brother?'

Both she and İkmen had knocked on the door for quite some time before the policeman suggested that she use her key.

The body of the shop was quite empty. Sad little pairs of plastic shoes sat on the shelves like gloomy reminders of a previous time. Handan Sarıgul shook her head. She didn't often come into the shop these days. 'It's only when Rafik orders some new trainers that anything remotely stylish comes into this shop. My brother lost heart long ago.' And then she shouted up the stairs that led up from the office at the back to the apartment above, 'Ali!'

İkmen, who was a little behind the shoe maker's sister, turned to Ayşe Farsakoğlu and said, 'Are you armed?'

She was used to this. Whenever a potentially violent situation was in the offing he always asked her. It was, she knew, because although he was wearing a gun, he was not. It wasn't loaded. If, İkmen always asserted, he couldn't talk his way out of trouble, he probably deserved to be shot. Ayşe, however, was another matter, in his mind, and he insisted that she was always ready to protect herself.

'Yes, sir,' she said.

'Good.'

They followed Handan up the stairs and into Ali Paksoy's apartment. They found her standing in the kitchen. It was a small, basic, intensely old-fashioned room. There was no refrigerator, just one of those old wooden cabinets covered with thin mesh to keep the flies out. Inside, İkmen knew, there would be either tiles or a slab of marble on which milk and butter would be placed in order to keep them cool. Even his own cheap kitchen was better than this.

Handan, looking around, still shaking her head, said, 'My brother has altered so little since our father died.'

'May I go into the other rooms, Mrs Sarıgul?' Ayşe asked.

'Yes, of course,' she said.

İkmen started to speak. 'Mrs Sarıgul—'

'They said that Edmondo Loya killed that woman,' she said as she looked down at the old, scarred table in the middle of the room. 'But then you let him go. Why was that, Inspector?'

'Lack of evidence,' İkmen replied. 'I cannot hold someone on no evidence, even if that person confesses.'

She walked once around the table, touching its surface as she went. 'Do you think that Edmondo and my brother, or just my brother on his own . . .'

'Mrs Sarıgul, until I can speak to your brother, I won't know what he may or may not have done,' İkmen said. 'Mr Loya, too, doesn't seem to be in the area at the moment.'

'You think they may be together?'

'I don't know,' İkmen said. 'Do they go out together much, do you know?'

'Edmondo is often out and about, everyone knows that,' she said. 'But my brother doesn't often leave the shop. When he's alone he sometimes doesn't answer the door because he wants to stay on his own. I offer to cook for him, but he rarely comes over for a meal. I do his washing.'

Ayşe Farsakoğlu came in from one of the other two rooms and said, 'He's not here, sir.'

A great roar of voices burst out of the kebab shop at the end of the street where a huge group of men were watching the football on the television.

'Not even a minute, by my calculation,' Krikor Sarkissian said as he looked down at his extremely sophisticated watch. 'Less than a minute!'

İzzet Melik sat down in his seat again and let his arms rest by his sides. Milan had scored! In, Dr Sarkissian was quite correct, less than one minute, Paolo Maldini had scored for AC Milan!

'He's thirty-six, you know!' İzzet said excitedly. 'Paolo Maldini, he's thirty-six!'

Natasha, frowning, said, 'That's not very old.'

'That's ancient for a footballer,' her cousin called across at her.

'Yes, I know, but . . .'

Krikor Sarkissian nudged İzzet Melik on the arm. 'Natasha is just bitter that the Italians are winning,' he said. 'But then they have come out fighting, haven't they?'

'Absolutely!'

'A fabulous goal.'

It had been. The entire Italian side of the stadium had risen to its feet in the wake of it. Whether in jubilation or despair, everyone had reacted in some way. The Liverpool supporters had booed and whistled their disapproval.

As play began after the celebrations, Natasha Sarkissian rose to her feet and shouted, in English, 'Liverpool! Come on, you Reds!'

'Sir, there's nobody in and I think I just heard someone score in the football,' Constable Yıldız said as he ran breathlessly up to Süleyman.

'Didn't I tell you to knock on the front door?' A scandalised Süleyman said. He'd only left the boy a few moments earlier.

'Yes, sir, but there's clearly no one in and—'

'Constable, he could be walking out of the front door right now! I don't care what's happening in the bloody football, get back round there and stay by that front door until I tell you to stop!'

Yıldız put his head down and began to walk very slowly down the small alleyway that led to the back of the Loyas' property.

'Quicker than that!' a disgruntled Süleyman shouted at him.

Once the young man had gone, Süleyman looked up at the thick walls that surrounded what İkmen had told him was a considerable garden. At the very back of the plot there was a thick, wooden gate which was apparently locked from the other side. Like so many of these old Fener 'palaces', the Loyas' great pile was in effect a small fortress, built to withstand both time and possible invasion.

Something else that İkmen had told him, of course, was that the chamber his officers had found underneath the basement, the one containing all those old bottles of opium, had a door which led out into the garden. According to İkmen it was a very small door and was hidden behind a dilapidated wooden garage, now no longer occupied by any sort of vehicle. There were no other out-houses or workshops and so if Edmondo Loya was on the property he was either in the house, the garden or the shed. Whether or not voices from outside could be heard from the chamber under the basement he didn't know.

For the second time since he'd been there he called out, 'Mr Loya, it's Inspector Süleyman from the police, can I talk to you, please?'

Again there was no response. Süleyman looked down at his watch. He'd give him another two minutes, then he'd go and get Yıldız. He looked up at the great dark wall to his left and tried to feel confident about scaling it. Maybe the young constable would be better suited to that task? Poor Yıldız. He had so wanted to see the football match. Süleyman himself had heard a roar from the streets round about that signified something a few minutes before. Not a half-deflated thing like the roars that sometimes accompanied missed opportunities, this roar had been wild and full-throated. Someone had obviously scored. For his own sake, if nothing else, he hoped it was Liverpool. Zelfa would be impossible if the Italians won this game.

*　　*　　*

Ali Paksoy wasn't in the basement either, which left only one place that he could be.

'He used to play down here when he was a child,' Handan Sarıgul said as she unlocked the door to the Byzantine chapel underneath the shoe shop.

'And you?' İkmen asked. 'Did you used to play down here too, Mrs Sarıgul?'

She looked to the side of the now open door for the torch her brother always had there, ready for use in the chapel, and found that it was gone. Leaning in to the darkness below, she called out, 'Ali?'

But no one replied. She turned to İkmen and said, 'The torch my brother uses down there has gone.'

İkmen looked at Ayşe, who raised an eyebrow before opening her handbag and taking out a small black cylinder.

'It's all right, Mrs Sarıgul,' İkmen said. 'Sergeant Farsakoğlu and I both have torches. If you don't mind us going in front of you . . .'

Handan stepped quickly out of their way. 'You're welcome,' she said and then, shivering slightly, added, 'Horrible place!'

'You don't like it?' İkmen lit up the stairs beneath his feet before training the beam from his torch on the massive vaulted ceiling above.

Ayşe, now at the bottom of the rough stone staircase, lit the steps for Handan as she descended. 'My brother liked to play here,' she said when she reached the bottom. 'But it was always too dirty for me. Father didn't encourage either of us to have friends when we were little and so Ali used to play down here on his own. He should've had a brother, poor Ali.'

İkmen, who was in the chapel for the first time, took a

277

few minutes to have a good look around. Like Süleyman, he tested the walls with his knuckles and the ground below with his feet. Everything sounded very solid. Ayşe was once again fixated on the fresco above the trough-like structure. Handan Sarıgul came over to join her.

'I think that maybe it was that picture that made me so dislike this place initially,' she said.

'It's not very good,' Ayşe replied.

'Whether it is or isn't, it's still a representation of a person, and in Islam we're taught to abhor such things aren't we?' Handan said.

İkmen, who had now come over to join the women, frowned. 'I think it's quite good, actually,' he said as he shone his torch directly on to the preternaturally rounded head. 'The exaggerated stylisation is typically Byzantine; look at the frescos in the Aya Sofya or the Kariye. Has the Ministry of Culture seen this?'

'No, sir,' Ayşe said. 'Apparently not. Inspector Süleyman informed Mr Paksoy it was his duty to contact them.'

'Indeed.' He then turned to Handan Sarıgul and said, 'Well, your brother isn't here, is he?'

'No.'

'I take it there's no alternative entrance to or exits from this place?'

'Not that I know of,' Handan replied.

'Oh, well, then, it would seem that your brother really is out, Mrs Sarıgul,' İkmen said and, ushering her in front of him with his torch, he added, 'Let's go.'

She moved forward towards the stairs and the light from the basement door above. İkmen followed. Only Ayşe Farsakoğlu didn't move from her seemingly fixed position beside the fresco. It was only when İkmen was halfway up the staircase that he realised that she wasn't following him. He turned. 'Sergeant?'

'Sir,' she said, as she shone her torch into the deep niche underneath the picture, 'this is the place.'

'The place you felt something?'

'Yes. It looks a bit different now.'

He shone his torch down towards her face and noted the strain that he saw there. This wasn't just a silly notion she was having here, this was something that could just be real.

He turned to Handan Sarıgul again and said, 'That niche, or whatever it is beneath that fresco, do you know what it is?'

Handan pulled a face. 'Another reason why I never would go down there.'

İkmen frowned.

'It's a well, Inspector,' she said. 'There's a wooden lid, it must still be there, underneath a lot of dirt and stones. You can, if I remember rightly, move the lid from either up here or down in the well.'

'That's why it looks different, I can see wood underneath the stones this time! Mr Paksoy didn't tell Inspector Süleyman anything about a well,' Ayşe said. 'He said he thought this thing might be a baptismal font.'

'Take it from me, it's a well,' Handan said. 'I've seen it. It's absolutely terrifying.'

Getting over the wall into the Loyas' garden had proved easier than Süleyman had imagined. He was actually rather fitter than he had thought – either that or Hikmet Yıldız was very strong. The boost the young man had given him to get him on top of the wall had been considerable, but he'd still had to get down into the garden under his own steam. This

279

he had managed with some ease, if not aplomb. Now standing on the small patch of grass in front of the great door at the back of the garden, he looked at the padlock that held it shut with alarm. It was not only new, but was huge and complicated and there was no handy key swinging from a rusty nail in the wall to be seen anywhere. He could of course shoot the thing off, but then he didn't actually have a warrant that allowed him to do so. He wasn't the only one who knew it.

'Sir, we're not supposed to be here, are we?' the now invisible Yıldız said from beyond the great wooden door.

'I need to speak to Mr Loya about how his fingerprints came to be on Ali Paksoy's car,' Süleyman said. 'I feel this is a matter of urgency. Also, in view of his recent experiences, I do have concerns for his safety.'

'You think he might've topped himself, do you?'

'I don't know.' According to İkmen, Edmondo Loya had been very, very depressed upon his release from police custody. Even when he was placed into a squad car to carry him home, he was still protesting his guilt. Whatever Edmondo Loya may or may not have done to or with Emine Aksu was not strictly Süleyman's concern. But whichever way one looked at it, Edmondo Loya was clearly, guilty or no, not a 'normal' everyday sort of individual. He was far too troubled for that.

'I'll just go and see if the back door is open,' Süleyman said as he made his way over to a solid red door just to the left of the derelict garage. But as it happened, he didn't need to go over to see that it was open. Although not swinging free exactly, the door was open enough to allow him to see the refrigerator as well as several other units in the Loyas' kitchen.

'It's open,' he called to Yıldız over the wall. 'If you go around to the front door, I'll let you in.'

'Sir.'

He remembered the main body of the house. The dark halls, the extravagant displays of Toledo steel. It was odd to Süleyman that after five centuries of living in Turkey the Loyas still surrounded themselves with memories of a country which they not only didn't know, but which also had actively rejected them. Even the speaking of Ladino, the Hebrew-Spanish elision still spoken by so many of the İstanbul Jews, was, when he thought about it, somewhat strange. His friend Balthazar Cohen had once told him that the speaking of Ladino was as much about not being understood by outsiders as it was about preserving identity. But even so, this overtly Spanish house was really quite creepy.

He opened the door to Yıldız just as someone, given the wild whoops coming from the coffee house in the next street as well as from the Loyas' neighbours, scored a goal over in the Olimpiyat Stadium.

Chapter 17

İzzet Melik looked down at Natasha Sarkissian and smiled.

'We scored again,' he said.

Thirty-nine minutes into the first half, a cross from Andriy Shevchenko found Hernan Crespo, who put a resounding second goal into the back of the net for AC Milan.

'I'm sorry to say so, Natasha,' Süleyman Arslan the geneticist said, 'but Liverpool are playing appallingly.'

'I know,' she said miserably. 'I know!'

İzzet, now most definitely on a roll of joy said, 'But Milano – Milano are just playing like a dream!'

'Steady,' Abdullah Ceylan the lawyer said. 'Not like this is one of our teams here.'

'No, but—'

'You're very keen on Milan, aren't you, İzzet?' Krikor said. 'Knowledgeable. Have you been interested in Italian football for very long?'

Play started again and so İzzet looked away from the doctor while he answered him. 'There's always been quite an Italian community in my home city, İzmir.'

Italians all over the stadium lit large and very bright flares.

'Oh, İzmir, yes,' Krikor said.

'My parents had a friend, a Jewish man, whose ancestors had come from Italy. He gave Italian lessons. My father paid for my brother and myself to go to him. I loved the language.'

A tense hum filled the stadium now as the Liverpool fans started to get themselves back together again for their team. Some of them began singing 'You'll Never Walk Alone'. Natasha Sarkissian, with an acid glance towards İzzet, began to join in.

'You've been to Italy?' Krikor continued.

'Venice,' İzzet said. 'But only once, unfortunately.'

'You liked it?'

'I loved it,' İzzet replied. 'Everything about it. The place, the food, the people . . . Of course, they dress so well it does make you feel a little bit scruffy, but I don't mind. You know D – Krikor, I think that I could just wander from city to city in Italy and be perfectly happy only to look.'

For an outwardly rough man like İzzet to express almost spiritual feelings like this was quite surprising and Krikor inwardly applauded him for it. But then something happened on the pitch that made absolutely everyone in that stadium rise to their feet.

It was pitch-black down in the well. Deep, too. When one or two of the stones that had been scattered over the top of the wooden lid fell into it, several long seconds passed before a faint 'plop' was heard as they hit the water below. But İkmen and Ayşe Farsakoğlu hadn't had to scrape much detritus off the lid in order to find it. Unlike the first time she'd seen it, Ayşe could now tell that the bottom of the niche was made of wood. Someone had obviously moved some little stones and soot on to the lid to make it appear undisturbed. But because they, in her opinion, had to apparently do this from below, the plan had failed.

All three of them leaned over the lip of the niche, staring into the utter absence of light.

'I can see why it might have frightened you, Mrs Sarıgul,' İkmen said.

'So let's close it up, then,' Handan said as she pushed herself away from the thing. 'Go and look for my brother.'

İkmen was about to follow her, when he saw the expression on Ayşe's face. 'Sergeant?' He bent back down again in order to speak to her.

'Sir, this is the place!' she whispered earnestly. 'The place I, you know, I had the feeling about.'

'Ayşe, it's a well. We can investigate it further later. But now we need to find Mr Paksoy.'

'Sir, there's a ladder going down the side of the shaft,' Ayşe said as she pointed her torch towards the left side of the old brick-built tube.

'For maintenance, yes.'

'Sir,' Ayşe moved still closer to him and said, 'someone has moved the lid of this well since I came here with Inspector Süleyman. There was no way you could have seen that wooden lid when I first looked at it. And Paksoy lied about what it was. It's a well, and he knew it was a well.'

'So what do you suggest that we do about it?' İkmen said.

'When we came in here, Mrs Sarıgul said that the torch her brother usually keeps by the door to the chapel was missing,' Ayşe said.

'Yes.'

'And with the dust and soot disturbed on the lid of the well . . .'

'You think he might be down there somewhere, don't you?' İkmen said. 'Ayşe, it's a well, it goes down into water and that's it.'

Still looking down into the hideous darkness, Ayşe said, 'We think that's it, but what if it isn't? What if there's yet

285

another shaft off from the main body of the well, what if, yes, what if he is down there? I think the lid of the well was closed from below. Sir, Mr Paksoy was, we know now, having some sort of fling at the very least with Mrs Aksu. We need to talk to him! Whether he's down there or not we need to speak to him. I am prepared to go down myself, sir.' She looked deep into his eyes. 'You know how I feel about this!'

He smiled and then placed a hand on her shoulder. 'Yes, I understand,' he said. 'But I can't let you go down into that.' He tipped his head slightly towards the well. 'I'd never forgive myself if anything happened to you.'

'But sir, you don't like heights!'

İkmen stood up. 'I don't like murderers and rapists but I have to come into contact with them because that's my job.'

'What's going on?' Handan Sarıgul said. 'What are you talking about?'

İkmen took a cigarette out of his packet and put it into his mouth. 'I'm just going to take a look down your brother's well,' he said.

Handan Sarıgul's eyes widened. 'You think he's down there? Ali?'

'Who knows?' İkmen shrugged. 'But we must explore every possibility.' He then lit up his cigarette and swung one leg over the niche and into the well.

'Mr Loya! Edmondo!'

Only God knew how many bedrooms were in that house! When he got to seven Süleyman gave up counting. All beautifully fitted out and decorated – or rather they had been about a hundred years before; the bedrooms were uniformly huge and, even in spring, decidedly chilly.

'Sir, I don't think he's here!' Yıldız called up from one of

286

the rooms below. 'It says on the television that it's half-time now and it's 3–0 to AC Milan. 3–0! Amazing! Sergeant Melik will be delighted.'

Süleyman, furious, lunged his head and shoulders over the banisters so that he could see the floor below. 'Constable Yıldız, have you switched on Mr Loya's television?'

'Well, er, yes . . .'

'A suspect's things! You're touching and using a suspect's goods in his own home! I don't believe you, Yıldız! You—'

'Sir, it's football, it's important!'

'No, it isn't!' Süleyman yelled down into the dark, echoing Toledo steel-lined hall below. 'It's a fucking game, Yıldız! Now switch that television off and then get into that old garage out in the garden.'

A barely audible recognition of what had been said slipped from Hikmet Yıldız' mouth. 'Sir.'

'When I've done here, I'm going to the basement,' Süleyman said. 'I'll see you in the garden, Yıldız.'

Although he couldn't exactly see what was happening, İkmen knew that the ladder he was on was very rusty. As he put his hands and feet on each rung, gritty, wispy bits kept coming off and falling silently into the water below. He knew his knuckles were white as he descended because he was gripping on so tightly that it hurt. Thank God for the cigarette that still burned brightly between his lips! At least while he was smoking he was on nodding terms with real life. Doing things on the say-so of his own intuition was one thing, but to do so much on the hunch of another . . .

'Sir, are you OK?' Ayşe called down.

The temptation to respond with the words 'Never better'

was strong, but he resisted. 'Fine,' he mumbled through his cigarette.

'What?'

'Fine!' he said again, louder this time, losing his precious cigarette to the oily water below as he did so. 'Damn!'

'Sir?'

'It's all right,' İkmen said. 'I've just lost my cigarette, that's all.'

'See anything?'

Now that he was over a metre down he needed to get his torch in order to see anything. As his mind reeled away from the horror of what he was doing, İkmen put one shaking hand into the pocket of his trousers and withdrew his torch. Logically he knew that holding on to the aged ladder with one hand was probably no less safe than holding on with two, but it still terrified him. In fact, once the torch was switched on, he could see that if necessary he could brace himself against the opposite wall of the shaft. He could also see that the ladder was indeed covered with rust, although wear was discernible on the treads too. Someone had been down here in living memory, he felt.

'So what can you see?' Ayşe called down.

'What, you mean beyond a ladder that is barely connected to the wall?'

'I don't know why you're doing this!' Handan Sarıgul said. 'Why are you doing this?'

'I wish I knew,' İkmen said. 'But for once it is not I who possesses a feeling, it is my sergeant.'

'It's ridiculous!' Her voice was further away now. She had moved back from the hated well, unable to stand it any longer.

After a pause during which he transferred his torch from his left hand to his right and then into his mouth, İkmen

288

began to make his way further down the ladder. If going down was this tough, what on earth would going up be like! His lungs were shot by so many years of smoking and he could hardly rely upon his poor white knuckles to take all of the strain. Had he carried on thinking about this as opposed to attending to his downward descent, he probably wouldn't have noticed when the toes of his shoes stopped scraping against the bricks at the side of the shaft. But fortunately Ayşe prompted him with yet another of her demands for an update and he stopped.

Moving very slowly downwards with the torch still firmly clamped between his teeth, İkmen noticed that the ladder suddenly went down past a cavity. What kind of cavity it was, wasn't immediately apparent, but that it was there at all was intriguing. As he descended he found, at first to his relief, that the toes of his shoes hit brickwork again quite quickly. Slowly the cavity came into view and would have gone, too, if something truly extraordinary hadn't happened. What looked like the uneven surface at the bottom of the cavity suddenly moved, rearing up with a violence that nearly made İkmen lose his footing. By the light of the torch in his mouth, İkmen could now see that the bottom of the cavity had a face and eyes that were looking into his pleadingly.

'Sir?'

Several minutes had passed since either of the women had heard anything from the well below and Ayşe, although she could still see İkmen, was concerned.

'Sir, what—'

'Sergeant Farsakoğlu, could you please call for back up and also alert the fire service. I think we'll need their assistance here,' İkmen said, his voice echoing sonorously up the shaft of the well.

Ayşe took her phone out of her pocket and then, calling down the well once again, she said, 'Sir, what shall I tell the station?'

'Tell them we've found Mrs Emine Aksu,' İkmen said. 'We will, however, need assistance from the fire service and their lifting equipment to get her out.'

Handan Sarıgul looked across at Ayşe and said, 'Is that the woman who was missing?'

Ayşe said it was before she began speaking into her phone, making requests on behalf of her boss.

Down in the well, İkmen still looked into the great dark eyes of what he could see was Emine Aksu but which possessed such a frightened, almost feral quality, that he was loath to move or even breathe too hard. God alone knew what she was doing down there, what she'd been through. But her arms were secured to the wall by what looked like a short chain. Fear and suspicion were the only emotions he could detect in her at the present. But once he heard Ayşe on the phone, he began to talk. Whether Mrs Aksu answered him or not wasn't important. If the fire service were to have any chance of getting her out of what looked like a maintenance shaft successfully, he had to try to ensure that she was calm.

'Mrs Aksu, my name is Çetin İkmen,' he said. 'I'm a police officer. We've been looking for you.'

She didn't move. Her still, shocked eyes didn't so much as flicker.

'My colleague at the top of the well is calling the fire service,' İkmen said. 'They have far more experience of getting people out of difficult situations than we do. But

290

I'll stay with you until they come. It's OK. You're safe now.'

'No!' The word came, he could hear, from a throat that hadn't been lubricated for a very long time.

'Mrs Aksu?'

She was shaking. Her feet, which were the part of her body closest to him, vibrated, making the heels of those very distinctive shoes of hers click and clack together like castanets. For one brief moment, İkmen took his eyes off her wild and bloodied face, propped up and straining to see him through the gloom, and watched as two little models of the Eiffel Tower floated up and down in her heels.

'You've got to go,' she said. 'Now!'

'And leave you? I'm not leaving you,' İkmen said as he looked down the shaft at her face once again. The chains at her wrists were shaking.

'Sir, we've got some uniforms on their way now and the fire service,' he heard Ayşe call down from above.

'Good.'

'Are you OK, sir? Do you want to come up and I'll take your place?'

He knew she knew how he was with heights. Not that she was any better, if she were honest.

'No, Sergeant, that's—'

'You must go!' the woman with the wild eyes said. Her teeth were clenched, muscles and veins standing out from her dirty temples.

'Mrs – I can't!' İkmen said. 'I—'

And then as he looked at her face he began to make out something that appeared to be moving about behind her head. A dark shape against the darkness of this shaft that stretched, God alone knew how far, horizontally underneath the shoe shop and the adjacent property. For a moment he didn't know what to do. If he told Emine Aksu that he knew she wasn't alone, would it cause the person with her to panic, maybe do something reactive and violent to her? He couldn't do or say nothing, but . . . it had been such a relief to find her alive that it hadn't occurred to him that she could still be in danger from anything apart from her current situation in the well. But she was. Now, as he looked as hard as he could at her face, he could see that there was a hand at her throat. It held something small, but chillingly metallic. The only person, as far as İkmen knew, to have real knowledge of the well and its secrets was obviously still in residence. He decided to speak directly to him.

'You know, Mr Paksoy,' he said, 'I realise that if that shaft you are in had an outlet into the street or even another building, you would have taken it. But it doesn't and so you are trapped. Maybe it's an overflow conduit for the well? Is that what it is, Mr Paksoy? Something to take up the water should the well flood, to protect the buildings up top?'

He heard a gasp from above, either from Ayşe Farsakoğlu or, more likely, from Ali Paksoy's sister.

'The fire service are on their way to get Mrs Aksu safely out of here,' İkmen continued. 'If you help them it will go easier for you, I give you my word. But if you impede us . . . I don't know what's happened here, Mr Paksoy, but I must urge you in the strongest possible terms to give yourself and that knife you're holding up – now.'

Chapter 18

'Crespo's scored again!' İzzet Melik was on his feet, screaming.

'Unbelievable!' Krikor Sarkissian, like all of the Italians in the stadium, was also on his feet.

'Amazing!'

'You couldn't make it up in your head,' Süleyman Arslan said. 'It's like some sort of football fairy story!'

'The English will never, ever come back from this now!' someone said against the deafening roars of both pleasure and pain that were coming from different parts of the crowd.

İzzet looked down at a very crestfallen Natasha Sarkissian and said, 'Sorry.'

Still sitting, hunched and obviously unimpressed, Natasha Sarkissian gave him an evil glare. All around the stadium despondent Liverpool fans texted their agony back to the northwest of England.

'Oh, well this is one match that is over,' Hatice Arslan said as she sat down once again to wait for play to recommence. 'What a shame it's so one-sided! I was expecting more from the English, I must say.'

As most people quietly resumed their seats and the players began to ready themselves for what was left of the first half, Natasha Sarkissian turned to her companions and said, 'Have any of you ever been to Liverpool?'

Krikor had once, many years before, but the closest anyone else had ever been was Manchester.

As play began again, Natasha smiled. 'Liverpudlians – "Scousers", as they call themselves – don't give up easily. It isn't over yet, not by any means,' she said.

The Loya brothers still hadn't had the wall İkmen's men had burst through repaired. The basement floor was covered with rubble: bricks, stone and plaster. Not that there was really very much in the basement anyway. The brothers, maybe because of its proximity to 'that' room that now lurked darkly at the end of the lighted basement, hadn't put a lot down there. An old push bike, some planks of wood, and a sack of coal seemed to be the main items stored. Edmondo Loya was most certainly not in here.

Mehmet Süleyman made his way to the end of the space and then clambered over the main pile of rubble by the wall. As he stepped through he shook his head, musing upon how so many of 'the men' so often left terrible messes in their wake. But then not all of their superior officers were that fussy about clearing up themselves. And, in truth, sometimes the owners of the property under investigation deserved no more than this. But not the Loyas. From what he'd seen of them they were a pair of rather eccentric, argumentative middle-aged men. Harmless, in most respects, except in Edmondo's case, to himself. Poor strange man, owning up to a crime he couldn't possibly have committed.

Süleyman took his torch out of his pocket and switched it on. Now emptied of their sinister narcotic bottles, the shelves around the walls looked just like normal racks used by normal people for storing tools and car parts and bicycles. There was no sign of any of the erotic magazines İkmen had told him about on the table. In fact, the only thing on the table was a large white envelope. Frowning, Süleyman approached it. It was then that he saw the shoes, old-fashioned brown brogues, above the table. He made straight for the door into the garden and flung it open.

'Yıldız!' he yelled desperately. 'Constable Yıldız!'

No immediate reply came from the person who held a knife to Emine Aksu's throat. In fact, so long did this total silence continue, that İkmen actually began to wonder whether he had been wrong to ascribe whatever was happening to Ali Paksoy.

'Mrs Aksu . . .'

'He's never going to let me get out of here alive!' she said. And then, in response to still firmer pressure from the knife, she first gasped and then became silent.

'We're all going to get out of here alive, including Mr Paksoy,' İkmen said.

He heard what sounded like a muffled argument from above.

'Ayşe?'

'I—' And then he heard her shout. 'No!'

'Ali! Ali my brother!' Handan Sarıgul yelled through her tears. 'Ali!'

Suddenly a face, dark with anger and meaty as a bullock, reared into İkmen's field of vision. He can't have heard his sister earlier. Now he had and he was trembling with the shock of it.

'Mr Paksoy,' İkmen said.

'Why is Handan here?' Ali Paksoy said as he continued to press the short skinning knife into the folds of Emine Aksu's neck.

'Your sister was concerned about you,' İkmen said. The metal ladder he was standing on was old and thin. Both the knuckles of his hands and the insteps of his feet were beginning to hurt now. 'We all wanted to know where you were.'

'Well, now that you do, I'd be obliged if you'd take my sister away,' Paksoy said. 'She's a good woman, a prayerful woman; she shouldn't be around things like this.' He looked down into the terrified eyes of Emine Aksu and leered.

'You think that Mrs Aksu is unworthy of your sister's attentions?'

Paksoy looked up, his several chins wobbling as he moved. 'She's dirty,' he said. 'With her dresses and her little feet and her shoes! Makes me dirty.' Then suddenly he shouted, 'She thought that she could just snap her fingers at me!'

'Mrs Aksu, you feel, was manipulating you?' İkmen said.

Somewhere at the bottom of the well something scampered into the water. Just briefly İkmen closed his eyes. He didn't have many phobias, but if that was a rat . . . In fact, there was only really the one and that was, possibly, scuttling about in the water below him at that moment.

'Oh, she thought she was manipulating me, but she wasn't,' Ali Paksoy said, his face sweating heavily as he spoke. 'I was manipulating her. Bitch. Thinks she's so wonderful! But I showed her!' He looked back down at her again and laughed. 'I showed you, didn't I lady!'

'For God's sake, he has sex with dead bodies!' Emine Aksu cried through shaking tears.

Ali Paksoy, silent now, failed completely to deny her words.

Süleyman's investigation. Paksoy's car had yielded evidence indicating that the so-called Kamondo Lady had been one of its more recent passengers. She had been assaulted. İkmen swallowed his revulsion and made himself

296

look into the face of this man he now knew to be a necrophiliac. His first ever case as a detective had involved one of this kind. He, too, had been a sweaty, leering and yet timid individual. A poor, pathetic inadequate. And yet from the bloodied and terrified state of Emine Aksu, it was clear that this example was not as benign as the creature İkmen had encountered all those years ago at the beginning of his career.

The sound of well-shod feet, as well as the deep tones of male voices coming from above, alerted İkmen to the fact that either his back-up or the fire service boys must have arrived.

'Mr Paksoy,' he said, 'my men have arrived. Unchain Mrs Aksu and move away from her now.'

'No!' He clung still tighter to her body, the knife in his hand now drawing a small trickle of blood from her neck.

Emine Aksu wept. 'I've been such a bad woman!' she said. 'Oh God help me!'

'Mr Paksoy,' İkmen said, 'you know that myself and my colleagues cannot let you leave here with Mrs Aksu as your hostage.'

He didn't answer.

'Inspector İkmen!' The familiar voice rang down into the well from above. It was that of one of his young fellow inspectors, Metin İskender. A boy from the slums originally, Metin had risen quickly through the ranks, had taken down several major criminals, and was famous for his uncompromising attitude towards offenders. İkmen looked up and saw Metin's young, handsome face looking down at him. He also saw the younger man's gun which was already in his hand.

'Ah, Inspector İskender,' İkmen said. Looking up now was beginning to make him feel dizzy and so he lowered his gaze almost immediately. 'We're all fine down here. Are the fire service men here yet?'

'Just arrived.'

'Good.' He looked across at Ali Paksoy. 'Mr Paksoy, in a moment I'm going to ask one of the fire officers to come and look at this ladder.'

'Why?'

'Because if they're going to bring Mrs Aksu up the ladder, the fire officers need to know it's not going to collapse underneath them. I'm basing this on the assumption that Mrs Aksu, from what I have observed, will not be able to get out by herself. I imagine her body must be quite weak. This ladder will have to hold the officer, Mrs Aksu and myself all at the same time.'

'You?'

'When Mrs Aksu has been taken away, I will remain behind with you,' İkmen said. 'You're not going to be alone in this, Mr Paksoy.'

'Don't treat me as if I'm some sort of child, some sort of lunatic!'

Obviously the empathic approach was not one that was going to work here. Maybe Ali Paksoy had had some sort of therapy for something in the past. From the sound of it, he hadn't been very open to that approach. But whatever had happened, didn't seem to have worked.

'And you're not having her, anyway!' the shoe seller continued angrily. 'At no point did I say that you could have her!'

Mehmet Süleyman slipped the knotted rope over Edmondo Loya's limp head and threw it to the floor. Constable Hikmet Yıldız, across the other side of that dark, poisoned little room, was telephoning for an ambulance. The small man propped up in Süleyman's arms blinked his bloodshot and swollen eyes slowly. The purple rope burns around his throat hurt and his still-constricted airway felt as if it would never work properly again.

'The constable over there is calling for an ambulance to take you to hospital,' Süleyman said. 'I'm going to leave an officer with you until the doctors have finished their work and then we're going to talk.'

Edmondo Loya made a few growling attempts at speech and then gave up. Weakly, he pointed at the envelope on the table.

'Your suicide note?'

Edmondo moved his head to indicate his assent.

'Should I read it now or do you want me to open it when I come and see you?'

He shrugged, as if it didn't matter. But then Süleyman imagined that it probably didn't now. When a person reaches the point where he's prepared to take his own life, little outside of that does matter. Poor Edmondo Loya. He had failed in so much during the course of his life: with women, with engaging with 'real' life, and now even this attempt to kill himself had failed. God alone knew how long he'd been hanging there slowly and inexpertly traversing towards an agonising death.

'Ambulance is on its way, sir,' Constable Yıldız said as he hunkered down beside Süleyman and his little, limp charge. 'Know why he tried to do it?'

'No,' Süleyman said. 'He can't speak yet and . . .' He looked down into those poor damaged eyes and then shook his head. Putting off finding out what was going on here wasn't really an option. 'Edmondo, once the ambulance arrives I'm going to have to read that note in case it contains evidence pertaining to your confession.'

Finally discovering something that approximated to a voice, Edmondo Loya rasped, 'It does.'

'I see.' Süleyman looked over at the table and then back at the man in his arms once again. 'Your confession was a lie, wasn't it?'

He paused for a moment before he whispered, 'Yes.'

'This is something you explain in your note.'

He indicated that it was, or rather he, inside, felt and hoped that it did. It had, after all, been written in haste and at a time when his brain had been literally boiling in his head. But then, when were suicide notes ever written under anything approaching calm circumstances? However worthless a person feels his or her life to be, death is never a thing that is easily embraced.

The chief fire officer was a man called İsmail Kanlı and, from the look of him, he'd been in the service for a very long time.

'It's as old as Byzantium,' he growled through his cigarette at Metin İskender. 'Not literally, you understand, but that ladder is dangerously corroded. I don't want to send anyone down there using that.'

They were far away from the well, over by the door that led back up into the basement of the shop.

'Do you think we should get Inspector İkmen out of there?' İskender asked.

'Definitely.' With his large fire helmet obscuring half of his face and his enormous moustache the other, İsmail Kanlı could have been any sort of age, from thirty to three hundred. 'The well itself seems sound enough,' he continued. 'Once your man is out I'll send one of my lads down on a rope. Do we know if the woman's badly hurt?'

'I don't know that she's hurt, exactly,' İskender said. 'She was a missing person and the opinion seems to be that she's been held prisoner down there, in that narrow shaft, for some weeks.'

'So she's unused to moving?'

'She must be weak and I imagine dehydrated, too.'

What could be seen of Kanlı's face, frowned. 'The man with the woman down there has a knife, you say?'

'Yes.' He sighed. 'As far as we know the shaft the two of them are in leads nowhere. It's a sort of maintenance platform – either that, or an overflow for the well.'

'So he's cornered?'

'Yes.'

'With a knife.'

'Indeed,' İskender said. 'And, of course, there's no way in that environment of safely taking a shot at him. I'll be honest with you, we cannot disable this man, nor can we be sure that he will not attack either that woman or whoever comes down on your rope. At the moment the woman is chained to a wall. But our man is trying to get the offender to release her.'

İsmail Kanlı nodded, thinking gravely through what was a very short list of options.

The sound of feet running on packed earth followed by a scream of 'Ali!' roused everyone from whatever thoughts or reveries they were having. In spite of Ayşe Farsakoğlu's insistence that she stay away, Handan Sarıgul was once again calling to her brother down the well.

'Handan!' Ali Paksoy looked at İkmen and said, 'I ask again what my sister is doing in a place like this!'

His hands were now so tightly fixed to the metal ladder, İkmen had serious doubts as to whether he could ever move again. That and his realisation that Ali Paksoy did not seem to be responsive to empathy brought about a change in his approach. 'Listen, Paksoy,' he said, 'if you want your sister to go, you'd better start co-operating. You can't escape. But you do have one choice here. That is for me to get your sister to go and we do this thing safely, and like human beings, or she stays and I tell her what I think happened here. Unchain Mrs Asku now, please!'

He didn't know for sure, but he imagined that sex of a type decent women like Handan Sarıgul would never even dream of had to be involved somewhere. If Emine Aksu were to be believed necrophilia had been involved.

'I have a very lurid imagination,' İkmen added.

The small rodent-like eyes darted from Emine Aksu's face to İkmen's and then back again.

'What she said, about loving the dead, it isn't true.'

'It is!' she countered. And then, as if suddenly and in spite of still being held at knife point nothing mattered any more, she said, 'Nothing more than a skeleton, it was! But he—'

'All right! All right!' Ali Paksoy's large face shook with both rage and misery. He looked across at İkmen again and said, 'Get my sister out of here!'

'Unchain Mrs Aksu from the wall and I will think about it,' İkmen countered. After a few seconds, the sound of a metallic lock being turned was clearly heard by Çetin İkmen.

The first Liverpool goal came in the fifty-fourth minute. Steven Gerrard headed it hard and fast into the corner of the net. Natasha Sarkissian rose to her feet and cheered with the rest of the Liverpool fans, but when she sat down again she was quiet. This seemed to represent, or so İzzet Melik felt, a new calm, if not downright smug, confidence. But then, ever since the start of the second half, Liverpool had been playing with far more confidence and élan. And when, just two minutes after Gerrard's triumph, Vladimir Smica put the Liverpudlians just one goal behind the Italians, even İzzet's faith in the Milanese began to waver.

'I told you,' Natasha said as she sat down from yet another bout of cheering, 'never underestimate the people of Liverpool.'

'That Smica is an Eastern European of some sort,' İzzet retorted. 'Not from Liverpool at all.'

'Oh, and all the Turkish teams have only Turkish players, do they?' Natasha shook her head playfully. 'When I meant Liverpool people, I meant everyone; all the supporters in the city and the team itself. Cities have vibes, you know. Like İstanbul has an ancient, melancholy air. Liverpool's vibe by contrast is very lively and argumentative and tough.'

'You think that İstanbul is melancholy?' İzzet said.

'To me it is, yes,' Natasha replied. Then, as she turned away to watch the match, she added, 'But maybe that's because I'm Armenian. Most things are melancholy to us.'

Except, apparently, for the city of Liverpool. İzzet wondered if that last comment of hers was meant to be a sort of veiled criticism of Turkey. Maybe it was her way of referring, albeit obliquely, to the alleged massacre of over a million Armenians by the Ottomans during the First World War. He personally had never believed in that story but maybe she, like a lot of the Armenian Diaspora, did. İstanbul wasn't melancholy! Vast, fast, dirty and totally absorbing, yes – or rather that was most certainly how he saw it. What was now becoming miserable, however, was AC Milan's football.

Liverpool continued to dominate the match from then on until, apparently in an act of sheer desperation, Gennaro Gattuso deliberately swept Steven Gerrard's feet away from him inside the penalty area. To an almost breathless silence inside the stadium, the referee awarded a penalty to Liverpool. As Xabi Alonso walked forward to place the ball on the spot, Natasha covered her eyes with her hands.

Stating the obvious, Süleyman Arslan said, 'If he gets this that'll equalise for Liverpool. Amazing! An hour ago, half an hour ago, who would have thought it!'

Chapter 19

That İkmen still wasn't out of the well when fire officer İsmail Kanlı was lowered into it was typical of the policeman. He had promised Ali Paksoy he would stay with him the whole time and he was determined to do just that. Even knife-wielding lunatics were due the odd break or two along the way.

'I understand this lady's got no injuries,' İsmail said as he drew level with İkmen's back.

'Not that I can see. She's unchained now,' the policeman replied. And then he said to Emine Aksu, 'Are you hurt?'

'I'm hungry and thirsty and my hands hurt where I've been chained up.'

'But you haven't actually been injured, bones broken or . . . ?'

'No.'

'So that nutter just sort of brought you down here and kept you, did he?' the fireman said with some anger in his voice. 'God, some—'

'Officer,' İkmen, his back locked so tight that he couldn't have turned to look at the fireman if he'd wanted, watched Ali Paksoy's features darken. The small skinning knife was still very close to Emine Aksu's jugular vein. 'Can we just get the lady out, please?'

'Certainly, although in order to do that, you'll have to get out of my way, Inspector.'

He was only partially blocking the shaft, but it was enough to impede any rescue attempt.

'Best thing would be for you to go down,' the fireman said. 'That way I'll have a clear passage up once I've got a hold of the lady.'

'Right.' He'd been holding on to the same rung of the ladder for a long time. Even moving down one step was going to be hard. As he did it, oh so slowly, he felt his arms, legs and even his head shake with terror. 'I'm sorry I . . .'

'Go at your own pace, Inspector. No hurry.'

'Sir, just be careful!' he heard Ayşe's urgent voice call to him from above. Not that her urgency was surprising. Every time he breathed hard a bit more fell off the ladder and into the dark water below.

After what seemed like hours, Emine Aksu's crazy shoes and the even more crazy sight of Ali Paksoy's face were replaced by deeper darkness and yet more small red Byzantine bricks. Above his head, İsmail Kanlı, the fireman suspended by a thick rope from the mouth of the well, swung himself over towards the maintenance shaft.

'I'm going to lift the lady out of here now.' İkmen heard him say.

Then Ali Paksoy said, 'I don't think that you are! Just because you're wearing a uniform—'

There was a terrible scream. Masculine, more of a bellow, really. İkmen, still tense and stiff on his rotting ladder, felt a terrible sense of foreboding. Against all of his instincts he looked up. The fireman, though at the shaft, with his arms actually in it, was shaking his head from which liquid appeared

306

to be pouring. It dripped down on to İkmen who knew immediately from its smell that it was blood.

'Ali Paksoy!' he shouted. 'If you don't stop this I will have your sister lowered into this well! I'll have her stand on this rotting ladder with me!'

Even if he hadn't known that Ali Paksoy was sensitive about his religious sister, İkmen would have used family to get to his man anyway. After all, what Turkish male would want his elderly mother or saintly sister to see him in an animalistic and compromised position? Whatever else might go by the wayside, family, even in modern Istanbul, was sacred.

'Officer,' İkmen called to the man up above him, 'are you all right?'

'Just a cut,' the fireman replied through tightly clenched teeth. 'I've got the lady.'

As if to underline this, İkmen heard a deep, female grunt. He then saw those peculiar shoes, stuck haphazardly on what he now noticed were swollen feet, curl themselves as far as they could around the fireman's calves. There was another grunt as the officer took her weight, and then he called up above, 'Get me out of this hell hole, will you! I've been fucking stabbed!'

Both firemen and police officers pulled on that rope like maniacs. Once at the top he heard the fireman say, 'The bastard went for my face!'

İkmen, blood-spattered and cold to the core, was now the only one left inside the well with Ali Paksoy.

Rather than climb straight up the ladder to get out of the well, İkmen only pulled himself up a couple of rungs. Level again with the shaft, he looked in silence at Ali Paksoy.

307

Metin İskender, who had spoken a few words to Emine Aksu, mainly to confirm her identity, now came to join Ayşe at the mouth of the well.

'Fire Officer Kanli's wound is only superficial. But to stab anyone in the face!' he shook his head in disbelief. 'He's going to go to the hospital along with Mrs Aksu.' He looked behind him as a group of fire officers lifted Emine Aksu up off the floor.

'I wish the inspector would come up now,' Ayşe said as she looked down into the well at the still silent figure of Çetin İkmen. 'That ladder isn't secure.'

'Someone needs to get that man out of the shaft,' İskender replied. 'He certainly wouldn't let you do it. You know better than any of us what your boss is like.'

What he said was true, if couched somewhat arrogantly, but that was just Metin İskender's character. İkmen was, for better or worse, getting the job done.

One of the younger fire officers joined them at the top of the well and said, 'Officer Kanlı has told a group of us to stay to assist you, sir. As you know, he doesn't trust that ladder and so we'll be on hand with our ropes and harnesses for your man down there and that "person" who stabbed our brother.'

Ayşe Farsakoğlu and Metin İskender exchanged a look. Firemen, like police officers, were very protective of their own. This young man and probably all of his fellows, too, could very possibly be bent on a little revenge should the opportunity present itself.

'In fact,' the young officer continued, 'what I'd like to do is throw a rope down for Inspector –'

'İkmen.'

'İkmen. He can tie it around himself. Extra insurance, sort

308

of thing.' He picked a coil of rope up from the chapel floor and made a large loop at one end.

'Good idea,' Metin İskender said. He called down to İkmen, 'Inspector! Fire officers are going to throw down a rope for you!'

İkmen looked up.

'Put it over your head and shoulders so it rests around your waist, sir!' the young fireman said as he began to lower the rope into the well. 'Extra insurance because of that ladder.'

'OK.'

While he was waiting for the rope to reach him, İkmen looked into the shaft at Ali Paksoy and said, 'The fire chief, the one you stabbed, doesn't trust this ladder.'

'It's OK,' the shoe seller muttered. 'It's always served me.'

'Hasn't it just!' İkmen grabbed hold of the rope and slipped it over his head and shoulders. 'How many women have you brought down here, Ali?'

'That isn't any of your business! That's a private matter!'

'I beg to differ.' Now that he had the security of the rope around his body and also now that he was alone with the shoe seller, İkmen felt more confident about taking a punitive stance. He couldn't after all pull such a large man physically out of the shaft, but maybe he could, with luck, persuade or even terrorise him to come out of his own volition. 'You can't stay down here for ever, Ali,' he said. 'You can't escape, and the longer this all goes on, the dimmer the view the judge will take of you at your trial.'

'I'm not going to trial!'

'Oh, I think that you are,' İkmen replied. 'And if you're thinking of harming yourself with that knife, forget it, because even halfway down this well I can save you. I may not be a doctor but I can staunch a wound and you and I both know if you cut yourself you'll be too weak to do anything about it.'

Ali Paksoy looked at İkmen with small eyes filled with hatred. Condensation on the side of the shaft dripped noisily into the well. 'I could throw myself down there!' he said.

'Into the well?' İkmen laughed. 'Do you know how deep it is?'

'Do you?'

'No. Why should I? I don't live here.'

It was rather like having a conversation with a truculent teenager. But then if Mr Paksoy was indeed a lover of the dead that would be consistent. The necrophiliac İkmen had come across early on in his career had exhibited, unlike this man, real arrested development, but Ali Paksoy was only a more intelligent and cunning version of that pathetic creature.

'The lady who had the shop before my father said that the well went on for ever,' Ali Paksoy said.

'Yes, she probably said it to stop little children, like you as you were then, from coming down here and hurting yourself,' İkmen replied.

'My father said it went on for ever.'

'Probably for the same reason,' İkmen said. And then losing patience with what to him seemed like wilful infantilisation, he cried, 'For God's sake, man, nothing goes on for ever! That is a fairy tale!'

'I—'

'Throw yourself down there and the chances are you'll drown if you're lucky, but more likely you will hit whatever is at the bottom of this well and break your back! Do you want to be a cripple for the rest of your life? A cripple in prison?'

Ali Paksoy's face was blank. But İkmen felt that something inside him was beginning to unravel. He looked up at his colleagues at the top of the well first and then he continued. It was time to get graphic.

'In prison, you know,' he said, 'men convicted of sex crimes can have a hard time. Other prisoners don't like them. The guards try to do their duty and protect them, but it isn't always easy. Let's be honest, they don't always want to. But if you're reasonably fit and mobile, you can generally protect yourself. Disabled men, however, well, they are very fair game, aren't they?' Ali Paksoy's eyes flickered with what could be shock. 'If you can't move they can do what they like to you, can't they? You can be everyone's "girlfriend"; a piece of meat to abuse and hurt and degrade beyond what I imagine even you can envisage, Mr Paksoy.'

'No.'

'Yes,' İkmen said. He heard that scuttling noise coming from the bottom of the well again, the one that could be the sound of a rat, and shuddered. He needed to end this thing before he went crazy himself. 'Not funny when it's you that's being used, is it?'

'Homosexuals!' Ali Paksoy put his head in his hands and began to sob. 'Unnatural!'

Coming from someone who had allegedly had sex with a corpse, the expression of such a prejudice was laughable. But İkmen wasn't even smiling now. Every bone, muscle and sinew was stretched to its limit as he flung an arm out to take the little skinning knife that lay in front of the weeping Ali Paksoy. Not that the shoe seller knew he had taken it until he took his hands away from his eyes and saw what İkmen was putting into his jacket pocket.

Gambling on the hope that Paksoy didn't have any other

311

weapon, İkmen said, 'Ali Paksoy, you have nowhere left to go. Let us get you out of there and then you and I can talk for a while. I need to know what has been going on here and I think that you, for once, need to face your life as a grown man.'

Süleyman opened the plain white envelope outside the room the hospital had allocated to Edmondo Loya. In accordance with what he imagined the man would want, he'd taken him to the Jewish Hospital – it was also the nearest, being within the confines of Balat.

The attending doctor, a tall, rather louche-looking individual, spoke to Edmondo in Ladino which he seemed to respond to with something approaching relief. Maybe it was the familiarity of the old? After all, someone of Edmondo's age would probably, just, have spoken Ladino at home with his parents.

'He'll be all right,' the doctor said to Süleyman after he had finished treating the wounds on Edmondo's neck. 'Luckily it was a very bad attempt at self harm. Most inept. There's no real damage done. I'll keep him in overnight. Got a brother, hasn't he? Where's he?'

Süleyman explained that Maurice Loya was currently at the football match over in İkitelli.

'No point trying to get hold of him, then!' the doctor said. 'Game's gone to extra time, so I've heard. Three-all. Amazing! You leaving a man here tonight or something?'

Süleyman told him that because Edmondo was implicated in a current investigation, an officer would have to be present outside his room until his discharge from the hospital. The doctor shrugged. 'OK with me,' he said. 'I'll get back to the TV now. Want to see some of this extra time, if I can. You can see yourself out, can't you, Inspector?'

Süleyman said that he could, but before he left the building he read Edmondo Loya's suicide note. It was addressed to no one in particular, but it told him about some things that he and İkmen knew or had surmised. It also told him some other things that were entirely new, if not totally unexpected.

Once outside the hospital, he tried to call İkmen on his mobile but found that he could only get through to his voice mail. After putting a card through the letter box at the Loya house asking Maurice Loya to contact him immediately, Süleyman got in his car and drove back to the station.

'Milan certainly have the best of the play,' Krikor Sarkissian said to İzzet Melik.

With the exception of a header from Shevchenko, which had been saved by the Liverpool goalkeeper Dudek in the 116th minute, the period of extra time had been mainly characterised by exhaustion. Two Liverpool players had been treated for cramp and now that it was both late and dark, the fans as well as the players were beginning to flag.

'Sadly, I think that it's going to have to go to a penalty shoot-out,' Abdullah Ceylan the lawyer said. 'That's most unsatisfactory! So little skill involved in that. Just down to the fickle finger of fate, I always feel.'

'Well, isn't everything?' Krikor said. 'Good God, Abdullah, you're a Muslim; you must believe that fate is the principal factor in every scenario, surely?'

Abdullah Ceylan wasn't a fool. He knew that the Armenian was only teasing him. With a very straight face he answered back, 'Ah, but Krikor, this is football! The beautiful game,

313

a contest of skill and endurance enacted between teams of modern-day gladiators!'

İzzet Melik, looking on, didn't know what to make of this till both Krikor and the lawyer laughed.

'Well, at least these men are really working for their enormous salaries for once!' the Armenian said. And then, shaking his head, he added, 'Gladiators! Good God, can you imagine these pampered creatures fighting for their lives!'

Natasha Sarkissian, who had been quiet until that moment, leaned across to İzzet and said, 'I bet you that if it comes to a penalty shoot-out Liverpool win.'

Frowning, İzzet said, 'You bet me what?'

She gripped his arm and winked lasciviously. 'Whatever you like,' she said.

Chapter 20

By the time he got back to the station, Çetin İkmen was exhausted. Grey and shaky, his appearance was, to Ayşe Farsakoğlu, cause for concern and she tried for some time on the journey back from Balat to get him to follow Mrs Emine Aksu to the hospital. But he wouldn't and, once he'd called Ahmet Aksu to tell him the good news about his wife and had had two glasses of tea and several cigarettes, he did indeed look very much better.

Ali Paksoy, now safely ensconced in a cell, had requested a lawyer, a Mr Eker. İkmen had never heard of him but that didn't mean that he wasn't going to offer the policeman a significant challenge. Although quite how Ali Paksoy could possibly mount any sort of defence based on anything other than insanity İkmen couldn't imagine.

'Çetin!'

He looked up from the paperwork he and Ayşe had spread across his desk into the face of Mehmet Süleyman.

'I tried to call you some time ago,' he said as he walked into the room and then embraced the older man for a moment. 'Now I know why you didn't answer. You were down a well!'

'A well with a very shaky ladder down one side,' İkmen said. 'If Sergeant Farsakoğlu hadn't been in attendance with her bottle of hand cream when the fire service pulled me out, I think that probably my fingers would have been clawed for all time. Massaging that stuff in brought them back to life. I tell you, Mehmet, I'm getting too arthritic for this job!'

'Nonsense!' He sat down. 'Where is Sergeant Farsakoğlu?'

'Downstairs waiting for Ali Paksoy's lawyer,' İkmen said.

Süleyman lit a cigarette. 'I heard you had him in custody. Found Emine Aksu alive, too, so I'm told. That must be a relief.'

İkmen, lighting up yet again, said, 'Yes. You know, when this investigation started, I was convinced that she was dead.' And then, as if to himself, he added, 'Maybe it was because she was indeed beneath the ground? In the well. It's one explanation. Unless I'm . . . unless I'm losing my skill . . .'

Mehmet Süleyman didn't usually get himself too involved in İkmen's more esoteric feelings and musings and so, sticking relentlessly to the known, he cut in, 'Çetin, I was at the house of Edmondo Loya earlier this evening. It was fortuitous.'

'Was it?' İkmen, still distracted by his own thoughts, said, 'I was going to go and see if I could find him myself before Ali Paksoy's nephew turned up at Cohen's and told us – Ayşe and myself – he'd seen Emine Aksu in his uncle's shop. He didn't know when but—'

'Çetin, Edmondo Loya tried to kill himself this evening,' Süleyman said.

İkmen looked up sharply.

'Tried to hang himself. Luckily he wasn't very good at it and young Yıldız and myself managed to save him,' Süleyman said. 'He planned it, however.' He pushed a piece of paper across the desk towards İkmen. 'Suicide note. I think that you should read it before you go in to interview Mr Paksoy.'

'We.' İkmen picked the letter up from his desk and said, 'We should interview Mr Paksoy. You and me.'

316

'My issue with him relates to his car,' Süleyman said. 'Nothing so serious as the false imprisonment of a woman.'

İkmen, reading, said, 'No? I think you'll find, my dear Mehmet, that it is.' Then when he had finished the note he looked up. 'Poor soul.'

'Edmondo Loya? Yes. But—'

'Emine Aksu has made an allegation against Ali Paksoy to the effect that she witnessed him having sex with a dead body,' İkmen said. 'I don't know how this happened but . . . one doesn't have to be a genius to realise that, given the evidence from Paksoy's car, that poor dead body could very well be your Kamondo Lady. And she in turn, if we look at Edmondo's note—'

'Incredible!' Süleyman put his cigarette out and then lit up another. 'He'll deny it, of course.'

'Of course.'

'You haven't got a statement from Mrs Aksu yet?'

'No, she's in hospital. But I have no doubt that she will be willing to give one,' İkmen said. 'And forensic are already all over that well underneath Paksoy's house. Mrs Aksu intimated that the dead body was kept in the same shaft where we found her and Mr Paksoy. This could be quite a tale, should Mr Paksoy choose to tell it to us.'

'If you like that sort of thing,' Süleyman said gloomily.

İkmen shrugged. 'It is our business my dear Mehmet. If people always behaved themselves and never ever gave in to their baser urges, you and I would be unemployed.'

Ayşe Farsakoğlu first knocked on İkmen's door and then walked in. 'Sir,' she said, 'Mr Eker is here. He looks a bit, well, agitated.'

İkmen took a deep breath and looked across at Süleyman.

'I wonder if he's angry at having been kept away from that football match?' he said.

The entire stadium erupted. It had been 3–2 to Liverpool with AC Milan to take one more penalty to keep them in the game. As Andriy Shevchenko placed the ball in front of the Liverpool goal and prepared to take the shot, İzzet Melik covered his eyes. If Shevchenko scored, AC were still in with a chance, if he missed . . .

A massive roar that mixed both pleasure and pain soared up from the crowd. Next to him Natasha Sarkissian screamed out something in English. He looked up and saw that she was smiling. Damn it!

'We are the champions!' she yelled. 'We are the champions!'

'Fabulous save by the English goalkeeper!' Krikor Sarkissian said to İzzet. 'It's a pity that you missed it, although I can understand why you did.'

'We lost!'

'Yes, but what a great match!' the Armenian said. 'I can't remember being this involved in a match and I wasn't supporting either side!'

In spite of himself İzzet smiled. After all it wasn't as if it had been his own team, Fenerbahçe, that had just dipped out on European honours. Italy was only his adopted second home and it had been a very, very exciting match. Out on the pitch the Liverpool players turned somersaults in delight in the churned-up grass.

'Thank you so much for giving me a ticket,' İzzet said to Krikor as they all waited for the presentation of the cup ceremony to begin. Supporters were waving dummy cups in the crowd now, but the real thing had yet to make an appearance.

'It's been a pleasure,' Krikor replied.

'And now, because WE won you must make good on our bet, Sergeant,' Natasha Sarkissian said as she sat down beside him and took one of his arms in hers.

'But we didn't set a bet or . . .'

'I think you should take me to dinner when we get back into the city,' Natasha said. 'Dinner and . . .' She smiled.

Her cousin, who had been watching her and listening to what she had been saying, asked İzzet if he would mind if he leaned across him. 'I need to speak to Natasha.'

'Of course.'

Even though his face was not turned towards him, İzzet could see that Krikor was frowning. 'Stop playing around, Natasha,' he said in English. 'You're not in London now. This man is one of Arto's colleagues. I know what you're like. Leave him alone!'

'Afraid I'll break his poor little heart, are you?' she said spitefully. 'Oh grow up, Krikor! He's a great big thing! He can take care of himself!'

'Maybe,' her cousin replied. 'But you leave him alone or you'll have me to answer to! I won't be embarrassed by you here. In England I don't care, but I have to live here, so leave the man alone!'

Pouting like a child, Natasha Sarkissian turned away.

'I'm sorry about that, İzzet,' Krikor said as he moved back into his seat once again. 'A minor disagreement.'

İzzet smiled. He didn't know much English but he knew enough. He had actually already got the measure of Natasha Sarkissian all on his own and in spite of that he would, he knew, have taken her very joyfully to bed. But not now. Dr Krikor was right, he was a colleague of Dr Arto's and so to do that would be wrong. Shame. It had been a long time since . . .

'Ah, here they come now! The gallant losers!' Abdullah Ceylan said as the exhausted AC Milan players stepped up to take their runner-up medals.

Krikor, enthusiastically clapping the losers, said, 'İzzet, when we leave here, would you like me to drive you straight home or . . . ?'

'Oh, Dr, er, Krikor, if you can take me to a tram stop that will be fine.'

'Nonsense!' he shouted above the roar of the crowd. 'My brother told me you live in Zeyrek. That's no problem. If you're not going on anywhere else . . .'

Natasha looked across at her cousin and smiled unpleasantly.

'No,' İzzet said. 'I'm going straight home.'

'Then that's settled,' Krikor said. 'My brother would never forgive me if I just dumped you in the street to contend with public transport. The idea!'

Of course it was what most people did have to do, İzzet on many occasions himself. But the Sarkissians, just like the lawyers and the scientists they were friends with, led a quite different kind of existence. It was one where clearly women, even when denied what they said they wanted, got over it and on to the next thing very quickly. Now that the Liverpool team were on the pitch Natasha Sarkissian was waving her arms, blowing them kisses and laughing as if she didn't have a care in the world.

İkmen sat down and began to read from a piece of paper that he had in his hand.

'False imprisonment of Mrs Emine Aksu, sexual assault on Mrs Emine Aksu, violent assault on Mr İsmail Kanh of the fire service, alleged desecration of an unknown corpse,

320

possible murder of same . . .' He looked up smiling. 'Anything else, do you think?'

Beside the squat and beefy frame of Ali Paksoy was a slim little man who, to both İkmen and Süleyman, looked as if he was about thirteen.

'If I may answer those allegations before we proceed,' the 'child' said.

'Mr Eker?' Süleyman asked.

His voice was high and slightly tremulous, just like a very young boy. 'Firstly,' he said, 'with regard to the false imprisonment and sexual assault: Mrs Aksu, the woman concerned, went to Mr Paksoy's shop of her own volition. Sex was consensual. Mrs Aksu is a woman of a promiscuous nature who gave herself to my client willingly. The "imprisonment" was also consensual and was part of what my client has described as a "sex game". Mrs Aksu's assertion that my client engaged in sex with an unknown corpse is, as far as I am concerned, pure hearsay. My client does, however, admit the assault upon the fire officer, but he was profoundly threatened by your violent intervention at that time. He is, nevertheless, truly sorry for his actions.'

Mr Eker might look like a child, but that wasn't, as İkmen would have been the first to admit, a bad start. He looked over at Süleyman and raised his eyebrows.

'Inspector İkmen?' Not a patient man, Mr Eker.

'Well, Mr Eker,' İkmen said, 'what can I say? I am of course delighted that your client has admitted to the assault upon Mr Kanlı. I am sure that all fire officers everywhere will feel reassured by his statement of contrition. But with regard to Mrs Aksu, who, by the way, has agreed to make a statement to me in the morning, I must take issue.'

'In what way?'

'Well firstly,' İkmen said, 'this lady's alleged immorality is irrelevant.'

Mr Eker shook his head. 'Inspector İkmen, I'm sorry but—'

'We know from testimony given to us by an independent witness that Mrs Aksu went to see Mr Paksoy willingly,' İkmen said. 'We know, from your nephew who saw you with Mrs Aksu in the basement of your shop, Mr Paksoy, that sex at that point was consensual.'

'What independent witness?' Ali Paksoy asked. 'Emine was very careful that no one saw her when she came over!'

'It was someone who knew Mrs Aksu from your shared past in the hippy hang-outs of Sultanahmet,' Süleyman said. 'Mrs Aksu was, it is true, being very discreet when she travelled over the Golden Horn to see you. She wore a long black coat and a plain green head-scarf. But then Balat is a place where one is better off appearing modest, isn't it? We don't yet know where or when she put them on over the gaudy clothes she left her home in. But she showed what she had on underneath to this man because, he felt, she wanted to taunt him. She told him she was going to have sex with you, too, Mr Paksoy.'

'Which proves consent,' Mr Eker put in.

'At that point in time, yes,' İkmen said. 'Or so it would seem.'

Ali Paksoy, who had been quietly agitated by what had just been said, blurted, 'Who? Who said he saw Emine? Where?'

'I don't know where he saw Mrs Aksu but see her he did on the day of her disappearance,' Süleyman said. 'It was his description of her clothing that caused us to almost believe that he had killed Mrs Aksu.'

'Edmondo . . .'

'Edmondo Loya tried to kill himself earlier this evening,' Süleyman said. 'Fortunately for his family he did not succeed.'

'Typical Edmondo . . .'

'What do you mean?' İkmen asked.

'He never succeeds at anything,' Ali Paksoy said. 'Never has.'

'He nearly took a murder charge for you!' İkmen said suddenly angry with this large, unpleasant man. 'Whether you were in fact imprisoning Mrs Aksu or not, you allowed him, your supposed friend, to admit to a crime you knew could not have taken place! Now why would you do that, Ali, if all you were up to with Mrs Aksu was just a game?'

Mr Eker was very quick to cover his client's sudden plunge into confusion. 'You don't have to answer that,' he said.

They all sat in silence for a few moments while İkmen considered where his questioning might go next. There was something else Edmondo Loya's suicide note had said . . .

'Mr Paksoy, Mr Loya named you as the possible murderer of Mrs Aksu.'

'But she's alive,' Eker said.

İkmen raised a hand. 'Hear me out, please,' he countered. 'He named your client, Mr Eker not just because he knew that Mrs Aksu was going to see him. He named him because Mr Loya, though possessed of no proof at all in this matter, has never been comfortable with the sudden disappearance of an old girlfriend of yours back in the early seventies.' İkmen looked down at the paper in front of him again and read out what was written on it. 'Charlotte Lloyd from Cardiff, which is in Wales, I believe.'

Ali Paksoy made no sound or movement, in fact no response whatsoever. 'Charlotte left,' he said, 'went off with a whole load of other foreign kids to Iran.'

İkmen shrugged. 'Well then, maybe Mr Loya was wrong,' he said. 'I have to tell you, however, that Mr Loya was sufficiently disturbed by the fact that a dead body may well have been transported in a car he knew you possessed to cite it in his suicide note.'

The shoe seller's lawyer just very briefly smiled at his client. 'It means nothing.'

'Maybe not, but we will be contacting the police in Cardiff, just to make sure that Miss Lloyd did indeed make it home safely,' İkmen said with a smile. 'For the sake of completeness.'

'Of course,' Mr Eker said brightly. And then suddenly frowning he said, 'This Mr Loya, why—'

'Did he confess to a murder he clearly didn't do?' İkmen said. 'Mr Eker, that is confidential information – between ourselves and Mr Loya – that I cannot discuss with you. I'd ask your client, he's known Mr Loya for years.'

Mr Eker looked across at Ali Paksoy who said, 'Edmondo is . . . he's never had a girlfriend . . .'

'An inadequate living in fantasy much of the time, given to lies that aggrandise his miserable existence,' Mr Eker said. And then, with a wave of his thin little hand, he added, 'Hardly a reliable source of information.'

Süleyman inwardly smiled. The 'kid' sounded just like his wife for a moment. Clearly an armchair psychologist as well as a lawyer.

'We'll find that out when Mr Loya's doctor allows us to interview him properly,' İkmen said. And then, leaning across the table towards the shoe seller, he continued, 'Mr Paksoy, I am going to conclude this interview now. It is late, I am exhausted and tomorrow my colleagues and I will see Mrs Aksu and Mr Loya, when I hope to have at least some of the forensic results from material found in your well back from the laboratory.' He fixed him with a hard gaze. 'You and I both know what was said in that well. We know what passed between us. Mr Paksoy, you are facing serious charges and could be looking at trial by multiple judges. Their opinions frequently divide . . .'

'Inspector İkmen!'

'But real contrition is always taken into account,' İkmen stood up and put his copy of Edmondo Loya's suicide note into his pocket. 'Always.'

'Don't listen to him,' Mr Eker said quickly to his client. 'He's only trying to frighten you.'

And from the look on Ali Paksoy's very white face, he had succeeded.

Chapter 21

The principal 'casualties' of the previous night's footballing celebrations were very big hangovers. There were fights at various points across the city, but nothing serious and most of the broken bones seen in hospitals resulted from drunken falls rather than aggression. Most of the fans were leaving the city that day or on the Friday and, with their departure as imminent as summer, Commissioner Ardıç had, apparently, been seen smiling as he fed the pigeons at his office window that morning. International football and not so much as a complaint about the noise! Soft policing at its finest! Who said that İstanbul wasn't up to it?

Ardıç wasn't the only one smiling that morning. Strangely, Emine Aksu beamed at both İkmen and, especially, Süleyman from her hospital bed. The indomitable human spirit in all its wonderful glory.

'Gentlemen!' she said as they entered her expensive private room at the International Hospital.

'A step up from the Taksim,' İkmen said as he settled himself down into one of the comfortable leather chairs beside her bed.

'It was very nice of those gorgeous fire officers to take me there,' she said. 'But Ahmet, my husband, insisted I transfer here.'

Money talking. Süleyman, who knew of money, smiled. İkmen, who had no relationship with it at all, also smiled.

'Mrs Aksu,' İkmen said as soon as his colleague had sat down beside him, 'I understand you wish to make a statement.'

Her face, which had been bright, now darkened. 'About Ali Paksoy? Yes,' she said, 'yes, I do.'

'Mrs Aksu, we realise that you've been through a terrible—'

'If it puts that bastard away, it all will have been worth it,' she said. And then propping herself up on her pillows as comfortably as she could, she looked over at the two men and said, 'Gentlemen, take full and careful note of what I say; this is quite a story.' And then, as an afterthought, she added, 'I do hope your stomachs are as strong as I suspect and hope your arms might be.' She laughed then. 'I expect you find me very forward, liberated, coarse – however you may wish to couch it.'

'We know something about your history, Mrs Aksu,' İkmen said. 'Inspector Süleyman and our team have spent many hours talking to your husband and your friends during the time that you were missing.'

'Yes.' She laughed again. 'You know I never meant to have anything to do with Ali Paksoy. I'd all but forgotten that he existed, to be honest with you. But then one day, about a week or maybe two after . . . I had this Italian lover . . .'

'Yes, we know.'

She acknowledged this statement with a nod. 'He left. I wasn't happy.' And then seeing what she imagined was a distinct lack of sympathy on the faces of the men in front of her, she said, 'If Ahmet has told you that he and I just swing

328

for the hell of it, then you should know that he is lying. There was a time, yes, but not now. My husband is impotent, has been for years. He runs the business, can't stand any kind of intervention from me. I'm bored! When we were young we used to hang out with all the foreigners and the freaks in Sultanahmet, but I'm too old to do that now. So many of the people from those days are dead and those who aren't should be. I met up again with Ali quite by chance.'

'Are you sure of that?' Süleyman said.

'Oh, yes. None of what happened was, I think, actually intentional,' she said. 'It became so, but . . . apart from that creepy Edmondo Loya, Ali Paksoy was the only boy in our group who never wanted to be with me. OK, when I met him again he was older and fatter and even, at the start, a little weird, but I am, gentlemen, a rich, bored middle-aged woman. To me he was unfinished business, a challenge. I threw myself at him, I admit it, and he reciprocated with some very animal-istic sex in the basement of his shop. He was very conscious of the fact that his sister lived next door and so I'd turn up, generally on Mondays when his nephew had the day off, covered in an ugly old coat and headscarf with my "finery" on underneath. Not that Ali bothered that much about my clothing, with the exception of my shoes.' She looked across the room to where her Eiffel Tower shoes stood below the window. 'He insisted I always wear those.'

'Mrs Aksu—'

'As a lover he was appalling,' she said. 'Didn't have a clue about how to pleasure a woman. I had to teach him. Nothing too odd there, though, as I trust you will agree. How many men know exactly "what to do", eh?'

İkmen looked at Süleyman, who was gazing very fixedly down at the floor.

'Being with Ali, however, wasn't just about sex. It was about flattery. He always shut the place up when I arrived and we had sex in the basement which was childish, funny and exhilarating. Also having him, an old friend, as a secret from Ahmet was delicious. I was going to tell him in the end, of course. I knew he'd laugh at the idea of my going with "soft" Ali.'

'"Soft" Ali?'

'Yes.' She frowned now. 'He had this girlfriend back in the old days, a European. Totally love struck, he was. Didn't even know I existed. When she left, he was very quiet, for a bit. All his friends worried – needlessly, as it happened.'

There was a silence after that, as Emine Aksu appeared to have to get her thoughts together once again. İkmen wondered whether this 'lost' girlfriend was the woman Edmondo Loya had referred to in his suicide note.

'On that "last" day when I went to see Ali, I met Edmondo Loya at the bottom of the hill,' she continued. 'Such a freak! He started in immediately about how the fact that I had rejected him back in the seventies had ruined his life! My first thought was to just tell him to pull himself together, but then I thought it might be more fun to rub a little more salt into his old, old wound. I opened my coat so that he could see my revealing little outfit and then I told him I was off to have sex with Ali Paksoy. I told him that he was now the only member of our old group that I hadn't slept with. When I left him I was laughing.'

'Mrs Aksu,' Süleyman said gravely, 'at the end of last week Mr Loya confessed to your murder. Then last night he attempted suicide.'

She looked down at the covers on her bed and shook her less than expertly coiffured head. Without make-up she looked plain and even quite old. 'I'm sorry for that,' she said. 'God, why did he confess to my murder? He knew I was with Ali Paksoy!' She looked up, her face furious now. 'He could have told you that! I could have been spared that hideous . . . Little bastard!'

'We have yet to speak to Mr Loya,' İkmen said. 'For the moment, however, we must concentrate upon you and your ordeal, Mrs Aksu. Mr Paksoy has engaged a very vocal and punitive lawyer and so we must gather as much evidence as we can in order to make our case stand up to his scrutiny.'

'I understand.' She swallowed hard. This was where, İkmen imagined, her story was going to get tough. 'On that day . . . when I disappeared, Ali took me down to the basement as usual, but then he asked me if I wanted to see what was below it. I said yes, provided it was somewhere we could, you know, have . . .'

'Sex.'

'Yes. And so there's this Byzantine church.' She shrugged. 'Pretty groovy. I start to do my thing, strip off . . . but then Ali said there was an even better place.'

'Down the well?'

She put her hands up to her head and said, 'What was I thinking? I am a risk taker, but . . .' She shrugged. 'He made me climb down that ladder in those shoes! He went first, looking up my skirt and at my feet, mainly my feet. There wasn't much room in that tunnel thing, but we managed to do it and it was kind of exciting having sex with your head over a great, big, deep well. Call me a bored spoilt rich girl if you must, but . . .' A tiny laugh was followed by a shake of her head. 'But then it got dark.'

'Dark?'

'Ali suggested we do a little bondage. I've been tied up before, I get it, you know?'

'But this was different?' Süleyman asked.

'He had chains, you know, there already. He started talking, as he was chaining me up,' she said. 'Referred to himself as "we", answered his own questions. For instance, "Do we think that's tight enough?" "Yes, I think it is." Then he's talking, to himself, about the "other one". "You have her, I'll have the other one." I was scared then and losing track of who was where, who was who, and exactly how many people there might be in that terrible dark place. I told Ali I wanted to go home. His response was to smack me so hard across the head that I lost consciousness.' She swallowed hard. 'When I came to, he was puffing and panting on top of something I couldn't see at the back of the shaft. But in the days that followed, I discovered what it was.'

'This dead . . .'

'He as one of "himselves" had me, and then the "other one" gave it to the skeleton. We were side by side, myself and the corpse. I was in my very own horror movie.' Only now did she begin to cry, stopping herself almost immediately after she had started. 'Silly bitch!'

'No.'

She ignored İkmen's one word of support and said, 'I had plenty of time to look at that skeleton as I lay chained up and gagged for hours, days on end. He never said who it was, but I think maybe it could have been that old girlfriend of his from the seventies. Some of the fragments on the body looked as if they came from that time. His girlfriend left very suddenly and, as we now know, Ali Paksoy is a terrible, twisted little man. He could have killed her. He could have killed me!'

'What happened to the body?' İkmen said.

'Apparently he liked me more than "it",' she said. 'My being fresh and alive, I guess, was a novelty. But anyway, there wasn't much space and he wanted to be able to manipulate himself with my feet in those shoes; he liked that. I also told him at one point, I think, that I was jealous of the thing. I wanted it gone, as you can imagine!'

'Mr Paksoy was a shoe fetishist, would you say?' Süleyman asked.

'Oh the shoes did it for him all right,' she replied. 'The thing about the body involved him and his alter ego chattering on about how "she" didn't have any shoes any more. I think that's maybe why she went.'

'Do you know where "she" went?'

'Maybe. Not that we talked a lot, he and the other he and myself, you understand,' she said. 'But when "they" said that maybe she should be moved and "discussed" where she might be transported to, I "gave" them a suggestion.'

İkmen frowned.

'I thought that if I could get him out of there and into the open with her, maybe he'd get picked up by the police. He was worrying about what to do with her, what might be appropriate, because he still loved her and so on and so on. I suggested he take her somewhere I used to go to when I was a child.'

'The Kamondo Stairs,' İkmen said.

'You found her?'

'Yes. But we didn't know that Mr Paksoy had put her there,' Süleyman said. 'We were getting close. We had found the car he took her in but . . .'

'Why the Kamondo Stairs?' İkmen asked. 'Why did you suggest there?'

'It's very public. He was likely, I hoped, to get discovered there – then maybe you, the police, would find me. Cool, aren't they, the Stairs? And arty, and a little bit Zen. An old hippy like Ali would go for that. I took a chance on the possibility the skeleton was his old girlfriend, and I said that if he, if *they* loved her, he should put her somewhere where her funky spirit would feel at home, make her a piece of art. He already didn't want to bury her. He felt she'd be sad if he did that. I got taken to the Kamondo Stairs as a kid by my grandfather who used to own a bank on Voyvoda Street.' She crossed her arms over her chest and then added, 'And yes, my maternal grandfather was a Jew, what banker on that street wasn't?'

'Did Edmondo Loya . . . ?'

'No, Edmondo never knew about my background. That I knew I had that one small thing in common with him was bad enough. My mother lived through the war, Inspector, when her father lost all of his money. She always told me to keep the Jewish thing dark. Maybe that was why Edmondo Loya always made my skin crawl. Maybe I was always frightened he might sniff me out.'

'Mrs Aksu,' İkmen said, 'Jewish people are protected under the law, you—'

'Two thousand and three.' She raised a warning finger up to him. 'One synagogue in Karaköy, one in Şişli, blown to bits!'

İkmen nodded his agreement. After all, his son-in-law Berekiah had been one of the victims of the Karaköy explosion.

'I'm only telling you about my own family now so you've absolutely everything you could possibly need to hang this bastard!'

'Mrs Aksu, capital punishment is no longer employed in the Republic.'

'More's the pity!' And then suddenly and dramatically she broke down into torrents of real, no-holds-barred tears. 'That, that fucker raped me again and again and again! With that . . . body still clinging to him!' And then looking up suddenly she shouted, 'Why am I not mad with it, eh? Why? I want to be mad! I must go mad to forget! I must!'

'İzzet!'

She had clearly been in the middle of writing something down when he came into the room. Now she was flying towards him, stopping only when she got really close, and putting her hands firmly behind her back.

İzzet? Sergeant Farsakoğlu never called him 'İzzet'.

'Ah, did you enjoy the match last night?' she said as she looked up at him with a sort of half-smile on her face. Maybe spending much of the previous evening, so he had been told, watching İkmen sway about on an ancient ladder halfway down a well had done something to her brain?

'Er, yes,' he said, 'thank you, Sergeant Farsakoğlu, I had a very nice time.'

'I heard it was a very good match. You didn't have any, um, any trouble . . .'

He sat down in what was usually İkmen's chair. 'There wasn't any trouble, not really. And anyway, I was with Dr Sarkissian's brother and his friends. Posh people, posh seats.'

'So you didn't have any . . . ?'

'No, I didn't have any trouble. What . . . ?'

She cleared her throat nervously. 'Well,' she said, 'we were very busy here last night, Inspector İkmen, Inspector Süleyman, me.'

'You have Mr Paksoy the shoe seller in custody.'

'Yes.' It was still as if she was waiting for him to say something, to confess, even. Why, he couldn't imagine, unless . . .

'Sergeant Farsakoğlu, have you spoken to Dr Sarkissian this morning?'

'Our Dr Sarkissian?'

'Either.'

He looked stern and so Ayşe turned her head away. 'Our doctor is due to come in soon,' she said. 'That body on the Kamondo Stairs, it may have been a foreigner. The police in Cardiff in Wales have faxed us through some photographs of a woman. Dr Sarkissian is coming in to—'

'Sergeant Farsakoğlu, has anyone spoken to you about my being at the match last night with Dr Krikor Sarkissian and his friends?'

He'd heard what Krikor had said to Natasha, how he had warned her firmly away from him. OK, in a sense it was treating him like a helpless idiot, but it was, he knew, well meant. Natasha Sarkissian was a very attractive woman whom he could have bedded very easily, but to do that would hardly have been professional and if Natasha really were a professional heart-breaker . . .

'No one has spoken to me about anything except work!' Ayşe said angrily now, her hands on her hips. 'Why should they?'

'Well . . .'

'Ah, Sergeant Melik, I understand you had a wonderful time at the Olimpiyat Stadium last night.' It was a familiar, male voice and it very successfully dispersed all the tension in the room.

'Yes, Doctor, it was great,' İzzet said as Dr Arto Sarkissian lumbered into the room.

'Good,' the doctor said and then he turned to Ayşe. 'Sergeant Farsakoğlu, do you have those photographs for me?'

'Yes, Doctor.'

She handed him a sheaf of papers and then went and sat silently down behind her desk. İzzet, after a short pause, left both her and the doctor to their own devices. Absorbing the fact that she'd looked, for just a moment, as if she was about to hug him was enough for his brain to consider for the moment.

'You are beyond belief!' Maurice Loya said as he watched his brother weep softly as he lay on top of his hospital bed. 'You lied to me, you lied to the police. A woman you actually know was in danger because you wouldn't tell anyone where she was!'

'I didn't think that Ali Paksoy would hurt her!' Edmondo said. 'I thought he might teach her a lesson . . .'

'Teach her a lesson! Teach her a lesson!' his brother cried. 'Edmondo, by your own admission, you've had your suspicions about this man for thirty years! You express your fears in your suicide note! You should have told the police!'

'He was my friend! Sometimes he let me sit in his car. It's a classic.'

'He is a raving lunatic if the police are right about him! You knew he was a fetishist yourself! A fucking weirdo!' Maurice said. 'Not to mention that he used the fact he did occasionally let you sit in the car to indirectly incriminate you. You could have been accused of necrophilia! He'd imprisoned that woman down a well underneath his shop!'

'I didn't know that Ali had a well. His dad would never let Ali have friends in the house.'

Maurice ran over, sat down beside his brother on the bed, and took one of his hands. 'Edmondo,' he said breathlessly, 'for God's sake, will you listen! This is no longer 1955. Nor is it 1972. You are neither a child nor hanging around with hippies any more. You have lied to the police – up to and including throwing one of our daggers into the Golden Horn – which has almost resulted in the death of a woman, you have tried to kill yourself and nearly given me a heart attack and for what? Eh?'

'Maurice!' Edmondo began to cry again.

'Did you want people to think that you were a big, sexy man, is that it? Crime of passion? Oh, that's a really sexy thing to do, isn't it?'

'Maurice!'

'It's squalid! Like all those bloody fuck books I found, with the police in tow, down in Father's old bunker. Your fuck books, Edmondo! What were they doing down there in that place of grim old memories and dark artefacts from the past? Did you think it was romantic to do that down there, eh? Why didn't you have your books in your room like a normal person?'

'Because, because I thought that you might come in and—'

'Well, if I had, then I would have soon gone out again, wouldn't I!'

'But Maurice, books no normal man—'

'Oh, normal men look at fuck books, Edmondo!'

'But you have girlfriends and women who go to bars with you and—'

'And I also use books from time to time, too,' Maurice said. 'I've used prostitutes! It's legal in this country, so what of it?'

'And if you had found out?' Edmondo said. 'Always laughing at me, Maurice! How could I? How could I ever do anything with you laughing at me?'

Maurice Loya sighed. He hadn't known that this particular day would come but he had often speculated about something of this sort. His brother was a pain, a worry at times, and an almost constant embarrassment. And he, Maurice Loya, had never been one not to express his impatience. Even when their parents had been alive and they had attended to most of Edmondo's quirks and peccadilloes, Maurice had still seethed every time his brother so much as spoke. He was embarrassing! Gauche and over-intellectual and scruffy. Living with him was impossible even if, as Maurice would have been the first to acknowledge, living without him was unthinkable. 'Edmondo,' he said shaking his head slowly as he spoke, 'the police will be here soon.'

His brother's eyes filled with fear. 'Are they going to arrest me?'

'I don't know,' Maurice said. 'I have no idea about what action or actions they may take against you.' He took a deep breath. 'But whatever comes, Edmondo, I want you to know that I will not desert you.'

Edmondo's eyes widened. 'After what I . . . I only wanted to disappear down the rabbit hole, Maurice. Like Alice. I knew I've always been in the rabbit hole in a sense, in another place from everyone else.'

'Yes, but . . . you are my brother.' Amid some awkwardness Maurice reached across the bed and placed his arms gingerly around Edmondo's shoulders. 'Whatever "Wonderland" you may inhabit, you are still my brother and I love you.'

'Oh, er, er . . .' Edmondo found this physical closeness as

difficult if not more so than Maurice. But he understood his brother's sentiment – just. 'Maurice,' he said, 'it's just been us since Mother and Father died, hasn't it?'

'Yes, Edmondo,' Maurice said as he gently disengaged himself from his sibling. Whether he would have married had Edmondo never existed, Maurice Loya would never know. But because his brother was as he was, that had never ever been a serious option. Now, unless he wanted his entire family life to be a total waste, he had to support his brother no matter what. 'Try not to worry about it,' he said gently. 'Just, er, just get better . . .'

A knock at Edmondo's hospital room door made both of them start. The door opened.

'Police here to see you,' the thin, lugubrious doctor said.

Maurice looked across at Edmondo, took a deep breath in, and then said, 'Send them through, Doctor. We're ready.'

Chapter 22

İkmen knew that legally he couldn't prevent Ali Paksoy from having his lawyer, Mr Eker, with him during questioning. The attorney was an essential source of advice and support for his client. But as an officer of the law İkmen was not obliged to either talk or listen to Mr Eker. And so, before they began to question Paksoy in earnest, both İkmen and Süleyman agreed that Mr Eker should be treated as, at best, a slightly annoying sound and, at worst, a piece of irrelevant furniture. Above all, İkmen wanted to see Ali Paksoy effectively alone and exposed. He wanted to hear for himself the two voices heard by Emine Aksu and the two witnesses who had seen the shoe seller's Fiat by the Kamondo Stairs on the night that poor old skeleton was propped up there. Stepping into the arena of the really, really strange.

Just before he and Süleyman went in to Interview Room 2, Ayşe Farsakoğlu handed him a printout of a photograph of a girl. 'Charlotte Lloyd,' she said, 'from Cardiff.'

İkmen raised a questioning eyebrow.

'Eighteen years old,' Ayşe said. 'According to the police in Cardiff she disappeared sometime during the course of a backpacking holiday in 1972.'

'Nineteen seventy-two?' İkmen frowned. 'Didn't Dr Sarkissian place the approximate time of death . . .'

'Late seventies, early eighties,' Süleyman cut in as he took the photograph from his colleague and looked down at it. 'Yes, and the age of the victim was approximately early twenties.'

'So yet another girl?'

'Or,' Süleyman said with a shrug, 'maybe the same girl. Maybe Mr Paksoy has had rather more than just water and rats down his well for a very, very long time.'

İkmen put Charlotte Lloyd's picture into the file with Ali Paksoy's name on it and then he and Süleyman walked into the interview room. Ali Paksoy and Mr Eker were both looking very relaxed.

İkmen, smiling, sat down opposite Ali Paksoy and looked straight into his face. 'All right, Mr Paksoy,' he said, 'let's not waste time haggling about as yet unknown elements and speculation. I'm going to tell you the facts that I have before me so far – things verified by witnesses and/or supported by scientific evidence. Then and, I suggest only then, we will talk.'

'Inspector İkmen—' the lawyer began.

'If you wish you can listen too, Mr Eker,' İkmen said.

'But—'

He ignored him. 'What is known is this,' he said. 'You were certainly having a sexual relationship with Mrs Aksu. She was witnessed going to meet you and then again together with you in your premises on the day that she "disappeared". I found Mrs Aksu chained to the wall, with you by her side, in a maintenance shaft attached to a Byzantine well underneath your shop.' He put a hand up to his head before continuing, 'I'm sorry, but even by the standards of my career, that particular sight was odd almost beyond belief. However . . . Mrs Aksu, according to her doctor, was suffering from dehydration when we found her. She had also been sexually brutalised over a considerable period of time.' Seeing that Ali Paksoy was about to protest, he held up a hand to silence him. 'That is what Mrs Aksu's doctor has observed, Mr Paksoy. The lady has sustained laceration and bruising that are, so her doctor asserts, consistent with resistance to sexual assault. Should your DNA match that of the semen found inside the victim you will, Mr Paksoy, be held responsible for those assaults.'

'Emine Aksu', Eker began, 'is a woman known to be free with her favours . . .'

'Irrelevant.' İkmen dismissed the lawyer with a wave of his hand. 'Other realities, Mr Paksoy, include the fact that you tried to prevent myself, my colleagues and members of the fire service from getting Mrs Aksu out of the well. You assaulted one of the fire officers . . .'

'I was frightened!' His little eyes began to fill with tears as his big face reddened.

'So you say, but that isn't a fact,' İkmen said. 'We are dealing in fact here and only that.' He took a deep breath. 'Apart from your family members and those of the previous owners of the shop, now, I believe, resident in Israel, no one knows about the well underneath your premises. This being the case, and provided the DNA testing on your sample proves positive for the semen inside Mrs Aksu, it would seem that you are the only logical culprit thus far.' He looked across at Süleyman. 'Inspector?'

'Mr Paksoy, do you own a 1972 Fiat 124?'

'You know that he does,' his lawyer replied.

'I would like him to reiterate it,' Süleyman said. 'Mr Paksoy?'

He was crying. 'You know that we do! We forgot to lock it up! You found it! You!'

İkmen hardly dared to breathe. Had Paksoy just made a mistake or was some sort of separation taking place inside his mind? Would they soon hear two distinct and separate voices?

'Tissue fragments recovered from that vehicle committed for DNA testing match that of the corpse found on the Kamondo Stairs last week,' Süleyman said. 'The laboratory is also looking at samples taken from the maintenance shaft of your well, semen found on the Kamondo Stairs corpse and attempting to establish whether the cadaver is this woman.' He stretched over and flipped open the file that was in front of Çetin İkmen. A head-and-shoulders photograph of a young girl smiled into the room. 'Charlotte Lloyd. Originally from Cardiff in Wales. Officially missing since . . .'

But Ali Paksoy was crying hard now, weeping in an hysterical, almost child-like way.

'Inspector İkmen!' Eker said as he attempted to calm his client. 'This is too much!'

But he was ignored.

'Charlotte Lloyd went missing in 1972,' Süleyman said. 'The body on the Kamondo Stairs died in the late seventies, early eighties, according to our doctor. We will find out anyway, Mr Paksoy, but can you tell us whether the Kamondo Stairs body and Charlotte Lloyd are one and the same? Did you keep Charlotte in that well, like you kept Mrs Aksu?'

'Or is the Kamondo Lady someone else?' İkmen said. 'She had, so our doctor tells us, cancer when she was killed.' He leaned forward, across the desk, towards the crying man seated there. 'Because she didn't die of cancer, Mr Paksoy,' he said, 'she was stabbed. Murdered. I can't tell you why, because I don't know. DNA from that body will be compared to that of any family Charlotte Lloyd may still have and . . .' He

344

watched the round childlike face sob. 'We' – he had referred to himself as 'we'. 'Ali,' İkmen said rather more softly than he had before, 'you need to talk to us. You,' he took a risk, 'both of you, have kept all of these secrets for far too long. It's time to—'

'Mr Paksoy,' the lawyer said, 'I would very strongly recommend that you make no further statements until we have spoken.'

'Ali,' İkmen smiled, 'tell me about the shoes. We've been speaking to an old friend of yours today. Back in the sixties and seventies when all the hippies began to arrive, one of the things that you really liked about them was their crazy shoes. Very pretty, some of the girls' shoes were, as I remember them.'

The crying hadn't stopped but it was abating now. Sniffing rather than crying – again in a very childlike manner, wiping his nose on the cuff of his shirt.

'Why don't we talk about shoes?'

'In this country back in the sixties and seventies, shoes were just like boxes. My father said that was how shoes should be.' The 'other', the personality or aspect of Ali Paksoy that was somehow detached from the rest of him, didn't speak in another or different voice. It just conversed with him while he remained fully conscious of it; it was just simply a part of him. It was a way of speaking, İkmen imagined, that had evolved out of very great loneliness. 'But I disagreed. NEVER TOLD HIM THAT. No, one didn't disagree with my father. WENT OFF TO LOOK AT ALL THE FOREIGN KIDS. SO MANY OF US WERE CURIOUS ABOUT THEM IN THOSE DAYS. They were beautiful. But it was the shoes that attracted me most of course. YES.'

Süleyman, fascinated, leaned across the desk and said, 'Ali, Charlotte? Charlotte Lloyd?'

'SHE WAS A HIPPY. She was beautiful. SHE GAVE HERSELF TO ME THE VERY FIRST TIME WE MET. She wore shoes that had pretty yellow daises on them. Cut out of the softest suede, stitched on to the leather covering the toes. MADE ME FEEL DIFFERENT, THOSE SHOES. I COULD . . . We all had girls back then, except Edmondo Loya.'

Mr Eker, now very much out of his depth, in fact frowning with the strain of trying to follow what was happening, said, 'Mr Paksoy, I must reiterate, you and I do have to talk.'

For a moment it looked as if his client might have heard him, but if he did, he chose not to acknowledge the fact. 'When Charlotte wanted to go back on the road again, I didn't like it. I TOOK HER HOME.'

There was a long silence as the two policemen, at least, absorbed what this might mean.

'For how long?' İkmen said. 'You took her home for how long?'

Another silence. Süleyman lit a cigarette. He'd have to share all this with Zelfa. Was it fetishism or . . .

'SHE GOT SICK. I DID WHAT I HAD TO. SHE WAS IN PAIN.'

After a few seconds during which he took in the information he had just been given, İkmen said, 'Ali Paksoy, are you telling me that you killed Charlotte Lloyd?'

'Dad was dead by then. Rafik didn't yet work at the shop. But if somebody heard . . . I COULDN'T LET THE DAISY-COVERED SHOES GO. SHOES HAD NEVER TURNED ME ON BEFORE. SHOES WERE WEAPONS.'

'Weapons?'

Suddenly Ali Paksoy laughed. 'And then, just a few months ago, my stupid nephew goes and sells them!'

Even İkmen was struggling to keep up now. A form of mania appeared to be taking hold. Eyes bright and shiny, words, from whichever source, tumbling wildly.

'Rafik. Sold the shoes.'

'How . . . ?'

'IT WAS MY FAULT. I CLEANED THEM. I ALWAYS DID, YOU HAVE TO LOOK AFTER SHOES. I GOT DISTRACTED. HE SOLD THEM! RAFIK.' He sighed. 'And then it wasn't the same. Then I couldn't love her.'

'Who?'

'My hippy. My . . . CHARLOTTE.' He looked down at the floor.

Çetin İkmen had always had a strong stomach, but the sight of this man being sad about his impotence with a corpse was something he was having to look away from just temporarily.

'How did you get, er, Charlotte down into the well?' Süleyman asked.

Ali Paksoy's face instantly brightened. 'Oh, she wanted to go there with me!' he said. 'We were very quiet going down there so as not to disturb my father – he was sick. But once the door of the church was closed we had a fine time!'

'Yes, but getting down to the shaft . . .'

'Oh. OH. Well, I took her down there. SHE WANTED TO GO BACK ON THE ROAD. I COULDN'T HAVE THAT. WE WERE GOOD TOGETHER. I could, I could . . . I made chains to bind her. SEX WORKED.'

'It hasn't "worked" before?'

'No. Yes! FATHER WAS A WICKED BASTARD, HE . . .' He swallowed hard and then said, 'I looked after Charlotte. I fed her and kept her calm and I cleaned her little shoes and then when the pain became too much for her to bear I put her out of it. You put animals down when they are in pain.' His eyes dripped with tears.

'But then you kept her body and her shoes,' İkmen said,' and—'

'I HAVE NEEDS, INSPECTOR!'

'And so what about Mrs Aksu?' İkmen said. 'How did you come to light upon her?'

'EMİNE WAS NEVER A HIPPY, JUST A TROLLOP! She was a hippy but a very selfish one. HER SHOES WERE AMAZING, I . . .' He put his head down as if in shame.

'The Eiffel Tower shoes?' İkmen asked.

'Mmm.'

'They aroused you, sexually?'

Another silence and then, 'SHE WAS CHEAP! SHE LET ME USE HER SHOES, ON MYSELF. SHE WATCHED,' he laughed. 'SHE SAID SHE WASN'T TELLING HER HUSBAND AHMET ABOUT US, SAID HE'S BE SO SHOCKED! IT WAS OUR SECRET.'

'So what happened?' Süleyman asked. 'Why did you imprison Mrs Aksu?'

'BECAUSE SHE WAS GOING TO TELL AHMET! SHE THOUGHT IT WAS FUNNY! LIKE SHE THOUGHT IT WAS FUNNY WHEN SHE REJECTED EDMONDO LOYA YEARS AGO.'

'You didn't want to lose her?'

'IT WASN'T WORKING WITH CHARLOTTE ANY MORE! BUT WITH EMİNE . . .' His eyes glazed over, this other, slightly more punitive voice. 'BOTH OF THEM!' He shuddered. 'IF ONLY EMİNE HADN'T BECOME SO JEALOUS.'

'What do you mean?' İkmen said, looking at the face of Mr Eker who was truly, truly horrified.

'EMİNE BECAME JEALOUS, TOLD ME TO GET RID OF CHARLOTTE,' he said. 'Not that Emine was uncaring. THE KAMONDO STAIRS LIKE AN ART EXHIBIT, SHE SAID. BEAUTIFUL.

It was fitting, right.'

'And then it was just you and Mrs Aksu,' İkmen said. 'You know, Mr Paksoy, I know you know that Edmondo Loya confessed to the murder of Emine Aksu. He was your friend.'

'There are no friends where love is concerned.'

'Mr Loya was coming to see you just after I released him from police custody,' İkmen said. 'I think my presence prevented him from doing so. We know, because he has admitted as much to us, that he saw Mrs Aksu on the day of her disappearance. She told him she was going to see you. She taunted him with that information. When he confessed his "crime" to us, Mr Loya suspected that Mrs Aksu might still be with you – or rather, that is what he has told us. After you took Mrs Aksu, for want of a better term, did Mr Loya at any time have certain knowledge of that?'

'No.'

'Did he ask you about her?'

'No! And even if he had, i wouldn't have told him,' Paksoy said. 'Emine wasn't for him! He fancied her! Why would I want him to know where she was?'

'You were quite happy to let Edmondo Loya take the blame for a murder that you knew had never happened though, weren't you?' Süleyman said.

Ali Paksoy, impassive, looked down at the floor in silence.

'Edmondo Loya is your friend,' İkmen said. 'You used to let him sit in that old car of yours, didn't you? That helped you, didn't it? When we found Edmondo's prints on your car, you told us he was never ever in it. But as we now know, you used to let him sit in it from time to time. He was, and remains, pathetically grateful for it. So it wasn't easy telling him you tried to lead us to believe it was he who had broken in and possibly stolen your car, he who maybe dumped the Kamondo body. Edmondo Loya cannot even drive!'

But nothing except a cold, fish-like stare met his gaze. 'FATHER NEVER LET US HAVE ANY FRIENDS,' Ali Paksoy, the shoe seller of Balat, said.

Chapter 23

They all met up at Balthazar Cohen's house, or rather in his garden. Spring was rapidly transmuting into summer and it was far too hot to be indoors. The 'guest of honour' was Süleyman's wife, Dr Zelfa Halman, psychiatrist.

'Haven't you had enough of them over the past week?' Balthazar said to İkmen as he pointed Zelfa towards a chair beside her husband. She had just finished one of her clinics and was a little tired and hot after a long, traffic-choked taxi ride over from Taksim to Balat.

'Those visiting Mr Paksoy only do so at the behest of his defence,' İkmen said. 'They don't want to say anything to me. Not now.' He sighed. 'Dr Halman has agreed to talk to us – unofficially, of course – because I think that after what we've all been through with the shoe seller we need a bit of professional insight. Mr Cohen here is included because he is a friend of Edmondo Loya – and of course he is a genuine man of Balat and so has an interest in local affairs.'

Ayşe Farsakoğlu and İzzet Melik made up the party and, after Balthazar's wife had served them all with tea and fresh water, the six of them were left to their own devices.

'Dr Halman?'

Unusually, when in a professional situation, Zelfa Halman didn't have any notes or files in front of her. All the information that she had about Ali Paksoy had come, unofficially, from either her husband or İkmen. No records, of either her opinions or even this meeting, were ever going to be made. Judges would decide Ali Paksoy's fate, but those who had been involved in his apprehension needed what Zelfa, İkmen knew, would call 'closure'. It was not every day, thankfully, that one came across a person whose life had telescoped down to just sick or pathetic fetishes.

'In order to understand Ali Paksoy we have to have a notion of what his parents were like,' Zelfa said. And then, waving away a somewhat doubtful look from Balthazar, she went on, 'I'm not getting Freudian on you, don't worry! How they were with their children explains a lot. Now, Inspector Süleyman,' she used his title because his subordinates were present, 'you interviewed Handan Sarıgul, Mr Paksoy's sister.'

'Yes.' He took a long drag from his cigarette and then leaned back in his chair. 'The Paksoys came to İstanbul back in the fifties. Old Mr Paksoy was a shoemaker from Bursa, very skilled; his dream was to have several shops staffed by dedicated artisans. Mother died when Handan and Ali were very young, the father, Faruk, basically raised the children alone. It wasn't easy. They were young, he was alone in a new city, and the world had started to change.'

'In what way?' İzzet Melik asked.

'This country began to open itself up to foreign markets,' Süleyman said. 'Imports from abroad and tourists, early on in the shape of, generally Western European, cultural tourists, then the influx of hippies in the sixties and the importation of new ideas and philosophies, even a new morality of sorts. Old Mr Paksoy was very threatened by all of it. He tried to keep his children away from it by forbidding them to have friends, by not marrying off his daughter, and by keeping his son where he could see him. But he became ill towards the end of the sixties and so Ali, at least, made a bid for freedom. He made friends with some other boys, including Edmondo Loya, and became one of those Turkish kids who hung around with the foreign hippies. One of old Mr Paksoy's last acts was to buy that 1972 Fiat 124 for himself and his son to drive around in. It was done to show people, and himself too, I imagine, that he wasn't a failure.' He looked across at his wife who continued where he left off.

'But Faruk Paksoy was a disappointed man,' she said. 'People didn't want hand-made shoes any more and so his skills were, as he perceived it, wasted. To Faruk, a hand-crafted shoe made of top-class materials was the most beautiful thing in the world. He did indeed pass on this enthusiasm to his son Ali, but unfortunately the boy had even less opportunity to practise his skills than his father. So in the Paksoy house what did we have? The old man seething with disappointment and the two children, motherless, but young and desperate for life. Paksoy senior was, I believe – and quite understandably – jealous. He was Mr Charm himself to all his neighbours and customers, but to his children he was a nightmare. In order to spend hours and hours learning a rapidly dying craft, Ali was made to sacrifice all friendships. He was alone for unreasonable amounts of time for a child! That other voice he uses isn't so much, from what I can deduce about it, another personality – it's company. He talks like that, I think, in order to stop the silence from crushing him. Handan was now the "mother" of the household, always away in the kitchen, and so she couldn't possibly marry or go out either. The slightest murmur of dissent on the part of either child was punished with a beating – generally with a very stout and expertly made shoe. Luckily for Handan she married very soon after her father died in 1973. Ali was happy to give her away to the boy who had always been her secret sweetheart, the son of the baker next door. She didn't manage to conceive a child for many years after that but eventually her only son Rafik was born in 1987.'

'What about this Welsh girl?' Ayşe Farsakoğlu asked.

'I'm coming to Charlotte Lloyd,' Zelfa said. 'From what Inspector Süleyman has told me, I've come to the opinion that Ali Paksoy, maybe as a result of the way he was treated by his father, which, no doubt, induced low self-esteem, suffered from sexual dysfunction. I don't think that his sexual experience pre-Charlotte Lloyd was extensive, but whatever it was, it was unsatisfactory. Then suddenly there is Charlotte, pretty, young and, most importantly for him, wearing shoes that are beautiful in both design and manufacture. They, as much as her, turn him on. Success in his mind has always been attached to well-produced shoes, so of course he can perform sexually with Charlotte and of course it is, in his mind, utterly perfect. It is his moment of revelation, everything he does from then on proceeds from it. When his father buys a new car in order to show off to the other tradespeople in Balat, Ali takes Charlotte out in it with his father's blessing. Not that the car is about the strange foreign girl at all to Faruk; it's about him and his wealth. He had cancer by this time and knew that he was dying; he had to get that showing off done and at any cost – even with a foreigner involved!' She, a half-foreigner herself, looked across at her husband with amusement and said, 'We do have our uses from time to time.'

'So what happened when Charlotte decided to defect back to the hippy trail, Dr Halman?' İkmen said as he lit up a cigarette.

'I don't know exactly, of course,' Zelfa said, 'only Ali

Paksoy will really know the answer to that question. But conjecture? By his own admission he didn't want to let Charlotte or her shoes go. His father was dying, he knew his sister should marry when that happened, and he was afraid of that silence again, I think. He also feared the prospect of trying to have sex with someone other than Charlotte and failing. He drugged her . . .'

'What with?'

'He says large amounts of cannabis did the trick, but we can't be sure of that now,' Zelfa said. 'Carried her down to the well, he claims.'

'And then had his way with her until her death?' İzzet Melik asked cringing and then correcting himself, 'Sorry, after her death.'

'I don't know how often or for how long he bound and gagged her,' Zelfa said. 'He fed her and, it's possible, eventually she adapted to the situation. Hostages can, the so-called Stockholm Syndrome takes effect, where the victim identifies and sympathises with the offender. Maybe this happened, we don't know. What we do know, however, is that at some point towards the end of the seventies, Charlotte became sick. She had bowel cancer and she must have lost a lot of weight as well as her youthful looks. Ali killed her – he stabbed her, he says – in order to put her out of her pain. This may well be so, but what has also occurred to me is that maybe around about the same time as Charlotte's physical beauty faded, Ali came to realise that she wasn't that important after all. The shoes, *her* shoes, were important, and as long as he had them and also some object upon which to focus the sexual effect from them, a live woman did not, as such, matter.'

'So her death changed very little?' Ayşe Farsakoğlu said.

'That's right.'

'Weird bastard,' Balthazar muttered under his rasping, cigaretty breath.

'Ali had seen his father suffer. He knew that was a bad thing. He convinced himself he'd done Charlotte a service. Where he stands upon right and wrong and whether he retains any religious values, I don't know,' Zelfa said. 'This is, I think, one of those cases where the sanity of the offender is difficult to assess. From what I've been told he possesses insight into what has happened and what he has done so . . .' She shrugged. 'Over the years Ali carefully maintained Charlotte's beloved shoes until one day, for some reason he left them somewhere he shouldn't and nephew Rafik sold them to some very grateful lady. From what I've been told the usual stock in that shop was either cheap or boring or both. Ali's days of necrophilia and even probably masturbation are over.'

'He can't, er . . .'

'Get it up without shoes? No,' Zelfa said. 'He's a shoe fetishist. He isn't strictly speaking a necrophiliac because dead bodies are not the prime focus of his libido. He generalises to necrophilia. Shoes are important, the holes he puts himself into whilst looking at shoes are not. So when he met his old acquaintance Emine Aksu it was not her appearance that instantly turned Ali Paksoy on but those very pretty, saucy little shoes of hers. He'd missed sex and so he really went for it with Emine.' She sighed. 'Then she went and spoiled it all by telling him she was going to let her husband in on their secret. Ali, of course, knew Ahmet Aksu from when they were all young and he knew that he and Emine always liked to sleep with all sorts of people. He didn't want anyone else involved in his fantasy, so he decided to have Emine, together with what remained of Charlotte, all to himself. Of course he's not worked out that space will be tight down there and so when he and Emine have what she thinks at first is a bit of fun, he is doing this with his back to Charlotte. But that, too, is exciting.'

'Do you think, Dr Halman, that Paksoy would have kept the body if Mrs Aksu hadn't claimed to, as he says, have become jealous of it?' Ayşe asked.

'Undoubtedly,' Zelfa replied. 'Mrs Aksu's statement contains details about Paksoy taking great pleasure in having them "both". Her "jealousy" was a very smart, albeit desperate move on her part and also demonstrates how far removed from reality Paksoy had become.'

'What do you mean?'

'The risk involved in taking out that old car of his and giving Charlotte probably the most outré send off I can recall in my entire psychiatric career! Emine Aksu was quite correct, he could have very easily been picked up by the police. He wasn't' – she shot both İkmen and Süleyman an accusatory glance – 'but he could have been. Apart from anything else he could have lost his nerve at any time. Although I think that he dealt with that by inserting the other "him" into his vocalisations that night. Didn't witnesses report hearing two men talking to each other?'

'Yes,' İkmen said, 'they did.'

A short silence followed while all concerned attempted to absorb the strange facts and theories they had just been exposed to.

'But what about my friend Edmondo?' Balthazar said at length. 'What about him?'

Zelfa sighed and shook her head sadly.

'The Aksus are not proceeding with charges against him,' İkmen said. 'Mr Aksu appreciates that Edmondo, rather than

357

needing prison, requires treatment of some sort. We, however, will have to take action. He withheld information that could possibly have resulted in the death of Mrs Aksu. For the moment, however, he is entrusted to the care of his brother.'

'Maurice!'

'Yet another thoughtless bully,' Zelfa said. 'Chipping away at Edmondo's self esteem year in and year out! Edmondo didn't just admit to killing Emine in the hope that his friend Ali would teach her a lesson. He did it also to prove to Maurice that he could be a man – with sex and women and passion and everything.'

'But Edmondo suspected that Ali had had something to do with the hippy girl Charlotte's disappearance, didn't he?' İzzet said.

'That was in his suicide note, yes,' Zelfa replied. 'But—'

'That thought, intuition, or whatever you might like to call it, was at the edge of Edmondo's consciousness,' İkmen cut in. 'It was, I think, one of his darker secrets. He has or had a few. The cache of opium underneath his house bought to deliver the Loya family from the Nazi hordes in World War Two, his lonely magazine-fuelled masturbation, the depth to which Emine Aksu hurt him all those years ago.' He frowned. 'Ali Paksoy was one of his very few friends. On occasion, he let Edmondo sit in his father's old car. That was a treat for an isolated soul like Edmondo. That's why his prints were found on the vehicle. Charlotte Lloyd disappeared suddenly, and after the initial shock, the devastated Ali recovered very quickly from this. Something in Edmondo knew that Ali was as "un-right", if you like, as he was – in a different way, of course. But, we know our own after all, don't we?'

'Some of us reject our own,' Balthazar said sadly.

İkmen, sitting beside him, put a protective arm around the back of his wheelchair. Although he'd killed no one, Edmondo Loya had contributed much to the complication of this now almost complete investigation. He'd loved Emine Aksu far too much and then he'd hated her with a passion. Her rejection of her heritage had caused her to despise the bookish little Jew as much as she did, a rejection born like most evils out of fear. Now though, Edmondo had paid her back – many times over. Emine Aksu, back in the arms of her impotent husband, had looked like a frightened mouse the last time that İkmen had seen her. So many old ex-hippies falling foul of their own pasts, hidden or otherwise.

But then later on, when all of his colleagues had returned either to their homes or to the station, İkmen found himself outside a doorway he recognised as one that used to lead into an old backpackers' hostel many years ago. It wasn't any place that his old love, Alison the little English girl, had stayed in. Just around the corner from the Pudding Shop it was very near to his apartment and was now a leather clothing warehouse and shop. There was a man standing, lurking in the doorway. Built like a short, stout bull, he would occasionally walk up to people who were clearly tourists and say to them, in English, 'Nice leather jacket lady, yes please!' Sometimes he would say things to other tourists – probably much the same things he said in English – in languages İkmen didn't understand: Polish, Czech or Russian maybe.

The world had changed. The hippy ladies were no more and the carpet and leather goods touts were as likely to try and tap up the tourists in Russian or Czech as they were in English or German.

As he let himself into his apartment building and then began his weary climb upstairs he remembered a saying he had been taught many years before in high school, in one of his English classes. 'Every dog shall have his day.' It made İkmen smile. That applied to movements too, he thought. The hippies, the frightened Jews with their caches of sugar or opium or whatever they thought they needed, the poor migrants from Anatolia in the 1950s with their few possessions and many, many dreams. It had all given way to mobile phones, multilingual tourist touts, topless beaches on the south coast and, by contrast simply because Turkey is Turkey and totally, utterly and infuriatingly unique, veiled women on the streets of the modern republican capital, Ankara.

Holding on to whatever was meaningful even if it was imperfect or wrecked was what life was about, he decided as he threw his house keys on to his armchair and then lit a cigarette.

Fatma his wife, always in the kitchen, called out, 'Çetin? Kemal needs new shirts for school. He's grown again. About forty lire should cover it.'

'God!' İkmen muttered and then said, 'Yes, OK.'

'And can you go and look at the tap in the bathroom? It's leaking again.'

Wreckage, like dripping taps and expensive children and invisible wives, was not necessarily a bad thing. They were not things that one had to go 'on the road' or on a mental 'trip' to find – not of necessity. It would have been nice if he could have done things like that, once, but not now. İkmen picked up his keys from the armchair and placed them on the table beside it, then sat down. Well, at least all of those foreign football fans had finally gone home. He had hardly noticed them, involved as he had been with shoe sellers and ancient hippies and poor, heartbreaking little Jewish intellectuals. İzzet Melik had apparently seen the match in question and had been what his friend Arto Sarkissian had described as 'stalked' by his cousin Natasha. İkmen smiled. Sex and sport just went on whatever happened. The former made him hopeful while the latter remained a mystery. But then he had always smoked far too hard for football, swimming or any other sport to ever be a real possibility. A lot of young people did eschew cigarettes now, however, in order to do the sport thing – even some of his own younger children. Turkey was changing – again. He flopped back in his chair, put his current cigarette out, and then lit up another.

Epilogue

He hardly recognised her. She could, had she had a daughter, have been her. But not, surely . . .

'I finally decided to have it all lifted,' she said as she drew her long, old fingers up across her new, young face and neck. 'I'm so pleased. What do you think? Do you think that I look desirable? Sexy? Young?'

'I . . .'

She laughed. So HIM, so annoyingly awkward, but she must be nice. He wasn't BAD, as such . . .

'It's OK,' she said, 'I know you liked me as I was but time moves on even for me!'

'Doesn't it just.' The other voice was deeper, graver and quite displeased.

Emine Aksu turned and looked into the eyes of another Jewish man who was very far from being timid. He also looked almost exactly like Edmondo.

'Oh.'

'Oh, indeed, Mrs Aksu,' Maurice Loya said as he grabbed his brother's arm and began to steer him across the other side of İstiklal Street.

'I didn't mean to—'

'Leave my brother alone,' Maurice Loya said.

'Goodbye, Emine,' Edmondo said in that half-asleep, drugged way that he always had with him now.

Transquillised. Forcibly medicated to make him 'normal'. Better than prison, but . . . she, this woman, had been the cause of it all, Maurice Loya seethed. Now he spent every moment that he wasn't at work attending to a drooling medicalised junkie, now his clever, if irritating, brother had no intellect. Because of her. Maurice Loya turned around quickly and, leaving his brother standing looking up at the sky in the middle of the street, he went back to Emine Aksu and he said, 'You did that! You! Thoughtless tart!'

Her mouth dropped open as her hands flew up to her very expensively reconstructed décolletage.

'You look like what you are,' Maurice Loya said, 'a sad old woman in a teenager's dress.' And then he added, 'A sad old woman on coke – I can see that drugged-up haze in your eyes – no longer a spoilt little rich girl, no longer a rebel or a hippy. Nothing.'

And then he went, taking his brother Edmondo along with him. For just a moment, İkmen thought about leaving the poor woman to cry off her make-up in the street. After all, her cruelty to Edmondo Loya had been the cause of his actions, had resulted in a team of psychiatrists recommending medication. Better than prison – just. Only.

But he went up to her and offered her his handkerchief and then his arm. There had been no winners when Ali Paksoy, the Necrophiliac of Balat, as they called him now in the press, had gone to court. He'd been given a life sentence, Edmondo Loya was – well, as he was, and this poor lady was still looking for men to counteract the coldness of her husband's impotence.

'Let me escort you to a taxi,' İkmen said as he began to lead her up towards the many cabs on Taksim Square.

'Escort? Oh, how gallant and quaint,' she said as she

dabbed her black-smudged eyes with her handkerchief. 'How very old fashioned.'

'Old fashioned?' İkmen smiled. 'No, madam, old fashioned is casual. Manners, of the good old Turkish variety, are what constitute hip and cool these days.'

'Really?' She frowned. 'I haven't heard that. My husband publishes a lifestyle magazine and he knows all the trends before they happen.'

'Really?'

'Yes.'

Across in the Old City the first muezzin to call the midday prayers began his request for the faithful to pray.

'Well this is a very new trend indeed,' İkmen said as he opened the door of the nearest yellow cab for her to climb inside.

'So who—'

'Oh, I originated it myself,' İkmen said. 'Just now, Mrs Aksu. I am an İstanbullu; like my city, I am always evolving.'

She climbed inside the cab, laughing.

'You!' she said theatrically. 'You?'

İkmen banged one of his hands down on the roof of the cab and then said out loud a word he remembered from many, many years ago. Alison had said it, often.

'Groovy.' It made him laugh. It was a word the hippies had used all the time, back in those days.

God alone in all his splendour knew what it meant.

Hippies

The hippy culture or phenomenon grew out of the Beat Generation movement of the 1950s. The Beatniks were principally American post-Second World War writers, artists and poets. They were non-conformists whose art and lifestyle included exploration of both the physical world, by travelling, and the inner life via the use of drugs. The most influential Beat writers were William S. Burroughs, Allen Ginsberg and Jack Kerouac, who wrote the ultimate Beat-journey book *On the Road* in 1957.

Exactly when the world of the Beatniks ended and when hippies came into being isn't clear. The first people whose lifestyle later became known as 'hippy' came from the United States. A combination of prosperity and Beat philosophy together with the, albeit short-lived, presidency of a very young John F. Kennedy, produced a generation of people who wanted to live 'different' lives. Exploring the inner world through music, drugs and art of all types was 'in', as was wearing unconventional clothes, practising 'free' or unmarried love, caring about the earth, and even, in some cases, travelling to what were then considered primitive cultures in search of enlightenment. At a festival called the 'Human Be-In' in 1967 in San Francisco, the famous writer, psychologist and drug user Timothy Leary exhorted his hippy followers to 'Tune in, turn on and drop out'. Millions of young people, not only in the USA but also by now in Europe and Australasia too, did just that.

Because such a large part of hippy philosophy was centred around the notions of travel and exploration, lots of young people took to the road in the early sixties and seventies. They were looking for personal enlightenment, experience and maybe even an encounter with the divine. The Hindu ashrams of India and the Buddhist temples of Nepal, particularly Kathmandu, were where most of them wanted to get to and the route for that journey, for both Europeans and non-Europeans, was a fairly standard one. In old buses, vans and sometimes on trains, too, the hippies would cross Europe into Turkey and then make their way across Iran and Afghanistan before entering Pakistan, India and finally Nepal. Some of them would make the entire journey, some just part of it. Some would die of drug overdoses, malnutrition or disease along the way and some would indeed find what they were looking for and many remain in these countries to this day.

Turkey saw a lot of hippies during the sixties and early seventies, particularly in İstanbul, which was the first stop on the hippy trail. At the centre of hippy İstanbul was and remains the Pudding Shop or Lale Restaurant on Divan Yolu in Sultanahmet. Started by the Colpan family in 1958, the Pudding Shop sold simple, cheap food that poor young hippies could easily afford. In particular, it sold a filling rice pudding called sütlaç, which was particularly welcome to those suffering from the cannabis-induced hunger known as the 'munchies'. Because of sütlaç the Pudding Shop became a favourite with the hippies who would arrange to meet there and leave messages for their friends on the restaurant's large and crowded notice board. The Pudding Shop still serves sütlaç but, as Çetin İkmen remarks in this book, it also serves designer coffee these days, too!

Quite when the hippy movement came to an end, no one really knows. Some say that it didn't and, given the still-large numbers of people who like to wear their hair long, care for the environment, compose poetry and go to rock festivals, they are probably right.

Turkish Alphabet

The Turkish Alphabet is very similar to its English counterpart with the following exceptions:

* The letters q, w and x do not appear.
* Some letters behave differently in Turkish compared with English:

C, c   Not the c in cat and tractor, but the j in jam and Taj or the g in gentle and courageous.

G, g   Always the hard g in great or slug, never the soft g of general and outrage.

J, j   As the French pronounce the j in bonjour and the g in gendarme.

* The following additional letters appear:

Ç, ç   The ch in chunk or choke.

Ğ, ğ   'Yumuşak ge' is used to lengthen the vowel that it follows. It is not usually voiced (except as a vague y sound). For instance, it is used in the name Ayşe Farsakoğlu, which is pronounced *Far-sak-erlu*, and in öğle (noon, midday), pronounced öy-*lay* (see below for how to pronounce ö).

Ş, ş   The sh in ship and shovel.

I, ı	Without a dot, the sound of the a in probable.
İ, i	With a dot, the i in thin or tinny.
ö, ö	Like the ur sound in further.
Ü, ü	Like the u in the French tu.

Full pronunciation guide

A, a	Usually short, the a in hah! or the u in but, never the medium or long a in nasty and hateful.
B, b	As in English.
C, c	Not the c in cat and tractor, but the j in jam and Taj or the g in gentle and courageous.
Ç, ç	The ch in chunk or choke.
D, d	As in English.
E, e	Always short, the e in venerable, never the e in Bede (and never silent).
F, f	As in English.
G, g	Always the hard g in great or slug, never the soft g of general and outrage.
Ğ, ğ	'Yumuşak ge' is used to lengthen the vowel that it follows. It is not usually voiced (except as a vague y sound). For instance, it is used in the name Ayşe Farsakoğlu, which is pronounced *Far-sak-erlu*, and in öğle (noon, midday), pronounced *öy-lay* (see below for how to pronounce ö).
H, h	As in English (and never silent).
I,	Without a dot, the sound of the a in probable.
İ, i	With a dot, the i in thin or tinny.

J, j	As the French pronounce the j in bonjour and the g in gendarme.
K, k	As in English (and never silent).
L, l	As in English.
M, m	As in English.
N, n	As in English.
O, o	Always short, the o in hot and bothered.
ö, ö	Like the ur sound in further.
P, p	As in English.
R, r	As in English.
S, s	As in English.
Ş, ş	The sh in ship and shovel.
T, t	As in English.
U, u	Always medium-length, the u in push and pull, never the u in but.
Ü, ü	Like the u in the French tu.
V, v	Usually as in English, but sometimes almost a w sound in words such as tavuk (hen).
Y, y	As in English. Follows vowels to make diphthongs: ay is the y sound in fly; ey is the ay sound in day; oy is the oy sound in toy; uy is almost the same as the French oui.
Z, z	As in English.

Now you can buy any of these other bestselling
Headline books from your bookshop
or *direct from the publisher*.

FREE P&P AND UK DELIVERY
(Overseas and Ireland £3.50 per book)

The Cruellest Month	Louise Penny	£6.99
Stalked	Brian Freeman	£6.99
Death's Door	Quintin Jardine	£6.99
Faces	Martina Cole	£6.99
The Templar	Paul Doherty	£6.99
The Takedown	Patrick Quinlan	£6.99
Silent Partner	Jonathan Kellerman	£6.99
After the Mourning	Barbara Nadel	£6.99
Point of No Return	Scott Frost	£6.99

TO ORDER SIMPLY CALL THIS NUMBER

01235 400 414

or visit our website: www.headline.co.uk

Prices and availability subject to change without notice.